Book I of the trilogy *Brotherhood of the Mamluks*, *Chains of Nobility*, was a finalist for the 2019 Colby Award "for first-time fiction or non-fiction that has made a major contribution to the understanding of military history, intelligence operations, or international affairs."

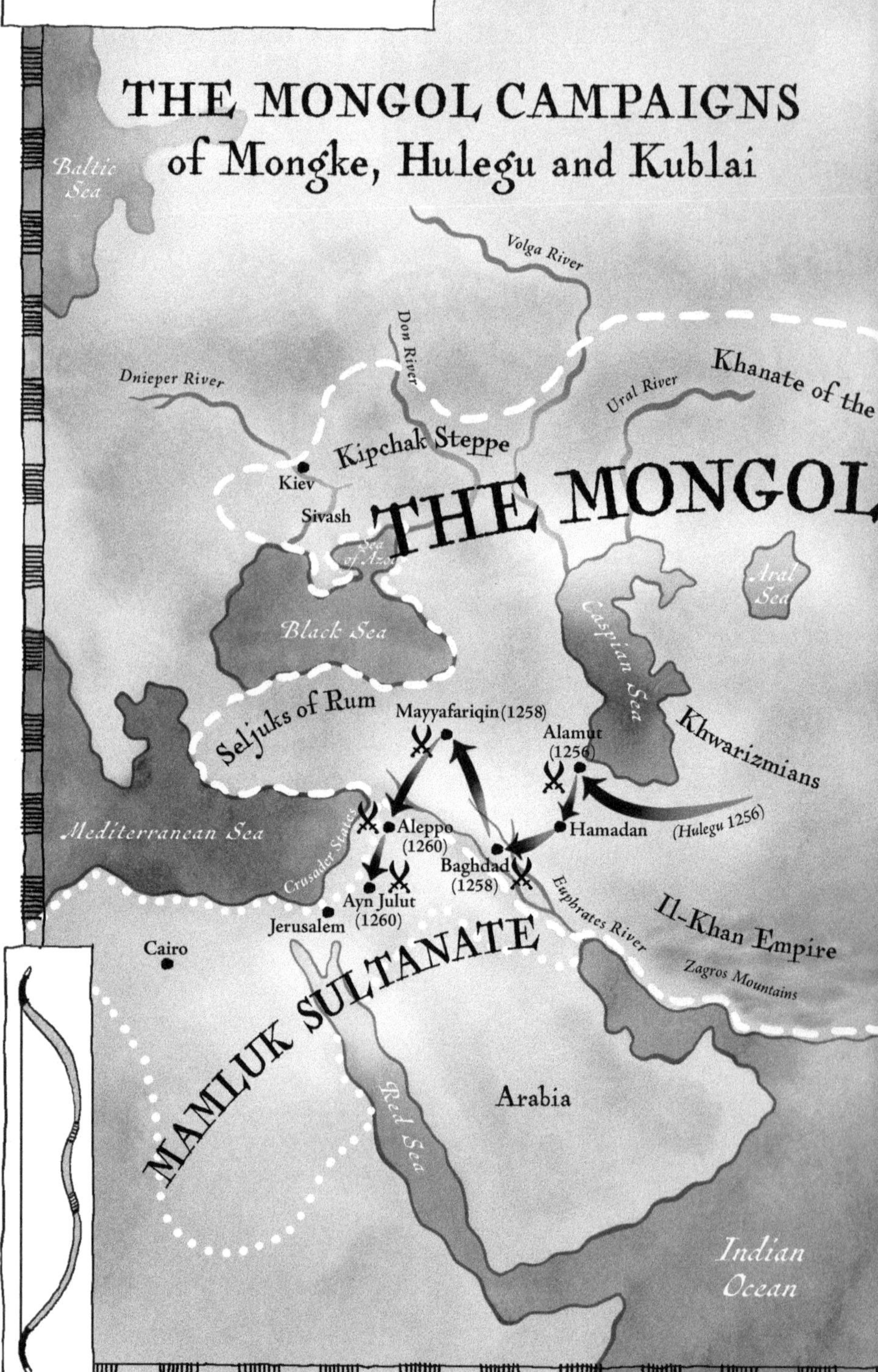
THE MONGOL CAMPAIGNS
of Mongke, Hulegu and Kublai
Baltic Sea
Volga River
Don River
Dnieper River
Ural River
Khanate of the
Kipchak Steppe
Kiev
Sivash
THE MONGOL
Sea of Azov
Aral Sea
Black Sea
Caspian Sea
Seljuks of Rum
Mayyafariqin (1258)
Alamut (1256)
Khwarizmians
Mediterranean Sea
Crusader States
Aleppo (1260)
Hamadan
(Hulegu 1256)
Baghdad (1258)
Ayn Julut (1260)
Jerusalem
Euphrates River
Il-Khan Empire
Cairo
MAMLUK SULTANATE
Zagros Mountains
Red Sea
Arabia
Indian Ocean

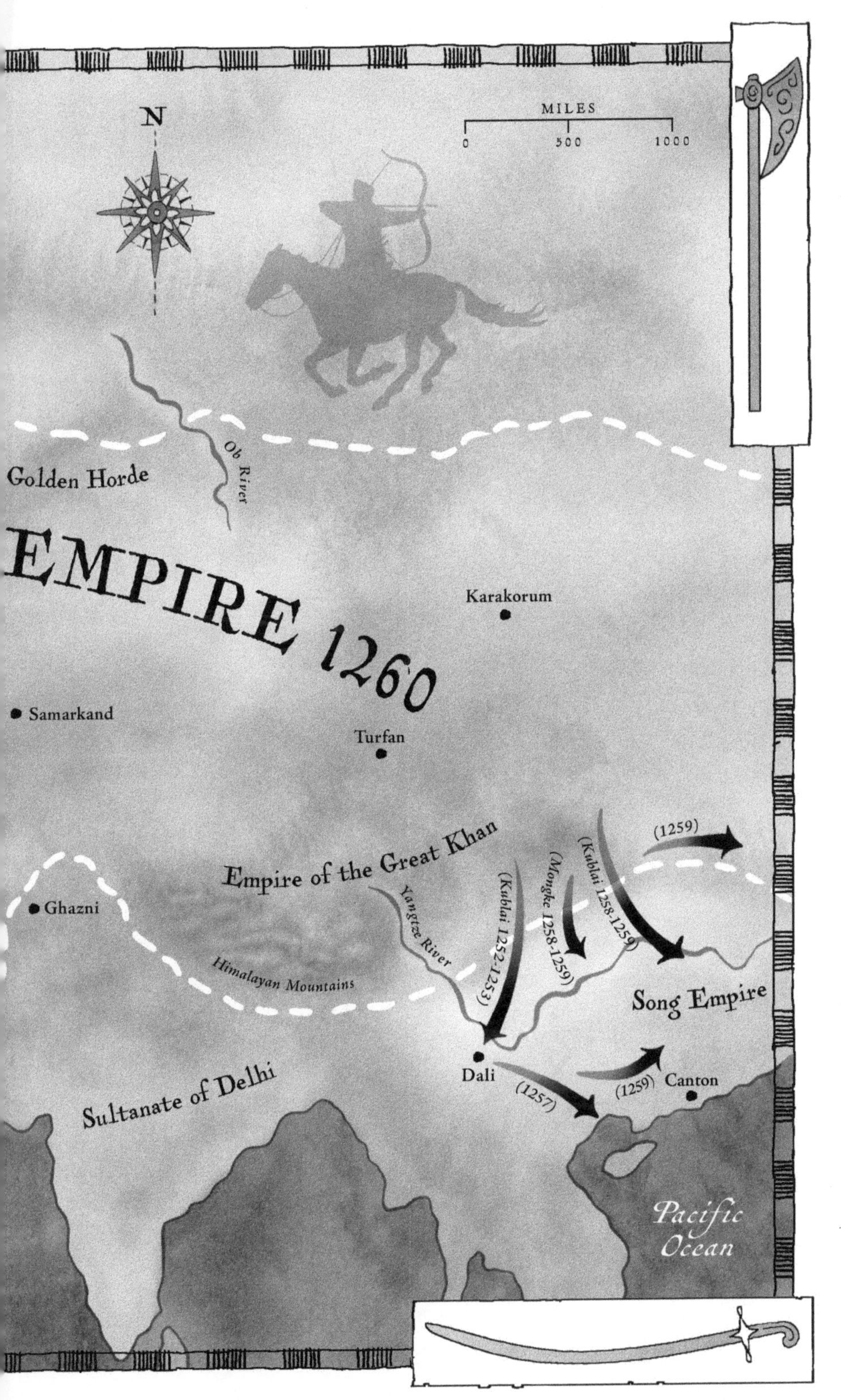

MILES
0
500
1000
N
Golden Horde
Ob River
EMPIRE 1260
Karakorum
Samarkand
Turfan
Empire of the Great Khan
(1259)
(Kublai 1258-1259)
(Mongke 1258-1259)
(Kublai 1252-1253)
Yangtze River
Ghazni
Himalayan Mountains
Song Empire
Dali
(1257)
(1259)
Canton
Sultanate of Delhi
Pacific Ocean

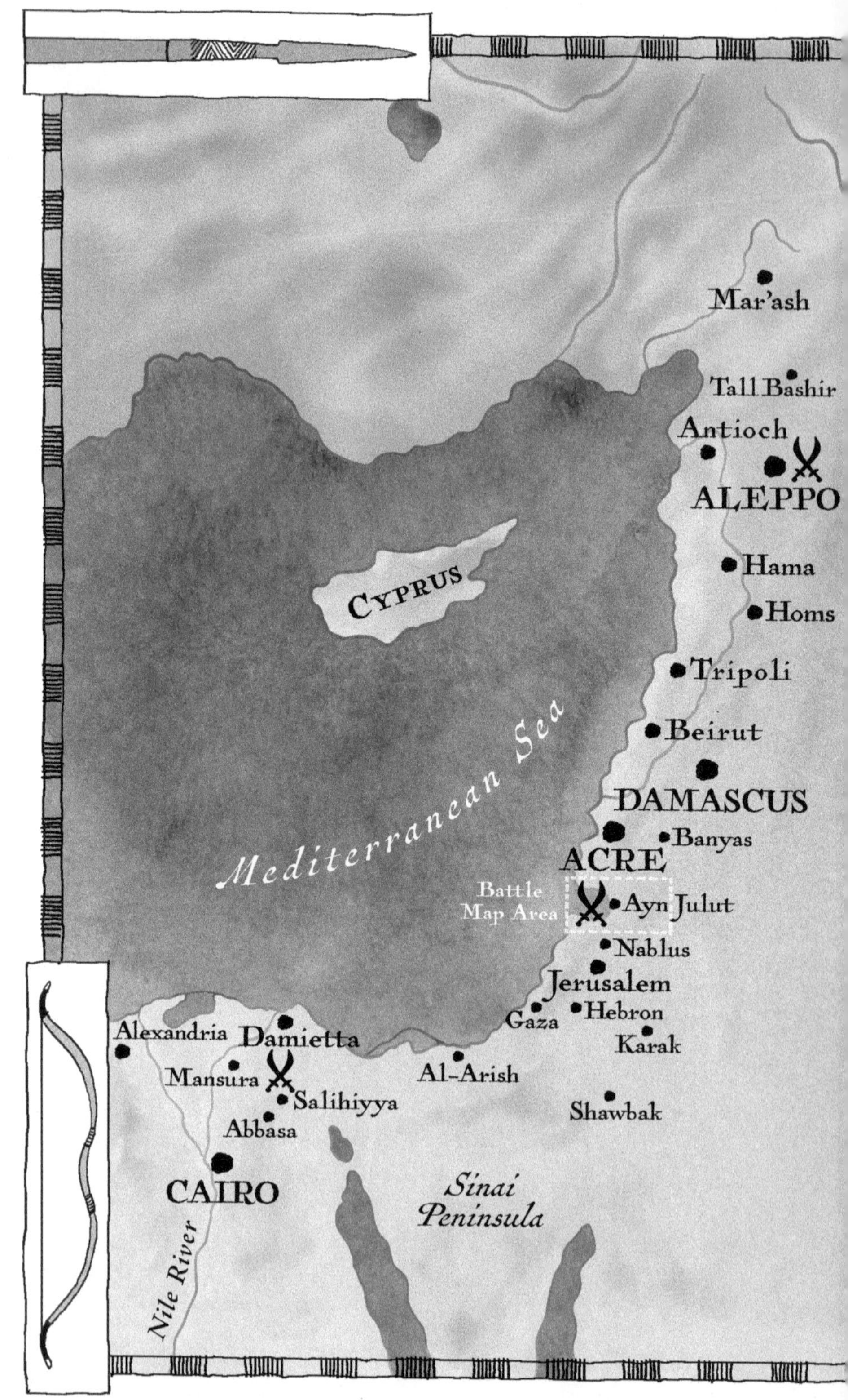
Mar'ash
Tall Bashir
Antioch
ALEPPO
Hama
Homs
Tripoli
Beirut
DAMASCUS
Banyas
ACRE
Battle
Map Area
Ayn Julut
Nablus
Jerusalem
Gaza
Hebron
Karak
CYPRUS
Mediterranean Sea
Alexandria
Damietta
Mansura
Salihiyya
Abbasa
Al-Arish
Shawbak
CAIRO
Sinai
Peninsula
Nile River

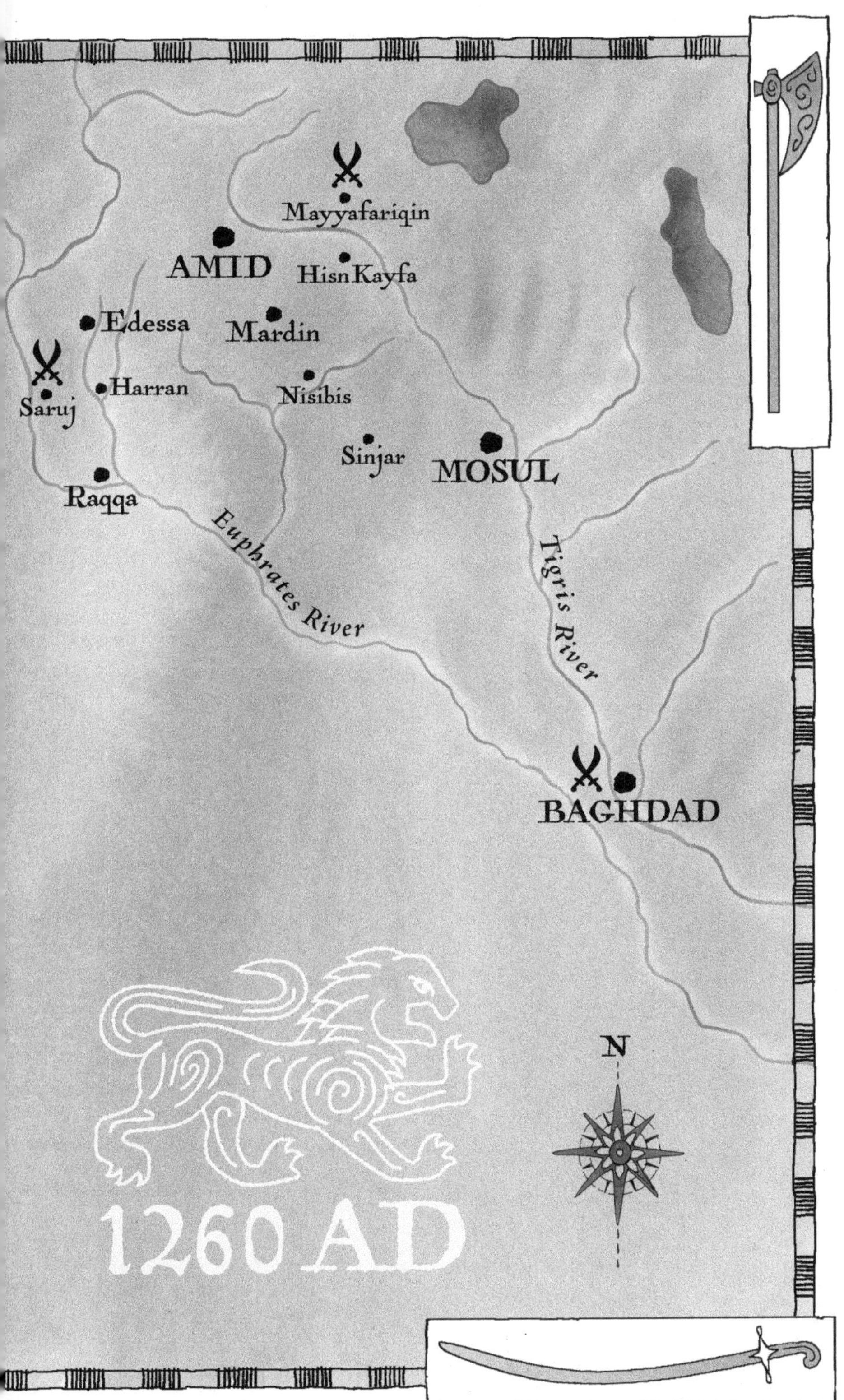
Mayyafariqin
AMID
Hisn Kayfa
Edessa
Mardin
Harran
Saruj
Nisibis
Sinjar
MOSUL
Raqqa
Euphrates River
Tigris River
BAGHDAD
N
1260 AD

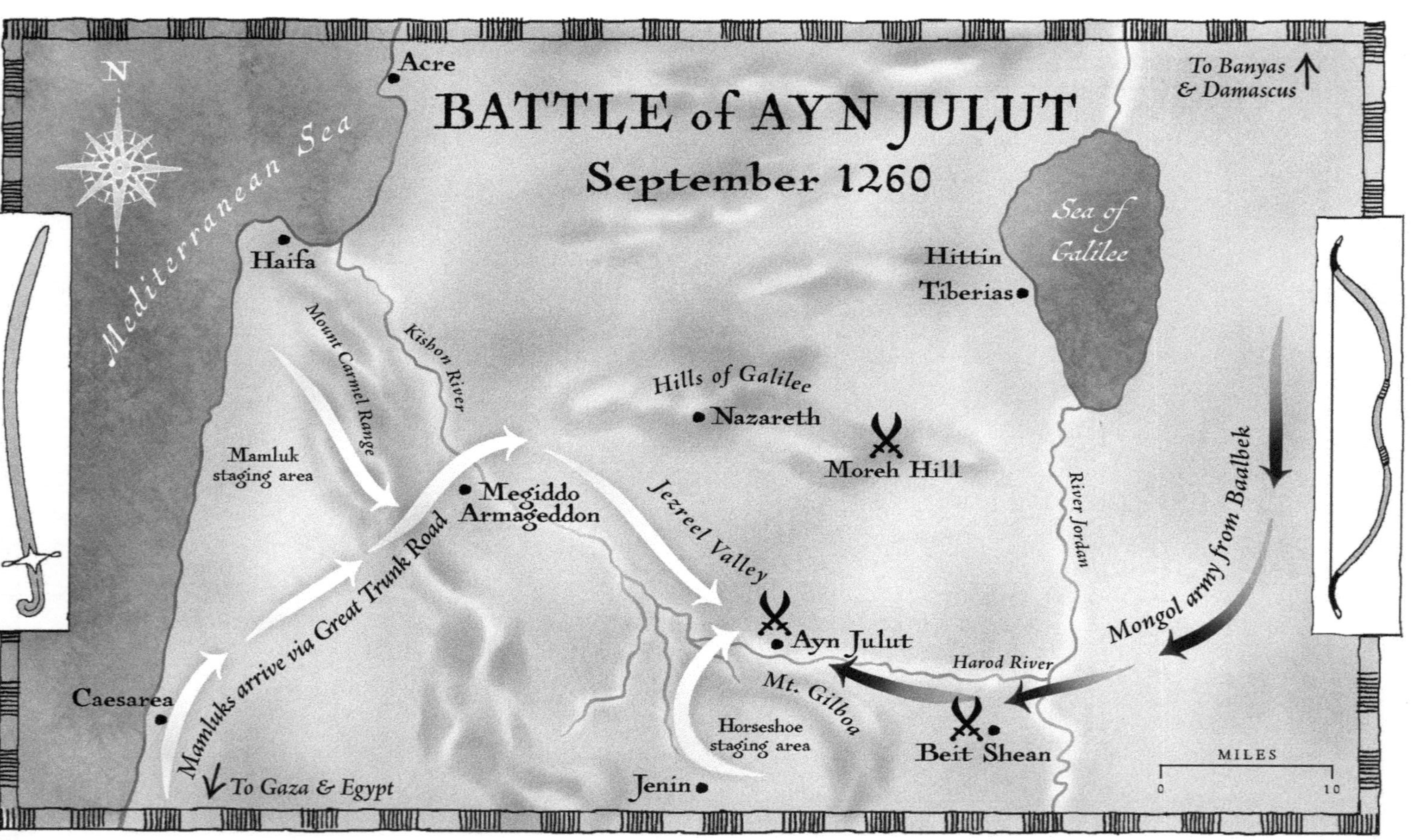
BATTLE of AYN JULUT
September 1260
N
Mediterranean Sea
Acre
Haifa
To Banyas & Damascus
Sea of Galilee
Hittin
Tiberias
Mount Carmel Range
Kishon River
Hills of Galilee
Nazareth
Moreh Hill
Mamluk staging area
Megiddo
Armageddon
Jezreel Valley
River Jordan
Mongol army from Baalbek
Mamluks arrive via Great Trunk Road
Ayn Julut
Harod River
Mt. Gilboa
Caesarea
Horseshoe staging area
Beit Shean
To Gaza & Egypt
Jenin
MILES
0
10

PRAISE FOR
Brad Graft and *Brotherhood of the Mamluks*

"*Chains of Nobility* abounds with evocative portrayals... Excitingly illuminates an ancient class of warriors."

—Kirkus Reviews

"*A Lion's Share* delivers gripping action scenes... A time of nearly unthinkable conflict is vividly brought to life."

—Kirkus Reviews

"Graft nimbly inserts the reader into the world and mindset of the medieval jihadi. From the Russian steppe to inside the citadel walls, he takes us where Mamluks are made and loyalty between comrades is sealed."

—Steven Pressfield, Bestselling author of *The Legend of Bagger Vance*, *The Warrior Ethos*, and *Gates of Fire*

"*Chains of Nobility* is a harrowing tale of comradeship and combat, providing an in-the-saddle look at the process of creating Mamluks—early Islam's military elite. A great piece of work."

—Nathaniel Fick, former Marine Officer and NY Times bestselling author of *One Bullet Away: The Making of a Marine Officer*

"A gripping saga of brotherhood and devotion, *Chains of Nobility* is a must-read for military history buffs. Author Brad Graft enlightens us on the little-known reason behind Medieval Islam's triumphs during the Middle Ages: nomadic youth enslaved by the descendants of Saladin and sharpened into the spear tip of Muslim armies."

—Michael Franzak, former Marine pilot and author of *A Nightmare's Prayer*, winner of the 2012 Colby Award

"In *Chains of Nobility*, Graft displays an exceptional writing style that captures the emotions, and often the harsh environment, in which the action is occurring. An enjoyable read."

—Ron Christmas, Lieutenant General, U.S. Marine Corps and past President/CEO, Marine Corps Heritage Foundation

"*Chains of Nobility* and *A Lion's Share* are rare finds in medieval historical fiction: novels that entertain, while aptly recreating the Mamluk ethos and their era. I am grateful for Graft's work. His academic approach captures the history; his military background and fine writing skills bring these vital stories to life."

—Mahmoud Sabit, historian, filmmaker, and authority on Egypt's Mamluk Period and 19th century political reforms

"An exacting, dramatic, and absorbing look at a world most readers have never encountered, not in books, movies, or history class: military slavery in the Middle East during the 13th century."—*Traverse City Record Eagle*

"The author has created an intriguing and believable world from ancient ideas, settings, and characters, a masterful job of both history and fiction."

—Military Writers Society of America

MORE BOOKS FROM BRAD GRAFT

Chains of Nobility:
*Brotherhood of the Mamluks (Book 1)**
by Brad Graft

A Lion's Share:
*Brotherhood of the Mamluks (Book 2)***
by Brad Graft

*A Finalist for the Colby Award, which recognizes "a first work of fiction or non-fiction that has made a major contribution to the understanding of military history, intelligence operations, or international affairs."
**Awarded a silver medal by the Military Writers Society of America: "The author has created an intriguing and believable world from ancient ideas, settings and characters, a masterful job of both history and fiction."

MORE BOOKS FROM THE SAGER GROUP

The Swamp: Deceit and Corruption in the CIA
An Elizabeth Petrov Thriller (Book 1)
by Jeff Grant

Meeting Mozart:
A Novel Drawn From the Secret Diaries of Lorenzo Da Ponte
by Howard Jay Smith

Labyrinth of the Wind:
A Novel of Love and Nuclear Secrets in Tehran
by Madhav Misra

Three Days in Gettysburg
by Brian Mockenhaupt

Miss Havilland: A Novel
by Gay Daly

The Orphan's Daughter: A Novel
by Jan Cherubin

Lifeboat No. 8: Surviving the Titanic
by Elizabeth Kaye

Shaman: The Mysterious Life and Impeccable Death of Carlos Castaneda
by Mike Sager

A Boy and His Dog in Hell: And Other True Stories
By Mike Sager

BROTHERHOOD OF THE MAMLUKS

BOOK THREE

EDGE OF ARMAGEDDON

A Novel

Brotherhood of the Mamluks: Book Three: Edge of Armageddon

Cover illustration and design by GRAFIT studio
Cover design by Siori Kitajima, PatternBased.com
Maps by Jenifer Thomas of Draw Big Design
Interior Design by Siori Kitajima, PatternBased.com

Cataloging-in-Publication data for this book is available from the Library of Congress.
ISBNs
eBook: 978-1-950154-70-8
Paperback: 978-1-950154-71-5

Published by The Sager Group LLC
www.TheSagerGroup.Net

BROTHERHOOD OF THE MAMLUKS

· BOOK THREE ·

EDGE OF ARMAGEDDON

A Novel

BRAD GRAFT

LIST OF CHARACTERS

Mamluk regiments in the sultanate

- *Salihiyya*, or *Salihi*: original Mamluks of Sultan al-Salih
- *Bahriyya, or Bahri*: Sultan al-Salih's "River Island Regiment"
- *Jamdariyya:* Sultan al-Salih's regiment of royal guards
- *Muizziyya*: Mamluks of Sultan Aybeg
- *Nasiriyya*: Mamluks of the Prince of Damascus, al-Nasir Yusuf
- *Aziziyya*: Mamluks of al-Nasir Yusuf's father, Prince al-Aziz of Aleppo

Mamluks of the Bahri

- *Aqtay*: Amir of One Hundred, leader of the Bahri 1249-1254, murdered by Aybeg and Qutuz in 1254
- *Baybars*: Amir of One Hundred, leader of the Bahri in 1254-1260
- *Zeki* (man of intelligence): Baybars' most-trusted Amir of Forty
- *Sedat* (just): Amirate Three Commander

Mamluks of the Muizziyya

- *Cenk* (combat): advisor to Sultans Aybeg and Qutuz, former amir in the *Jamdariyya*
- *Tarkhan*: Mongol advisor to Qutuz
- "*Ox*," nickname for *Balaban* (robust): amir of the guard

Family Esel served in Damascus

- *Gamal* (handsome): Esel's master, father of the family
- *Rashida* (righteous): mother
- *Saja* (the silence of the night): daughter
- *Esel* (windy land): family slave

Mamluks of Leander's Reconnaissance Team

- *Leander* (lion): interpreter
- *Duyal* (perceptive person): commander
- "*Singer*," nickname for *Halis* (pure/clear/real): Amir Duyal's old friend

Cenk's family

- *Fidan* (young plant): wife
- *Inci* (pearl): daughter
- *Turkmani*: Cenk's first patron; amir killed near Aleppo

Jacinta's family

- *Jacinta* (hyacinth flower): Egyptian spy
- *Kaphiri* (hill): Jacinta's father
- *Zane* (well-born, or noble): Jacinta's boy

Ayyubid Royalty/ Middle Eastern Rulers

Dates refer to reigns

- *Salah ad-Din*, or *Saladin*: Sultan of Egypt (1174-1193), founder of Ayyubid dynasty
- *al-Salih*: Sultan of Egypt (1240-1249), grandnephew of Saladin
- *Shajarat al-Durr:* wife of Sultan al-Salih, Sultana of Egypt (1250)
- *Aybeg*: Mamluk Amir of One Hundred turned Sultan of Egypt (1250-1257)
- *al-Mansur Ali*: fifteen-year-old son of Sultan Aybeg, Sultan of Egypt (1257-1259)
- *Qutuz*: Vicegerent to Aybeg turned Sultan of Egypt (1259-1260)
- *Shaykh Rukn al-Din Khurshah*: head of the Assassins in Persia
- *al-Nasir Yusuf*: Governor of Aleppo (1236-1260) and Damascus (1250-1260), great-grandson of Saladin
- *al-Zahir Ghazi*: brother of al-Nasir Yusuf of Damascus
- *al-Mughith Umar*: Governor of Karak/Transjordan (1250-1263)
- *al-Mansur Mohammad II:* Governor of Hama (1244-1284)
- *al-Ashraf Musa:* Prince of Homs (1246-1248 and 1260-1263), Prince of Tall Bashir (1248-1260)
- *Alam al-Din:* Governor of Damascus after Ayn Julut
- *al-Muzaffar*: Governor of Aleppo after Ayn Julut

Mongol Leadership

Dates refer to reigns as "Great Khan"

- *Genghis Khan*: (1206–1227) uniter of the tribes
- *Mongke:* (1251–1259) Great Khan, son of Tolui, grandson of Genghis Khan
- *Hulegu*: brother of Mongke, tasked with the western offensive into the Middle East
- *Ketbugha*: brother of Mongke, led attacks in western Persia, Damascus, Baalbek; Mongol commander at Battle of Ayn Julut
- *Kubilai*: (1260-1294) brother of Mongke, tasked with southern offensive in China, candidate for Great Khan in 1260
- *Ariq Boke*: brother of Mongke, candidate for Great Khan in 1260
- *Berke*: leader of the "Golden Horde," grandson of Genghis Khan
- *Baydara*: commander at Gaza in 1260

Mongol's Christian Allies

Dates refer to reigns

- *Hetoum:* King of Cilician Armenia (1226-1270)
- *Bohemond VI:* Prince of Antioch and Count of Tripoli (1251-1275)

PART 1

BETRAYAL

"At three things the earth shakes; under four it cannot bear up: a slave turned king..."

–Proverbs 30:21-22

CHAPTER 1

Esel

Damascus, Syria

March 7, 1257

Esel plods along Straight Street in the dark, a splintered yoke resting wide across her shoulders. Empty water bags dangle from each end of her load. Her eyes stay fixed to the Umayyad Mosque's spires, the towers reaching like outstretched fingers, craving to touch the stars blinking in the Great Sky. She turns south on the narrow road leading to the *Bab al-Saghir*, the "Small Gate" on Damascus' south side.

The guard in the sole tower allows her passage with a casual wave through the lattice work, her master having given his permission for her unaccompanied departures for morning chores this week. Her heavy footsteps echo within the arched outlet. Old feet drubbing the timeworn cobbles.

Exiting the gate, she takes the cart path toward the cemetery, past the empty vendor stalls stretching west along the high southern wall. She crosses the blocky mausoleums with their blue-domed roofs, where the Prophet's companions are said to lie, a pair of them enshrining two of Mohammad's wives.

She passes the multitude of round-topped stones peppering the dark flat on both sides of the path, white-pocked slabs with their strange black scribbles faded from the sun. The farther south she travels, the smaller the headstones become, the last of them being the graves of the poor. Unmarked rocks for the weariest, finally resting; boulders and irregular stones, hastily pressed into the graveled soil.

She enters the southern suburb, the mud-bricked homes hugging the narrow strip of road leading to Jordan and Palestine. The warm smell of dough and the burn of cedar fill her nostrils. The early risers prepare their *Saj* by candlelight, the bread named for the vaulted metal surface on which it is baked.

The sound of wet dough being slapped on cooking stones escapes through shuttered windows. She pictures the women inside the mud walls, sitting cross-legged, spreading the white ball, tossing it in the air from hand to hand to get the round shape—the women calling this process the *lougha*, the same name applied to their Syrian folk dance—and then laying the drooping span of dough atop the curved baking tins, blocked above their fires.

Although every woman worth her salt in a Syrian kitchen can throw the bread, Esel never mastered the skill. Tired of their Saj being misshapen and torn, Esel's master had years ago directed her to purchase the family's bread from the market.

Esel reaches a grassy mound between two hills where a scattering of goats graze, one of the few lush areas on her route. She leaves the trail and trudges up the nearest hill. She smiles upon feeling the stalks brushing against her shins. Near the crest, she tips sideways to remove the yoke from her neck. She stretches, rubbing the pain from her back, while taking in the last of the fading stars.

She looks over her shoulders. Seeing no one, she faces north, opposite Mecca, in the direction of the distant grasslands northeast of the Black Sea. She drops to her knees and buries

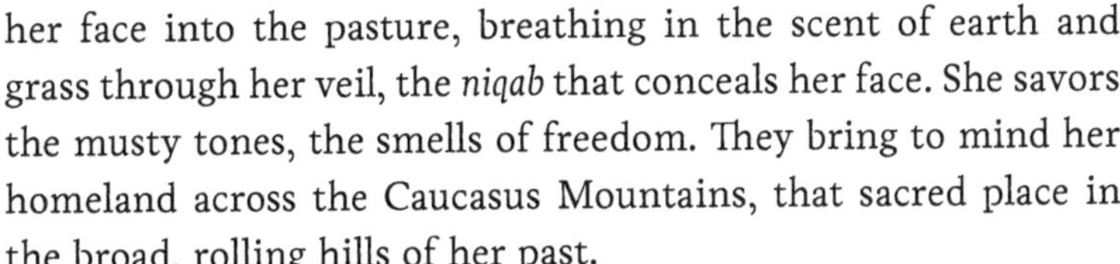

her face into the pasture, breathing in the scent of earth and grass through her veil, the *niqab* that conceals her face. She savors the musty tones, the smells of freedom. They bring to mind her homeland across the Caucasus Mountains, that sacred place in the broad, rolling hills of her past.

She pictures the "String of Hills" in her steppe birthplace. She envisions climbing up the second mount, past the sun-bleached bones from prior sacrifices and half-rotted arrow shafts protruding from the ground shot by passing shepherds in reverence. She imagines wading through the drooping plumes of Stipa grass, weaving about the gifts left at the flattened hilltop, and prostrating herself at the foot of the stone figure.

As a child, she had made an immediate connection with the chiseled form on the second hill, whom her tribe, the Goker Kipchaks, named simply, "Respectable Woman." Legend spoke only of a great woman doing man's work. Round-faced, wide-hipped, and with large breasts, the sculpted rock had been on the hill as long as the Kipchaks themselves.

In one rock hand, the Respectable Woman held a mirror of polished obsidian to protect her back. In the other hand, she held a cup, stained brown from the blood sacrifices of bull, sheep, and dog provided by worshipers so the spirit could eat with the visitors' dead relatives.

The Rus to their west called the row of life-sized statues on the hills *balvan*, translated from their native Turkish as "stupid." Yet Esel's people knew such words only angered the spirits. The Kipchaks prayed to these effigies regularly for strength against such enemies.

The Rus seemed so strange to her back then, the soft-willed peasants who rolled and stacked the stones between their farm plots and pegged wedges of timber upon their mud-walled houses. But even these pitiful folk were robust, compared to the average city dweller here in Damascus.

Esel meditates for a moment and then quietly chants her morning prayer to the Respectable Woman:

"Oh Noble One, oh Wise Spirit, please bless the precious girl in my care, asleep in the stone house. And also my people of the steppe, those scattered in every direction like errant seeds blown far across the plains in violent storms. Bring us herders together soon, just as the close of winter summoned us to gather in joy, before our move to spring grass. Please comfort our Kipchaks—those pushed west from our lands, living under the Tartar's fist. Also those sold into servitude as children and forced to toil for their merchant and princely keepers in these dusty lands.

"Please forgive me, Respectable Woman, for falling short of your ideals those sixteen summers past at the Isthmus of Orkapi, when my eyes went temporarily blind, when my mouth was unable to speak, when the hunting skills you bestowed upon me were lost, when my cursed silence helped seal the fate of my tower."

She rises and slowly peeks behind her. She affixes the yoke to her shoulders and continues down the path. Rounding the bend, she grins, pleased to see no other at the well. She unstraps the empty bags from her yoke.

Hand over hand, Esel pulls the abraded rope atop the well, the large bucket twisting and thumping the stone sides, the old pulley yelping its familiar squeak in the quiet dawn. She ignores the dull ache in her lower back. She sucks in the cool air emitted from the wet rock down in the hole. She closes her eyes. Pull, pull, pull.

The rusted hook atop the bucket handle clunks against the pulley's half-rotted wood. She steps on the rope and pulls the bucket to the stone edge. She pours the precious water into the leather bag without spilling a drop. When the skin is full, she folds over the worn edge twice and lashes the ends. She secures the bag to the end of her yoke and does the same with the second bag.

She wads her gray hair into a fist on the back of her head and reties it with a thin piece of burred hide. She shrugs the stiffness from her shoulders. The star-specked sky transitions to a bluish-black; a dull pink appears hemmed in by the dark clouds on the horizon. She sighs, blowing aside stray curls from her frizzy hair, those that refuse to be restrained by the *hijab* across her head.

As she crouches to pick up her yoke, another woman approaches with a single bucket strapped over her shoulder. Esel winces in the dark. A tightness fills her chest. Tomorrow she will get up even earlier. She recognizes the gait of the thin Albanian slave, one of the chattier women, who seems to spend far too much time here. She tries to remember the woman's name, which she should already know, but it escapes her.

"Good morning, Esel. Up early, I see," the woman says, easing down her load.

"Good morning. Yes, yes, things to be done."

The Albanian struggles to untie the knot holding her strap.

"Let me help," Esel says. She kneels and unsheathes a small knife banded to her calf with the deftness of one accustomed to wielding a blade. She uses the point to quickly loosen both ends of the leather strapping and reties it with loops she used in the old country when fashioning a choke strap.

The Albanian eyes her warily. "My, thank you." She appears eager to engage on a domestic topic. "Gamal's well still dry? Makes for a long walk here."

"Maybe a little long for an old lady," Esel says. "I think he is making arrangements for a new one to be dug." She tightens the binding on one of her bags, hoping the Albanian will see this as a signal that she has little time to chat.

"And how's your little Saja?"

Esel warms, just hearing the name of the beautiful child. "Growing up quickly," she says, her smile waning as she recalls her duties. She must return to get her master's little daughter up and fed.

The woman squints, her smile likely gone sour behind her veil. "And Rashida, the privileged one. Gamal managing to keep his gifted poet content?"

Esel recoils. She knew the gossip would arrive in short order. She will not be drawn into trading slurs on her master's wife. She will not jeopardize the working relationship that has lasted nearly a decade, Gamal treating her about as well as she could hope. He has never touched her, sexually or violently. Perhaps he knows better. While he has not once asked of her background, she suspects that he knows the blood of a warrioress runs through her veins.

"Oh, both are doing well. I must be off," Esel says.

Esel ducks under the yoke, its hewed edge bearing a crack along its entirety. A staple and pole ring remain attached on one side, where the device was once connected to the tongue of a cart, the contraption towed years ago by another of her master's subservient creatures. She squats, her buttocks nearly touching the ground, the curved beam now centered on her neck. She lifts the water containers with a groan.

"Until next time," the woman says, a look of dejection in her eyes.

"Yes," Esel replies. "Good day."

Esel departs for home. Each step away from the well, the tension in her head and rib cage loosens. She lumbers up the dusty road toward her master's house, more comfortable with the pain in her feet and knees than that caused in enduring such encounters with women like the Albanian.

She shakes her curly head and chuckles. Whether fellow slave, wife of a rich man, or a poor widow, she feels equally put off by them all. Whether Circassian, Albanian, Georgian, or a Syrian orphan, Esel often agonizes similarly in their presence.

Even the fellow Kipchak slaves she comes across in the market offer her no solace. Many of these nomadic women have understandably become more Syrian, more Muslim than Kipchak over the years. Esel supposes she could blame her social awkwardness on her previous life, those precious years, before coming to Syria.

Esel had not always been a slave. Born forty-eight years ago on the Kipchak steppe, many said that she was one of the most respected bow-makers in the entire confederation of clans, those who inhabited the vast grasslands between the Black and Caspian Seas. While she never let compliments go to her head, some said that she had all of—some said even more than—her father's skill. And warriors from many tribes acknowledged him as one born with talents seen once every other generation.

She grew up his apprentice, following his instruction, watching his steady hands, and doing precisely as he asked. Year after year, her father taught his daughter every secret of their trade.

She stops to dump a pebble from her slipper, balancing on one foot with the heavy load. The guard nods her approval and she passes through the gate. The worn footpath turns from dirt to cobbles. She trudges along, reminiscing.

When her father became too old to work, he sat hunched by the fire in her felt-walled hut, her *ger*. Wrapped in fleece, he watched her toil all day. After finishing her day's labor, she handed her craftwork to him for inspection. Even once bent over with frailty, he ran the tillered horn and wood through his knotted fingers, holding the curved limbs just beneath his eyes, which had gone cloudy-white.

Occasionally, he gently pointed out a flaw with his signature grin and crinkled eyebrows, probably just to let her know that he could still see, that he still cared. But most of the time he just nodded and handed the creation back to her. It was those moments that motivated her. It was those instances that kept her at the craft after his death. For once he passed on to the Great Sky, she felt the good man's presence most strongly while at her worktable.

She wipes a tear from her cheek with the veil.

Yet it was not just the intricate detail and the soul of the trade that she acquired from the old man. Through her father's dealings, she learned how men thought. She discovered some were good-hearted, while others connived endlessly. She learned the difference between a man of sincerity and one prone to deceit. Her father never spoke of such matters. But as the warriors left his ger, she later understood that his sideways glances flashed to his only child were to see if she was absorbing these lessons in human nature.

She trudges on, the chain ring knocking repetitively against the hard wood of her yoke. Attempting to block out the pain in her back and legs, she plans her day, mulling over which vendors might have the freshest goods, when she will clean the floors, and the best time to pull weeds from the garden. By the time she dumps the last of the water off at the house, the market stalls will be open and she will be able to purchase what is needed for the family's evening meal—some goat, spices, and the few vegetables that she does not have growing in her master's courtyard plot. She looks forward to seeing Saja and hopes the sweetheart is still asleep.

The sun crowns the horizon in a dull gold. She wipes the sweat from her forehead. The yoke digs into her neck, her shoulder muscles tighten. She rests her arms atop the contraption, sticking her swollen thumbs into the two holes drilled across the grain of the wood, where the bow once fit beneath the ox's neck.

She fights the urge to stop and rest. The quicker she moves, the sooner she will be home. At her pace, the rhythm of chain ring against yoke brings to mind a song from her childhood. She grins, quietly humming the sweet melody. The thump of metal on juniper recalls the hourglass-shaped goblet drums of her homeland, fish skin stretched tightly across their hoops, and the fir-necked tamburs of past festivals.

She sings softly in her native tongue, turning occasionally to make sure no one hears. Always expected to use her master's language around the family she serves, when alone, she engages in self-talk, make-believe chats with Yagmur, her deceased husband, and these Kipchak tunes, which keep her fluent in her language of origin.

Esel smiles, recalling her aunt singing this very song as she milked the cows that had lost their calves in the spring. While Esel puts her heart into the melody, she cannot match the clarity of her kin's voice, which not only calmed the beasts, but was often known to make the cows low softly.

She looks into the vast blueness. The Great Sky. She laments the days of old when at her feet was not the dusty stone path of her current life, but the abundant grass of the steppe; days when she heard not the clunk of metal on yoke, but the musical jangle from the tack of her stout-legged pony, the beast taking her not to the stone house of her keeper, but to the felt-walled security of her riverside shelter.

And to that big ger of hers—that haven of her previous craftwork, that place the Goker Kipchaks made especially for her. Her ger. She smiles thinking of that specially-made workplace on the steppe so many years ago, so far away from this scorched desert land in every way.

CHAPTER 2

Esel

The steppe, northeast of the Black Sea
July 26, 1236

Gers, shelters of the Kipchak people, were unique in the fact that they lacked uniqueness. Each had a frame formed from willow, its shell of mushroom-colored wool laboriously crafted from pounded fleece. The entrance flap faced south, welcoming both guests and the warming sun. Most gers spanned nine paces in width, the exception being the khan's, whose shelter exceeded fifteen paces, enough space to hold his meetings with the elders or occasional visitors.

The typical dwelling was void of items unnecessary, holding only crucial possessions, adapted over the centuries by a people who continuously moved between pasture lands. A fire pit centered the structure, capped with an iron tripod that held the family pot, if fortunate. Otherwise, three blackened stones supported their crock. A flap overhead vented the space. Pine-logged beds of the male inhabitants lined the west wall and those of the females occupied the east wall.

When mare's milk was abundant, the nomads suspended a single leather vessel near the entrance, filled with the fermented beverage, *koumis*. In season, yogurt curds also dangled in balanced pairs to dry, looking like ornaments, swung over wooden supports with horsehair twine. At the north wall stood a bureau, holding the family's belongings.

Six years ago, when she was but twenty-three, the tribe—or what her nomads called a *tower*—built Esel her own ger. This hut was like most, yet bigger than all, save the khan's. Her standing chest anchored the room. Taken from the Kievans during a raid several autumns prior, its painted coating had peeled, leaving only chipped hints of flowers and winding stems. Hinged doors veiled shelving on the right side and a massive compartment on the left.

Yet Esel's bureau was not packed with fur-lined mittens, wool garments, and her family's modest cookware. Instead, hers was piled with tilted spires of wooden cups, blackened pots, tangles of dried tendon, heaps of hewn maple limbs on tilt, long rolls of white-pocked bark, and entwined ram horns in varying lengths. She opened the doors to this wobbly piece of furniture cautiously, on the alert to catch bundles of material that often tumbled from the heavily-loaded shelves.

Atop her refuge was a vent hole twice the size of that of most gers, designed to both accommodate a large drying fire and maximize workspace light. Beneath and just offset from the opening was a worktable built specifically to her short height, as she would hardly reach the shoulder of a yearling colt. In the colder months, a dung-fueled fire burned almost always, but rarely was Esel the one to start or maintain the flame. No matter how early she rose to ply her craft, she arrived to warmth and a pile of wood, or worm-holed dung, stacked against the felt wall like saucers.

When entering Esel's ger, guests watched their step or risked tripping over heaps of wooden limbs and coils of sinew, lying in various stages of unpacking. In Esel's domain there were no beds or sleeping rugs, but rather thick oaken benches abutting the walls east and west. Hanging above and around these were bows, arrows, and components of each, in all stages of production. Guests coming to speak with Esel peeked through drying wood limbs bent in elegant arches, flattened sections of wild sheep horn stored on dowels, and around webs of stretched hide and twisted sinew, used for bowstrings and sizing.

Visitors' eyes invariably wandered about the structure, as each visit provided one with an interior view altered since their previous call. Each day, Esel hung more completed bows for their year-long drying process, the limbs at rest in their c-shaped curl, packed like bats in a cave. And in this ger, a guest's eyes could stray without insulting the dweller. Friends who tried to converse with Esel found themselves talking to the bushy top of her head. She kept her eyes down upon her handiwork, her tiny feet often covered in twisted shavings of bone or wood.

Instead of reading her facial clues to clarify the meaning in her speech, her fellow Kipchaks grew adept at taking in more obscure hints, picking up the nuances of her locks. The wriggle of long curls in one manner confirmed an idea. The sway of her dirty-blonde tresses in another discouraged a discussed course of action. The shake of the entire heap meant a yarn well-received, a sign recognized by the astute long before the snorting laughter left Esel's throat. If told an exceptionally funny tale, the little woman could be heard guffawing through four layers of felt, and the tips of her hair—at times shrouded in clumps of dried glue—danced the merriest of jigs, clicking about her mottled tabletop in glee.

The absence of eye contact and face-to-face communication in Esel's ger did not deter tribesmen from entering in a continuous stream. Rarely were there not two or three warriors present.

The tower's children found her ger a place of endless fascination: the abode mounded with an ever-changing collection of animal parts; the haven where the smiling lady cleverly hid shin-high works in progress from searching eyes; the sanctuary where the kids might eventually be run off by the older visitors, but never by the sweet resident; the hut where precious gifts of pared maple and dried gut string were presented with regularity. Callers had to be careful when entering. At any moment, children could burst from Esel's wool lodging, like caddisfly bugs from their underwater shucks, with wide eyes and fluttering arms, one hand grasping its first simple bow, the other small fist stuffed with crude arrows.

At mealtimes, the felt walls of most gers held in the savory scent of fatty sheep or the occasional chunk of horsemeat boiling in the pot. But during all waking hours, Esel's ger emitted only the smell of wet maple, boiling horn, or the subtle tang of fish and sinew glue bubbling in her tiny pot. And while she often awakened at her workbench, with her arms asleep, unaware if it was day or night, Esel did not routinely sleep in this ger. She only worked in it during the cold weather or early mornings. On calm days, she preferred to labor outside. To work with fewer interruptions, she took to starting before sunup, even though the candlelight stressed her eyes.

Humming to herself this day, with half-dried fish glue covering her fingers, she pushed the unruly hair from her face with the back of her hand. Spotting her hemp hair tie on the bench, she chided herself for forgetting her husband's teasing advice. "My darling, you may want to put a strap on that osprey's nest," Yagmur often said.

Squinting in the flickering light of the tallow candles, she pulled another section of pre-measured leg tendon from a wooden bowl of water and laid it flat on her table. She combed the stringy mass until it was flat and then dipped and re-dipped the white sinew into a pot filled with syrupy goop. After each dip, she squeezed the excess glue from the soggy mass between her thumb and forefinger. After repeating this process again and again, she flipped the strip and did the same, ensuring every fiber of tendon was saturated.

Turning to the clamped bow frame beside her—the weapon thickened in the center at the grip and tapering perfectly to the tips—she carefully placed the dripping ribbon of sinew atop the upper limb. She smoothed the sinew along the full length of the stout birch—grip to tip—careful to keep the tendon strands perfectly flat and even across the width of the limb.

She contemplated the carving she would add to the horn section of this piece. While the children were always ecstatic to see their names etched into one of the limbs, for the adults she occasionally engraved the likeness of a warrior's favorite dog or trusted steed into the bone. Often the recipients left her ger with wet eyes, her bows destined to become cherished family relics to be passed down through the generations.

But her weapons were not wall decorations. She built each with the realization that her pieces were the lethal determinants of life and death for her Kipchak tower's slice of the steppe. Even the children's bows, the devices of endless games, were often placed in the hands of toddlers before they could walk, so they came to know the feel of bow grip in hand.

And no one in the tower knew better how a drawn bow should feel than this woman with the wild hair. For the finely crafted weapons she built, any variation of thickness in the layers of wood or sinew or bone on the recurved limbs of her bows—any error in the consistency of the sinew scraps mixed into the fish glue—made bows unbalanced, created weapons that were too soft or too stiff, or caused the materials to separate and fall apart.

Poorly-crafted weapons created missed arrow shots. Missed shots turned into lost game, surviving predators that lived to maul their flock, or undispatched enemies who would return later to threaten the tower again—all of which produced starving Kipchak children and dead warriors. Her father beat these topics home when Esel was very young, the only times she could recall his mellow speech turning stern. "We are not allowed to have a sloppy day's work. Good enough often is not," he always said.

Running the flat of her finger down the smooth length of the bow limb, she tried to picture his smiling face, recall his jovial ways. Her father had been the tower's master bowyer. More than that, he had been a good man, consistently guiding her, never once raising a hand to her in anger.

She grew up completing bow-crafting tasks better suited to her youth and vigor, or taking on those monotonous parts of the trade that were beneath him, although he would never treat them as such. She busied herself roaming the bottomlands for birch-bark of proper consistency, prepping deer and moose tendons, or cleaning the impurities from fish bladders. Her happiest moments recalled from youth were those sparkles in her father's eyes when he looked over her shoulder to see her batch of bubbling glue made to the right consistency, or when he peeked out the ger flap to see a hunk of elm she had dragged back from her explorations, which they both knew would make the perfect bow frame.

As the years passed after her father's death, she grew more competent in her craft. She ignored the generous words poured upon her—that she had become the most respected bowyer in the entire confederation. She was not interested in praise, but only in perfecting her craft.

Regardless, she made the bows because the tribe needed a good bowyer. She made the bows because the tower could not survive without accurate weapons. She made the bows because her father would have wished her to do so. She figured this life of hers was destined by the gods. Her path was to be about stick, string, and feather—and applying this deadly combination to hunt the prey and predators, which also roamed their cherished steppe.

CHAPTER 3

Esel

Damascus, Syria
March 9, 1257

Esel sets aside her axe and tosses the last of the split pieces into her cart, a mix of gnarled terebinth, scrub oak, and well-dried fir. She wipes a dirty sleeve across her brow, eyeing the shadow cast by her load—almost as long as the object itself, almost time for the afternoon prayer.

She pushes the handcart to the front door of Gamal's home, the sprawling house flat-roofed and plastered with elegantly painted stucco. The master will be home soon. She pivots, centering the blocky wheels of her cart in the door frame. Slipping under the worn leather strap between cart handles, she leans her back into it, grunting while pulling on the thick grips. She pulls the cart inside.

With a glance over her shoulder, she takes quick stock of the room. Well-swept floors. The chairs about the family's table spaced evenly. Two clay vessels filled to their lips with drinking water sweat in the corner. A bundle of kindling lies waiting in the firebox. All exactly the way Gamal's wife, Rashida, insists. Esel unloads the cart, neatly stacking the wood upon the hearth. She picks up the stray pieces of bark and drops them in the empty cart bed.

"Esel!" the young Saja bounds in, beaming.

Esel grins, her eyes going to the wildflowers splayed in the girl's tiny fist. "Well now, look at those lovelies. Will not your mother be tickled?"

"I picked them for you," the girl says, setting them carefully atop the table and then skipping her way into her room to stow her bag.

Esel bites her lip, hopes Saja will not say such words in front of Rashida. Esel pulls a ceramic vase from the shelf, adds a ladle of water, and tidily arranges the stems. "Thank you, but these may be too pretty for just one person—maybe I will set them on the table for all of us to enjoy."

"All right," Saja says reentering the room with a book in hand.

"Did your dolls find their way back into the bin as your mother asked?"

"Yes, *nene*."

Esel grins at the girl's recall of the Turkish words she shared and the grandmotherly allusion. "How were your teachings today?"

"Mathematics, nothing hard," the girl says.

"Not for you."

"Ha!"

The recognizable voice of the *muezzin* flows through the open door of the home, the crisp rise and fall of his call reverberating about the hard floor and tight-blocked walls.

Esel had grown tolerant of the "call to prayer," only once swapping, in her mind, the *adhan* sung in Arabic with the also often-undecipherable chant of their *saman*, their Kipchak holy man, droned those years past on the steppe. She only pretends to be a Muslim, refusing to let go of her steppe peoples' gods.

Yet she is under no illusion whose religion reigns here. Islam rules. Many locals refer to Damascus as *al-Sham*—"the north"—in reference to the city's location, relative to the Muslims' cradle of religion on the Arabian Peninsula. Not far enough north for her liking, she thinks.

"Time for the *Asr*," Esel says.

"Can we go to the mosque for prayer this time, before Mother and Father come home?"

"Ah, we might best stay here," Esel says smiling. Saja is still naively unaware that a household slave entering the mosque with a money man's daughter may raise some eyebrows with the local wives, as well as among Rashida's fellow teachers.

A sadness falls upon the child's olive-skinned face. "Why do you always prefer the *Du'a*?" she asks, her green eyes squinting.

Esel grins, knowing this question would come one day. The child puts more and more together each moon, finally wondering why Esel seems to be consistently busy, or rarely near the mosque, during the five prayer times.

The houses of worship are places for only the men to appear publicly, the women crammed into partitioned sections of just a few mosques to revere Allah. Esel prefers the Du'a—the less formal prayers—acceptable for Muslims traveling and encouraged for overburdened slaves.

"Well, you know my list of tasks is long," Esel says. "Taking the time to get to the mosque and back is often difficult for me. Not best for the family."

"But the other women talk before and after prayer. Friends share views. It is fun."

"That is true."

She looks at Esel solemnly, as if just coming to some determination. "But you would rather not see them, would you? The other women."

Esel grins. "Oh, I do not know."

"I watch you keep to yourself at the bazaar, too. When we are there, you do not gab with the others."

"I am there to buy supplies for this household, not cackle with the local hens. There is work to be done. Do you think your father would have kept me here for ten years if I did not complete the things he asked? I would rather be unfamiliar with the happenings in Damascus and have my tasks finished than otherwise."

"But what about friends? It is hard to keep friends when you do not talk to them."

Esel nods.

"Do you have girlfriends? You never speak of any."

Esel wipes the table. Saja waits for the answer.

Esel sighs. "I suppose I do not have many friends."

"Why? You are very nice."

"Everyone is different. Where I came from, my best friend was a man, my husband."

"What is his name?"

"Yagmur."

"But you had girlfriends there, too?"

"Things there were not as they are here. My mother died of the fever when I was younger than you. No other woman took me under her wing to teach me all of the things needed to become a woman. I spent very little time with them."

"So, you are mad at all women for this?"

Esel laughs. "No, my plum. But I was raised more around men."

"Men?"

"Yes, men." She tries to remember one invitation from the Kipchak women in the old country—a single offer to join them in scraping hides, repairing felt, drying meat, or breaking down gers during the tower's moves. Not one summons comes to mind.

"Like here, people concentrate on certain things in the northern tribes," Esel says. "There is food to gather, animals to kill, and such. I did these things instead of what most women were doing."

"With the men?

Esel laughs. "Yes, yes. With the men."

"What about cooking? You must have cooked back home with the women. You know how."

"My, you ask many questions from your nene today. I learned to cook later in life. Luckily, you were not around to eat the food I prepared during my first years in Syria."

During Esel's first six moons in Syria, only the patient tutelage from her first master's wife kept the old merchant from chucking Esel back on the slave block. When this previous master died six years into her servitude, he left his struggling business and personal possessions to his brother. While the brother took all her master's household items, he turned his nose up at Esel, the slave who ran the house.

Esel was taken back to the same trading station on the northern outskirts of Damascus, where she started her servitude, sixteen years earlier in 1241. That day, she was exchanged for seven hundred dinars. Her strong back but mediocre cooking and house-tending talents, placed her worth at fifty gold pieces more than a pack donkey, eight hundred less than those Arabians ridden by the Mamluk warriors who served the Prince of Damascus.

Even now, only Gamal's patience with her culinary ruins, or perhaps his realization that his prized wife was no more talented at the cook fire, kept him from dragging Esel back to the slave merchants.

The second call wails, the *Iqamah*, summoning the Muslims to line up for the beginning of the prayers.

Saja pouts. "So you and I will never go to the mosque together, will we?"

"Well. You and are I are friends and we talk right here. And we still pray together. Are not those the two important things?"

Saja smiles.

"Just remember the verse from the Koran: 'If a Muslim prays without the right attitude of mind, it is as if they had not bothered to pray at all. Woe to those who pray but are unmindful of their prayer, or who pray only to be seen by people.' You don't want nene worried about her work here while in the mosque, do you?"

"No, but the Koran also says that prayer at a mosque brings twenty-seven times more blessing than a prayer outside a mosque."

Esel beams. "We will hope that God forgives me. Maybe those twenty-seven times are more than God needs to hear. Talking to God is a personal thing. Appreciating our differences and how another worships—maybe it is one way we show respect for each other."

Saja fetches her rolled prayer mat and Esel sets hers beside the child's. They face southward toward Mecca and bow, resting their hands on knees. They kneel. Assuming the prostrate position, Esel turns to watch Saja close her eyes, the girl bending down to set her forehead to the floor.

As Saja does so, Esel makes a quarter turn north, closer to the direction of her homeland, the heaving grasslands, along the *Su Basi*, their tributary of the great Volga. Esel puts her head to the stone. Curls enshroud her face, providing a comforting sanctuary, an assist in bringing her to that sacred place in the String of Hills. She breathes in the dusty odor of the rock floor, recollecting a more heartening scent far to the northeast, the smell of cold stone and charred dung from ritual fires set at the base of the Respectable Woman's legs.

Esel and Saja return to the kneeling position, opening their hands to the sky, palms up, moving their lips as they mutter prayers. Saja whispers through her second *raka*, her tiny brow furled. Good. Let the dear child become a devout Muslim; let her be blessed by this land's God.

Esel again bows, making her afternoon prayer. Her mind stays fixed on the last line of her hushed recitation: "Please forgive me, Respectable Woman, for falling short of your ideals those sixteen summers past at the Isthmus of Orkapi, when my eyes went temporarily blind, when my mouth was unable to speak, when the hunting skills you bestowed upon me were lost, when my cursed silence helped seal the fate of my tower."

She keeps her head down, the thoughts of those events on the Orkapi narrow shoving the prayers from her mind, quashing the peace granted by the Respectable Woman. Her people thereafter called that place *Kıyamet Isthmus*, or "Isthmus of Doom." Her memories of that day pervade, preventing her from finishing her devotions.

She sits upon her ankles in contemplation, waiting for the child to finish her personal prayer to Allah. Finish your prayer, little one. Make sure you stay in the better of graces of your God than I am with mine.

Amid Saja's prayers, muttered beneath her breath, Esel attempts to drive out the negative. Her mind floats northward to the undulant hills, to the infinite grass waving so joyously in the wind. She daydreams of time spent with her young nephew, Baybars, the closest thing to a son she ever had, her own womb incapable of producing a child.

She muses how it might have been if the Mongols had never attacked their lands, if Saja had been born many years ago as a Kipchak, not a Syrian. How enjoyable it would have been if Saja had been Esel and Yagmur's child, one near the age of her sister's boy. How nice it would have been if Baybars and Saja had been like brother and sister. Life-long friends.

As bright as the pair were, how well they would have gotten along. Perhaps the sweet girl would have taken some of the edge off her serious nephew, maybe gotten him to laugh a little more. Probably not. She smiles.

Brother and sister. Her daydream is pure illusion. A profound sadness comes over her as she tries to envision the boy, his features mostly lost to her. Baybars, that young prodigy she helped raise those decades past.

CHAPTER 4

Esel

The steppe, northeast of the Black Sea

July 26, 1236

Esel rose from her worktable, tiny coils of shaved ibex horn tumbling from her blouse as she stood. She laid down her blade and elbowed open the ger flap, looking back at the six unstrung bows on her bench as the morning's first rays cast orange upon the wood and horn. With a parting glimpse, she picked out the imperfections in each of the curved weapons, none of which would affect durability or accuracy. Looking at the dry glue splotches covering her table, she grimaced. Her father would not have been pleased.

Her mind wandered back to his thick hands. She had marveled at the remarkable delicacy in his meaty fingers, at his speed in shaving down the birch or maple, his precision when joining the grafted layers of bone. When finished, he would leave not a drip of fish glue in the pot or splattered on the worktable. She remembered the exactness in his bows, knew she would never be as talented as he. She still missed him, having spent more time with him than her own husband. She nodded, thankful for all that the old man had taught her.

For years, he repaired any bow brought to him, regardless of its condition, often holding the mangled weapon up to the light and tilting his head back with that permanent grin to assess the damage. "Hmmm, ah well, I see. We should be able to get this one back to sticking deer and spreading fear," he would say, his frown turning into a large-toothed smile when meeting the eye of a relieved warrior.

Even though his wife passed many years ago, her father refused to take another mate. He comforted himself through complete immersion in his work. As a young man, he would often look up from his table to realize he had eaten nothing all day. Later in life, the tower's women, aware of his ways, alternately brought him a portion of their family's evening gruel each day, so that he would be assured of at least one good meal.

The men would also feed him—critical raw materials, that is, goods from which he created his magic. In return for the highly-prized bows made from his hand, and at times in an effort to put their needs ahead of the others, men in the tower would duck into his ger routinely. They brought him: horn from the upland ibex, used for the inner belly of the bow; tendons stripped from the rear legs of wild game for the sinew layer applied to the bow's back; leather hide from their ponies slaughtered for meat, used for weather-resistant bow strings; swim bladders from fish, which produced the best glue. As a nearly-unnoticed observer at his side, Esel was raised witness not just to her father's skills in the bowyer craft, but also to his dealings with the tower's warriors, and she was ever observant of their exertions to stay in his good graces.

Only when ibex, deer, and moose were scarce, did her father compromise and use the horns and tendons from the tower's rams or traded cattle. Looking at his finished work made from livestock one day, he picked at the glue on his fingers until the skin came with it. Oblivious to the blood wrung into his hands, he said, "I do not like this. Wild material is superior to that from the domesticated beast. Just as on the field of battle, the wild and hardy will always defeat those raised soft and docile, all else being equal."

She knew that her father and the rest of the tower were disappointed that he had no sons, although her father would never say as much to anyone. Only his exceptional standing allowed him to break the gender rules in the tribe, teaching Esel, his only child, every secret of the craft. More as a tribute to him, as opposed to a love of the art, Esel stuck with it. She probably had little choice. Aside from the hunt, what else did she know?

She walked a few hundred paces away from the cluster of gers, gaining a view of the rocky hummocks, the rising sun warming the swelling grasslands. Heavy seed heads bent the stalks at the same graceful arc as the bows she crafted. She smiled at the field of little golden bows.

The precious summer grass now held on to the last of its green, as a middle-aged woman held on to the last of her youthful allure. Soon the tower's flock would consume the feed in this broad meadow, compelling the expedient breakdown of gers and a move to fresh grass.

A dark figure moved on a hillside, catching the corner of her eye. A pulse of panic sped to her core. A sole form, riding bareback. She sighed in relief as the rider leaned to take a shot into a chest-high target made of an old deerskin, crudely attached to a makeshift tripod. A boy, his target riddled with a tight group of arrows, looking like the nose of a dog after giving chase to a porcupine. He made a wide sweep, squeezed his calves, switched hands with reins and bow, took aim when his pony found a steady gait, and released another arrow. All of this done in one flowing motion.

He pulled his pony to a halt, patted the animal's neck, and instinctively checked his quiver for remaining arrows, all the while scanning the hilltops. He waited for the fatigued stallion to recover, the lad rolling his neck to remain loose in the way of her eight-year-old nephew, Baybars. Reluctantly, he allowed the pony to dip its head to indulge in a taste of grass, seemingly frustrated that the animal did not share the rider's focus on the task at hand.

She nodded in relief, remembering Baybars' comment last week. "I am unsatisfied with my ability to shoot with the bow in either hand," he had stated in his sober tone, foreign to most others of his age. She was not surprised to see him working at her recommended drill in solitude, while the other children—even the tower's best warriors—were still curled on their sheepskins.

Five years prior, her nephew had charged out of her ger with his new bow in hand. From the first moment he drew back, she pegged his talent as innate. His bow arm and drawing forearm naturally formed a line as straight as the arrows in his quiver. His release was unvaryingly smooth. She thought then that he shot and acted more like five than three years old. She recalled Baybars three years later, at age six, deadly accurate with the bow.

> *The shooting match finished, Baybars unstrung his bow and placed it into its oilcloth cover. Two older boys approached him after Baybars' victory.*
>
> *A push. A kick. Baybars took one step away to feign retreat, and then pounced on the first attacker, grabbing a leg and hurling a punch at the boy's face. The second boy, smirking, dove into the fracas, eventually pinning Baybars down and punching him several times until her nephew surrendered.*
>
> *When the ordeal was done, Baybars rose and caught his breath. Without a whimper, he went back to his weapon. Dropping to one knee, he carefully inspected its condition, worried more about a scratch to his bow than his swelling eye and the blood dripping from his nose. Pleased his bow and quiver were fine, he blew the blood from his nose, carefully holding his prized possessions away from the spray.*

She had noticed then that while the older boys still attempted to keep her nephew at bay, many of the kids his age and younger had begun to naturally trail behind him, like a mob of fawns. They watched his every move. They emulated his mannerisms. While preferring seclusion, he seemed at ease in this role, or at least cognizant that it was best not to fight the natural order of things. During games, Baybars corrected the younger boys' bow technique, mimicking the instruction taught by her and the tower's best warriors. He turned away none who were willing to learn.

Esel reckoned this boded well for the tower, as many of the young boys were better shots than some of the older warriors were at this age. She refused to take any credit, dismissing the thought that their performance was a direct result of the improved quality of the bows she made for the tower. The lads' proficiencies were tied to the vigor in their practice. Her nephew's fire was contagious.

The boy finally showed mercy on the tired pony this morning, securing his mount with the others. He strolled toward his mother's ger, yet changed his course once spotting Esel.

"My nephew must have the eyes of an owl to have gotten in so much drill before first light," Esel said.

"Arrows are most often shot at game and foes during low light. Why would one practice during high sun?" Baybars asked in jest, quoting a line from one of the tower's best hunters. He smiled. "If you like, I will help you strip those tendons today."

"Yes, good." Esel nodded as the boy walked away. Perhaps the tower would remain strong for another generation, if so desired by the spirits. Just maybe her Goker Kipchaks would not have to continue living their entire lives on the run, pushing farther west to escape the enemy's wrath. She turned again to the rocky mountain bluffs, scanning the southern crags until she found the outline of a warrior on watch. He sat erect, half-hidden by a boulder; his bow laid across his thighs.

She looked east to the near slope of a large knoll, where last moon a warrior answered the holy man's call, sacrificing himself to the River Spirit on behalf of his tower. Tears welled in her eyes as the morning bronze slathered the earthen mound and the grave's only adornments: a wooden image of the enemy he had slain in battles past and the martyr's spear stuck deep into the steppe. A clump of tail hair from his favorite pony fluttered atop the shaft. She recalled the morning the saman read the cracks in the sheep's burned shoulder bone, telling of the bold action needed in return for the she-spirit's protection from the Mongols, those hordes from the east also known by many as Black Tartars.

The warrior who had offered his life was unmarried, thus his burial was modest by Kipchak standards, but proper, as this young man had surrendered his future and had proven himself virtuous. When the warrior's heart stopped, his fellow nomads went straight to the pony herd and led his favorite animal away. They first sliced the animal's shoulder and in ceremony drank blood from the cut. They then killed and dressed out the animal, presenting the meat to the entire tower.

The women took the pony's head, tail, and legs and prepared them for ritual. They stretched the hide on a wooden frame, eventually stuffing the skin with dried grass. When all was ready, the warrior's kin dressed him in a belted tunic and put a wooden cup in his hand. They laid him and his pony in the hole with their heads facing west. Also beneath the dirt with him was all else he would need on the other side—his bow, a dozen worn arrows, and a wooden vessel of *nabiz*—wine made from dates. The warriors he had slain, represented by the carving above, would serve him in the next world.

She bowed her head in prayer to the Great Sky, asking again that this warrior's selfless act be well received and help protect them from the enemy. She opened her eyes.

A flock of blackbirds swooped down in unison over the hillock, a quivering black tapestry dispersing wide to the consistency of fleas in air, only to bunch up in seconds, dark as mud. They landed in a throng of chirping, screeching bedlam. Some perched atop the carving, while others surrounded the weapon shaft, the birds equally unafraid of the hair waving in the wind as the sculpted human form beside it. They bobbed their squawking heads, their clamor producing an energy that felt capable of pulling his spear from the ground.

One bird departed, causing all to vanish over the hill in a shimmering wave of shrieks and flapping wings, leaving the thick tuft of ponytail, rising and falling in the stiffening eastern breeze. She turned back toward her ger, as a shudder moved through her.

CHAPTER 5

Cenk

Cairo Citadel

April 10, 1257

With one eye closed, Cenk peers along the edge of the sword, the blade resting on the stub of finger on his left hand. He grunts in self-confirmation that he has filed the proper angle along its length. He nudges aside his sharpening stone.

"I can find you a skilled trooper to put a proper edge on that blade, if you wish," Tarkhan says, his elbows upon the same table.

Cenk raises a lip. "You forget I was years as an amir in the *Jamdariyya*." He waves his hand about the axes and swords in their racks, the red-coated uniforms hanging stiffly on rods. "This guard hut was where I taught my men the right way to whet steel back then."

The Mongol Tarkhan raises his eyebrows in mock fascination. "Hmmm. Way back, when you were a real soldier in the royal guard and not a scroll-scribbling advisor. I am surprised you even remember which end of the sword to sharpen now," he says, fighting off a grin, the man dressed in the traditional Mongol *deel*, his overcoat no different than that worn by the herders in his rugged homeland.

"This from a used-up, spit-out commander. Like you ever employed any practical skills, once reaching your *lofty* level of command," Cenk says. He looks up to meet his comrade's eyes with a wink.

Tarkhan shakes his head, smiles broadly.

Even though Tarkhan shares the ethnicity of the empire's most lethal enemy, Cenk cannot help but like the old man, his fellow counselor to Aybeg, the Sultan of Egypt. Perhaps it is because this Mongol refugee—this *Wafidiyya*, as the Mamluks call them—has so much in common with Cenk himself. Raised as a common herder and hunter, Tarkhan rose through the Tartar ranks quickly, eventually leading a battalion of a thousand horsemen, the Mongol *mingan*.

Cenk puts his eyes back to the blade. "Just a few more years of this staff life, my brother, and then we will both be put to pasture, eh? Once we bring some security back to Mother Egypt. Then maybe we will actually take that hunt we have been chattering about for so long. We will then see if you remember how to ride a horse, see if you actually have any soldierly competencies left."

The Mongol grins, but his eyes go quickly serious. "One too many enemies circling to think of those frivolities now."

Cenk nods. During all of his thirty-one years of service, the empire—encompassing a swath of North Africa, Syria and the upper Jazira—continually had threats to fret over. But Cenk struggles to remember a time more perilous than now.

As usual, Cairo faces an assortment of Ayyubid royals opposed to the sultanate, Kurdish princes with Saladin the Great's blood coursing through their veins. Each Ayyubid monarch had always felt it his destiny to rule, even when a cousin, uncle, or brother led the empire. Yet no Ayyubid can stomach the present situation: the realm guided by the infantile Mamluk Sultanate, military slaves who murdered their patron's heir to take power seven years ago.

Currently, the Sunni princes of Karak and Damascus resist Mamluk control. Plus Allah knows how many of the other less powerful governors covertly scheme or ally with either. Last year, the Caliph al Mustasim, Islam's spiritual leader in Baghdad, completed a rushed peace deal between the Mamluk Sultan Aybeg and al-Nasir of Damascus, the realm's second most powerful leader. Yet this treaty is little more than a temporary fix; a soft-hand cleric's naive desire to achieve harmony.

And, of course, there is still the exiled *Bahriyya* Mamluks, known as the *Bahri* or "River Island Regiment." Cenk's patron of fourteen years, the Sultan al-Salih Ayyub, formed this elite unit once the Mamluk ranks in his Egyptian army swelled, naming the elite unit after the Nile River, *Bahr al-Nil*.

Since being chased out of Cairo three years ago, the renegade Baybars al-Bunduqdari leads the Bahri. This relentless prick roams the Middle East, attempting to manipulate any Syrian prince with a treasury big enough to support his motley collection of Bahri and their quest to take down Sultan Aybeg.

But Cenk worries most about the immense Mongol horde. The sultan's emissaries in Persia recounted that the Mongol's commander, Hulegu, has nearly finished off the sovereign Assassins there, rooting the Shia from their high mountain fortifications. Many feel the Tartars will not be satisfied until they have the entire Middle East under boot heel.

"Duty," Tarkhan says, squeezing his temples.

Duty. Cenk has surely done his share. A Mamluk's life is all he knows. While most slave soldiers from his era are of Kipchak descent, Cenk is one of the few Bashkirs.

Yet Kipchaks have not always dominated the Mamluk ranks. For generations, Ayyubid royals purchased boys from throughout the vast Eurasian steppe—Turkmen, Circassians, Armenians, Georgians, Albanians, and more. In the barrack schools throughout the kingdom, these hearty lads were transformed into Muslims and expert cavalry. Ayyubid princes adored their Mamluks' battle skills, but it was these soldiers' intense loyalty which prompted monarchs to commonly refer to their personal Mamluks as sons. And while Cenk has few regrets, the burden associated with keeping his elite corps' reputation has weighed heavily on the forty-seven year old.

This onus was almost alleviated seven years ago. Cenk was but a whisker away from leaving the service once King Louis IX of France and his Crusaders were beaten in Mansura. This victory undoubtedly saved Cairo from infidel occupation. Things were better then, when Cenk's daughter, Inci, was little more than a toddler.

But then the wheels came off the Egyptian cart. The Sultan al-Salih died. Shortly afterward, the Mamluks murdered al-Salih's incompetent heir, Turanshah. Then hostility broke out among al-Salih's elite regiments of Mamluks, the *Salihiyya, or Salihi*, and the Bahri. All of these turbulent events hit almost simultaneously and violently, like a tempest, turning the Mamluk brotherhood and the whole empire upon its head.

Yet it was less these events and more the unlikely rise of Aybeg which prevented Cenk from hanging up his sword for good. He and Aybeg had braved hardships together in decades past. As mere boys, they were bought off the slave block by Amir Turkmani. Ranked as "Amirs' Mamluks," the pair were disadvantaged to the "Royal Mamluks," who called al-Salih their only patron. Cenk and Aybeg were seemingly fated to serve humble careers.

After graduation from their initial training, their manumission, the two served Turkmani, enduring three campaigns throughout the Jazira and Anatolia. When Turkmani died on a patrol twenty-one years past, their status dropped further. Their entire amirate assumed the dreaded title of *sayfiyah*, orphans of the military order.

Yet almost miraculously, Sultan al-Salih snatched both Cenk and Aybeg into his ranks of Royal Mamluks, essentially rescuing them from middling futures. This was the only break they needed. From there, the pair's shared trait of tenacity kept them competent, relevant, and hungry for ascension. Against the odds, both of their careers bloomed. Going forward, they proved themselves political survivors.

Once al-Salih's ranks of Mamluks swelled, Aybeg remained with the sultan's Salihi, while Cenk was elevated to the Jamdariyya, the sultan's personal bodyguard. And while the two were never personal adversaries, their units were rivals.

But despite serving in contending regiments, Aybeg never forgot Cenk, especially once the military slave turned sultan. Aybeg embraced Cenk during the infancy of his improbable ascent to the top. And even though Cenk lacked the qualifications to advise at this level, the ruthless sultan begged for Cenk's counsel, his "horse sense," as Aybeg called it.

In an attempt to overcome his shortfalls in matters of diplomacy and higher-end strategy, Cenk showed his appreciation to the sultan with long days and extreme devotion. For years now, Aybeg has reciprocated by granting Cenk *iqta*—income-producing farmlands to the north. These have made Cenk wealthy beyond his dreams. Yet such has come at cost. Motivated little by coin and the comforts it yields, many times Cenk wished that he had just quit.

He wonders how differently his family life would have been the last eight years if he had just retired in that little house on the Mediterranean that he and his family had visited. Even though he slept at least half of these nights in his own bed, he has missed nearly the entire childhood of his little Inci, his thirteen-year-old girl, now more woman than lass. For most of the last decade, he has spent so much time at work that he may as well have been deployed.

He changes over to the whetstone, adding a drizzle of oil to the coarse surface. He runs the entire sword's length back and forth across the stone, concentrating to keep the slant of his blade true. After six uniform strokes, he turns the weapon over and repeats the process. To test, he rubs a stubby thumb across the sharp blade.

"Why does the sultan like to meet in this place?" Tarkhan asks.

"As it does for us, it reminds him of simpler times, better circumstances, when he was a troop, or at least when he led in closer proximity to them."

"Odd that he is late. Did he not say that he would be here after his bath?"

"Aye, but he looked a little ruined after polo." Cenk shakes his head. "Still thinks he can compete with the young troops. Maybe he laid down for a bit."

"Let us wait a little more and then head over to save him the trip," Tarkhan says.

They eventually leave the guard shack, lumbering their way across limestone pathways under high vaulted ceilings—each roofed structure supported by stone-blocked ribs, sprawling out and downward like the chunky legs of a spider—into a courtyard where serious-faced men in red tunics stand atop high-walled ramparts, manning their stations. Up the stairs, the two aging warriors climb on rickety knees, the pair negotiating the short rise to the sultan's quarters with snorts and groans.

Walking abreast, they stroll through another long corridor, making the final approach to the sultan's bath. In the distance, a eunuch lies balled up at the door to the chamber. A knot forms in Cenk's gut.

"Where is the guard?" Tarkhan asks the eunuch.

The castrated advisor only wraps his arms tighter about his shins. He jabbers something indecipherable, shaking his head.

Cenk growls and kicks him out of the doorway. He raps twice on the heavy-planked door and enters.

Flickering candles ripple firelight upon the giant white columns and fan-shaped rock overhead, which surround the raised bath. Between the columns, eerie shadows are cast upon the band of Arabic script chiseled across the stone. The tails on the lion-shaped heraldry of their former patron appear to twitch nervously in the dusk.

No guards. Steam still curls from the bath. Cenk glances at Tarkhan, a look of dread falling upon the Mongol's face, his eyes on the surface of the water.

"Where is he?" Cenk asks.

Tarkhan's eyes go wide. Then Cenk, too, sees the bristles just breaching the surface. A form bobs in the water below.

Cenk runs to the bath, latches onto the Sultan's arm and struggles to pull out the still-muscular sixty-year-old. Tarkhan grasps under the other armpit. They drag the dripping body atop the smooth-rocked ledge.

Aybeg lies expressionless, his vacant eyes looking through them. Cenk flips him over and frantically presses on his back to pump the water from his lungs. "Breathe! Breathe!" He pushes lifeless gurgles from the sultan's mouth. "No!"

In time Cenk feels Tarkhan tug him away. The Mongol turns over the naked body. No obvious wounds.

"He must have passed out. Drowned," Tarkhan says.

"The guards, where the hell are they?" Cenk asks.

Tarkhan points to the sultan's neck. Red marks across his throat. A scrape across his chest, chafed skin about his wrists.

"Multiple men. He must have tried to fight them off," Cenk says.

The Mongol nods.

Cenk drops to a knee, slumps forward, his head resting against the polished rock. He had warned the sultan before of his vulnerability, but Aybeg never took him seriously.

For a while, the sultan had gotten into the habit every Tuesday of riding through the Egyptian camp at 'Abassa, escorted by the *Aziziyya*, the Mamluk regiment who once served the father of al-Nasir of Damascus. These cavalrymen had abandoned al-Nasir during a battle six years past and had served Aybeg since.

Cenk had cautioned Aybeg not to pattern himself, not to be alone with these men. But his mentor continued. This past October, Egypt's moles informed Cenk of the Aziziyya's plan to kill the sultan. When confronted, these scheming Mamluks fled Egypt and rejoined the Prince of Damascus.

Enemies and underhanded soldiers within the ranks wished Aybeg dead. Cenk became adamant about restricting the sultan's public appearance, had his food tested, even requested guards continually at his friend's side.

> *"From now on we need a pair of guards near you," Cenk said.*
>
> *Aybeg snarled, slid lower in his bath, gulped a mouthful of water, and discharged it like a fountain.*
>
> *"I am serious. These threats to your life are real—they will not strike where we expect, will hit when you are vulnerable. Like here."*
>
> *The sultan smiled. "By Allah, a mother hen you have become." He raised his sword from under the water. "You forget that I am clever, too, that I was a Mamluk before I was a sultan." Aybeg smiled, admiring his dripping blade.*
>
> *"You overlook that a sixty-year old's speed and skills are no match for a young man's. So, yes—cluck, cluck, cluck goes your mother hen."*
>
> *Aybeg grimaced. "So then you suggest we emplace a guard in order to guard the aged guard." He smiled.*
>
> *"A guard to shield the old, stubborn guard, who is too damn valuable to die now," Cenk said, shaking his head.*

Cenk looks to his side. Aybeg's sword and belt hang just out of reach, draped over the back of the royal's chair. The guard. Had the sultan excused them, or were they absent from their duty station? There will be hell to pay. Al-Nasir and the Aziziyya—did they pay others to execute their murderous plan?

His forehead goes back to the stone. Without warning, a sob bursts from him. Another admired patron gone. His old friend of thirty years, murdered. Cenk should have done more to protect him, should have—

Tarkhan puts a hand to his shoulder. Cenk buries his head into the crook of his arm.

Aybeg had never forgotten his *Khushdashiya*, the cohesion and loyalty among his brothers in manumission. He had stayed faithful to his brother, Cenk, until the end. But now, another blood brother is no more. The invaluable one among them is gone.

The sultan is dead.

Tarkhan pulls Cenk to his feet. "Come my friend, we must alert the guard and secure the citadel. We must tell al-Durr, too, let the queen know of this wicked act."

CHAPTER 6

Esel

Damascus, Syria

April 21, 1257

Setting the dish of *kibbeh* atop the table, Esel eyes the faint stain at the corner of the tablecloth and then the plump Rashida. She hopes her master's fussy wife has not noticed the spot that Esel frantically scrubbed out earlier. Steam twirls from the platter. Gamal grins, the dish of cracked wheat, ground lamb, and spices being one of his favorites.

With the meal fully served, Esel moves to the end of the table with hands folded across her front respectfully, waiting for Gamal. He nods her release and she moves to the kitchen area, where she waits from her station.

"So, good news today," Gamal says, scooping a side of *mutabbal*, a mashed eggplant blended with tahini, olive oil, salt, and garlic from their garden. "My council at the palace went well. Al-Nasir provided another large order and a hint of more to come. I may be able to keep my bladesmiths and the armorers busy for eight months or more."

Rashida answers through a mouth full of kibbeh. "Good. Al-Nasir puts the tax coin to good use. Your brother will be happy. How many swords?"

"Only sixty, but two hundred and fifty of the lighter style of *jawshan*—Kalid's version of the chest armor—for al-Nasir's Mamluks. The best made."

"Did you not supply those cuirasses last year?" Rashida says.

"Those were for the Aziziyya Mamluks, once they left Cairo and returned to our prince. This new lamellar armor is for the Bahri, you recall, the River Island Regiment. From Cairo."

Rashida sniffs. "I have a hard time keeping the Turkish brutes straight."

"Thankfully, the only way al-Nasir can keep the Bahri on his side, and prevent them from serving al-Mughith in Karak, is to continue supplying them."

"Keep tossing scraps to the steppe dogs," Rashida says.

Little Saja looks over to Esel woefully, seemingly shamed by her mother's comment. Esel turns a shoulder, neatens a stack of herbs, and pretends she has not heard the slight.

"Equipping those 'dogs' who roam the dangerous hinterlands on our behalf is what's keeping your old friend al-Nasir, in power, what's keeping us in this house." Gamal waves his hand about him. "And what will help prevent the Mongols from one day putting all of Damascus to hoof."

Esel turns her back, sweeping out a corner of the kitchen that is already clean. "Equipping the steppe dogs," she mutters. These customers he disparages, her brave kin, are the people who have turned Gamal into one of the wealthier arms merchants in Syria. If the Kipchak-born Mamluks are dogs, then Gamal is little more than a greedy vulture. Too round-bellied to fly, he gets fat off the steel and leather implements needed for the endless string of wars in this dry land.

Gamal's father, Latif, had been a proficient bladesmith, skilled at pounding the steel ingots into swords. The precursors to these blades served the armies of Allah, even before the days of Mohammad. Damascus was known for producing the hardest, sharpest, and most shatter-resistant of swords. And men such as Latif made a decent living from the trade for centuries. Gamal's father, and his before him, each raised three children in a modest home on the west side of town.

Yet Latif's niche in the trade was not his skill in forging and working the steel, but his ability to spot the highest-quality of raw Wootz nuggets, which steadily arrived on camelback from India. Latif taught Gamal which Indian vendors he could trust and which iron additives and plant masses in the proper quantities were most effective in maximizing the magic-like hardening process that took place when heat and hammer were applied. These ingredients and methods became the family's guarded secrets, gaining them a competitive advantage. Even though blessed with just average smithing skills, Latif created some of the most reliable blades in the Levant.

Today, Gamal's oldest brother continues to hammer and fold the fine steel into the wispy, mottled pattern that distinguishes Damascus steel, reminiscent of rushing water. The thin-armed Gamal ducks the hot work and forearm burns inherent in the craft, sticking to the business side of sword making. He also expands the family trade to lance heads, lamellar armor, imported helmets, and recently, even bows.

"Our population of young men is robust now," Rashida says, wiping oil from the side of her mouth. "Al-Nasir has grown our allied army to thousands. Why must the prince continue bringing in these rogue slaves from the other side of the empire, paying so dear a sum in kit and fiefs for these white-faced murderers? Over and over they have proven themselves disloyal."

Gamal laughs. "There is a reason the military slave trade has lasted hundreds of years. You of all people should not go sour on it just because a couple of Mamluk regiments snubbed your poet friend al-Nasir—or because of the Sultan of Egypt's murder."

Rashida pouts.

"Nothing has changed," he says. "Al-Nasir and every prince in the Middle East will always fill their elite ranks with the Turkish tribesmen—solid stock, sturdy men. Not all are white-skinned. But they are all reliable fighters. It is that simple. You know this."

Rashida appears chastised.

He looks up grimly. "Reared on horseback with bow in hand in those harsh lands, growing up hand-to-mouth, born to kill. Face it, our young men. . ." He shakes his head, chewing contemplatively. "They will never be of the same resilience as the Mamluks. Our sultan needs elite cavalry and none are superior to the steppe nomads. They are worth double the coin our prince pays for them. They have always been worth it."

Rashida raises her palm. "But the Aziziyya, who al-Nasir welcomed back. His father's Mamluks left our prince five, six years back, when he was most vulnerable on the battlefield at al-Abbasa. They spent years serving our enemy, the Egyptian Sultan, afterward. And same with the *Nasiriyya*. Even our sultan's personal guard abandoned him when our friend needed him most. The slave business seems broken."

Gamal shakes his head. "Maybe for al-Nasir. Problem for him is that it would take years to buy a fresh batch of fresh youth to train, those who would be completely faithful to him. His quandary, our quandary, is time. Our sultan needs seasoned, choice troops now, not in the four years it would take to stand up a new force in the citadel schools. The Mongols are on the empire's doorstep, my dear. Plus al-Nasir faces Egypt and Karak and more. Our friend is not short on enemies."

She nods, reaching across the table to push the hair out of Saja's face.

"And, of course, it always comes back to coin," he says. "The Mongols have already managed to trade, butcher, or assimilate into their own forces many of the Kipchak youth. The supply of young pagans is starting to lean out. The price has grown dear and al-Nasir's treasury is too thin to afford fresh military conscripts now, even if he had the time."

She sighs. "So he is forced to embrace the old ones—men of shifting loyalty—from wherever they may come, despite whatever wickedness they have committed."

"Wickedness? Tsst. It is war. Cheaper to buy their allegiance with new weapons and armor and assign their leaders the iqta of his former subjects than to buy and train hundreds of new lads."

She scowls.

Gamal takes a bite of kibbeh and swallows. "The Nasiriyya, al-Nasir's former Mamluks. Those men of questionable devotion are the oddity, not the norm in conduct for these regiments. And while the Bahri of Egypt are not perfect either, you cannot argue their loyalty to their original patron, the sultan, al-Salih. Through thick and thin. For decades. The Bahri simply refused to serve al-Salih's son when he proved himself inept and unwilling to support them."

Rashida snorts. "So they killed him, killed the heir chosen by their father figure. And again, the slave queen, al-Durr, has just done the same to the Mamluk sultan they elected."

Gamal shrugs. "So we hear. But the queen was also loyal to al-Salih, her first husband. Her marriage after al-Salih's death to the new sultan, Aybeg, was purely political. We all knew Aybeg would not last."

"They are all boors, unable to shake their pagan brutishness. Evil," Rashida says.

"Listen, you are the philosopher, the writer. I am merely a weapons peddler. War has always been a messy business. And fortunately, it is not going anywhere. Poets write and killers kill. You can deem these Mamluks barbarians, or evil, if you like. But if evil, they are a necessary evil. And remember, they are still Muslims, and no other Muslims in this land are more skilled with the weapons I sell than they."

Esel stows her broom. A necessary evil. Where would these clean-handed merchants and competing princes be without the Mamluks in their armies? She wonders why the Mamluks remain mysteriously chained by obligation to the Muslim princes, once graduated from their barracks schools and freed. If she were them, she would leave, go back to the steppe.

Esel moves in to clear their plates. She brings forth the *Kanafeh*, a flaky pastry dessert stuffed with sweet white cheese, nuts, and syrup. When Rashida looks away, Esel widens her eyes, licks her lips, and winks at Saja, who smiles.

"So, who leads these Bahri Mamluks that al-Nasir has taken on?" Rashida asks dejectedly. "Who will wear our armor?"

"Baybars al-Bunduqdari," he says, taking a swig from his mug. "And, fortunately for us, his regiment keeps growing and his Mamluks are accustomed to only the best light armor and weapons. Our specialty. And they train much and are, thankfully, rough on their gear." He smiles.

At the sound of his name, Esel's heart flutters. A rush of blood goes to her head. She struggles to show no expression. She puts her back to the table, busies herself by wiping down a ladle. She had heard fragments of conversation from the gossiping women at the well of this growing horde of Mamluks in the Sinai, yet never a name as to who led them. Her nephew, Baybars. A tinge of pride runs through her.

The family gobbles their dessert.

Rashida pushes aside her plate. "This Baybars. If he was willing to slay his patron's son, Turanshah, could he not do the same to our al-Nasir? By Allah, he has already proven himself willing to slay a sultan to further his selfish aims."

Gamal belches. "Do not worry, your star pupil is safe. Al-Nasir is no fool. He keeps the Bahri at arm's length. And thank Allah the sultan of Damascus and Aleppo is a poet, or he might not be buying kit from the husband of his favorite teacher." He winks at his wife. He then looks to his daughter. "Enough talk of weapons and war and Mamluks. How is my daughter this day?"

Esel walks deeper into the kitchen. She fills both kettles and begins to wash the stack of plates. Baybars. Surely they speak of her young nephew, now grown and turned commander. She smiles. He lives, still attracts his peers. "Of course, he does," she mumbles.

She grips a pot handle as one would a bow, conjuring the wood in her fist into the stout birch grip on a weapon made from her own hand twenty years past. And beside her on the stalk, Baybars, the young nephew whom she helped make into a hunter and young man, both.

CHAPTER 7

Esel

Steppe, northeast of the Black Sea

August 2, 1236

Esel and Baybars leapt across a small ravine, making their way up an adjacent hill toward the tower's herd. Turning to look behind, she watched Yagmur's staff slip in the mud, toppling him into the gully. She ran back and peered down the embankment.

"You all right?" she asked her husband.

"Good thing I am not a pony," he said, struggling to right himself, using a fist full of grass to regain his feet. "You would have eaten me long ago." He grasped his nearly-useless leg and flung it upward, fighting his way over the muddy ledge. He looked up at her, forced a grin. "Sometimes I think we should have just lopped off this dead weight."

She clutched his outstretched hand with both of hers and helped him up. "Ah, we should not have gotten so far ahead. Sorry."

She recalled the sight of him two years past, draped over the back of his comrade's mount, unconscious after a fall from his own pony. She was certain her man was dead. It was a wonder that he had even survived.

Before that raid on the Rus, Yagmur had been the nimblest of runners and a fine rider. In hunting deer and antelope, he had no peer in their tower. That tumble left his right leg hanging limp and awkward, his knee joint rigid as an oak limb. His damaged right shoulder prevented him from pulling back a bow. For nearly a year after his injury, her gregarious man went silent and mostly inactive, quietly suffering his fate.

Yet in the last few moons, Yagmur had come around, determined to remain of service to the tribe. While no longer able to join his fellow warriors on raids and hunts, he relegated himself to leather craft and took a greater interest in the tower's sheep and goats, directing the young herders. On occasion, he prepped the bone slabs, wood sections, and fish glue for Esel's own work, but only when he initiated these jobs on his own. She refused to task him with boy's work.

Yagmur stopped smiling and pointed to the cloud of flies that roiled above two carcasses lying in the drainage. "*Kurt*," he said. "Wolf," in their language. They walked over.

One of the lambs had been hamstrung, only her entrails devoured; the second lay contorted, its throat torn out, but otherwise uneaten. This animal's belly bloated in the low light, the soft breeze wafting the rot in their direction.

Esel knelt nearby, inspecting the five-padded impression made by the attacker's forelimb paw. She traced the depth of the base pad, where it pressed deep into the mud, her hand nearly fitting within the print.

Shooing away the flies from the second carcass, Baybars parted the lamb's wool to examine the incisions about its neck. "This wolf is inexperienced, an adolescent," he said.

Yagmur spat. "Can't recall a summer with so many sheep mauled. The wolves must have bred like hares this spring."

"This is just the start. Soon the bitches will have their young out every evening," Esel said to the eight-year old.

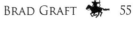

Yagmur shook his head. "Teaching pups the art of the kill, but not even taking the time to eat. We—you—best stick some arrows in them or we will have but rats in the pot by spring."

A twinge of unwanted responsibility filled her gut. She turned west; the sun perched just above the cliff they called "Crows Feet" for the etchings on the cliff face. She stared at the gray slab of mountain until her vision clouded. She closed her eyes, visualizing the distance and rough location of the howls she had heard the last two evenings.

She lifted her chin and turned, until her nose bisected the wind. She pictured the outlying terrain in her mind, envisioned the hunting stand they must make, using the northeastern wind to their advantage.

Yagmur was right. Soon the juvenile wolves would shed their role as novices. In just two moons, they would join ranks as lethal killers in the pack, further decimating the tower's flock.

"Shall we find these killers?" Esel asked her nephew, interrupting the boy's study of the lambs.

Baybars nodded with a gleam in his deep-blue eyes. She looked at the single white spot in his right eye, the size of a small beetle, wondering how the blemish seemed to have no effect on his vision.

She smiled and handed him her work bow. "Then off! Fetch my hunting weapon and quiver, your reed call and mine."

Baybars slipped from under his bow and bundle of arrows and departed for her ger at a sprint.

"I'd best go back to mend your tunics and put on the pot, while the hunters go afield," Yagmur said, leaning on his staff.

She elbowed his arm and chuckled to put him at ease. She knew her status in the tower was unusual for a woman and it wounded his pride. Early on, she had used her advantage as the master bowyer's daughter to learn the secrets of the tower's best hunters.

At first, the warriors invited her on hunting trips merely to win her father's favor. As a young girl, she was allowed on hunts only to observe the performance of the bows and make the most basic of field repairs. Initially, some of the Kipchak hunters refused her company. Yet as she became more gifted in crafting the recurved bows they preferred, all held their tongues, not wanting to displease one with a talent so critical to their own success in the tower.

As the summers passed, she gained knowledge and skill in the pursuit of game, becoming proficient in stalking deer and antelope. Yagmur taught her. By her mid-twenties, she had developed into one of the tower's most able bowshots and stalkers, the only woman in the tower to hold such a distinction.

Now, at twenty-seven years of age, Esel has also grown into a strong game caller, equally gifted at both creating and employing the various mouth calls of reed, bone, and hide. Most of the tower's best designs at luring in the wolf came from her hand.

The elders had discussed the possibility of redirecting the efforts of another hunter or two onto the wolves, yet so far the Saman—he with access to and influence in the world of the spirits—received no sign from the gods that harmonized with such a change. So for now, only she and one other hunter have been bestowed the title of *Kurt Alici*, "Wolf Taker," sanctified by the tower's spiritual leader to kill the mystical predator.

"My Yagmur, do not worry. I know who the man of the ger is." She looked into his eyes.

Yagmur beheld the lean figure of his wife and pulled her in for a kiss. "Shoot true, my love." He limped away, looking back only once.

A subtle shift of wind triggered a shiver down her spine and put her mind to the task ahead. She faced toward the place of her birth, a five-day ride northeast across the rugged steppe. She dropped to her knees, burying her head in the turf, pressing her nostrils deeper, drawing in the comforting scent of yellow grass and dirt.

She prayed to the Respectable Woman, the hallowed statue from her birthplace. She requested blessings upon her people and their flock and an opportunity for a clean kill this night. She asked for pardon in having to assume this grave duty of slaying the wildest of creatures, the best hunter on the steppe, in her attempt to learn the unknowable, the desires and whims of the fanged ghosts of the steppe.

Esel whispered to the far-off sculpture, knowing in her heart that the noble goddess was behind every well-aimed arrow, and that the mirror of volcanic rock in the figure's hand was the set of eyes covering her rear from snapping canine jaws. She wondered if the effigies still stood, or if the Mongols had destroyed them all.

She opened her eyes, startled to see Baybars waiting patiently on one knee only a few steps away, his chest still heaving from the run to and from the ger, Esel's gear laid beside him. He had changed to his gray-colored tunic and olive cap, the dun colors helpful in fooling the wolf's sharp vision.

He walked to the ravine, dabbed his fingers in the soft mud, and smeared stripes of muck onto his nose, chin, and cheek bones to remove glare and simulate shadow on his face's protrusions. She nodded, pleased that the lad always applied the lessons learned from previous hunts. She could not recall giving identical instruction to him twice. Her nephew slept with his gear staged on the ger frame entrance in anticipation of a spontaneous invite from any hunter.

Esel grinned, heartened that Baybars shared her preoccupation with the particulars of the wolf hunt. For countless nights at the table, her nephew inquired as to wolves' habits and past hunters who excelled at killing the clever beasts. She emptied her brain to fill Baybar's insatiable appetite for every aspect of this hunt: camouflage and concealment; creating mouth calls from the best reeds, hollowed antlers, and wing bones; the mating and stalking habits of the canine; and the particulars in using the calls to mimic not only the challenge and interrogation howl of the wolf, but also each of the wolf's food sources. Long into the evenings, he listened with furrowed brow until Esel pointed the tired-eyed youth in the direction of his own ger.

Nevertheless, Esel preferred hunting the wolves alone. While some argued that two sets of eyes were critical in covering every approach, two hunters also created twice the noise and double the scent column. And few could argue with her success. Yet Baybars' quest for knowledge caused her to stray from her solitary inclination. The Saman also tolerated the boy joining Esel on the hunts, likely more concerned with preserving the life of their prized bowyer than in her grooming of the prodigy.

She donned her gear and glanced at the sun dipping on the horizon. Baybars ran his fingers down his bowstring, checking for nicks and proper connection to the bow's limbs. He patted his pouch, verifying the location of his battered reed call.

For moons he practiced, mimicking his aunt by placing his tongue on different parts of the reed and blowing through the device with varying force, all the while changing the position of his lips. He was soon tolerable at simulating the wail of a distressed fawn, the whine of a wolf pup, and even the dining call of a single crow.

"Well, then," Esel said.

They stepped off, trotting quietly in line as would the wolves themselves. Staying below the ridgeline and shadows cast by giant outcroppings of crumbling rock, they covered the hills, moving steadily upwind into the fading light. After putting several rises between them and the main flock, they eased over the crest of a mount, sneaking close to the trunk of a scraggly pine so as not to catch the gaze of any predator below.

Esel halted to verify the direction of the waning northerly, savoring the sweet smell of the dried grass sweeping across the valley. They continued, with softer feet than before, careful not to break a twig or kick a rock, knowing that on this final approach, they no longer had the hillside to buffer their noise.

She looked left and upwind at the steppe to the north, discerning the kind of terrain preferred by a wolf pack—a gully filled with abundant rodents and deer, a long strand of rolling spruce and junipers for daytime beds, the winding creek, and of course, a large flock of sheep to their south. She figured this was the approximate location of the previous howls, perhaps the pack's assembly area.

Over her shoulder, the sun set auburn on the swaying grass. She tapped her chest and pointed to a thick shrub, only feet away. She then patted her nephew's shoulder and pointed him toward a tall juniper farther downwind from her spot, just above a shallow draw. Baybars nodded in confirmation, the lad acknowledging the two natural shooting lanes crosswind of his position, places where a wolf circling downwind would cross.

With the sun to their backs, they snuck into their improvised kill stations, backing slowly into bushes until both were nearly swallowed by branches. They nocked arrows with tails of carved horn.

She looked down the draw and struggled to locate him, the youth's outline completely broken up by the stout trunk and sprawling limbs. He faced southeast, oriented on both gaps in the brush, their prey's likely approach. She had his backside covered, but she left hers exposed uphill, confident in the grace of the Respectable Woman.

She waited for the environs to settle to their presence. A pair of jays squawked from the pines and then went silent. The sun dropped behind them.

The soothing oranges and golds in the valley surrendered to a cold blue, giving advantage to the hunted. An owl hooted to locate his companion. The northerly, which had earlier lapped at her left cheek, now turned to gentle, inconsistent kisses. The wolves would soon leave their daytime beds.

Esel placed the thin caller to her lips. Focus. She pushed the reed to the roof of her mouth and began her blood-chilling wail, forcing the sound out the side of her lips to accentuate the death song of the wolf's prey. Her fawn bawl ricocheted through the dotting of rocky mounds, softening as it filtered across the pines and grass in the valley. She continued for only moments, alternating moans with guttural pleas.

The two stood motionless for a couple of moments, bows down, but at the ready. A red squirrel nearby chirped and wheezed a warning call to his fellows with an intensity that quaked his entire body, adding credence to the death struggle she created.

Moving only her eyes, Esel focused on nothing in particular, rather looking for any subtle movement in the scrub to her front and sides. Several hundred paces away, a flock of sparrows spooked from a juniper, but the dimming light and thick undergrowth obscured the cause of their alarm. Baybars stayed disciplined, unmoving.

Again Esel produced her heart-wrenching whine, this time increasing the volume and extending her lips into a cone shape and moving her head slowly from side to side, projecting the sound in all directions. She ended her call with a pathetic, dying whimper.

A crow scouting overhead believed, dipping his wing to turn and signaling to his distant mates that he may have found an evening meal. Two from its murder abandoned the preparation of their roost and swooped in, circling only feet above her head. The three crows held above her, pushing air through their wings in great huffs. They rattled their mutual frustration in not spotting the wounded animal.

As the crows extended their search area, she resisted the urge to look up, recalling her own guidance to Baybars. "The wolves will not come from the air. A warning cry from a crow will send a wolf retreating as quickly as a shout from your mouth."

Nature's chorus chattered and squawked, continuing to add realism to her faux scene of carnage. She repeated her calling sequence, movement in the scrub catching her eye and cutting short her muted cry.

Six hundred paces east of their position, a shadow moved slowly from bush to bush—closer, the dark specter coalescing into the sleek profile of a canine. The lone male turned, taking a wide route downwind from the perceived meal to determine how this fawn had come into harm's way and whether it was just a babe separated from its mother or the wounded prize of another bold wolf encroaching upon his defined territory.

The wolf snapped to a rest, testing the air with a subtle rise of his nose and check of the country both left and right. Sensing nothing out of ordinary, he loped into open country, his head large as a helmeted Rus, bobbing only slightly as his muscular legs rolled in an effortless rhythm.

A dominant male. Here was death incarnate, the beast drawn to the desperate cries by instincts honed and sharpened by centuries of ancestors. His summer coat was still thin, highlighting the thick muscle in his chest and shoulders.

A regret filled Esel, as it always did upon initially spotting the graceful beast. A sadness born in the truth that she must pursue the very animal that epitomized all that was free and uninhibited. The ultimate hunter. She tried to quell any tenderness that competed with her devotion to the tribe. She reminded herself that in comes the devil, the one who killed her people's sheep and caused their children to go hungry.

Approaching the shallow drainage, the silver-black brute attempted to make himself small, keeping his head and hindquarters low, forming a slinking arch of fur and fangs. Using every stretch of low ground, every branch to mask his approach, the wolf disappeared for moments at a time, only to reappear twenty paces closer when exposed by a void of cover.

While a master at hiding his large frame and movement, the creature was unable to veil his anger. Gray guard hairs atop his shoulders bristled like needles on a frosty pine bough.

He stopped, looked behind him. Then forward. His ears stood erect and rotated, permitting their white cups to absorb every vibration. He lifted his nose for one last taste of the air, exercising caution, restraining his inclination to close with the sound of distress and attack.

She looked to Baybars. She fretted for his safety, questioned whether she should have brought him here. Her heart pounded steadily in her chest. This animal was a killer and not a foolish one. "Settle," she told herself.

Knowing a pack of wolves roamed this ground, she listened intently, as another predator could likely breach the high ground behind her to gain visibility of the entire valley.

She emptied her lungs slowly, trying to replace the anxious breath inside her with fresh, calm air. Killing a dominant male would be a morale boost for the tower. She figured only the pack's alpha male would have such size and aggressive posture, and move with such confidence and vigilance toward a potential confrontation. Alone.

The wolf trotted into another dip in the terrain and quickly closed the distance between himself and her nephew. She worried the youth did not see the approaching animal, as Baybars remained motionless.

The giant head and pointed ears popped up from the eroded bank. Over he came, even bigger than she thought, heading at a diagonal toward her, having pinpointed the source where he last heard the sound.

Their wind remained good for now, her scent blowing crossway and short of the wolf. With the male only forty paces from Baybars, she bit her lip. If the dog moved only slightly uphill from the draw, he would "wind" her nephew.

She must do something. If the wolf caught Baybars' scent, the beast would realize his folly with a quick exit and never come to a reed call again. At times unpredictable, the wolf might even choose to close on a single hunter.

When the predator turned his head, she shifted her feet and eased her bowstring back in one movement. She waited. She would rather not, but would take this fifty-pace shot. She aimed.

Baybars turned his head as the wolf pounded across a skinny clearing, its tail held vertical. Esel froze, her nephew having the closer shot.

As the wolf slunk forward into thick cover, Baybars squared his body and drew his bow, taking aim at the next opening. The dog then exposed himself in this sliver of open country. Esel's shoulder muscles burned, but she took the pain, as to slowly release her draw might be noticed by their prey.

"Squeak, squeak," Baybars mimicked the sound of a small rodent.

"Perfect," she whispered to herself. He chose the perfect time to stop the creeping wolf's progress. The creature halted his powerful legs with a jerk and snapped his white-masked head toward Baybars, the male's hair now prickled along its entire spine, from snout to tail. The wolf swiveled his ears to the location of the new sound, confused for a moment. The familiar twang of bow shot broke the calm.

Whack. The sound of iron penetrating flesh.

She stepped from her cover, swung her bow, and aligned her feet toward the beast downhill, her heart seeming to stop beating.

The animal tipped to his shoulder, kicking his rear leg at the exposed fletching stuck deep into his upper lung. She moved farther left for an even better shot and reset her feet. The wolf clawed in violent lurches at the shaft, swipes that soon diminished to lethargic grazes.

She slowly released her draw and lowered her bow, keeping the arrow nocked. If a second shot was needed, she must be ready. She rubbed her shoulder vigorously.

The brute crumbled. He arched his back and extended all four legs, as if taking a morning stretch. His muscles contracted and he shuddered in a death quiver. She took a deep breath, trying to still her own shudders.

She moved back into her tree and pressed the tip of the reed into her mouth with quivering hands. She sent a strong burst of air through pursed lips, replicating the sharp cries of a wolf pup in distress. She scanned the area for a second predator, which may have approached undetected from another direction.

Baybars remained poised, ignoring the downed animal, scanning the valley with another arrow already nocked in his bow. She lessened the push of air through the reed, creating the miserable whimper of a dying wolf.

A growing patch of black saturated the grass beneath the male's chest. Seeing no movement and with darkness upon them, Esel made her way down the slope on shaky legs. As she approached the beast, her pulse quickened. The wolf seeming to grow larger with each step. His tongue protruded through ivory incisors.

Baybars came up beside her, arrow still nocked, holding another in his draw hand. He approached his kill from the back and poked him in the haunch with the arrow tip. He pulled open the rear leg to confirm the animal a male.

She half-expected a jubilant grin and a whoop from a young boy, who had just outdone himself. Instead, he dropped the leg and stared at the beast, his face calm and expressionless, like that of a seasoned killer.

Baybars scanned the horizon for the summer archer in the sky. Finding the faint collection of stars low in the darkening heavens, he laid his bow across his thighs and sat cross-legged. He invoked some words to the twinkling image. When finished, he returned to Esel's side. "We made a good kill, my aunt."

She chuckled. "*You* made a good kill. I only watched."

She gaped at her nephew, confounded by the image of this lad of small stature, standing over his kill, the wolf likely weighing three times the shooter. She wondered how many boys his age had called in and slayed such a prize, the beast owning the keenest senses and highest intellect of any creature on the steppe. Few. Baybars had just done what most men would never do in a lifetime.

"I wonder how many of our sheep this one ate?" he asked.

"Some, I am certain of this. But never again," She knelt before the wolf and ran her fingers through his stout guard hair. She bowed her head, and with palms pressed together, recited the prayer of thanksgiving to the Respectable Woman. She rose.

They stood a few moments in silence as the darkness enshrouded them. She reached into her pouch and pulled out the *ugur*, the ankle bone of a she-wolf Esel had been carrying for moons during their hunts together.

She pressed the lucky talisman into his palm, the charm blessed by the saman last year.

His eyes grew large. "Thank you, *Teyze*."

"You know the full meaning of it?" she asked.

"I know the wolf's ankle bone assures safe travels for the few men who carry it. No warrior ever mentioned how he got one."

She nodded. "You also know that wolves travel great distances vigilantly, over harsh terrain and into perilous conditions," she said, pulling her own ugur from the flap on her belt, the yellowed chunk bestowed upon her by an old Wolf Taker a dozen years past when she was but fifteen years old.

She was the only woman known among the Gokers privileged to own one, and younger than all; most of the ugurs were held by old hunters, men who also pegged the beasts' fur to their gers' north wall, the most respected side of their shelters.

"Remember that this charm is not really gifted by me, but rather offered by the gods, through me, once earned," she said. "This is true for all who possess one."

He nodded.

"Wear this ugur always," she said. "It is an honor and will impart to you some of the wolf's bravery and her cleverness in escaping danger."

He rolled the beige-lobed talisman in his hand and then met her eyes.

She nodded. "Now you know."

CHAPTER 8

Jacinta

Cairo

April 22, 1257

Jacinta enters the courtyard of her parent's home, the entrance shaded by a sprawling Sycamore Fig that she and her brother climbed as children. The tree looks bigger, its trunk and smooth-skinned branches more knotted. She ducks under a low-hanging twig. A green pigeon feeding on the marble-sized figs flushes. Zane, at her side, jumps.

The little boy looks up at her with wide eyes. Seeing her smile, a grin widens across his face. They laugh and continue walking past her mother's broad beans and radishes. She frowns, having never seen the plot so choked with weeds.

She knocks twice on the door and walks in, following the scent of spiced lamb and rice to the kitchen. Her mother is making *fattah*, her daughter's favorite dish. Jacinta removes her hijab and shakes out her shiny black hair.

Her mother turns. Her once firm cheeks have begun to sag with age. Her eyes are glassed, reflecting a lingering discomfort that her smile cannot conceal. "Jacinta!"

She flings her arms around her daughter, squeezing her. She releases, palming each of Jacinta's sharp cheekbones. The squatty woman looks up at her. Jacinta sees new bags of skin sagging beneath her mother's eyes. She rubs her daughter's olive skin with each thumb. "So nice to have my flower back home."

Her flower. The daughter's name means "Hyacinth" and her sweet mother has treated her as this precious, beautiful blossom for as long Jacinta can remember. Jacinta smiles, a comfort setting in as she breathes in the familiar scent of her mother's skin, mixed with the same, cinnamon-heavy *susinum* oil that the woman had worn for years.

Her mother backs away. "And look here." She drops to her knees and grabs both of the boy's hands. "This is the precious Zane that we have heard about."

The russet-skinned lad smiles and then shies away, burying his face in Jacinta's thigh. She combs the boy's dark hair with her fingers.

"What a handsome boy he is. How old is he now?"

"Almost two years."

"Oh, such a healthy lad." Her mother's grin shrinks as her husband, Kaphiri, enters, straight-backed and formal as always. He is dressed in a merchant's robe, as if just having met a vendor.

He glances momentarily at the boy and then meets his daughter's eyes. "So glad you are home safely." He hugs her stiffly then opens his hand to the sitting room. "More than three years away is too long. We were worried. With Aybeg gone, that is enough of this spying work so far from home." Kaphiri looks away.

She nods. "With a son to raise, that is enough of that work altogether."

He bends over with palms on thighs and rubs his hand atop the child's head. "Yes, yes, a new son to raise." He looks to his wife, who leans under the arched entranceway. "Could you help get Zane washed before our meal?"

She smiles. "Of course."

Jacinta nods to her son and he hesitantly clutches the hand offered by her mother. Jacinta and her father sit rigidly in his wooden-back chairs.

"So, how was your time in Hama?" he asks, his face gone serious.

She waits until she can no longer hear her mother's footsteps. "Fine, just like after Damietta and Mansura here. They placed me in the infirmary, where I could hear what the sick and injured Mamluks said." She shakes her head. "My work there was mostly uneventful, hardly productive. I was more nurse than mole."

"I would rather have you bored and safe than otherwise."

She nods. "And Mother, she is fully recovered from her sickness?"

His eyes flash to the kitchen. "Mostly. She will have the occasional coughing spell, but we pray she has gotten past it."

"Good," she says, unconvinced of her mother's recuperation.

Kaphiri looks down the hallway and lowers his voice. "Your son. You took an orphan. Why?"

"Because I took care of his mother for several months and watched her die of the fever—her lad just off the tit. She had pleaded with me for days to not let her boy be placed in the squalor of the orphanage if she died. Over and over she said this. It was her last wish, her only appeal."

"But you have witnessed such for years in the infirmaries. You are not obligated to inherit such an encumbrance. What was this woman doing in the military hospital?"

Jacinta's heart sinks. He called his grandchild "an encumbrance."

"She was the new wife of a Bahri," Jacinta says. "A good woman."

"Where's the father? The Bahri are well paid. Surely he could have hired a girl until he found another wife, got a slave? I could even help in such arrangements." He raises an eyebrow.

"Zane's father was one of Aqtay's Bahri who fled to Hama. Aybeg's thugs had found and killed him moons prior. For some reason. I do not know," she says.

Her father nods. "So his mother was Egyptian, his father a Mamluk from the northern steppe?"

"Yes," she says, recognizing his attempt to hold back the look of disgust on his face.

"There is an orphanage outside of Cairo that is much better than those in Hama. The one run by that Syrian woman. You... " He seems to read the crease in her forehead.

"Dalila's place. I know of it." She stares at him blankly, willing away the tears.

He looks up at the ceiling.

She sighs. "I made a promise to a young widow whom I had grown to respect. I did what I thought was right."

"I understand." He strokes his beard with one eye half closed, his most common gesture when thinking of solutions. He always has solutions.

She sits up straighter in the chair. "The Prophet said that a person who assists and aids an orphan is on the same footing in heaven to the Prophet himself. Are not you happy that I honor our family this way—that I honor Allah?"

He looks to the floor, crosses his legs.

"While I hated being there, I feel God placed me in Hama for a reason. Zane is now my charge and I will not be giving him up."

Kaphiri stands and paces thoughtfully with his hands crossed in front. He stops, considers the books lining his shelves as he speaks, his back to her. "I have worked to build a solid reputation in Cairo for this family. I, too, made a promise—to your grandfather—to honor this family's name, to cherish it second only to the Prophet's."

"I know," Jacinta says. "And I will follow the law. Zane will not take your name. He will retain his father's. Do not worry, my boy won't be looking for his share of your wealth, depleting that to be inherited by 'the glorious one.'"

He nods his head slowly.

"That is most of your worry, yes? That my orphan would eventually be in a position to receive a portion of the family wealth—take away coins from your favorite, Sachi?"

"Speak respectfully of your brother. Twice I arranged marriages for you with promising merchants from good Egyptian families. Both times you refused. I could have easily forced you into either one, but did not, respecting your wishes. And in return, you do this?"

She feels another stab in her chest, followed by profound sadness. She addresses the back of his head. "Yes, our family's reputation. I will be the next generation of spurned hermit woman. But unlike mother's sister, I will be raising this urchin alone."

He turns to face her, scowling.

She looks him in the eye. "You were not so worried about our family's reputation when you offered my services to al-Salih. Is it any worse for you to be the grandfather of a mixed-raced child than it is to be the father of a woman spy?"

He glances to the kitchen to ensure his wife is not nearby. He shakes his head. "You willingly accepted that line of work. You would not be a wife. The Franj were on our shores back then." He takes a step closer. "You could have declined the position. As I recall, you felt it the duty of every Egyptian to do their share to expel the Crusaders."

She crosses her hands across her knee. "Could I really have declined? And if I had, how well would that have served your business? How many irrigation canals would you be managing now if I had rejected the sultan's 'gracious offer?' I was part of the deal—the services of the daughter in return for your increased management of his amirs' farmlands. I had no choice, especially once Aybeg became sultan. I sacrificed for the family, for our reputation, so that you could grow your purse."

A flush of anger creeps up his neck. "That purse has grown from your brother's toil and mine. And some of that silver will one day be yours."

"Had you ever thought that I care little about silver?"

He looks at her with mouth agape, saying nothing for several moments. He looks to the floor, his features softening.

She sits content in his discomfort, letting him stew. She stares at her father, noticing the lines etched at the corner of his eyes are much deeper than when she had seen him last.

He pleads. "You are twenty-seven years old now—no longer a young girl. How will you find a respectable husband being past your prime and now toting an orphan boy?"

"I worry little of such things. I am a mole—I was not meant to be a trader's wife." She sees the sorrow in his eyes and tries to ease her tone. "I harbor no ill will for you choosing my path. I only ask that you harbor no ill will toward my son. That is not asking much, is it?"

"Yes, it is asking much. I do not need vendors and fief holders talking behind my back of my only daughter raising a cross-raced grandson. I do not need Qutuz's amirs—the Muizziyya fief holders—knowing that I have a Bahri's urchin in the family." He clenches his lips, lowers his voice. "I do not. . ." He stops himself, looks down at her.

She nods. "I know. You do not need to give Aybeg's vicegerent any reason to think your judgment is lacking. You do not need to look bad in front of Qutuz or his amirs, the same men who murdered the Bahri's leader and sent hundreds running for their lives across the Sinai, splitting up families. This Qutuz did to fellow Mamluks, the same men who helped save Cairo from the infidels eight years ago."

He looks away.

"Qutuz is why Zane's mother—and many like her—fled across the desert alone, worried for her life and that of her unborn child's." She looks down. "You do not need a daughter who acted out of decency to keep one innocent child out of the orphanage."

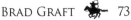

"I did not say that—and it is not that simple."

"It is that simple, Father." In her gut, she somehow recognizes this will be her last conversation with him. She feels little sadness in it.

She clenches her teeth and meets his eyes. "Perhaps you should have thought twice about placing me in the service of our illustrious sultanate—an occupation easier to enter than it is to leave. A position where they insist on sending me to foreign lands, sticking me in miserable infirmaries where I am forced to pull secrets from dying men. Maybe if you had not done so, I would not have picked up all of these useless, coddling tendencies, would have heartlessly allowed this baby to live in the horridness of an orphanage, as you now wish. For once, I thought I was doing good, I. . ."

She hears her mother's footsteps. They wait in silence for her to enter with a tray of tea. She seems to sense the tension between them. The corners of her mouth droop. Jacinta hopes her mother did not hear the last exchange.

"Where is Zane?" Jacinta asks.

"He is just finishing washing his face."

"I think he is tired, Mother." She fakes a smile. "I appreciate your invitation and work on the meal, but we'd best leave. I have a meal prepared for him at home. Leaving now will get him to bed on time."

Her mother looks down at the tray and then at her husband. The dark circles under her eyes looking more pronounced than earlier.

CHAPTER 9

Cenk

The Red Tower, Cairo Citadel
April 27, 1257

Cenk stomps up the winding passage leading to the "Red Tower," his shoulder grazing the block wall. He follows Amir Qutuz, the former Sultan's second in command, and three of his guards. Behind him at a distance, the hollow thumps of cavalry boots on stone echo through the tight overhead, a full squad of twelve from Aybeg's Muizziyya, his personal Mamluks, and Allah knows who else behind them. The dank smell of wet rock fills his nostrils.

A Mamluk's blade scrapes the stone.

In the dim light, Cenk pulls his own sword from its scabbard. Tipsy, he skims his fist across the wall to help keep his balance. The rough block abrades his knuckles, leaving a streak of blood on the gray slabs.

Cenk teeters, stumbling on the narrow stairs. Tarkhan catches him under the arm while avoiding Cenk's blade, likely anticipating such.

"Quick hands for an old coot," Cenk slurs to his fellow advisor.

The sober Tarkhan shakes his head.

Cenk chuckles, burps up the rancid taste of wine. He bites down on a wad of mint leaves in a half-hearted attempt to mask the smell of grape on his breath.

The wine. He had not touched a drop of alcohol in eighteen years, knowing the liquid was the devil's brew. He knew back then that continuing to drink would have ended his marriage and likely his career. But since pulling Aybeg's cold body from his bath last moon, he has cared little of such things.

Once his patron's *ghilman*, slave boys, had wrapped the dead sultan in white linen, Cenk went straight to the sultan's cellar. Alone, he guzzled a full wineskin. Puking it up immediately, he drank another slowly in the dim light. He smashed a cask against the wall, watching the deep garnet trickle down the limestone blocks.

He has stayed drunk much of the last seventeen days. He knows it is not good. He knows that Allah, plus all three of Cenk's dead patrons, would not approve of his recent conduct. Yet he allows himself to slip back into the destructive compulsion.

This damaging habit was born after a tragic ambush in a canyon between Aleppo and Hisn Kayfa. In that Khwarazmian trap twenty-one years ago, he lost his first patron, Amir Turkmani. That day, most of his closest mates were torn from him, many in his amirate killed or severely wounded.

Afterward, al-Salih, still the prince of Hisn Kayfa then, dispersed the survivors from Turkmani's Amirate of Forty. Perhaps wishing to dispel the unit's bad luck, the prince spread the remaining men across the empire to other Mamluk amirs. Only Cenk and a few others were blessed to join al-Salih's personal Mamluks at the citadel in Hisn Kayfa, defending the northern reaches of the empire.

For years in the Jazira, memories of this attack haunted him, manifesting themselves in nightmares and fits of rage aimed at his young wife and the unfortunate novices he trained. Too often back then he drank himself into a stupor, a feeble attempt to mitigate his losses. He still wonders how the *koumis*, the fermented mare's milk he bought in the back alleys, did not pickle his guts. He remains amazed how his drunken furies and unyielding pursuit to cull the weak from his training ranks did not end in his own banishment. Why his battered Kipchak wife did not sneak away in the night back then lingers as a mystery to him.

He thought he had left the koumis behind. Over a decade ago, he mended the relationship with his wife and yoked his anger into a fitting ambition of molding competent Mamluks. He figures it was their daughter who saved him. The birth of his precious Inci had been his true impetus to quit drinking. Or perhaps it was purely shame. He tired of insulting Allah. He refused to become the abusive parent that his father was. He would not subject Inci to living with a tyrant.

He wets his dry lips, spits a wad of saliva against the wall. He understands the alcohol could consume his life again, yet no longer feels a disgrace in it. He worries little that it may again stress his marriage, that it will further strain the relationship with his teenage daughter. The empire has bigger problems than his personal life. What does he matter?

Perhaps he drinks again to dull the ache in his heart, to stop the bad dreams that have returned. He consumes the spirits to blur the memories of his friend, Aybeg, being placed into his grand mausoleum. He will drink. He will be drunk.

Winding his way up the last of the stairs, he belches out loud. He thinks back to his loyal service with the sultan, serving under Aybeg for nearly seven years, right from the start of his tenuous rise to rule. Despite the challenges, they had accomplished the improbable in holding the empire together. Perhaps they were bonded together by more than their shared planning and schemes to snuff out the opposition and raise taxes. They were soldiers together first.

His thoughts drift back to the summer of 1234, when al-Salih's father, the Sultan al-Kamil, convinced sixteen Ayyubid princes to snake their way up the Euphrates to steal territory from the defending Seljuks. Endlessly, they attacked the enemy's barriers, their meaningless assaults resulting in the death of six friends and maiming of nine training mates, his Kushdashiya. He and Aybeg—back-to-back at one point—desperate and gore-covered, slashing their way out of a Seljuk counterattack.

Cenk's mind flashes to just days ago at the mausoleum, as the slab of stone was slid across his pale-faced comrade at the burial chamber. Aybeg had survived vicious battles, dodged assassination attempts, and braved ceaseless criticism from fellow Mamluks and Ayyubid princes—all jealous men, convinced that Aybeg had no business being sultan. Regardless of his perceived flaws, the sultan had survived it all. Cenk wipes the tears from his eyes.

Amir Qutuz reaches the landing at the top of the stairs, where two Salihi, Mamluks still loyal to the queen, stand guard. The pair are part of a small guard, who have watched the queen over the past weeks, while Qutuz and his advisors investigated the sultan's murder.

"You know why I am here," Qutuz says. "Unlock the door."

The guards look over the amir's shoulder to the tops of the black-enameled helmets sloping down the stairs and then at one another. They look fearful and confused.

"Your commander has come to his senses," Qutuz says. "There will be no reaction force of Salihi sent up these stairs. You are relieved of your duty here."

The older guard tightens his grip on the lion-etched axe that he holds chest-high at the ready. He glares at Qutuz disbelievingly.

Those Salihi who declined to join Aybeg's personal line of Royal Mamluks have remained faithful to the Queen, Shajarat al-Durr, or "Spray of Pearls." And for good reason. The queen was the favorite wife of their former sultan, al-Salih. No man had been more adored by all of the Mamluks in Egypt. In fact, both the Salihi and Bahri still hold observances and ceremonies for their graduates from the barracks schools at al-Salih's gravesite.

But the common troopers had more reasons than this to admire the queen. She came from roots as humble as theirs, al-Durr being a common slave, her dark beauty and intelligence quickly charming al-Salih those long years ago. More importantly, the strong-willed woman had managed Egypt when it was on the edge of collapse during the Frankish invasion seven years past.

Prior to the most decisive battle of the Seventh Crusade, the sultan died from a lingering respiratory illness. Knowing her husband's death would not only cause his soldiers emotional distress at the loss of their father figure, but also embolden the southward-encroaching Franks, al-Durr kept al-Salih's death a secret. She prevented the Franj from rallying their forces and snatching Egyptian territory during the leadership void.

Later, Mamluk amirs voted her the first woman ruler in the Middle East. Only to appease the caliph in Baghdad and Ayyubid balkers did the army make Aybeg sultan. Only for the appearance of legitimacy in the newfound Mamluk Sultanate, not love, did al-Durr marry Aybeg.

The men behind Qutuz part to make way for a quartet of thick-shouldered Mamluks, who push their way up the stairs, each grasping a handle of their battering ram. Tarkhan shoves Cenk aside to keep him from being run over.

Qutuz glances behind and then pulls his ivory-handled sword from its scabbard. He addresses the guards, "There is no decision for you to make here. I have a squad of Muizziyya behind me, plus another at the bottom of the stairs to assist if needed." He sighs. "This is not a day for foolish bravery from the Salihi."

The senior guard gives a nod of resignation to the younger of them. He reaches into his pouch to remove a cumbersome key, which he inserts into the metal housing. He lifts the key upward, displacing the pins with a heavy clunk. He cracks open the hefty door.

Qutuz raises his sword and pushes upon the metal-banded timbers. The door creaks open. His guards flood in around him.

CHAPTER 10

Cenk

The Red Tower, Cairo Citadel

April 27, 1257

Al-Durr turns from the red tower's shuttered window and takes in the scene with a tight-lipped shrewdness. Her women slaves scamper to her side, distress etched upon their brows.

The soldiers form a half moon about her. Another of Aybeg's wives stands behind them with her attendants. Nicknamed *Obur* by the Mamluks for her great desire to have her bloodline occupy the throne, she is the mother of Egypt's heir apparent, the fifteen-year-old al-Malik.

The queen smiles coyly. "I see the brave leader of the Muizziyya comes with reinforcements. Did you think you would need a full amirate to fetch one woman?"

"The scorpion is but a small creature," Qutuz says, "yet it packs much poison. So yes, I am forced to lead my men up these stairs because you, the most cunning of the scorpions, organized our legitimate leader's death. And 'fetch' you say?" Qutuz chuckles darkly. "We have not come to fetch you."

Her grin transforms to a sneer. "You slayed al-Salih's last true descendant to snatch the sultanate—now you come to finish off your patron's innocent wife. Wouldn't al-Salih be proud of you?"

"Innocent?" Qutuz asks rhetorically. "At least al-Salih's son was merely a drunk, an incompetent commander, a lazy womanizer. Turanshah got what he deserved back then. But you. Your sins are far graver than his."

Qutuz waves his hands toward the floor, where the dust and chips from the queen's pearls lie scattered, evidence of the queen sensing her fate and the selfish woman having pounded her jewelry into bits to ensure that no other would wear her ornaments.

"And, of course, greedy, till the end."

"Evil bitch," Cenk thinks. From the start Cenk and the sultan's advisors had known the political marriage between Aybeg and al-Durr stood on shaky ground. Al-Durr had been running all of Egypt's civil affairs since al-Salih's death. She still saw herself as queen, filling the role of sultana, the position she had been elected to hold seven years prior. Of course, Aybeg saw himself as not only the leader of the army—the true source of power—but also the sole sultan.

Al-Durr moves two paces closer. She puts her hands on her hips.

Qutuz steps up to meet her. "Did you arrange the murder of your husband, Aybeg, the Sultan of Egypt?"

"No, he died naturally," she says.

"Naturally," Qutuz mimics in her female pitch. "So it must come as a surprise to you that in the chop room last week, two of your servants shared the same story, each saying that you instructed them to strangle Aybeg in his bath?"

"It would not surprise me that they would say anything you suggested, once you strapped them to the board and pulled out your axes and branding irons."

"Both said there was a third servant who took part, Fabian, who has disappeared. Where is he?"

"It is not the role of a sultana to track the comings and goings of her slaves."

Qutuz sighs. "But apparently it was your role to task three of them with murder. Two of these now hang outside the citadel gate. And what of our commander of the guard? Ox is nowhere to be found. Did you also arrange his death, so that our sultan would be unguarded at his bath, or did you convince him to join your plot?"

Her eyes narrow. "I do not know what you're talking about."

Qutuz's jaw tightens, his fist curls about the hilt of his scimitar. "Our patron, al-Salih, should have kept his lovely tramp as a common slave. You were never fit to be queen."

Obur, the mother of al-Malik, steps forward to address the queen. "Did you kill Aybeg because of his refusal to divorce me? Did you fear that my son's accession would take power from you?"

Al-Durr looks at the woman defiantly.

"Or did you have him slain because Aybeg was to also marry into the house of Mosul, saw himself as deserving of another, more suitable wife? A royal, not some vicious slave queen?" asks Obur.

The queen crosses her arms.

Obur shakes her head. "But you are too self-absorbed to have seen the selflessness in Aybeg's deed, our husband taking this step in Mosul for the benefit of Egypt, to form an alliance with another strong prince who could help us against the Bahri and Mongol threats."

Cenk raises his eyebrows. How did Obur know that Aybeg had been courting the daughter of Badr al-Din Lu'lu', Prince of Mosul? This was all done in secret. Cenk recalls his conversation with Aybeg. "It is non-stop disputes with the queen," Aybeg said. "She hates me. Not that I care—her beauty has been halved since al-Salih's time, but her ambition and wickedness have tripled. She needs her tongue cut out. Or one day, an axe blade across her neck."

"Is this brilliant hag one of your new interrogators?" al-Durr asks Qutuz.

Qutuz puts the tip of his blade under al-Durr's chin. "Let us skip the theatrics. Did you think your letter to al-Nasir of Damascus would not be discovered? That your goal to reunite Cairo and Damascus by murdering Aybeg would somehow remain undisclosed? That nobody knew you were hiding part of al-Salih's treasure from Aybeg?"

At secrets uncovered, the queen's face goes pale.

He flicks his wrist, slicing al-Durr. A drop of blood trickles down her neck.

"The Bahri will crucify you for this," the queen says. "They still respect their father's queen. Still know I am the able hand at the tiller here."

"Tsst. Baybars and the rebel Bahri." Qutuz shakes his head. "They will never see Cairo again. They will continue to whore themselves out in Syria, until too old to fight. In the barren desert, they will wither and fade into oblivion."

Qutuz looks at the mother of al-Malik and then to her slave girls. He seems to measure them, as a confident fighter would an opponent prior to a spar. He turns to Cenk and smiles. "Sword work is sloppy business. And so impersonal, eh Cenk?"

"Yes, my Amir. It surely is."

"Our Sultan Aybeg was a brave man," Qutuz says. "He wore countless scars from enemy steel. Who could have imagined that he would meet his fate from the bare hands of house slaves?"

"Surely not the warrior's death he deserved. And so slow and miserable," Cenk says.

"Methinks the planner of such an assassination would also desire a similarly intimate ending, wouldn't you say, Cenk?"

"Certainly, my Amir. Plus, we could not think of spilling *royal* blood in our palace. Who knows the future evil that doing so might bring to Mother Egypt." Cenk looks to Tarkhan.

The Mongol finds no humor in Cenk's sarcasm. The Tartars believe this notion concerning royal bloodshed more so than Cenk's native Bashkirs.

Qutuz turns to Obur. "So happens that another of Aybeg's wives brought a few servants with her. We know their fidelity is unquestionable."

Obur removes her cloak, letting it fall to the floor. The largest of the three servants slips off her wooden clogs. She palms the hefty shoe like a grinding stone. The other slaves follow her lead. They eye al-Durr.

Cenk raises his eyebrows, shrugs his shoulders. Al-Durr's attendants slowly back away.

Obur and her slaves need no more permission. They fall upon the queen, who receives them with raised fists. Obur's maids swarm al-Durr like attacking wasps, their clog-hits stinging her with strikes against the head, back, and arms. Obur claws at the queen, crumbling al-Durr to the rock floor.

Cenk laughs, his bellowing chortles rising above the din of the women's scuffle. He looks to Tarkhan and the sober Mamluks about him. They stand expressionless. Cenk finds this equally hilarious and his guffaws now double, echoing against the rock walls.

The large slave straddles one of the queen's arms and pounds her clog against the royal's head. Some of the Muizziyya mumble. Al-Durr's Salihi look away.

The queen squirms free of the hold and regains her feet. She flails, fewer of her punches now hitting their marks.

The clog-strikes fall like hammer blows. The queen bee loses her orientation, her fists lower. A clog to the back of the head drops her again. A servant kicks the queen in the head and back with her callused feet.

Qutuz steps in. He elbows aside the kicking slave and throws a knee to another woman. Obur backs offs, huffing.

The queen peeks through her elbows up at Qutuz, her arms wrapped over her head, her chest heaving.

"I can save you now," Qutuz says calmly. "Just tell me the truth. Where is the third servant, this man, Fabian?"

"I do not know. Truly."

Qutuz steps upon her ankle. "Did your goons murder my Commander of the Guard, keeping him from posting his men that day?"

"No," she says.

"Was the Ox embroiled in your ploy?"

She hesitates, then looks at him sideways, the queen likely calculating her death as imminent, regardless of whether she lies or speaks the truth.

Despite her condition and his drunkenness, Cenk understands the queen's look, knows instinctively that Ox, his former novice in training twenty years ago, is implicated. Cenk mumbles to Tarkhan, "The Ox did it. He is the one who relieved the guards from Aybeg's bath."

Tarkhan looks at him skeptically.

Cenk hiccups. "I will take care of him."

"Answer now," Qutuz says to the queen.

She closes her elbows tighter across her face.

Qutuz steps aside. The cloggers rush in. The queen struggles to her knees. She is quickly overwhelmed by a flurry of kicks and blows. The room echoes with the slaps and dull pounding of wood upon bone, skull upon rock. Their clogs, once the color of sand, turn to red.

Two of the wasps shred the queen's royal garb, tearing at her like hyenas upon the belly of a fresh kill. They smash in one side of al-Durr's head, the white of skull now exposed through the queen's tresses.

Obur pulls the big slave from the carnage. Another girl rolls off. The four stand, their garments splattered in gore. Gasping, they stare at the naked queen.

Al-Durr's hair lies snarled upon the rock, her bloodied face unrecognizable. A jagged edge of collarbone nearly punctures her dark skin; her shoulder props unnaturally against her ear. Crimson oozes from her body into the cracks in the floor, dispersing to a growing puddle in the corner of the room.

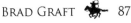

One of al-Durr's servants moves to the queen's side carrying a shawl over her shoulder. With a single tear running down her cheek, she brushes back al-Durr's matted hair and ties the garment around the waist of her mistress. She pecks Spray of Pearl's forehead, leaving the blood of a queen bright upon her lips.

At least one enemy gone, Cenk thinks. His Mongol friend gapes at al-Durr with sad eyes.

Qutuz thumbs toward the open window. He squares himself to the corpse with sword in hand, as if still not trusting that the wily scorpion has been slayed.

Two thick-armed men come forward.

Cenk looks down at the battered corpse. An unanticipated sadness sweeps through him, as he remembers that this is al-Salih's wife. His patron, the man he loved. The kin of Saladin, the father who had saved him and his other mates from obscurity. How miserable the Sultan al-Salih would be if he were alive to see his beloved wife now.

When al-Salih Ayyub became a Sultan in 1240, al-Durr came with him to Egypt and gave birth to their son, Khalil. Cenk recalled seeing al-Durr so proud to be carrying royalty in her arms. After the birth, al-Salih married her. Perhaps his patron felt somehow obligated to do so, maybe guilt got the best of him. Perhaps the sultan never really loved her; maybe she was merely breeding stock to him.

Cenk rationalizes. If al-Salih had seen the malice and conspiring his slave queen had brewed since his death, surely he would not oppose what he and Qutuz have just done. Yes, al-Salih would have wanted this.

The Muizziyya drag the queen by her bare feet to the window edge. They each grasp her under thigh and arm and then look back at Qutuz for confirmation. He nods, almost casually.

The pair awkwardly heave her out the window. They step away quickly, neither man likely wishing to view a sultana mangled below.

Men begin to move toward the door. A growing clod of boot stomps resonates down the stairs. Cenk walks over to the window and looks out as a cloud passes over the setting sun.

Below, the queen's body lies doubled over on itself, having rolled face-down into the fortification's ditch.

With both of al-Salih's sons long dead and the former sultan's Mamluk regiments split and hostile toward each other, Cenk reasons that in one way, al-Durr represented the last living piece of al-Salih. Perhaps the queen was the last fragment of stability in Cairo. Yet now, she, too, has been destroyed by the Royal Mamluks, men whom the old sultan treated as his favored sons.

CHAPTER 11

Esel

Damascus, Syria
May 10, 1257

Rashida pushes away her plate, nary a scrap of lamb or flake of pastry left uneaten. Esel meekly steps in to clear the last of the jade-colored dishes, keeping her attention on the table to avoid meeting the glance of tonight's dinner guest, al-Nasir Yusuf, Prince of Damascus. She returns to her station and quietly places the greenware on her silver platter.

Ornate flowers and meandering vines grace the rims of the glazed tableware. On the center of each plate, the image of a dark-bearded rider draped in chain mail raises his sword to a cowering enemy. Beneath the drawing are inscriptions in both Turkish and Arabic: "Al-Nasir—Warrior of the Ages."

Esel resumes her position, lacing her hands across the beltline of her full-length tunic, the fancy kirtle provided to her by the prince's *wazir*, his chief advisor. Her eyes flash to al-Nasir, the noble seated at her master's table and whose form is depicted on the dinner plates.

The dark-skinned Kurd wears a fur-trimmed robe, which fails to hide his belly fat. A sparse beard. A balding head. His slender fingers end in well-trimmed nails that are lovelier than those of a woman.

Esel doubts the overfed caliph ever suffered a callus from toil in his privileged life. Warrior of the Ages? Does he put the inscription in Turkish so his Mamluks eating from the same plates can be reminded of his greatness?

For years, Esel has overheard Rashida speaking highly of al-Nasir. Esel looked forward to seeing this powerful man, the royal who governs Damascus, Aleppo, and the other lesser cities of Syria. Yet in front of her is the opposite of the man she imagined.

She feels pity for the broad-shouldered guards outside and the hundreds of other Kipchak warriors turned Mamluk soldiers, duty-bound to serve this aristocrat. She doubts the fighting men of her old tower would have followed this prince anywhere, regardless of his lineage. Sure he has gold, but does he possess any fighting skills? Has he demonstrated a scrap of bravery on the field of battle? Ever?

Al-Nasir throws his head back in laughter at a flattering comment from Gamal. The prince folds his delicate hands across his lap. A disgust rises in Esel that she has not felt since her first weeks in Syria. The enslaved men of her bloodline deserve a more honorable commander than this. Perspiration dampens her pits. She must leave his presence for a bit.

She shoulders the tray and heads for her master's kitchen, her garment's hemline dragging upon the floor. She concentrates on each step, nervous that she might trip on the borrowed tunic and break the expensive items she carries.

Al-Nasir's wazir had taken every precaution earlier this evening. She was forced to disrobe and redress in the presence of another slave. He personally searched Esel for weapons before allowing her inside the house, lecherously running his hands inside her thighs and between her buttocks. She took this conduct with clenched teeth, fearful that to lash out would mean a thrashing, or worse.

She was forbidden to cook or be near the food when serving the royal. The wazir insisted on using the glazed Chinese ceramic plates from the palace, as apparently the ceramic possesses some mystical ability to detect poison by its sweating or breaking.

Reaching the bench table, she stoops beside it and deposits the platter of soiled cookery. Al-Nasir's slaves pay her no attention, busying themselves at the washtubs and repacking their crates with the silver and pottery they brought. They leave the family with the spare foodstuffs brought with them from the palace.

With the other slaves' backs turned, Esel snatches three legs of lamb and wraps them in linen cloths. She gathers the hem of her oversized kirtle and slips out the side door. She pushes one of the bundles into the hands of a Mamluk guard, who stands in the shadow. He smiles and bows his appreciation.

She continues to the front of the house, to where the pair of Mamluks she chatted with earlier stand watch at the front door. These men do not wear their customary uniforms of scarlet and gold, but rather the common robes of the trader-class. Their swords rest in the small of their backs, hidden behind them, so as to not alert passersby to the importance of the man inside the merchant's house this evening.

She hands each Kipchak a shank of still-warm lamb.

"Thank you," the larger says.

She nods, acknowledging his gratitude.

"You are not enjoying the tender conversation between old friends?" the older guard whispers.

She rolls her eyes. "In this nice breeze and out of earshot of the jabbers, you two may have the best job tonight."

They smile and tear into the seasoned meat.

"I have lived in Damascus for almost eight years, yet I still find the mentality of these people bizarre," he says.

"How so?" she asks.

"Maybe I just miss the people from my Dnieper territory. Conversation at evening meals back home was scant, mostly about the next day's work and lore from the elders on the most courageous before us. We left our dinner mats aiming to be more like the best of our ancestors. But people here. They know and eat too much. The more they have read, the more they chatter, the more they are sidetracked from what is important," he says, gazing into the darkness.

She nods, contemplating the rugged people in the country west of her tower's homeland that the guard mentions, plus the prince's life and how he became what he is. Certainly al-Nasir's regal upbringing ruined him. But she reckons the Damascenes' way of thinking of extends beyond the royal order, encompassing all classes. "I have lived here much longer. I think the walls that surround this city also play a part in creating people like them."

The Kipchak pivots his gaze to scan for eavesdroppers and turns back to Esel. With a nod of his head he invites her to continue.

"Seems most people here feel the ramparts are the blessed divider between civility and barbarism," she says. "The separator between the tamed and the untamed who live outside the gates. But behind the walls, they—even we, in time—lose the awareness that living in the forest and open grasslands compel. Our hardness fades. Our senses, our connection to the wilds become dulled."

The older Mamluk concurs. "The locals are content in being detached. Nature for the city dweller is a stroll through a manicured garden. Ask them to stalk a deer, set a snare, or break a horse—they would be lost."

"Yes," she says.

The younger guard shrugs. "It is about security. And gold." He glances to his mate. "Figure how many more of the prince's soldiers it would take to guard Damascus, if it were not surrounded by high block."

"Yes," she says. "But in return for the supposed refuge provided by the walls and the efficiencies gained in its defense, the town folk become nothing but penned animals, docile and complacent."

"As the prince desires," the young man says. "Fat and comfortable."

"Yet does he want the same for his soldiers?" Esel asks. "Those who stand atop the walls?"

The young man looks at her mutely.

She grins. "Even the guards' task of shielding the population is a sedentary one, requiring neither the mobility nor cleverness required of your fathers on the steppe."

The older guard chuckles. "She is right. Second-tier soldiers will suffice with nothing more strenuous than guarding a palisade. Aside from the Nasiriyya Mamluks, too few here have decent skills with bow on horseback."

"Unlike those who protected our towers back in the open country," she says.

"Where all men lived on horseback," the older Mamluk says. "Warriors willing and capable to take the offensive against an enemy in a moment's notice."

Esel nods. "That feels natural to me. These bulwarks. . ." She sighs. "Since my first day here, they felt like the boundary between those who really live on the outside and those who are but waiting to die on the inside."

She hears more jollity inside. "Well. I'd best get back to the 'safety' inside my master's mudded walls. This modest teacher's philosophy class is ended."

They raise their shanks of pilfered lamb in thanks.

As she ducks back into her master's home, her grin sours to a glower. Walls and cities and coerced religion. Combined, these turn hardy women into kept dolls. The blend converts men into women. Warriors become artisans. Hunters transform into soft-handed merchants. And a pathetic, false harmony hums between them all.

How is it that the Kipchak Confederation, filled with thousands of capable women, rough-hewn men, and warrior khans, has been beaten down and separated like cattle? Meanwhile, the cities of the Levant remain vibrant, despite so large a portion of their population being little more than sheep?

She groans. Who is she to throw stones? She has not lived on the steppe, beneath the Great Sky, for nearly two decades. Sadly, she, too, has mostly changed into one of these enfeebled city people.

She returns to the corner of the dining hall, waiting for her masters and guest to empty their teacups. She again observes the turbaned prince.

Rashida leans forward and places her hand upon the prince's arm. "I am so happy you came here. A change of scenery. A gathering like old times."

The prince flashes a smile of white teeth, none broken or missing.

"So, I understand that you are still writing. More poetry?" Rashida asks with raised eyebrows.

Al-Nasir's face brightens. "Yes." He reaches into his nearby satchel, rummaging. "I could not waste your precious instruction and let my skills tarnish."

Rashida and Gamal both force a chuckle. Her agenda is clear. Rashida exploits the old friendship for the benefit of Gamal's business. How fortunate for Gamal that Rashida's and al-Nasir's bond in the arts, formed a decade ago when Rashida taught al-Nasir poetry in Aleppo as a youth, has apparently held strong through the years. Esel hopes the royal weasel will not read his poems aloud. The prince finds the papyrus sheets he seeks and hands them to Rashida. "For later, when my good teacher has time."

"I look forward to them," she says. "When *I* have the time? *You* are the one who has few spare moments. It makes me happy to know that you still take the time to put quill to paper, given all your responsibilities."

"We all must rise to that required by our positions." He sighs, his eyes heavy from his burdens or from the evening's wine. "Between us, I miss those days in Aleppo, when I was just a governor of one city and not the ruler of Syria. Back when life was less serious. What I would give to be writing poetry daily, rather than engaging in endless administration and fielding lines of advisors and commanders, all elbowing for my time and favor. It is wearisome." He takes another sip of tea.

"The burdens of being the great-grandson of Saladin. Most think of only the grandeur in it," Rashida says.

"We have tried to be one less worry for you," Gamal says. "My craftsmen have been hard at it. We should meet the target date you set for us."

"Ah, I have been meaning to speak with you on this. I must cancel the requisition we made last month," the prince says.

Gamal's face goes blank.

The prince admires the winding vines on his cup. "The tribute we pay the Mongols is draining our treasury."

Gamal squints. "I thought you sent emissaries to the Mongol capital years ago to meet with their new Great Khan, Mongke? I thought we were already paying a set duty to keep the barbarians out of Damascus?"

"I did. Six years ago, shortly after Mongke and I both took power in our kingdoms. After al-Salih died, when the Crusaders still occupied Damietta." He takes a sip. "I thought by sending an embassy to Karakorum, I was being preemptive—that doing so would keep the tribute modest."

Gamal leans forward, resting his elbows on the table.

"But I sense Mongke may have seen my initial response as weakness. He just tripled the duty required in return for their protection. And I doubt even this satisfies the Mongols."

"Cannot this be negotiated? Gamal asks. "That increase is not reasonable."

"Reasonable," al-Nasir says dejectedly. "I fear the Mongols have no understanding of that principle, no reason to be such."

Al-Nasir looks to Gamal. "Khurshah, the leader of the Assassins in Iran. He and his family were recently executed, his armies destroyed."

"Yes, we have heard," Gamal says, glancing at his wife.

Al-Nasir slouches in his chair. "The Mongols see me as their vassal now." He turns his nose up at the thought. "The Tartar threat is now real. Imminent. Surely Mesopotamia is next. And then where?"

"Oh, dear," Rashida says.

The prince twists the hairs of his thin beard. "At this rate, my treasury will be empty in two years. I cannot continue to spend, equipping these Mamluks from Egypt with the best armor and weapons, and still afford the Mongol levy."

Beads of sweat dot Gamal's forehead. "I ... I understand, my Prince. Yet I have already paid for camel loads of the best Seljuk leather and many carts of Indian Wootz—materials for making swords and metal plates for the lamellar armor. My contacts in Italia have already acquired your requested helmets. They are aboard ship—on their way across the sea."

The prince sips his tea and absently rubs the smooth surface of his cup.

Gamal continues. "The bamboo arrived just yesterday for the two hundred lances. I have hired three more bladesmiths to produce your Mamluks' swords."

Al-Nasir cuts him off. "Those Bahri are not my Mamluks."

"Yes, my Prince. Of course, I mean the materials needed to arm your new warriors from Egypt. Your request was so large. I have no other ally of yours to sell the arms to. My vendors must be paid. Sitting on this much equipment for even a short time would put me out of business."

The prince nods his head in half-hearted sympathy. "We will raise taxes soon. But I have little choice now but to conserve our gold—for the good of the principality. I have tried to lighten the army's burden and expense by striking temporary accords with the weakest of our adversaries." He grimaces.

"But Allah knows who will rule Egypt with the Sultan Aybeg murdered, and if their next sovereign will honor the treaty between Egypt and us."

Gamal surveys al-Nasir from behind the lip of his cup.

Al-Nasir sighs. "And this Baybars of the Bahri. At first he seemed God-sent, arriving when I needed skilled troops. And more Mamluks flocking to him each moon, castoffs from the Salihi in Egypt and other Bahri who were serving al-Mughith of Karak. But increasingly, Baybars has become a thorn in my side. Expensive to keep and demanding."

"Yes, you have been wise to keep him down south, away from Damascus, isolated in the desert," Gamal says.

"I have done everything possible to keep him agreeable," says al-Nasir. "As I have no mission for him yet, Baybars trains with a vengeance. He shreds their gear in less than half of the time of my father's troops. And Baybars thinks only of taking Egypt. He challenges me endlessly for my assistance in such. He has spoken of nothing else since coming to me three years ago. His will has doubled now since the murder of Aybeg and his slave queen."

Esel smiles inside. They forget the ears of slaves surround them; they are unaware that she and Baybars are kin. Her nephew has not changed his ways after all these years. And it is no wonder that more of the hard-edged men from the steppe now flock to him, no different than the boys did when Baybars was young.

"At least Egypt and the Prince of Karak—even the caravan thieves—will learn that you have an able troop of warriors stationed in the desert," Gamal says. "This will mean less chance of conflict, fewer raids on your caravans, loss of fewer goods, and more gold in the merchants' purses to pay taxes," Gamal says, angling to the positive in arming the Bahri.

The prince shrugs. "Yes, but I cannot afford Baybars, cannot continue supplying his growing pack of rogues. I begin to wish I had never embraced him."

"But are not these the type of men you need to defend Syria? Perhaps with the Mongol threat, you could shift Baybars' obsession from Cairo to the north and east—to the more lethal and immediate foe."

Esel hides her smirk as her master squirms. Again Gamal maneuvers, surely willing to say anything to maintain his trade and the gold that fills his pockets.

The prince shakes his head in doubt and drains his cup. "More and more I feel the Bahri may be the pebble in my boot, the arrogant nomads. I suspect they wish to depose me, usurping royal authority for themselves, as they and their rival regiment did in Egypt against Turanshah."

Gamal considers. "Perhaps. What if you hedged a little, as men as talented as the Bahri are best working for you rather than another prince, yes?"

Al-Nasir rakes his thin beard and straightens as he considers Gamal's counsel.

"What if we still provided Baybars' troops with the promised weapons and armor—as even the best troops using broken gear are mostly useless—yet slashed their pay?" Gamal asks. "This would conserve dinars."

Al-Nasir raises an eyebrow. "I could pay Baybars his promised salary, and then offer to pay his troops later. Drag this arrangement out. Maybe not pay his men at all." He shrugs. "The Bahri have no future in Egypt. And Baybars' options in Syria are few."

Gamal nods, some relief beginning to show on his face. "Surely Baybars cares more for the jingle of coin in his own pouch and new kit for his throat-slitters than the decimation of his ranks in a war against his fellow Mamluks in Egypt?"

"Perhaps."

Gamal leans forward. "Maybe you could also lessen the iqta the Bahri receive from Nablus and Jidin? Skim some of Baybars' gold from the croplands for yourself. This coming winter, tell him the harvest was poor. He will not be in a position to know."

Rashida shifts in her seat uncomfortably and sets down her empty cup. Esel moves in and clears the cups and saucers. She busies herself in the kitchen, within earshot.

"I must do something," al-Nasir says. "Perhaps your ideas could string Baybars along for another year—maybe longer. And you are right. Having him idle near my camp is better than having him active against me in al-Mughith's camp in Karak."

"Yes, my Prince," Gamal says.

"Well, enough of that," al-Nasir says. He reaches for his satchel. "Maybe we have time to share one poem."

Rashida returns the prince's grin. "I was hoping you would." She looks over the cleared table and then to Esel at her station. "Esel, we are finished here. You can leave."

Esel bows her good evening. She turns from them, fuming. They scheme to mislead her nephew at every turn. She exits the side door and takes in the evening.

The stars shine brightly. She looks for the summer hunter in the sky. Finding him, she traces the curve of his bow with her finger. She follows the lower limb of the weapon downward. She nods. Down. South, where her nephew now dwells.

She walks the rocky path to her quarters. She lights two candles, setting one upon her shelf. She reaches underneath her bureau and unhooks the leather bag of silver hanging from a nail. She holds the sack to her chest, squeezing her life's savings. Inside the pouch, her accumulation of the occasional coins given to her by Gamal over the years, usually when he was drunk or feeling sorry for her—a *dirham* coin here and there to buy a warmer cloak or a bit of colorful fabric to brighten the clay walls of her room. She rarely spent any of it, knowing some day she would need it.

She bites her bottom lip. She walks straight to the Mamluk guards at the front door, the bag of coins clenched in her fist. The Kipchaks greet her and return the bread cloths, the lamb bones picked clean and set atop one.

"Thanks for the lamb," the older says.

"Yes, of course. Earlier, you said you would both be working gate duty during all of June," she whispers to the lead guard.

"Yes, he says.

"Do you know which one?"

He looks to his mate. "The Roman Jupiter Gate."

"You know this for certain? It will not change?"

"It is for certain," he says.

Her heart begins to race. "In the dark, guards do not always see all who pass through their assigned portal." She pushes the coin bag into the Mamluk's hand. "I wish to be one of those unseen at night, early next moon."

The guard looks to his friend. The younger soldier purses his lips.

"If agreed, not a word of this would pass my lips," she says. "No matter what. An oath between fellow Kipchaks."

The younger guard nods.

"I swear it upon my life." She places a hand over heart, a determination written upon her squinted brow.

The lead guard tucks the leather bag under his belt as he scans the empty street for prying eyes.

She looks him in the face, until he meets her eyes. He nods.

"Thank you," she says.

She returns to her hut, her chest pounding. She again finds the bow in the sky. A smoldering reek from a dowsed cookfire wafts between buildings. The foul smell takes her back to that cursed place. The tight country near the Rotten Sea, far west of her Kipchak homeland. Sixteen autumns ago in the year 1241. The year that her tower fled the Mongols to the Isthmus of Perekop. She hopes the implicit promise from this pair of Mamluk guards is truer than that provided by Anas Khan back then.

CHAPTER 12

Esel

Orkapi narrow, base of the Crimea

September 24, 1241

A hand on her shoulder shook Esel awake.

Her husband stood above her, leaning on his crutch, shielding his eyes from the late afternoon sun. "They return," Yagmur said.

She propped herself up on an elbow and looked east. Dark clouds roiled and tumbled over an undulant carpet of sea aster and the ribbon of path bisecting it.

Their khan and his bondsmen rounded the bend, their ponies at the canter. Upon seeing them, Esel and roughly two hundred from her tower struggled up from the ground, where they rested. Dust-covered Kipchaks re-shouldered their loads. Those tending carts arose from their wagons' shadows with switches in hand. The few warriors with ponies stepped into mudded stirrups and took to the path. Teenage boys prodded with long staffs what remained of the tower's thinning herd of sheep and goats.

For the past seven days, the nomads from Esel's tower had traveled south and west, driven by the Mongols, the invaders who continued to slay all who would not submit to their rule. While Esel's tribe of Kipchaks had eluded the Black Tartars for years, fate and the Mongols had caught up to them. There was no more safety in staying to the upland plateaus, where the grass grew scant, away from the major drainages. Now, the Black Tartars tracked and pushed the last of the renegade nomads over every inch of the steppe, like wounded game.

The beginning of their journey led them quietly through the lands of the Don River Kipchak, allied tribes on the great river who had succumbed to the invaders long ago. There, Esel's tower paid the newly-implemented toll in return for safe passage.

Of course, these people, and the rest of the Kipchaks farther north, no longer ruled the land. They merely administered it for the Mongols. All of the confederation's Kipchaks were now just one part of what the Tartars called the Golden Horde, named for the yellow tents used by the descendants of Batu Khan, grandson of the legendary Genghis Khan. These men ruled the massive grasslands from the former lands of the Rus to the west, clear to the old Bulgar and Bashkir territories to the east.

The last three days, the tower traveled west across the northern edge of the *Sivash*, a large system of shallow lagoons, which nearly severs the Tauric Peninsula from the mainland. These seemingly endless wetlands served as a natural border between the Kipchaks and the Turkmen nomads to their south. The swampy terrain stretched from the Sea of Azov on the east, clear to the Black Sea on the west.

Here at the base of the Tauric, Esel's tower sought permission to enter the north-south-running Orkapi Narrow, governed by the Turkmen khan, Anas. This thin neck of land, known to Esel's people as *Tauric kapisi* was the gateway to the massive peninsula.

The isthmus comprised the primary jut of navigable coast between the Black Sea to the west and the Sivash, or Rotten Sea, to the east—a place where the smell of spoiled eggs predominated. This far west along the Sivash, the grazing land gave way to hollow reeds, marsh-loving grasswort, and saltbush—less than ideal for livestock.

Yet this three-mile-wide strip of ground to Esel's south was more valuable than any fertile paddock back north. For centuries, whoever held this finger of land controlled the most navigable route south into the heart of the Tauric, the most likely approach of any enemy. With its occupation also came authority over trade between the vast steppe to the north and the broadening peninsula southward.

The Kipchaks huddled about their khan, their leader's face concerned.

"Anas said he will allow our crossing of the narrows in return for sixteen ewes and two of our mares," their khan said.

The tower stayed silent, looking at him with vacant faces. A baby cried. A sheep let out a "Meh-eh-eh-eh."

"Our men will unstring their bows and place them in the carts. Those with ponies will attach their leads to the back of the carts and walk with the others."

Hushed grumbles arose from some of the warriors.

"They have agreed to post guides at the main intersections to show us the best way south." Their khan turned from them with no intention to hear their concerns. He walked his pony to a cart and secured his lead to the rail. He strolled back in the direction from which he had come.

The cluster of warriors and travelers behind him hesitated. Before long, the mass of them tromped west along the trampled path and through the white flowers adjacent to it.

Yagmur limped beside her on his crutch. "Hope this is the last deal struck. Any more and we will be walking barefooted."

Esel nodded. Earlier in their trip, another Turkmen tribe had stripped them of half their livestock and all but a dozen of their horses.

With the low-hovering sun in their faces, they trudged the flat country between the two seacoasts, the road following the higher ground. As they made the turn south, the eastern wind carried the putrid scent of the Sivash across them, adding a fitting odor to the agreement made by their khan and what their lives had become.

Overhead, black clouds began to fuse into a thick layer of murk. Sunlight punched through one of the few remaining gaps, drawing her eyes back from where they came. The rays highlighted the north shore of the Sivash behind them, stretches of rolling scrubland peppered with sea lavender, the purple-blue flower bunches covering the upland shore for as far as they could see.

Crimson-tinged whitecaps curled in the giant lake, the foul red algae giving the water a rusty tinge. Waves spilled over the salt-encrusted shore. A blood-tinted version of winter on their cherished Volga River, far to the north, complete with shelf ice and frosty-capped boulders.

Yagmur saw where Esel looked. "A menacing landscape—to both the eyes and nose."

"Agreed." Esel wiped her arm across her sweating brow, wondering what awaited her people on the mainland of the peninsula, most having never seen a single blade of grass west of the Don River, much less the Tauric, where their khan's cousin supposedly welcomed them.

They crested a small rise. The first gers of the Turks appeared, their rounded shelters becoming more numerous as they followed the path south.

Passing through the congregation of huts, several of the Turks' women glanced over their shoulders at the pathetic herd of Kipchak refugees and their nine squeaking carts. Most of the dark-skinned women stayed to their tasks of scraping hides and milking their mares.

More gers. Few women for so many shelters. And the place was oddly free of children. And their men—where were their men?

They continued, more Kipchaks heads looking left and right as they trod, more eyes going to the tops of the dark-rocked hills, which gradually rose to their west. The road funneled the migrants into a tighter file, with flatter hills also emerging to their east.

Two old Turks on Esel's right shoveled a pile of chunky salt into a rickety cart bed. Not until half the Kipchaks passed them, did one of the Turks glance in their direction.

"I do not like this," Yagmur said.

Esel did not either. When the entire column passed the pair of workers, the old men leaned on their shovels. Should she run to the front of the column to warn her khan that she felt something amiss? No, their khan was no fool. He had an agreement.

When the last of the carts were a safe distance from the shovelers, both Turks pulled reed whistles from their pockets and blew loudly. They ran uphill toward a saddle in the dark hills.

Several of the Kipchak warriors sprinted back to the carts, anticipating what was coming.

Before the old Turks breached the low spot, archers appeared by the dozens atop the western ridgeline, their silhouettes dark against the setting sun. The arrows staged between their fingers, plus those in quivers upon their backs, splayed radially—the Turks appearing as armored with porcupine quills.

Esel looked back the way they had come. Over the foothills, more Turkish warriors materialized. She snatched two children by the scruff of their tunics and ran to the nearest cart, unsheathing her knife as she ran. She sawed at the straps securing the yoked ox to the cart. The ox spooked, nearly toppling the wagon. It landed on its wheels, crosswise to the path.

Cutting through the last of the leather, she kicked the beast in its ass. She shoved the kids beneath the cart, then dove under it, lying atop the kids.

A hiss of arrows thumped into the wooden bed overhead. Iron warheads smacked into flesh. Orders shouted by their khan.

Men screamed. She winced. The press of bodies became tighter under the cart as more women and children sought the only available cover. Soon Esel was wedged between bodies, unable to move. Children sobbed. She peered from between the blocky wheels.

The legs of Kipchak warriors ran past. To her right, a seated man grimaced as he bent the limbs of his bow across his knee, while another set his string. More projectiles buzzed in from the west, pinning some of the men to the wood of the cart before they could employ their weapons. Warriors hid behind the opposite wheel, nocking arrows.

Those men in the front of the column ran up the hillsides with daggers in hand, surely knowing their task was madness, yet cognizant that they would not survive the scramble rearward to fetch their bows. They sacrificed themselves, likely hoping they might buy their mates some time with this diversion.

Kipchaks unable to find cover scampered toward the eastern hills. The Turks ignored them. A woman with a baby strapped to her front breached the farthest hill. Looking over the opposite rise, she turned and ran back west, urging the others to do the same. More Turkish bowmen appeared over the eastern horizon.

Time slowed. A numbness engulfed Esel's brain and deadened her hearing. She laid with her head buried in her arms. A girl's scream brought her back to the present.

She thought of her father at his table, a fine bow in his hands. She must help fight. A bow. Find a bow. The tower needs you.

She screamed in rage, scrabbling at the dried grass to free herself from the tangle of arms and legs beneath the cart. She crouched and looked about.

Turks were already atop the carts, some inspecting the weapons made from her hand. Others looted sacks of yogurt curds.

She turned. Dead Kipchak warriors laid strewn about the hillsides, most of their quivers still full of arrows. Hundreds of Turkmen strolled about the bodies, poking at them with the tips of their bows, slitting the throats of the injured. Turkish boys dotted the tussocks, grouping the livestock with shepherd hooks, their yapping dogs in to assist.

She stood slump-shouldered. The slaughter was over before it started, the Kipchaks outmanned four to one. Her blood boiled, driving tears to her eyes. "Anas deceived them. The devil."

Yagmur. Where was her husband? Seeing him nowhere, she ran partway up the western mount and followed a game trail, side-straddling the ridgeline. She stepped over dead Kipchak and Turkmen, one pair who looked to have died in embrace, fighting hand-to-hand.

She sobbed. A bad dream. Could this just be a bad dream? Then ahead she saw him, recognized by the gnarled staff at his side. He bore a single arrow in his side, his tunic saturated in blood. She hurried to him, stumbled and fell, rolling back to her feet.

She threw herself beside him. He groaned. His hand groped where the shaft was embedded below his ribs. She wrapped her arms around his neck. "You are alive." She laid there weeping, breathing in his scent, having thought for certain he, too, was dead.

"They saw me struggling up the hill," he muttered. "I was not even worth another of their arrows to finish me."

She squeezed him tightly. "Luckily."

A kick to her rump. "Get up." A Turkish voice from behind her. "Get your ass up and join the others." She sprung to her feet and faced him, a tall man in a turban, a black beard frizzled upon his chin. His front teeth were rotted and his breath reeked of dead animal.

She spit at him, tears running down her cheeks.

He looked down at her spittle upon his leg. "Go to that cart and join the others," he said, pointing with his sword to sixty women huddled about an overturned wagon.

Two carts beyond this cowered the tower's girls. Near it stood the teenage boys, the most-prized of the Kipchaks' valuables. Esel knew well the lads' fates. The Turkmen would sell them to merchants at the trading hub on the east coast of the Black Sea, the fittest of the boys becoming military slaves.

She looked past the stinking man and saw her nephew, Baybars, watching her, a look of despair on his face. She rose, grabbing Yagmur's forearm to help him to his feet.

"Not him. Get away," said the Turk, raising his sword.

"No!" Esel argued. "You will need him. He can doctor any horse and his skills with leather are unrivaled."

The Turk regarded her, then furled his lip. He looked to see if any of his comrades were watching. Seeing none, he slowly lowered his sword and walked away.

CHAPTER 13

Leander

Zagros Mountains, western Persia

May 13, 1257

Leander, a former Crusader from the Kingdom of France, leans on the pommel of his saddle. He and his mates trek uphill toward the setting sun, the graveled trail blotched with patches of shortgrass and sprinkled with flickers of shade from overhanging oaks. Shaded folds of high country encase them. The lazy clop of hooves from the horses draws a wide yawn from him.

Singer hooks his riding stick under Leander's arm in a good-natured attempt to unseat him. His comrade flashes a boyish grin, but Leander knows this skilled cavalryman's jest is grounded in purpose. Despite the long ride, the long days, they must remain alert.

"Thank you, amir," Leander says, shaking his head in disgust for his indolence. He takes a swig from his water skin and splashes some across his face.

Singer raises his eyebrows, not expecting Leander's display of respect in uttering his fellow rider's title.

Singer and Duyal had insisted that such formalities, necessary when back among their regular units, were needless for their small team here in the mountainous hinterlands of Persia. The rigors of their assignment and close working conditions the past six moons made such conventions impractical.

Yet Leander slips the "amir" title into his conversations with them every so often. He reminds them that he respects their rank as well as the men. While Duyal commands, both Duyal and Singer are "Amirs of Forty," soldiers who earned the privilege to lead forty Mamluks in battle—plus attachments—the second-highest tactical grade in the Mamluk Corps. And Leander's comrades are senior—even superior—to him, Leander feels, in nearly every soldierly measure.

While Duyal and Singer are thirty-five and thirty-seven years old respectively, their white-skinned faces appear older, having been darkened and weathered from constant exposure to the elements. They wear herder's cloaks over their short-sleeved mail shirts and simple felt hats, with pieces of cut turban wrapped under their chins and around their necks in the way of the locals, hiding their brown and blond hair. What shows of their light-colored beards is masked in dust. They could pass as Bedu, Persian, Syrian, or most any race or creed in these parts.

Leander grins. What had he really done to deserve serving on a scouting team alongside these two salts? What had he accomplished in his twenty-nine years to be chosen for such an important assignment by their commander, Baybars al-Bunduqdari? Not enough.

He sits up straighter in the saddle. How blessed he is to be riding beside these warriors, perhaps the very best of the Bahri regiment's original five-hundred cavalrymen.

Singer and Duyal, like many of the Bahri Mamluks, are of Kipchak lineage. They were taken by the Mongols as adolescents from the vast steppe north and east of the Black Sea when the conquering Tartars decimated and scattered their towers in the 1230s. Some of the nomadic youth were impressed into Mongol service. Singer was such. Yet he managed to escape his captors, finding his way to then Prince al-Salih in the Jazira, who embraced Singer for his martial skills and knowledge of the Mongol ways and language.

Most Kipchaks, like Duyal, were led to the slave blocks and sold to Muslim princes around the realm, the boys sought after for their reputation as capable horse archers. Having been too many times abandoned on battlefields by his regular cavalry and auxiliary troops, al-Salih knew the value of these hardy lads from the brutal grasslands.

At his tibaqs, the barracks schools, al-Salih equipped his military slaves with the best gear. He honed their crude talents into battle skills, converting ḥerds of novices into his prized knights of Jihad—masters of the bow, lance, and sword.

Although snatched from their parents or taken as orphans, the Kipchak lads—like those Circassians and other Turkmen taken decades before them—eventually embraced their sultan, not just as soldiers would their commander but as sons would their new birthfather. Young warriors emerged from the tibaqs with unquestionable loyalty to al-Salih.

Al-Salih's father, nephew of Saladin the Great, had also fielded hundreds of Mamluks as elite cavalry during his reign. But when the Mongols flooded the slave markets with these relatively low-priced Kipchak boys twenty years ago, Sultan al-Salih saw even greater opportunity in the nomads. He was the first of the Ayyubids to stock his army en masse with Mamluks. He enlarged his hippodromes, the arenas where his novices were instructed.

Leander, too, endured this instruction, this vetting of recruits. At the tibaq in Cairo, Leander was the sole Frank in his training class, older and strange amid the Kipchak adolescents around him. Leander came into the region serving a French lord, but soon lost faith in the Crusader mission of conquering the lands of Islam. All the while, a growing admiration for the local population took hold of his heart, along with a respect for the unified Mamluks who protected them. Before a major battle, he switched to the Muslim side, al-Salih giving him an opportunity to earn a spot in the exclusive Bahri.

And after four years of sequestered instruction, the novices he trained with evolved not only into men, but also into Leander's Khushdash—the allegiance among brothers in common servitude and manumission, the bond of those who shared both years of preparation and the same theoretical release from slavery.

Leander looks to the cloudless sky and thanks Allah for His part in nudging him toward the Bahri. He reaches down and scratches behind the ears of his mare, a burly chestnut he named *Ayi*, meaning "bear" in the Turkish language of his warrior sect.

"That sand crack does not seem to be bothering her," Leander says to Singer, about his mare.

"The one climbing upward from the left hoof is fine," says Singer, his brows furling. "But there is a quarter crack spreading on her right hoof that is deeper."

"Probably from her toeing out," Duyal says.

"Aye. And the constant change from wet to dry up here," Singer says, looking skyward while patting the wet neck of his white-splotched sabino.

Baybars traded for these mounts with the Bedouin outside their Syrian camp. Knowing the team's mission would require them to cover long distances over steep and rugged terrain, Baybars insisted on leaving their Arabians behind and riding this sturdier lineage of horse from Cyrenaica, in northeastern Libya. Gifted with stout legs, this animal was a favorite of al-Salih's: a breed that offered the strength of a pack horse with much of the spirited temperament of their beloved Arabians.

A lump sets in Leander's gut. He misses his gray Arabian, Luna, now stabled near Damascus. He received this mare as a gift from al-Salih upon the completion of his training at the tibaq. The horse is of the cherished al-Bahrayan stock, originating from Eastern Arabia. Most Bahri feel this Arabian is the superior desert horse, the massive peninsula yielding the most agile warhorses, who are light of foot and perfectly suited for most engagements in the arid regions of Syria and Egypt.

Egypt. Al-Salih. The magnificent Nile. The food vendors and shops that lined Cairo's streets, offering savory roasted fish and tasty chickpea pastes. The sea. For Leander, the Nile Delta feels a thousand miles away from these Zagros Mountains where they now ride. A dream, a tale nearly forgotten to him. He finds it hard to believe they have been living away from their beloved Cairo for over three years now.

Back in 1248, when Leander graduated from his initial training, al-Salih ran the empire as his sultan father and grandfather had before him. He held the other princes at bay, assigning his kin governorships in the various Syrian cities within the realm. The empire then was a collective sovereignty, with shifting factions of Saladin's Kurdish descendants grudgingly ruling under the Ayyubid banner in Cairo from their own principalities.

Al-Salih's benevolence and charismatic personality kept his competitive Salihi and Bahri Mamluk Regiments from each other's throats. Like a nervous mother lion endeavoring to control her den of weaned cubs, al-Salih held the tenuous kingdom and Mamluk factions together for a decade.

But when al-Salih died in 1249, the glue bonding the empire disintegrated. To complicate matters, King Louis' Crusaders had snatched the coastline at Damietta and were on Cairo's doorstep. Even once the Crusader threat was checked in Mansura, Egypt could not right itself. Mamluks from both regiments murdered the incoming sultan, al-Salih's son, Turanshah. In the resulting disarray, Aybeg of the Salihi Regiment weaseled his way into the sultanate. Soon after, Aybeg tricked his rival, the Bahri's leader, Aqtay, into a meeting at the Cairo citadel. There, Aybeg and his henchmen murdered Aqtay and literally chased Baybars, Leander, and several hundred of the Bahri out of Cairo and into the desolate Sinai.

Until this mission took his team nearly a month's ride from Damascus, Leander and the Bahri simply followed the man who had surfaced as the most capable amir among them: Baybars al-Bunduqdari. Living in austere desert camps for years, the Bahri trained for one thing—war against Aybeg's Muizziyya in Cairo. Toward this end, Baybars continually prodded the indecisive al-Nasir of Syria to deliver more troops and gear to augment the Bahri's small force.

"Once over this pass, let us find a spot to camp on the other side, closer to the stream," Duyal says, eyeing the slabs of jagged stone that line the path ahead.

Leander and Singer agree with their leader.

While the Zagros Mountains had been harsh for both man and beast this past winter, the steep country had been kind in its own way. Its craggy elevation provided ample hiding spots for the Mamluks and its rock-shelved overhangs afforded sanctuary during the cold rain and snow. In this way, Leander dreads leaving the mountainous parts of Persia for the open country to the west, its rolling plains devoid of gorges or defiles from which to attack, or rocky redoubts from which to defend.

The road narrows and steepens into a series of lazy switchbacks. The trio draw their swords, laying them atop their thighs. They round a sharp curve abreast, the terrain compressing their formation. A rising wind courses across their front. Beside Leander a sheer face drops, choked with jagged rock and juniper—not much to break a fall.

As his eyes return to his front, Leander's horse nearly collides with another heading toward him. Foes, he thinks.

A bay stallion among the strangers rears. Others strive to control their steeds, while pulling swords from their scabbards.

Their beasts' eyes peel wide, their hooves scrabble at the loose stones.

These men also wear drab robes with no markings. Only one of their riders is light-skinned. Leander's eyes go to their tall horses and tack and then to their sword belts. A mishmash of weapons typically carried by fighters from Armenia or Italia. His eyes lock on the scabbard and stirrups on the nearest mount, gear recognized as that worn by the French. He raises his gaze to the man's white-skinned face. A fellow Frank, he hopes.

Ayi jumps sideways into Amir Duyal's mount. A surge of adrenalin courses through Leander. He pulls left on his reins to keep Ayi from tumbling over the edge. Singer's horse bucks. Spinning his mare back to the front, Leander counts seven men opposite them.

Once settling their mounts, the opposing warriors back their horses slowly and come alongside each other, their eyes quickly sizing up their potential opponents.

Leander pushes his horse in front of his commander's and whispers to Duyal in the uncommon dialect of Duyal's Kipchak tribe, "One is a Frank. Let me work this."

Duyal nods, his eyes urging Leander's vigilance.

Leander flips the tip of his blade to the rear and approaches slowly with both palms forward. He calls out in French, "I am a Frenchman. A knight from Ramerupt."

The white-skinned man across from him blurts a few words over his shoulder in the language of his comrades. He turns back to Leander, cracking a skeptical grin. He speaks in the Frankish tongue. "What would ragged, French-speaking shepherds be doing in the middle of this domain on such fine mounts, and not a single wailing sheep to move? Who do you serve?" he asks with one eye squinted.

"King Louis," Leander lies.

One of the dark-skinned men opposite Leander slowly eases a dagger from his saddle scabbard and holds it against his thigh. Behind Leander, Singer's horse rattles a snort of alarm.

"And you?" Leander asks.

"I attend Bohemond of Antioch and Tripoli. Who are you?"

"Leander. My former Lord, Henri of Brienne-Ramerupt, was killed in Mansura." He again concocts. "The king wished my services temporarily. Seven years later, well, here I am."

The man gauges the words, firming the grip on his sword.

"I saw your prince knighted by King Louis in Acre. What was that—five years ago?" Leander asks.

"That is about right." The stranger slowly lowers his sword to his side. "I am Edmond, a Templar Knight."

"Well, serving Bohemond, I figured you were not a Knight Hospitaller," Leander says with a half-grin.

Edmond chuckles, as every Crusader in the Levant knew that despising the Hospitallers was a family tradition in Antioch, with Bohemond VI's hatred going back at least two generations. The Templar stows his sword. One of the dark-skinned men at his side expels a sigh of relief. The others lower their weapons.

Pegging the Templar's comrades as Armenian, Leander holds back a jest about the elder Bohemond, father to this present Bohemond, and the senior's revulsion for the neighboring Kingdom of Armenia. That generations-old rivalry was quelled only three years ago through a marriage between royals.

"What is your affair in these foreign parts?" Edmond asks, surely knowing the answer.

"Same as you. There are more than a few snoops cloaked as herders wandering this country, trying to keep their leaders informed."

"So your king sent you here to put eyes on the Mongols."

Leander looks to the Armenians and then back to the Frenchman. "It is better than stacking stones in Jaffa, probably no worse than interpreting for the king's emissaries—dealing with the Saracens in Damascus or the Mamluk heathens in Cairo."

The Templar nods, seemingly aware that King Louis had improved the fortifications in both Jaffa and Caesarea and conducted some diplomacy with the Islamic powers of Syria and Egypt before departing the Levant in 1254.

An Armenian interrupts, wanting to know what Leander says. Edmond tells them.

"Appears you and I share the same gift—or perhaps the same curse." Leander says.

Edmond looks at him quizzically.

"Having the trust of a lord and the skill of knowing many tongues can put a knight under a millstone in a hurry."

The Templar laughs. "Or at least put him in the middle of nowhere."

Leander leans on his saddle. "King Louis may be as obsessed as your royal in sending emissaries to the Mongol capital." He shrugs. "At least with the Black Tartars making their way to the Levant, we do not have as far to ride."_

Edmond nods sadly, while looking over Duyal and Singer. "Who are your friends?"

"Guides. Turkmen. They do not know our language, but understand well the song of the bowstring."

"Their damned recurved bows. We have learned to respect their archers."

"And they know this country far better than we." Leander sighs, continuing with his ruse. "I have had enough of it. Been wishing I was back in the hills of Ramerupt."

"You are a long way from that sleepy place."

Leander tilts his head toward his comrades. "They are good enough company and reliable. As long as they are getting paid."

With his former countryman buying his story, Leander must probe for more. Baybars and Duyal both would expect such from him. "Both our sovereigns wish to grasp the capability of this Mongol enemy, before considering submitting. I cannot see the Kingdom of Jerusalem becoming a vassal to any pagan. Will Bohemond submit to the Mongols as his father before him did?"

"I do not know. We have seen little of the horde yet," the Templar says. "But by the looks of you and the direction you came, I am guessing you have seen them?"

Leander nods grimly. "We have been trailing the Mongols for nearly six months."

"Are the rumors true—that the grandson of Genghis Khan has sent two large armies in opposite directions?"

"Mongke, their Great Khan, has sent his brother, Kublai, with the 'Army of the Left' south of Mongolia to attack the Song Dynasty. While he has tasked his older brother, Hulegu, the 'Army of the Right' to expand the empire southwest."

"And you have seen Hulegu's army?"

"Plenty. But in bits and pieces. The Lurs and Bukhara fell first. Since then, the Mongols have taken nearly every stronghold in Kuhistan—those held by the Nizari Ismailis."

"Bloody?" Edmond asks.

"Somewhat. But only a few of the bastions were taken by force."

"The Assassins surely did not just hand over each fortress?"

"No. The Mongols captured the Persian Grand Master. They dragged the Imam from castle to castle, causing the Assassins in each fortification to surrender. One by one. So the Assassins are finished, too. Khuzistan is now a Mongol land."

Edmond quickly passes this information to his cohorts. An Armenian smiles. Leander figures the grin is because of the Persian loss, not the Mongol gain. The Assassins are equally despised, by both the Sunni Mamluks and Christians alike, for the Assassins' Shia faith and reputation for slaying adversaries in public places by dagger. The others whisper among themselves, their brows chiseled in concern.

"How large is the Mongol force?" Edmonds asks.

Leander shrugs. "Hard to know, for sure. We saw maybe four thousand Mongol cavalry—plus another thousand conscripts from China—engineers and surgeons, dozens of craftsmen from Rus and Czech lands. Bridge builders. Scribes and clerks. With allies, Hulegu might have five times as many warriors laid up at Hamandan."

The Crusader's face goes white. "Twenty thousand."

"Maybe more—including allies. I am sure you have heard that the Mongols are augmented by Christian forces—the King of Armenia, Antioch, and the Georgians' force have joined with the Tartars. These allies apparently wait for Hulegu's call, for the next stage of the campaign."

Edmond scowls. "Yes."

"Anyhow, when we first arrived late last year, twelve thousand captured Assassins were misled to believe they would be formed into a militia. They were sent from Khurasan to Khuzistan. And then slain en masse."

"Slain for cooperating with the Mongols?"

"Well, we doubt the Great Khan appreciated the Assassins sending a throat slitter to the Mongol capital. Mongke likely told his brother to exact some retribution. Hulegu did just that."

Edmond nods.

"But largely, it is the same old story with the Mongols," Leander says. "You resist, you die. One good thing is that for once, they are in no hurry, burdened as they are with a heavy train of supplies and baggage, plus attached personnel." He deceives. "And at least they are slaying Muslims."

"True."

"But it seems clear what they are up to. The Mongols are serious about this *Ilkhanate*, this expanded empire in the Middle East. And they are assembling an army to win it. Mongke appears to have given Hulegu plenty of leeway. The Tartars may see this 'House of Hulegu' as including all of Syria and Egypt."

"So the Mongols took those Persian forts to secure their rear, enroute to the Jazira and the Levant?"

Leander shrugs. "Seems the caliph in Baghdad ignored Hulegu's demand for troops in Persia. The Mongols would not see that as proper behavior for a vassal."

Leander senses Duyal's impatience to move, his dislike with so many words being passed without his comprehension of them.

"We are looking to stay just forward of Hulegu's vanguard." Leander says. "We figure they will be scouting for adequate pastures west of here, bridges needing repair."

"If they take Mesopotamia, could Acre and Caesarea be next?" Edmond asks.

"If. Who knows? Given the size of the Mongol army, I wonder if all of Outremer might be wise to unite with the Muslims to beat back the horde?"

"The enemy of my enemy is my ally," Edmond says.

"Right." He looks to Duyal and then to the Templar. "I am sorry, but we'd best go—should not be seen here together. At the bottom of the mountain, take the path right. Hulegu's vanguard may soon be pushing this way, so careful there. May God grant you success."

"And you."

Duyal's team continues down the hill in silence. They curve around the bulk of the mountain.

"Some quick thinking again from you, I am guessing," Singer says. "Who was he?"

"One of Bohemond's Templar Knights, Edmond," Leander says.

"What did you tell them about us?" Duyal asks.

"Aside that I was from Ramerupt, mostly lies. I said that I was one of King Louis' Crusaders. You two were Turk escorts. But I said nothing but the truth on the Mongols. I figured talk on the common enemy might keep their minds off us," Leander says.

"Good. We don't need them circling back," Duyal says.

"And as Baybars had urged, I suggested the Crusaders assist in fighting the Tartars, rather than bowing to them," Leander says.

Duyal nods. "Good. We may soon need all the help we can get. Even Christian help."

CHAPTER 14

Cenk

Cairo

May 14, 1257

Cenk closes the door behind him and eases down the stoop of his home. Dizzy from drink, he braces himself with the railing. He strolls north along the canal street in the dark, the glimmer from the watchmen's slipper lamps wagging ripples of light upon the cobbles. The fecund scent of river water feathers in from the west, where the mighty Nile flows, black and powerful.

He weaves through town, his palm resting on the pommel of his sword, content in the just punishment levied on the traitorous sultana two weeks past and primed to do his part in exacting the unfinished justice that remains.

He walks with a stiff-legged erectness, an attempt to hide his inebriated staggering. Taking the western path away from the buildings, a waxing quarter moon throws muted sparks across the dimpled flow of current. He passes the outline of papyrus-reed boats and flat-keeled barges tied up for the night. Deckhands sleep atop the mounds of cargo.

Waving fronds from the date palms crinkle in the wind, flicking moon shadows along his path. The few pedestrians he approaches duck into cul-de-sacs or vendor alleys. A man crosses to the opposite side of the street.

He leaves the neighborhood of the Mamluk amirs, stone houses lined with tight shrubbery and fence pickets pointed at the top like lance heads. Small placards adorn their gates, one bearing crossed swords, another a quill, another a long-necked Arabian—the emblems depicting each amir's role in the empire.

Approaching the senior amirs' homes, he eyes the vacant house of the Bahri's Amir Aqtay, Aybeg's past challenger for the sultanate. Aqtay's home has sat vacant for three years, no amir willing to occupy the place since the Amir of One Hundred met his fate by Muizziyya sword.

Cenk spits in the general direction of the house as he passes.

He rambles through a smaller souk, the bazaar now quiet, its cotton and hide-covered booths segregated by trade. Snores croak from beneath several of the empty vending stands and the flat-roofed shacks. He passes the long hall, where the cloth merchants meet each morning.

He reaches the old Pearl Palace, where the Fatimids once ruled. He recalls with a measure of distaste the stories of heretical behavior allowed during the previous dynasty's rule. During the Narwuz, the fall festival celebrating the height of the Nile's rise, the Fatimids permitted the commoners to engage in their old pagan rituals: citizens wore colorful masks in parades, men slapped each other with leather mats, folks walked the streets clad only in loin cloths, drunks killed one another, and hermaphrodites and whores clanged bells and raised their voices in the belvederes of the palace, so as to be heard by their Shia rulers.

Cenk shakes his head, thankful that the great one—Saladin, a fellow Sunni noted for his austerity—put an end to these practices.

Moving through Kafur's Garden, he draws his sword. Too many hedges and tall grasses. Places for a highwayman to lie up in ambuscade.

He heads northeast for the massive dual towers that bisect the northern skyline, the *Bab al-Nasr*, Arabic for "Gate of Victory." The rectangular columns catch the moon's rays, glowing in a dull almond against the evening sky, flanking each side of the semi-circular portal.

An arm rises from the rampart of the left turret, the man seeming to have picked out Cenk's stride, even in the dark. A pair of Mamluks on the ground swing open the northern gate. Cenk stomps beneath the giant arch, exiting the protection of Cairo's walls without altering his pace.

Once outside the gate, he raises an arm of farewell to his old troops, catching a shadowed glimpse of the two rotting forms hanging from the wall, the first of Aybeg's murderers caught and executed. Beside them, a stone engraving protrudes from the towers. A shield atop the diagonal sword, anchors each side of the arch. The engravings symbolize victory in protecting the city against invaders and malevolence.

Cenk nods. Evil. Conspirators. These have always threatened Mother Cairo. What al-Durr and her fellow connivers brewed was nothing unique. While the queen's ploy was discovered too late to save Aybeg, at least it was found in time to preserve the sultanate. He wonders what would become of the city and empire if there were not men like him to safeguard her? Stalwarts who step up and handle the dirty business of upholding rule.

He treks four miles north of town, his twisted knee eventually causing him to limp. He comes upon the half-crumbled stones of an abandoned house. He seats himself upon a block behind a short wall and amuses himself by recalling the interrogation two days past, gratified at how the location of his destination was realized.

Cenk looked the servant in the eye and then lied. "Your two other cohorts already disclosed that Ox, the Commander of the Guard, participated in the murder. Confirm their story and you will be spared. You have nothing to gain anymore. Only things to lose."

Fabian, the last of Aybeg's stranglers, turned away from Cenk, shivering on the huge block of wood where each of his limbs was secured by strap. Five plain-dressed Muizziyya had snatched him from his cousin's shack in Alexandria, a four-day's ride north from Cairo. With Fabian's hiding place found, the Mamluks bound the murderer to a mule, with neither bread nor water, and marched him to the Cairo citadel.

Cenk nodded to his guard. The axmen swung, his heavy blade landing with a thump, skillfully taking two fingers off Fabian's right hand at a diagonal.

Fabian howled.

"I guess we will not have to worry about you strangling the new sultan, al-Malik, like you strangled his father, Aybeg," Cenk said.

The servant wailed, thrashing on the wood, the chains about his ankles and wrists clanking against the stained timber.

Cenk strolled about the room, eyeing the brands and forks and rippers and blades neatly hung—implements designed to loosen the lips of those damned to the chop room.

"This will not get any more pleasant," Cenk said. "Cooperate."

Fabian calmed himself, his limbs shaking, his chains gone to a soft rattle.

His eyes followed Cenk, the amir coated in his summer uniform, spotless white.

"Where is the Ox?" Cenk asked.

"I do not know," Fabian said.

The axmen came forward. With a clunk of the blade, two fingers and a thumb dropped to the floor.

Fabian sobbed, looking at his ruined hand and the blood pooling upon the dark wood. "I heard Ox was holed up north of the city."

Cenk put a boot atop the chop block, resting his forearm upon his knee. "Where?"

Blood and spittle hung from Fabian's lip. "You will kill me regardless of what I say."

Cenk strolled the perimeter of the room, the breast rippers holding his attention.

Fabian eyed his severed fingers lying on the stones. "At that empty stone house a ways out of the north gate. The one with the crumbling arches near the dogu kolu *(east arm irrigation ditch)."*

Cenk turned to Qutuz, who sat on a stool with his elbows on spread legs. Qutuz lifted his chin. Cenk turned and strolled toward the door.

"Wait! Please!" Fabian said.

Cenk unlatched the door and bit down on the mint leaves in his mouth as Qutuz approached. Allowing his senior to depart first, Cenk looked back to Fabian. The man craned his neck to see him. Cenk slammed the door.

Strolling down the corridor in thought, he heard Fabian's muffled protests cut short by the thwack of steel on wood, like a butcher's cleaver on a block. Followed immediately by the thump of skull on stone.

Cenk rises from the stone block and elbows open the half missing door of the house. Finding rat shit, a soiled blanket, and an empty wineskin, he exits. He leans against the collapsed arch, disappearing into a shadow made by it, an adjacent wall, and an overgrown samwa bush.

He uses his heel like a rake to soften the pebbled soil about him. He picks out the biggest of the rocks and tosses them aside. He tests the ground for silence and then settles back into his corner.

He unbuttons his coat and gives his corked flask a shake. He tips the decanter to his lips, savoring the koumis. As a teenager on the steppe, he would sneak sips—later cups—of the intoxicating beverage from the leather bag hanging next to the ger flap, usually when his abusive father was away or too drunk to notice.

He lays his blade across his lap, ready to spring to foot. Let the Ox return to his hovel. Let the reunion between old troop and former instructor commence.

CHAPTER 15

Cenk

Cairo

May 14, 1257

Cenk leans against the deteriorated wall, gazing at the last standing section of a fallen arch and the stars above it. He breathes in the sharp fragrance of the samwa bush next to him. He associates the smell with his first patron, Amir Turkmani. This burly Mamluk used to carry a small pouch of the dried stems and leaves, doling it out to his troops like a caring mother to soothe stomachaches, fevers, and internal infections.

When Turkmani had access to the fresh leaves, he would rub the oil from the menthol-scented leaves upon his troops' snake bites, rashes, wasp stings, and scorpion bites. Especially when traveling in the Sinai, one could find Turkmani's hooch with his eyes closed, simply by following the smell of his samwa. Clumps of the plant were always found drying inside the apex of his small tent.

With sadness and longing, Cenk remembers the last time he saw Turkmani on the upper stretches of the Euphrates River, near Aleppo. Where have those twenty years gone? They laid his wounded amir across a samwa, the bush growing out of a tight crag between the sharp boulders. The incongruity. His master had died atop the plant that he had used for years to comfort his troops, those who were like sons to him. Cenk's mind wanders to that barren place.

> *With his back to the blowing sleet, Cenk sat within the protection of the jagged rocks. He shed his cloak and laid it upon his patron. He cradled Amir Turkmani in his trembling arms, Cenk's horse tugging the lead wrapped about his leg.*
>
> *Turkmani burped a mouthful of blood and swallowed it. "If only they could all be like you, my son."*
>
> *Cenk's patron spoke again, but this time his words were garbled. Cenk leaned closer, so as to hear over the beat of hooves and the shouting. But then he felt no breath on his neck. He lowered the head of his master to his knee and looked squarely at the ashen gray falling upon his patron's face.*
>
> *Amid the flying arrows, Cenk glanced skyward. "No. What have we done?" He looked down. His master's blood dribbled across the dark hair on his forearms, saturating his yellow trousers with puddles of wet scarlet. Cenk buried his head on Turkmani's shoulder and wept, the aroma from the dried samwa beneath him strong in his nostrils.*
>
> *Their unit's lack of awareness and inability to put arrowshot on the Khwarazmian enemy at the critical moment had caused Turkmani's death. While the shafts sunk into his master's body came not from Mamluk bows, they had still killed their patron. There, consecrated by his master's blood, Cenk made a promise. "Father, oh, my Father, I will make this right. I will cleanse the weak from our ranks."*
>
> *Though the life had left Turkmani's eyes, Cenk knew his master heard him, if not in this life's form, then in the one drifting above him.*

Cenk pulls a small yellow flower and leaf from the samwa bush and rolls the oil between his fingers. He breathes in the scent with eyes closed, picturing the bull-necked Turkmani. Those paternal eyes, almost out of place in his leathered face. Cenk gruffly wipes a tear from his cheek, takes another guzzle of fermented mare's milk, and stares bleakly ahead into the open desert.

How easily Cenk could have become a common slave, like most of the other dark-skinned stock gathered from the north. Turkmani saved him, purchasing the last boy on the slave block that day, decades ago. Surely his amir never could have imagined that Cenk, that lowly Bashkir lad, would become a trusted counselor at the top of the sultanate.

Cenk takes another swig, his eyes skyward. Drifting puffs of cloud periodically cover the moon, dark-centered and rimmed in iridescent white. He sighs. Surely Turkmani hovers there, maybe among those dusty-looking stars, with Mohammad and Allah—all three of them on fine Arabians—watching him at this very moment.

He pulls up the collar of his chain mail hauberk to block the cooling breeze. Eventually the pain in his legs forces him to walk in place and then sit on a half-crumbled block, his shoulder against the wall. He rubs his knees, trying to work the ache from them.

In time, his head bobs. As he snores, the dream that dogs him returns again, the dream that seems to intensify the harder he drinks.

> *Cenk looks across the table at Turkmani in their grubby-walled cell. "Before becoming a Furusiyya instructor, I promised you I would remove the weak from the ranks. I did this." Cenk clenches his fist. "But my Father, I no longer think weakness in our ranks is Cairo's biggest problem."*
>
> *Turkmani looks up briefly and then out the barred window. Blood drips from his thighs into pools forming about his*

feet. The arrow shafts, buried in his chest, rise and fall upon each breath.

Cenk exhales. "I feel Cairo, our army, is being girdled by evil—the darkness slowly strangling us." He leans forward. "And too many of us are unaware, or do nothing to stop it. Sometimes, I feel alone in my burden to rid the empire of wickedness, those who sow chaos, those who would do harm to our governorship."

"The Black Tartars?" Turkmani asks.

"Them, as they surely wish to snatch every dinar in Egypt's treasure. But everywhere. Evilness abounds—all threatening Mother Cairo, even Islam."

Turkmani looks up. "These problems are bigger than you. By Allah, let the young men fight our enemies. Maybe you should retire instead."

Cenk shakes his head. "Respectfully, my Amir. With things changing so quickly, those with the experience and gumption are critical. I know you would not retire right now."

Turkmani scowls. "Look at me. I am retired. Permanently." His eyes burn into Cenk's. "What of those you love and who still live—your family?"

Cenk winces, "I have come to terms that I may never retire. The empire needs me. I can already see in Qutuz's eyes that he will lean on me as Aybeg did, maybe harder. We all know Aybeg's young son will not be up to the job of becoming sultan."

Turkmani meets his eyes. "Just like empires, do not families also need guidance?"

Cenk looks down. "Of course. But Inci is nearly a woman. She is mostly Fidan's responsibility going forward. Do teenage girls listen to a father's direction anyway?"

Turkmani looks at him with sad eyes, itching absently at the arrow fletching that protrudes from his chest.

"I sometimes wonder if none of this has been my choice," Cenk says, "that it has all been the hand of Allah. He tasks those

who must step up during ominous times." He takes a sip from his wineskin.

"Do not pull Allah into this. You make this choice and I feel it is a bad one for you and your family. And this drinking. It will ruin you."

Cenk shrugs his shoulders. "But I like being drunk. I am forty-six. Who cares? The command does not."

"You do not think your wife and daughter care?"

He nods grudgingly. "I suppose."

The manic yip and cackle of a hyena in the distant papyrus awakens him. His eyes flash about. Fool. Falling asleep on his own watch. He struggles to his feet and peers around the wall. The wind has ceased and the moon hangs atop the western horizon, casting shadows long and ghostly.

He ducks back into his nook. He pulls the stopper from his spirits, takes a swallow, and rocks his head back against the stone wall.

It is getting very late. Perhaps the thick-skulled Ox is smarter than Cenk gives him credit for. Perhaps the brute sensed a trap and has found a new hooch. Maybe his last chance at the Ox is spoiled.

He stares into the night for a long while, the numbing of the koumis returning to him.

Sounds of distant scuffling come from the road to the north. Cenk reaches for his sword. He peeks around the arch. The lone figure on the road nears, his bull shoulders and slothful gait confirming the intended target. Cenk eases back into the corner.

Out of sight, Cenk slowly raises and lowers his shoulders to work the cold from his joints, turns his head left and right. He tries to shake off the last effects of the spirits. "Be sharp," he mumbles to himself.

As Ox's footsteps draw nearer, Cenk stills himself, his breath slow and steady, his pulse unaffected.

A few feet from the house, the man stops and waits. Cenk remains motionless, silently urging the goon to come forward, the coward. As if this insult was heard, the footsteps come slowly closer. Cenk closes his fist around his sword grip.

The grind of leather sole on tiny pebbles. One step. Two. The man very close now.

Judging the oaf to be one step past the wall, Cenk quietly treads heel-to-toe on the dirt he cleared earlier. He confirms his target, the man cloaked in the ragged tunic of a laborer. Cenk swings at the man's hamstrings with a backhand stroke.

Cenk feels his razor-sharp blade cut through the light robe and trousers and then the muscle. Sensing the hard strike of bone, he arrests the power in his stroke.

Ox yelps and crumbles to the ground. A clang upon the rocky soil as his weapon drops. "By Allah!"

Ox crabs forward on his elbows in an attempt to gain some space and then flops to his side to see who has surprised him. He squints, gawking into the faint moonlight.

"Who?"

"Who else?" Cenk says, moving fully into the moonlight. He steps on Ox's sword mid-blade and, grasping the grip, bends the steel severely. He chucks it over the wall.

Ox buries his turbaned forehead in his elbow. He attempts to rise, grunting. Unable, he settles again to his side.

Cenk steps closer. "Not hard to track your dumb ass—just follow the trail of coin, or where the lazy one sleeps."

"Just pull my root, you goat fucker," Ox says.

"Still as disrespectful as ever. Did you look forward to being a criminal on the run? Or did you somehow think you would live as a rich man in a different kingdom? A spy for the Crusaders, perhaps? The Armenians? Did you somehow think that we in Aybeg's Khushdash would not hunt you down, forever? Fool."

"You have the wrong man," Ox says.

"Uh huh." Cenk slowly circles the giant Mamluk. "How many Mamluks can brag they were responsible for slaying the leading amirs of both Mamluk regiments in Egypt—one a sultan and the other close to becoming one?"

"I only slew Aqtay—and he at Aybeg's order."

"Yes, yes. You were almost a good man then. The good soldier, following orders," Cenk says.

Ox fights to get to his knees, but topples in pain.

"Did you think the queen's servants would stay silent, that they would not squeal once we started detaching their limbs? You thought you would just walk away with the dirhams?" Cenk asks.

"I only received payment from the queen for my military service, nothing more. I just wanted to retire."

"Lies. Al-Durr is dead. All taking part in her scheme are dead. We know of your part in the assassination."

Ox looks up with a long face. He claws the dirt, pulling himself into the main road—a half-hearted attempt to escape or a useless try for some bystander to see him. He groans at the helplessness of his situation.

Cenk follows him for a few feet then stomps on Ox's severed hamstring.

Ox hollers and then shucks his disturbed turban, revealing sweaty hair matted to his massive head, a patch of baldness near his crown. "Let me live and the silver is yours. I will crawl away from here and not say a word of it."

"Yes, the silver. How generous of you to offer. Unselfishness was always one of your finest traits."

He stoops beside Ox, whispering. "Killing Aybeg is how you repaid him for all he had done for you? We promoted you to Amir of Forty, gave you command of my old guard, doubled your salary. You got the fief you wanted. Hell, Aybeg still let you plow his own concubines. But the greedy Ox still chose to murder our patron, despite his sultan's generosity."

"I killed no one," Ox says.

"I know. You are innocent. Did you know the bitch Queen had been in contact with al-Nasir of Damascus? She connived to put that coward atop Egypt. Al-Nasir—this is who you wanted leading Mother Cairo, rather than one of our own?!"

"I knew nothing of that," Ox says, locking his hands beneath his hamstrings, a hapless effort to apply pressure against the deep slashes. Ox appears as an immense infant, cradling himself as a growing circle of blood darkens the dirt about him.

"You knew nothing. You know nothing," Cenk says.

Ox looks in all directions, likely searching for something, anything, that could serve as a weapon or shield to protect himself. But he finds nothing.

Cenk walks over and kicks Ox's locked hands.

Crouched into a pitiful ball, the Ox cringes. "Finish me and be done with it."

Cenk kicks him twice in the forearms. "Almost fitting that the one who erred in allowing your birth in the regiment will be the same one who takes you out of it. The one who created you will destroy you."

"Figures you would hide in the shadows, rather than face me like a man," Ox hisses through clenched teeth. "You and Aybeg the same. Loud-mouthed, scroll-shuffling pussies. The devil's own."

Cenk smiles. "The devil, yes. You two will soon make good friends."

Ox tips to his back, the puddle about his solid thighs enlarging. He no longer has the strength to hold his wounds, or has decided to let himself bleed out. His bull-like chest slowly rises and falls.

Cenk raises his blade and brings it down across the ogre's neck. "To hell with you," he slurs.

Turning his back to the Ox, Cenk looks to the stars. "I am sorry for letting you down, my Turkmani. If I had just been more forceful at the tibaq twenty years past. If I had just been bolder as a young man, I could have faced down Aqtay and had this scoundrel ousted from the training ranks in Hisn Kayfa, never given him the chance to poison our corps, or kill Aybeg, another of your sons."

Cenk wipes his blade across Ox's tunic and returns his sword to its scabbard. He turns for the citadel.

CHAPTER 16

Esel

Damascus

June 2, 1257

Esel exits a side street bazaar with a basket in hand, heavy with root vegetables and a wedge of Saj. Above the niqab covering her face, her eyes stay locked forward in faux submission, ignoring those who pass in the opposite direction. Nearing the same stalled donkey that she has observed for weeks, she slows. Her eyes flit to the right, taking in the beast. He still looks healthy—no sores about the face or mouth, a flat back, and a healthy amount of fat. His legs and hooves remain in a respectable condition. She continues on.

She ambles toward home, the sun slipping behind the highest of the flat-roofed buildings. The vendors begin to stow their wares—women folding blankets, turbaned men placing wooden covers atop their spice bins, old peddlers loading trinkets upon their carts. She is oblivious to it all. Her thoughts turn, her furrowed brow concealed by her headscarf.

The muezzin's call to evening prayer, the Maghrib, intrudes on her thoughts, the pleading chant reverberating over the flagged streets. She hums a Kipchak tune overtop his vocals, drowning out his ghostly voice with the sounds of her own homeland. She pictures what remains in her memory of her grandmother, the wrinkled woman pounding wool into felt, darning garments, and butchering animals to the same song.

Reaching the clay-packed trail leading to her shack, she enters the cramped quarters. A straw-filled bed butts up to a straw-laden wall. A swept floor and a fireplace free of ashes. Two chairs flank her table; crooked shelves hold her few clothes, neatly folded.

She sets her veil on the same peg near the door and lies on her bed, staring at the thatched-reed ceiling. When darkness comes, she rises and peers out the door. Some laughter from the men down the street at their gaming tables. The smell of cooking fires hangs in the air.

She closes the door and stuffs her clothing into a leather bag, clearing the shelves. Reaching under the bed, she removes the linen pouches of dried meat and fruits, bits taken slyly from her master's house over the past weeks and sun-dried behind her hut. She stands on the bed and eases her dagger from between two bundles of thatching on the ceiling. She places her food and the waterskin atop the load. She cinches the bag and leans it against the wall, beside the door. She sits on the edge of the bed, waiting.

A knock on the flimsy planks.

A tingle radiates to Esel's fingertips.

"May I come in, Esel?" The child Saja whispers through the slots.

"Come."

The latch lifts with a soft clunk and the door inches open. "I just came to say good night," the little one says. She looks about the room. "What are you doing?"

Esel looks away from her bag, hidden from the young girl's vision by the inward swing of the door. She smiles at the child. "What am I doing? What are you doing still awake?"

"I could not sleep."

Esel smiles. "I see this."

"Why are you still awake?" Saja asks.

"Oh, I am just tidying things up here, but soon to bed."

Saja looks about the room. "Will you always live with us?"

Esel feels a flush across her brow. She wonders if the girl has noticed her clothes missing from the shelves, or perhaps sensed Esel acting differently the past few days.

"Well, nobody lives forever. But even when I am gone, I will take my thoughts of you to heaven with me in my heart. This I know. So in that way, I will always live with you. Always."

Saja smiles. "Good. I will do the same."

They talk of the girl's schoolwork and the coming birthday celebration for Saja's friend. The child rubs her eyes, yawns.

"My little plum, it looks to me as if bed is calling again. If your mother were to check on you now, you can imagine her worry."

"All right. Good night."

"Good night, my princess."

A hollowness fills Esel the moment the child closes the door. Her thoughts drift from Saja as a baby to her first spoken words. They linger on Esel's memory of the girl's first day at school. All of these maternal treasures—and more—enjoyed not by the child's mother, but by the child's nanny slave.

When darkness has set in, she peeks outside. Quiet. She hefts the bag across her back, closes the door behind her, and silently lowers the latch. She walks to the donkey stall at the edge of town, taking the back route she had walked a dozen times prior, slipping into the alley shadows when she sees another approach, or hears any footsteps.

Reaching the stable, she approaches the animal slowly. Eventually, she pets the donkey's neck and speaks to it softly.

When he calms, she looks both ways and enters the enclosure. She pulls tack from the wall, silencing the bit in her grasp. She slides the metal into his mouth and works the crown and browband into place. She leads him out, her eyes wide and scanning for movement on the street. She walks him southward, avoiding the watchmen and passing no one.

Near the western wall, she rubs the donkey's withers, then mounts him barebacked, her leather bag still across her shoulders, but resting atop the donkey's rump. Her eyes water at the thought of her leaving the child behind. A lump forms in her stomach.

She fights the desire to turn around, put the animal back into its stall, and run back to her shack. She continues west along the back streets as far as possible, eventually entering Straight Street, the old Roman road, the main artery running east to west through the city.

She rides through the western side of the *Midhat Pasha Souq*, its stalls covered in blankets and flaps of dried camel-skin tent. The high pillars of the *Bāb al-Jābiyya*, the Roman Jupiter Gate, loom ahead in the blackness. She heads for the giant doors between the pillars, the central carriageway used for carts and riders.

She reaches the gate. Seeing no one atop the rampart, her head begins to spin. Will the Kipchak pair she met during her master's dinner with the prince be there? Could the soldiers have changed their minds? Had she read the men wrongly—surely they would not take an old woman's coin and then deny her exit as they agreed? Has their schedule changed, putting strangers instead at this portal tonight?

She imagines her groggy master answering his door to see Esel in the soldiers' clutch. Her breathing becomes labored. She squeezes the worn leather reins.

A thump of boot steps echo in the stairwell. But the huge doors do not budge. Her heart flutters. She begins to think the worst. She catches the outline of a helmeted man atop the northern tower. She must dismount and run.

A smaller side door, flanking the bigger one, cracks open noiselessly, just wide enough for her and the donkey to pass. She ducks under the beamed overhang and the beast claps through the cobbled way. The pedestrian door closes behind her. The locking bar finds its seat with a thud.

She closes her eyes and heaves a sigh. Her pulse gradually settles. She looks up to the Great Sky and quietly recites a prayer of thanksgiving.

She takes the path south into the open country. She looks behind. No one follows.

She digs out her belt and dagger and secures the weapon to her side. A rising three-quarter moon emblazons the southern spur of the Anti-Lebanon Mountains in buttery light. To her northwest, the snowy peaks near Mount Hermon bask in the glow.

She spots two riders atop a rise ahead. She leaves the road and circles around them to avoid an encounter.

The moon ascends behind her shoulder, shedding its radiance upon the crisscrossing stripes of apricot and cherry orchards. A red fox bounces between rows. He halts to look over his back at her before vaulting into his wooded sanctuary.

The scent of apricots predominates, the first fruit of the harvest having already dropped to the ground. Gathered apricots lie in open spaces, some spread on large straw mats for the start of the drying process, others sit hand-pressed into round disks, waiting for the sun to bake them fully into a ruby red.

She leans over. "I knew you were a good donkey. I hope you are a lucky one, too. Do not you worry, I will treat you well. Will one day have you returned to your stall."

She passes fields of grain and cotton and rolling country shrouded with olive trees. On the moon-shadowed landscape ahead, she spies the foothills rising to meet the Anti-Lebanon Range to the west, the hummocks she yearned to explore since her first days in Syria.

Her donkey trundles along.

Once away from the seven branches of the Barada River and its web of irrigation ditches, the terrain transitions to scrub-covered hills and dry grassland. Juniper and cedar pock the hillsides. She rides through patches of iris and poppy and saltwort, some of it chopped ankle-high by the roving herds of goats and sheep.

Her confidence grows a mite with each mile she puts between her and *al-Ghu⍰ah*, the "oasis" of Damascus proper, and finally, she enters the wild terrain. Open country, its vastness unobstructed by man-made constructions, its scent free of urine and filth and man-planted crops.

A jackal yaps its high-pitched yowl to locate its mates. She looks up to the dull flecks of light, softened by the gleaming moon. She finds the arc of stars encompassing the summer huntsman's bow. She orients herself to its sweeping recurve, and satisfied, she inhales a great breath of dry desert air.

As a young woman, she had her own hunter on the Kipchak steppe. Perhaps the most talented one she ever knew. She addresses the flickering configuration in the sky. "Hello, Yagmur, my husband. Oh, how I still miss you. As much today as when you were taken from me."

Tears fill her eyes. "I am a little scared down here tonight."

She pulls back on the reins and waits for a few moments. Hearing nothing, she releases and gives the donkey some heel. She looks heavenward. "If the slave catchers nab me, it will mean death. But since our parting, have I really had life? I could not stand the thought of finishing my final years among these people and in that place. Being there has already eaten too much of my soul." She nods. "Like you, I will not let them take me alive now."

She sits erect on the animal's back, still at home there, after all these years. Breaching a prominence, she again halts below the crown. She takes in the country ahead. Juts of dark rock in the distance cast shadows on the high-shouldered scrubland. Seeing no movement, she pats the donkey and continues.

She looks skyward. "I am sure you wondered why I stayed so long in the dreaded city, why I did not try to run off earlier."

The donkey goes to the canter on his own. She reins him in, pulls his head nearly to her heel and calmly walks him into a tight circle. She leans down. "Cannot do that. We must stay at the walk," she says, rubbing his shoulder. We may have a ways to go."

Her eyes elevate. "Life in Damascus. You probably saw that my conditions there were better than those of our other enslaved Kipchaks. Of course, you would have hated it. I should have bolted earlier, but once Gamal's child was born . . . the girl kept me there. I stayed for her."

A single tear rolls down her cheek as she thinks of the young Saja. What will the pleasant child think when she awakens to no nene? She wipes her face, knowing the girl will be fine. Saja still has a mother—and soon another slave will be bought to tend her.

She approaches a tighter section of path where the hills converge. If she were setting up to waylay a traveler, this would be a spot she would pick. She unsheathes her dagger and holds it blade-back in her fist. She enters the defile, looking about the dark forms of prickly bushes, any of which could hold bandits.

"Would they kill an old woman to claim her blade and few pieces of dried meat and fruit?" She shrugs her shoulders. "Just the quicker I would be back with you, my husband."

She rides in silence for a while, the short-grassed path eventually widening again to the open expanse of the barren pan below.

She sheathes her weapon. "So you know why I stayed." She grins. "I doubt I need to tell you why I left."

The donkey snorts.

"I know, I know, you would say the tragedy at the Isthmus was not just my fault. Plenty of us had an inkling that things were awry. An ambush was coming." She tastes the salt from a single braid of tears.

"But I knew something was wrong from the start. Should have said something to our khan. Insisted we go back. But I did not. And because of this, you are dead, my love. And all of our warriors, too. And the women and young in our tower—all enslaved. This wound does not heal."

She sits up in the saddle. "So tonight I start anew in honor of you and our people. I am keen to make it right now, for at least one in our tower, who stays strong. Baybars. I will find him."

A chill fills the air. She pulls her shawl from the bag. Her eyes are drawn to the horizon ahead. Two dozen specks dot a hillside. A dark blotch among them. An old tree trunk amid stump heads? Or perhaps a man leaning against a rock? As she nears, the dark forms morph into a herd of black goats. The tree trunk transforms into a shepherd. He waves to her. She returns the greeting.

When out of earshot, she again eyes the constellation. "I was unable to provide you with child, my love. But our nephew, Baybars," a smile comes to her face. "He was mostly ours, eh? My younger sister, Pembe, had her hands full with her younger ones. Baybars would have gladly shared our ger."

She sets her face firmly. "And he is in trouble now." She shakes her head. "But why do I keep speaking as if you do not know? You see all from above."

She looks over her shoulder to the "Ladle," the form of stars low in the sky. She follows them up to the North Star, confirming her southern direction.

"Is what I do any different than tending our herds, Yagmur? Me, no more than a shepherd in this case. How often does a wolf enter a herder's ger and disclose the predators' schemes? Surely my hearing of al-Nasir's evil words was fate. It would be sinful to take no action against this wolf. What kind of shepherd would knowingly let the marauders harm the dearest, most valuable one in her flock?"

The breeze picks up, driving broken clouds across the face of the moon, roiling the short grass into a sea of shifting purples and blues. Thicker clouds pass over. Black splotches traverse the valley and stone faces, and blots of distant shrubs come into view upon the flats. She pulls the shawl higher around her neck.

"I am sure you worry. What if I do not find Baybars before the slave catchers find me?" She chuckles darkly. "Worry little. I doubt my keepers capable of detecting my true aim. They know nothing of my past. How much effort will they put into catching an old woman, one of declining worth? Just another hag, tired of the heavy work."

Before a broader haze shrouds the archer in the sky, she reaches toward the sparkles and calls into a gust, knowing this may be her last view of the archer this evening. "And Yagmur, am I not the right one for the task—childless, few good years left, a growing desire to be with my husband in the Great Sky?"

The donkey stomps onward.

In time, the moon parts the clouds, unveiling the landscape in a bluish-white light, looking as if she were home on the steppe. Their broad valley to the north, covered in a dusting of snow. She shivers, then grins, the scene taking her back to a time when Baybars was just a boy, before their enslavement.

Her lips purse. She feels emboldened. She does the right thing. She would not even be alive if not for her nephew's action on that snowy day. All those years ago.

CHAPTER 17

Esel

Steppe, northeast of the Black Sea

December 9, 1236

The wind whistled across the ger's vent flap, grabbing the lazy smoke as it exited, blasting it into oblivion across the steppe. Esel rose from her bed, rubbing her shoulders with crossed arms. She shuffled to the fire, grabbed two pieces of dung from her pile, and leaned them on edge in the half-starved flame.

The spine of her shelter moaned under the force of a squall, yet the blaze at her feet hardly flickered. Four layers of felt cocooned their ger, its bottom edges covered in snow and frozen soil, nearly melding it to the earth. She closed her eyes, thankful for the wool, hoping that no Kipchak was stuck outside this evening. Looking at the bundle of fleece on her bed, disheveled from her sleepless fussing, she speculated on the condition of the tower's herd. Their goats and sheep, their few cows, exposed to the storm's ferocity.

"If this keeps up, we could lose them all," Yagmur said, hunched over a candle, his eyes fixed on the thick bone needle he worked through the punched holes on a friend's worn dagger sheath. He seemed to read her mind.

"Hopefully they did not scatter too far," she said. She laid down and pulled the cover up to her chin. She dozed off.

A strange silence awakened her. Long shadows from their fire fluttered across the felt. The blizzard had lost its passion. She looked through the smoke at Yagmur, who set aside his work.

He cracked a smile. "Finally, you were able to get a little sleep."

"Yes, but you?"

"Ehh."

"Has it finally ended?"

"Maybe so."

They rose and unlashed the flap. She closed her tunic against the bitter cold that rushed into the refuge, over a waist-high drift.

A yellow-gray light shrouded the landscape. The air was still, yet a brisk wind lingered far above the ground, pushing stubborn clouds, stacked high and translucent. Replacing them were wispy cirrus, unveiling a waning moon above the western hills, just a sliver short of full.

The gray radiance switched to ice blue. Blown snow formed tapered additions to the backs of gers and etched river valleys of white upon the grassland.

The tower stirred. Men burst from ger flaps like oversized birds, kicking their way out of their snow-formed shells. Others toddled in fleece and fur, bows slung across their shoulders. Up on the hills, children swathed in sheepskins used pronged sticks to pry up freeze-dried dung in areas blown clean by the gales. Strapped on their backs were woven baskets, the creels on some hanging down to the gatherers' calves. From a distance, they appeared as pious turtles, alternately bowing to the ice-covered tundra for salvation.

Hunters saddled their ponies, the grumble in their bellies and cry from their babies likely providing the only motivation needed for an early start to the day. Herdsmen departed on foot for a race against the wolves to locate their animals, both the still-wandering stock and those unfortunate beasts already frozen.

In turn, the hunters circled the saman, the holy man sitting cross-legged, thinly clothed in wool and deerskin, his bare head topped with a band of equal-sized hawk feathers. He swayed, in one hand holding the rack of a giant buck at its mushroom-shaped base, the other gently beating the stretched goatskin of his davul drum with an exposed thumb and forefinger. Unmindful of the cold, he focused on his communication. Through the contented soul of the big deer, the Saman chanted an appeal to the steppe's living animals to surrender themselves for the tower.

Finishing their second circle around the gray-haired holy man, the men spun off in opposite directions for adjacent hunting grounds, the hooves of their ponies squeaking in the snow. Above them, parallel trails of forked breath from beast and rider caught the moon's rays, mixing into one thinning mass of rising vapor.

"Anything with legs and fur will be looking for a meal," Yagmur said. "The entire steppe has been bedded down too long." He pulled the flap closed.

Esel agreed, backing away from the opening with a shudder. She pulled on her rabbit-lined tunic and boots. She threw a sheepskin shawl about her shoulders. She donned her pouch, snatched her strung bow, and ducked through the flap into the evening glow.

The air bit and froze in her nostrils. Stars spattered the blackness, dulled by the moonlight. She made out the sweeping arc of the hunter's longbow in the formation of stars and exhaled a frosty plume. As she did, a deep-voiced wolf cracked its menacing howl over the adjacent ridge, signaling to his pack that a hunting party gathered.

She sighed. They too will take advantage of the moonlight. The wind would have kept them burrowed under the snow for two days. They would emerge ravenous from their encrusted caverns. Down in the valley, two wolves answered in unison with long cries barely audible, the male's deep call likely rousting the responders from their snow-covered slumber.

While the roving Mongols had not found the tower's winter encampment, two packs of wolves had. These lurked about its periphery for nearly three moons. As game grew scarce, the wolves grew bolder, willing to risk the lethality of the tower's bows to prey upon the livestock. Fourteen sheep and three goats were killed this moon alone, despite the increased diligence of the shepherds in posting night guards and stuffing animals into the few small pens that the sparse woodland allowed them to build.

She knelt and prayed to the Respectable Woman, so far away. She asked for peace and ample food for her people, and an arrow to find its way into the heart of their herd's canine plunderers.

She walked to her sister's ger, passing a rider with his hooded sparrow hawk on his arm. She knocked twice on the wooden frame. She jumped, as Baybars pulled the felt section open. He stood ready with bow and quiver, a bone call hanging from his neck, mutton tallow spread evenly across his cheeks, nose, and lips.

"You sleep with your back against the entrance flap?" she asked.

Her sister, Pembe, came forward with tired eyes, her young daughter on the teat. "Your nephew has been pacing a like an expectant father, longing for your invitation."

Baybars steered the little brother at his leg back to his mother. He looked up to Esel. "I just heard the big male howl from the northwest and a reply from two others straight east," the eight-year-old said, stepping into the cold.

She grinned. "Yes, the wolves will have a big feed on their minds."

"The brothers have already left for the carcass site," he said. "They figured you would know."

She reckoned the other two hunters would have been eager to take advantage of the dying wind. "All right."

Last moon, the saman bestowed the title and obligation of "wolf taker" upon two more hunters. Brothers. Both men were quiet ones, serious hunters who kept to themselves. Over the last few weeks, while the brothers watched her hands bond horn to birch, they made plans to kill wolves. A war declared upon the canines who ate the meat and milk that her people needed to live, the wool that kept her tower robed. The three intertwined generations of wisdom into strategies that were put to use in every corner of the wolves' vast hunting grounds.

One approach served as their base tactic. They regularly placed animal carcasses low among the rolling hills, at a site which gave the wolves only lightly-covered ingress and egress from every direction, yet provided the hunters an elevated view of the ambush site in adequate cover.

Although the predators sensed the location was trouble, nonetheless, the wolves were eventually drawn in by the convenience of an easy meal, especially on cold winter nights, when more meat was needed to fuel their internal fires. Occasionally the conditions gelled—the wind and light conditions providing opportunity for arrows to fly.

"Let us push away from camp and work another angle," she said, pulling a length of coiled hemp from her pouch.

Baybars nodded in agreement, eyebrows raised. He slipped back into his mother's shelter, returning with a riding blanket over his shoulder and a different quiver, full of heavier, broad-headed arrows.

They went to the pony herd, beasts with their asses still pointed in the direction of the dying wind. She patted her mare's curly hair. "You will be happy to get moving, eh?"

They shook the snow from their ponies' woolen covers and replaced them with their riding blankets and saddles. At a pen, Baybars elbowed a ewe aside and snatched a lamb. He roped the lamb's legs and gagged the bawling animal. Wrestling it to the rear of his pony, he cinched a loop of hemp and secured the lamb to the frame of his saddle.

They rode away from the tower toward a valley abundant with wolf sign three days past. Esel raised her arm twice to notify the bundled watchman of friendly passers in the area. They crunched their way over the windswept grassland, the moon firing occasional glitter on the undulating terrain. On either side of them, spruce trees doubled over with snowy loads. A creek twisted through the darkness, its rough course outlined by pockets of moonlight cast upon icy-banked riffles. They passed lofty taiga pine on the sides of mountains, the pines' sturdy needles grasping clumps of suspended snow.

Her pony stumbled. She lifted up on the beast's head to keep him from falling as they punched through a three-foot drift.

They hobbled their animals midway up a hillside, concealing the mounts on the reverse slope. Baybars untied and shouldered the lamb. They continued on foot, stepping lightly across the hardpack. She crossed wolf tracks and two piles of curled dung. She leaned down to inspect.

The older pile was frozen hard, black, and well-laden with deer hair. Around this pile were nail marks, scratching an angry border around the excrement. Adjacent was a second mound, pointed on both ends and much bigger in diameter, tufts of wool packed and twirled. Steam rose from it, the moon adding shimmer to its slimy glaze.

"Just happened. The big sheep eater warns the others to stay away," Esel whispered, pointing to the older pile. "We want him."

Baybars nodded.

"Slow and quiet. Just up and over." Knowing the terrain over the opposite hill to be steep, she secured an anchor knot about her waist with one hand. She handed Baybars the running end.

He rolled the lamb off his back and pinned it with a knee. With his shorter rope, he tied an overhand loop in one end and quickly pulled his tail end through, tightening the slip high above the hock on the lamb's rear leg. He again shouldered the animal.

Prepared, they slunk over the ridge, hugging a rock outcropping on the edge of the broken-timbered valley. They zigzagged down the slope, clenching jagged stone ledges with their uphill hands to keep from slipping.

Esel halted with her back against a large pine to take in the wind and put eyes on the land. She pointed at a large rock three quarters of the way down the slope. Baybars nodded his understanding that this was where they would set their trap, stroking the lamb to calm it.

She took a step. Then nothing. She felt the sensation of falling, yet was unable to comprehend how. She had trod the ground many times before.

She plunged down the hill headfirst, somehow tossed to her back, her face plowing through the powder.

The timber. Turn yourself. Turn. Quickly. She twisted while tumbling, struggling to get her feet downhill. A crash of branches. A stab to her side. A scrape across her face like the claws from a big cat.

Then a cinch of pain as the rope caught her just under the ribcage. She stopped, her breath knocked from her. In time, she opened her eyes. A thick cluster of trees only feet below her.

"You all right?!" Baybars called from above.

She knelt on the sharp face, leaned over and fanned her coat collar to remove some of the packed snow. "Yes." She placed her hands on her knees to recover, eventually looking up at him.

"Set your feet and lean forward to lessen the tension and I will pull you up," he said.

She rubbed her mitten across her brow. A dark patch of blood streaked the leather. She removed the mitten and clawed the packed snow from her ears. She then stood, testing her feet on the tilted ground, looking down at the sharp rocks at the bottom.

Regaining her confidence, she huffed and took three steps up, the ache of new-found bruises on her hip and shoulder now noticeable. She waited for the rope to grow taut.

She fought her way uphill, step by step through the knee-deep snow, Baybars practically pulling her up the final vertical stretch. Reaching the top, she tipped to her butt, exhausted. She looked up at him.

The lamb still rested across his neck, the length of rope opposite its leg buried in the snow. The separate running end from her rope was still wrapped about Baybars' waist and an adjacent tree, the trunk having acted as a makeshift pulley to carry her weight uphill.

"I do not believe I did that," she said, panting.

"The ledge was covered, widened by drift. You could not have known. I am just glad you are not injured badly," he said.

She traced her tracks to the final step before skidding down. "If I had been alone, my head would have been smashed on the bigger trees, or those rocks farther down. You saved me."

"I just happened to have the other end of your rope," he said almost nonchalantly. "But you cheated the wolves."

She gaped at him.

"Instead of a tiny lamb to be used as bait, they almost had a real meal," he said with a straight face. "How they would have enjoyed eating the Kipchak bowyer whose weapons have been skewering them for years." He grinned.

They both laughed, Esel holding her bruised ribs to lessen the smarting.

PART 2

DARK TIDE RISING

"An arrow from a warrior, shot at an unbeliever, counts more than the endless prayers said by a pious hermit."

—a Fourteenth-Century Mamluk war manual

CHAPTER 18

Jacinta
Cairo Citadel
June 3, 1257

Jacinta walks the long passage to the vicegerent's office. She halts, takes a deep breath, and knocks three times on the thick-planked door.

"Enter."

She pushes open the door to see Qutuz, Cenk, and Tarkhan turn toward her. She stands in the doorway, waiting to be summoned.

"Sit, sit," Qutuz says, motioning her in.

She takes a seat at the last available chair, facing Qutuz.

"We have another task for you."

A dread fills her. She can tell by his look that he will send her away again. She looks Qutuz in the eye.

"Al-Nasir." He scowls. "I need your ears and eyes in the souk of Damascus. With Aybeg's death and the queen's removal, the prince there—and the governors throughout the realm—will be smelling opportunity, weakness in us. No different than after Sultan Turanshah's death. Al-Nasir may have his sights on Cairo. We will need to know where loyalties and threats lie, to provide early warning of an attack."

Her shoulders slump.

"The Bahri will be pressing al-Nasir to strike. We need to get someone close to Baybars—to notify us of his intentions and the Bahri's doings."

"And you think a woman with child-in-hand is that person?" she asks.

"Yes," Qutuz says.

"After Hama, you told me I would not have to leave Cairo. That I would only be used on occasion for 'little things.' This does not sound like a little thing."

Cenk leans forward across the table. "Needs of the corps." He glowers, scooches his stool closer. "Nothing has changed. Surely you understand the threat to Mother Egypt? Surely you remain a faithful subject?"

She knows the direction this conversation will go. Qutuz is the same as Aybeg. Assignments from them are not debatable.

"I will do what is needed of me," she says, addressing Qutuz, ignoring Cenk. "But why me? If any of your spies is compromised among Baybars' force—it is me. I know you have not forgotten my role in your botched attempt at killing the translator, Leander. He surely told his command of my participation in this. If the Bahri saw me in Damascus now, they would kill me straight away."

Cenk scoffs. "If the Bahri knew you were involved, you would have been dead long ago, like some of your fellow moles. Leander must have said nothing of your suspected involvement. A real bright one, protecting the tramp who took part in trying to murder him."

She disregards Cenk's jab. "I care for a child now. I am a mother. With all of those at your disposal, why would you task one who already failed in a similar assignment with the Bahri?"

Qutuz smiles. "Always the same from you. You did not fool Aybeg, you do not fool me. You are as talented as any at this game. It was those Bedu knifemen who blundered in Cairo that night with Leander—not you."

She recalls the night.

> *The servant came to their table with her hands folded politely across her abdomen.*
>
> *"Bring us the fattah. Enough for two," Leander said.*
>
> *She bowed and turned back to the kitchen.*
>
> *A queasiness took hold in Jacinta's stomach. She looked about the other tables, people pretending not to watch them. Qutuz's plants, acting as if all was normal.*
>
> *A wave of guilt and shame passed through her. No. She will not let them go through with the capture. She must do something, anything, yet not alert Aybeg's diners, collaborators paid by the sultan. The hired servers. They, too, would be watching her every move, would report back to Qutuz and Aybeg. Think. Think. She kicked Leander under the table, hoping he understood the silent warning.*
>
> *She pushed back her chair with no expression. He looked at her quizzically, seemingly unsure if she kicked the table leg while moving to stand.*
>
> *"I should not have drunk so much from that spring. Will you excuse me for a moment?" she asked, looking at him gravely.*
>
> *She rose and headed for the door, her mind whirling. Unsure of what to do next, she closed the door behind her. She walked to the alley and sat against the wall, fretting. She prayed to Allah for forgiveness and for her conspiracy in this business. She hoped Leander was on to this scheme, or was at least less distracted with her away and more likely to defend himself.*
>
> *A smash.*
>
> *The window shutters? Frantic voices from the hired Bedu, those posing as servers. A slam of the door against the building.*

She peered around the corner.

The Bedu gave chase. A flash of red and Leander's boot heels disappeared into the dark. She eased farther into the alley and sank to her knees, crying.

"But I have a child now," she says.

Cenk leans back in his chair. "Yes, how self-sacrificing you became while away these years—taking in a Bahri's urchin." He sits forward and glares at her.

Qutuz looks sideways at Cenk and then meets her eyes. "More reason to send you. A peddler wench toting a mixed-breed brat will not be surmised to be a spy. I am not asking you to infiltrate Baybars' desert camp and slit his throat. Just snoop around Damascus and learn what he is up to. And al-Nasir, too—your specialty."

Jacinta looks down. "I still suspect they will know who I am." She regrets saying these words as soon as they are out of her mouth.

"At least one does," Cenk says. "Your old love, the Franj. Leander."

"You are still on that?" She asks. "He was my best informant, nothing more."

"Well, given the timing of your work with him and the closeness of it, your son could have been his, right?" Cenk asks.

She scowls at him. Qutuz's face brightens.

Cenk laughs. He turns to Qutuz. "Ha, I told you back then he was rooting her."

Both men guffaw. The Mongol advisor, Tarkhan, glances at Cenk and then watches her with serious eyes.

"Does it matter?" She asks. "You asked me to gain the Frank's trust and find out if he was dangerous to Sultan Aybeg. I was permitted to determine how I went about it."

Qutuz nods, his brows scrunching together. "True. But Cenk is right. The Franj, Leander. He could be your excuse for going to Damascus. If exposed, you explain that you are done with the spying game and have come to bring the Frank his child."

Qutuz leans back. "And I agree with Cenk. I doubt the other Bahri know you were a mole. If Leander suspected you, he obviously told no one of it. Leander remains Baybars' best translator. If you could get close again to Leander then we can learn what Baybars is thinking, planning."

"Oh, a very clever plan," Jacinta says. "Except what happens if Leander receives me? Will I then marry a former Crusader?" She crosses her legs. "Plus, while the mother of the child was an Egyptian, the true father of the child was Mert, a Kipchak, not a Frank. Zane is not even two years old. It would have been hard for the Frank and me to have made a baby while a ten-day's ride apart."

Qutuz frowns.

She meets his eyes. "I was nowhere near Leander when Zane was conceived. The Frank is not stupid."

Cenk shrugs his shoulders. "Details. Do not both Franks and Kipchaks have light skin? And plenty of Mamluks are not very good at math."

She rolls her eyes. "The Frank is educated. He is no fool. Zane bears no resemblance to him. Leander would know immediately that the child was not his."

Jacinta sits straight-faced, staring at the red-lioned pennant on the wall, Aybeg's Muizziyya retaining al-Salih's colors as a tribute to their old patron. She misses al-Salih and the simpler times when her assignments were merely to communicate to the grandfatherly sultan who were the most dutiful of his Mamluks. Only when Aybeg took the throne did the distrust and backstabbing and assassinations begin.

"Listen," she says, "Leander would know the child is too young to be his. And if not, at some point the Frank would learn the truth of Zane's real parents—that the child is an orphan."

Qutuz scoffs. "I care little for this chatter about inherited traits and speculation on baby ages. Leander would have to get to Cairo or Hama to learn the truth. We do not intend to let Baybars and his Bahri back into Egypt. Plus, the Crusader has already outlived most Mamluks. Chances are Leander will not survive long enough to figure out that the child is not his." He shrugs. "We just need him to live long enough for you to wheedle from him what we need to know."

She shakes her head, looks down. Cenk chuckles.

"Another small complication," she says. "The Frank knows I took part in that assassination attempt. He will spurn both me and child, even if he is duped into believing Zane is his."

The room goes silent.

"Take it from me. Offspring have a way of making couples mend fences," Cenk says, his face softening.

For a moment she is touched by his comment, as all in the room are aware of how the birth of Cenk's daughter salvaged the relationship with his wife.

She looks straight at Qutuz. "This assignment is a death sentence. If you wish me and my child dead, then just kill us now. Save us the scorching trip across the Sinai, where on the other side I can look forward to little more than being found out and killed by the Bahri."

Qutuz leans over the table. "You think I would send one of my most valuable into harm's way, on a job I did not think she could handle?"

"Yes, I do," she says.

"You are clever." Qutuz sits back. "You will find a way back into the Crusader's trust. You have done more difficult things before."

She squeezes her temples. She wishes she had never started working for al-Salih those eight years back, wishes she'd never met Aybeg or these others.

Cenk looks to Tarkhan. "Are not concubines being moved soon—a caravan departing for the Trunk Road?" Cenk asks.

Tarkhan nods. "But not for another forty days."

Qutuz stares at Jacinta's shoulders and small, firm breasts. He meets her dark-brown eyes above her veil. She looks away.

"Yes, she is smart and pretty enough to be mistaken for a woman of the harem," Qutuz says. He teases his beard. "This will be your last mission. I promise."

They sit.

"Is that all?" she asks.

"You may go," Qutuz says.

"No parting threat of death to me or my family this time, if I should attempt to flee or later refuse the work?"

"Please. Are we not past those kind of warnings by now?" Cenk asks.

CHAPTER 19

Esel

Outskirts of Damascus

June 3, 1257

Esel splashes across a rocky creek. The donkey scrabbles up the far bank. Having carried her nearly all night, the beast resumes his weary gait, his head nodding in time with the drag and stomp of his hooves.

The moon sets large and pale in the western sky, south of Damascus. Looking into the dawn, she wonders if she has come as far as the Baniyas, the grasslands which could support a horse army.

Movement catches her attention from the west. Two mounted archers emerge over a small rise, spurring their horses with bows in hand. She wonders from where they came. A fear rises in her, as she tries to make out their armor. Mamluks or brigands?

A regret in taking this chance leaches into her core. These men will shoot her. She has been too bold.

She turns the pony to face them, showing the palms of both hands before her, in the way of the Kipchaks. She hopes that she is close to the place of the Bahri. She hopes they are Mamluks. She hopes she has entered the edge of Baybars' camp, the location overheard in her masters' conversation with the prince last moon.

Her heart drums upon her breastbone. She waits for the men to arrive, or for the twang of bowstrings to signal the end of her wretched life.

The arch-necked Arabians strut in, high-hoofed and at the oblique, the haughty gray protesting the bit in its mouth. The horses look down on the big-headed donkey and pathetic rider upon his back.

The Mamluks rein in, walking their steeds toward her with arrows still nocked. They slowly lower their bows to their thighs. Their cuirasses look similar to those of al-Nasir's guards, yet turbans anchor the base of their pointed helmets. An instant of optimism surges through her.

The soldiers halt twenty paces away, their Arabians snorting impatiently. The chestnut mare fights the reins and stomps a hoof. She drives the likeness of a white dagger bisecting her forehead repeatedly downward. Even the horses seem to want her dead.

Esel takes a deep breath. What if her nephew has changed? What if her input is not welcome? What if these men do not believe her?

"Why do you come here, woman?" the man on the light-colored horse asks.

"I come to speak with the Amir, Baybars."

When she answers in their dialect of Turkish, the men look surprised.

"Where are you from?"

"The Su Basi," she says.

Her answer appears to grant her no favor with the man. "You are a Volga River Kipchak?"

"Yes, Goker," she says.

"You did not ride that donkey clear from the Kipchak steppe. Where do you live?"

"Damascus. But I am not going back."

"Why do you wish to speak with Baybars?" he asks.

A subtle relief comes over her. These are her nephew's men. "He is the son of my younger sister. I come to bring him a message—one he will find of great importance."

"From whom?" The Mamluk is unconvinced.

"I know what the Prince of Damascus has planned for him."

The Mamluk on the chestnut moves forward. "We could have easily shot you dead. Do you not have a herd to tend? Maybe a husband who would raise a switch if he knew you were out in the middle of the night speaking with us?"

"I come to the aid of your leader. You could say he is the last in my herd. And my Kipchak husband is long dead."

The Mamluks look at each other. They give their horses a touch of calf and stop five paces from her. Both men look sturdy, their white skin tanned dark. Each man carries two white-handled swords, one hanging from his belt, another upon his saddle. The scabbards are curved similar to the limbs of a bow. Moonlight reflects off the soldiers' fluted helmets.

"What is your name?" the older of them asks, looking at her ragged clothes.

"I am Esel. I knew Baybars many years ago, as a boy."

The younger raises his eyebrows. The other Mamluk narrows his eyes, as if to perceive any deception. The pair exchange a glance.

"I understand your apprehension," she says. "I am what I appear to be—a slave. An escapee, but one bearing valuable word. I speak the truth and only need to talk with your leader for a short while before you will witness such."

"If you are found deceitful, they will flay the skin from your back. Drop the bag. Get off that ass," the older Mamluk orders.

Esel ducks from the straps and eases her sack to the grass. She grabs the donkey's mane and lowers herself painfully to the ground. The senior Mamluk draws his sword, while the second man tosses him his reins and leaps down from his horse.

"Remove those layers of clothes. Leave just one," the young man says.

She does so and stands in tunic and dress, shivering. "The dagger on my belt is my only weapon."

"Lift your arms and stand with legs apart," he says.

He dumps the contents of her bag. He squats and feels through each garment, stowing each back in the kitbag. He then searches her, avoiding her breasts and discreetly rubbing the back of his hand between her legs in his check for hidden weapons. He tosses her sheathed dagger to his senior. He finishes by inspecting the insoles of her slippers.

"Dress and then remount," he says, throwing her shawl back to her.

She hefts the bag to her shoulders and pulls herself atop the ass. The older Mamluk grabs the reins to her donkey and the younger man follows in trace, his bow at the ready.

They ride a short distance, Esel being led like a child. As dawn approaches, the rising light illuminates the soldier to her front. Beneath his scaled armor is a white overcoat soiled to russet. Chainmail extends just below his sleeves. His trousers are a mustard gold and neatly tucked into cowhide gaiters, which bear inscriptions to their god and their leader. She observes the tooling in his finely-crafted saddle; the leather of his scabbard equally fine.

Cresting a small hill, she sees the Bahri camp stretched before her. Black lean-tos and dun-colored tents stand secluded amid clusters of pine and juniper, thickest along the course of a gurgling stream. Half-brown grass covers their valley, where over a hundred hobbled Arabians feed. The horses' ears prick up as the riders descend.

The lead Mamluk raises his bow well above his head, likely a signal for friendly riders in. They ride to the closest watchman, who sits camouflaged against a ledged rock, his horse tied to a juniper.

"We have a woman who says she is Baybars' aunt. Claims to have knowledge of the plans of al-Nasir. She is clean of weapons. We must take her to Amir Baybars."

"He is not here. He accompanies Amirate Two on their patrol to the east. They are due back soon," the watchman says.

"Then you take her until he is back. We have our own patrol to finish."

The watchman looks at Esel as if just he was burdened with unwanted goods. He shakes his head. "I cannot be chasing around some woman who might choose to run."

The mounted men look about the camp and eventually to each other.

"By Allah," the older Mamluk says, with disgust. He dismounts and pulls a hobble from his saddlebag. He affixes it to her donkey. He offers Esel a hand to dismount.

She slides off the other side of the beast.

"Just drop your bag and wait here with him."

She lays it to the ground and sits atop it. The riders depart over the same hill from which they entered.

Soon Esel is shivering.

The watchman sighs. He pulls a horse blanket from his saddlebag. He stares at her pitifully and places the blanket across her shoulders.

"Thank you," she says.

He turns to face his area of responsibility.

She curls into the dirt, pulls the blanket tightly around her, and drops into sleep.

A nudge to her shoulder. Another more firm. She opens her eyes. Light pierces them. She rolls over. Dusty boots just inches from her face. She shucks the blanket and rises to a seated position.

She looks up at the watchman and another like him, squinting momentarily, the sun between the two men's shoulders. She turns away. The events of the previous night slowly seep into her memory like rain into moss.

"It is time for you to see him," the watchman says, stowing his blanket. He looks to his relief and tells him, "I will take her to the amir."

He hauls her to her feet. She hefts the bag to her shoulders, her legs sore from her night's ride.

He draws his sword and holds open his other hand. "His is the biggest tent. Go."

They walk downhill through shin-high grass, dozens of men filling canteens in the stream, looking up at them from their crouches. Men saddling horses glance over their shoulders. Fingers point in her direction.

"Digger, only you could draw a woman while stuck on watch," a soldier calls.

Deep-voiced chuckles from those about them. The watchman ignores them.

"Stop," the watchman says about fifty paces from the camel skin-walled tent. She turns to face him.

He grabs her tunic and wads the collar in his grip. She can smell the dried goat on his breath.

"Behave," he says. "Raise a hand to him and your head comes off your shoulders, faster than you can feel the blade. His guards will not hesitate. I will not hesitate."

She nods in understanding.

They continue toward the big tent, where two guards stand.

Seeing their approach, one guard knocks on the framed entrance. He slips into the tent. In seconds he is back out. He nods a confirmation to the watchman. The guards pull their swords from their scabbards, both shooting her icy stares.

The watchman enters first. Another guard holds the flap open for her. The second guard steps in.

Baybars looks up from a small table, littered with stacks of papyrus and rolled maps.

She looks into the same blue eyes of his youth, the white spot in his right eye confirming his identity. Crow's-feet wrinkles and deep forehead creases appear bizarre to her upon the boy's face, which she last saw sixteen years ago in Anatolia. His skin is as tan as the others, but perhaps his features more handsome; his beard thicker than his men's.

He gazes at the old woman before him.

One guard steps closer to her, likely sensing that Baybars does not know her, that her story is a lie.

Esel reaches for the flap of her belt. A guard lifts his sword across his body. She draws the chunk of yellowed ankle bone from the leather and holds it up for Baybars to see. "Surely you remember this, Nephew, as it appears you no longer recognize your auntie with gray hair and a weathered face?"

He seems to look through her. Perhaps old memories flooding into his brain. Perhaps not.

His face lightens. He reaches to a band of hide around his neck. He pulls from his tunic an ugur hanging from the lashing, the ankle bone polished smooth from rubbing against his skin for twenty-one years. It is the talisman she gave Baybars after the eight-year-old arrowed his first male wolf.

He bursts from his stool, catching his table with a quick snatch before it tumbles, the stool tipping over at his feet.

His grin flashes, still boyish. "Ha! Ha! Teyze!" He rushes over and scoops her up in both hands and hugs her tightly. The ankle bone around his neck mashes into her chest. She feels her toes drop, her feet dangling.

She wraps her arms around his neck and squeezes, the air gone from her lungs. Tears pool in her eyes. In his embrace, she feels his thickly muscled shoulders, smells his dusty scent that brings her back to fond recollections of the two back-to-back in wolf stands, and laughs shared while grinding deer tendon side-by-side in her ger.

He grasps her shoulders and holds her at arm's length to get a look at her. He stares into her eyes. "Ha! What a day! By Allah, what a day!" He shakes his head, as if in awe of the impossibility of this reunion. "I never thought I would see you again. Never! What a blessing!"

She wipes the tears from her eyes, giggles spurting forth between her sobs. His voice so deep now. Her nephew now a man.

Baybars spins her to face the swordsmen who a moment earlier were poised to take her head at the first false move. "This is Esel, my teyze from the Volga country. The finest bowyer. Wolf taker. The best woman known to man."

Tears in his eyes, her watchman from last night stands with mouth open, his sword held loosely now, its tip resting on his boot. He shakes his head in disbelief.

CHAPTER 20

Jacinta

Sinai

July 19, 1257

A branch snaps. Jacinta props her elbow into the cool sand, trying not to awaken the boy Zane, who lies beside her. A Bedouin youth collects firewood from the deadwood nearby. He smiles an apology for waking her. She grins back at him while shooing flies from Zane's head.

The midday shadow cast from the cliff at her back has lengthened during her nap. It stretches past both strings of camels—forty-two beasts tethered by a series of ropes, from the rear saddle horn of one animal to the bridle of the next. They rest on their padded knees in the identical, leg-folded position.

Some camels are saddled for riding. Others carry panniers of freight destined for Palestine and Syria—stone, pottery, linen, papyrus, ox hides, bags of lentils, and dried fish. On the return trip to Cairo, the beasts will likely tote cedar wood, silver, copper, and other valuables.

Beyond them, the sun casts gold against a distant ridge of craggy rock and crumbling massifs, amid the rolling sand of the Sinai.

Jacinta sits up and yawns, leaning against the smooth face of a rock. She dreads her coming assignment in Damascus. She had been so content after finishing her work in Hama—so pleased to be home in Cairo with her boy, supposedly done with this spying business.

She pulls the satchel closer to her. Qutuz provided her with a measure of coin, yet she knows this supply in the bag will not get her through the mission. She must somehow determine what type of vendor she will pretend to be in this next foreign city. And once buying her space in the souk in Damascus, she must be shrewd enough to make at least some gold from this sham profession in order to support herself and Zane.

Her stomach turns. And once she is established in the bazaar, then will come the nasty business of probing those Syrian merchants and soldiers whom she deems knowledgeable, and then finding ways to make them agreeable to divulging what they know. That is when her nightly prayers to Allah will double, asking to be granted the perceptiveness to avoid sources who would flinch under her pressure, and the insight to steer clear of snitches planted by another ruler or those who would alert al-Nasir's moles to her, Jacinta, the prying newcomer in town who asks so many serious questions.

She grabs a fistful of sand and lets it slowly drain into her other palm. How long can her luck hold out in this treacherous game that she has despised from the start? She rubs her hands clean and strokes Zane's head. It is not just her life that she risks now.

The wind swirls, sending the comforting scent of smoke across her nose. Three small blazes crackle in the wind nearby, stacked stones holding blackened kettles of steaming water. A Bedouin squats beside the closest fire, lost in the pulse of flame on wood, as if the whispering flickers were divulging secrets of this barren place.

A Bedu beyond the camels checks his string of kangaroo rat traps—crumb-laden sticks laid across dug holes. He stands over one, lowering his staff, while moving it side to side. He strikes at the unseen rodent, plunging the blunt end of the stick into the bottom of the hole. He reaches down and snatches the skull-crushed rat, placing it in the fouled pouch on his waist.

Nearby, another camel tender scrapes the cinders from his two spheres of bread with the flat of a stick, his thin loaves having finished baking beneath the half-spent coals in his fire. He sets one loaf on its side and smacks the stick against its face. He then stands the bread on edge and lightly scrapes his blade across both surfaces, occasionally slapping his hands either side of the stout dough. He tosses it gently, spinning it, catching the round loaf in his hands, the last of the ash falling from the bread in chunks.

With no prompting, Bedu lads roll from blankets laid atop their rocky beds. They walk to the baker's fire and flick charred hunks from his fire with sticks, preserving the precious Sayal, or acacia wood. Once the pieces cool in the sand, they place the apricot-sized nuggets and larger pieces into sullied bags hanging from their waists. These they then dump into a larger carrier aside one camel.

Jacinta spots four Muizziyya Mamluks sitting straight-backed against the elevated rocks, their positions giving them a view from each direction. Each sits with bow resting across his lap, a quiver of arrows at his side.

Under the second acacia tree, forty feet away in the wadi, lies the most precious cargo in the caravan: a dozen women from the sultan's harem. These ladies lie curled beneath the sprawling branches in their identical tan cloaks, unmoving amid their luggage. Not one of these bright concubines has acknowledged the presence of Jacinta or her son in their nearly four days of travel through the Sinai wilds.

Unsurprising, given the concubines' station. The harem is not some collection of courtesans used by the sultan to satisfy his fleshly desires. Its members are cultured, skilled professionals. Once evaluated and trained, women of the harem are able to not only speak a number of languages, but do so intelligently. They regularly sway a visiting dignitary toward the sultan's position on a variety of serious matters. Many of these women are not just smart and attractive, but rich, paid depending on their rank and performance.

"Are you hungry, Mother?" Zane asks, looking up with deep-blue eyes.

She smiles and straightens his hair. "A bit. And you?"

He nods, nestling against her shoulder.

The Bedu brushes the last of the dust from his flat loaves and lays them on a rock face beside bowls of dried meat and wild figs. With a sober-faced bow, he invites his riders to the blankets spread across the sand.

They eat, the women of the harem sipping tea from ceramic cups in their usual dignified manner, sitting in cliques of three and four.

Jacinta wraps her hands about her wooden cup, savoring the rich aroma of the Bedu tea, heavy on the *bardagoosh*, or sage plant, and light on the rare black tea. Zane chews on his dried goat in silence, sitting on the corner of the blanket, watching the camels moan and bite at the tormenting flies.

When all have finished, the Bedu pack up their few utensils and pots with their usual efficiency. The cameleers look up to the location of the setting sun, the elongated silhouettes of trees and beasts now stretching into the crags and upon the sheer faces of tan rock adjacent to them. The riders know the caravan leaders' unspoken signals. They rise wearily to their feet.

Jacinta points to the monolith on their right, where the low sun highlights the shoulders, ears, eyes, and even jagged teeth of a rock-formed monster.

"Dragon," she says with raised eyebrows, opening and closing her mouth, pretending her teeth are fangs.

Zane looks up with wide eyes, smiling.

She takes his hand and they walk through the soft sand to the same camel they have ridden since the first day of their journey. As they near, the odor of the beasts predominates—a meld of urine, dust, and musk.

Just as the camels are fussy about where in the string each is positioned, so are the Bedu adamant about which person should ride which animal. Back in Cairo, the Bedu sized up all in the party and paired the riders and beasts according to riding ability and camel temperaments.

Jacinta lifts Zane atop the seated animal. The boy grabs the front horn and swings his leg over.

"Watch his mouth," she reminds him, knowing that some ornery camels have been known to bite the fingers clean off of green riders. Their camel turns an eye toward them. His cheeks fill and he spits up regurgitated vegetation.

She seats herself behind the lad. A hiss of gas peeps from the animal's rear. Zane laughs, burying his head in the saddle blanket, conditioned to avoid the reek.

Once the riders are saddled, the eldest of the Bedu ambles toward the line of camels. He raises both arms and begins chanting in the song he uses to roust the beasts. He bounces up and down and leans side to side. Some of the camels stand on his first verse. Others roar and grunt their displeasure. As the old man passes the standing animals, he kisses each on its forehead.

Jacinta grins. Many Bedu treat their camels better than they treat their own children. She recalls a story learned on her ride to Hama about someone's old uncle. When he died, his camel cried for a month, all day and night. The best of the camel tenders need only words to gain cooperation from their animals. Usually only the lazy, impatient, or ill-tempered Bedu apply the switch to motivate their beasts.

"Hold tightly," she says. She holds Zane with one arm and places the other on the rear horn. She leans back in preparation as the gap-toothed Bedu approaches. The camel hauls itself to its feet awkwardly.

A stream of urine runs down the camel's legs, the creatures doing so purposely to cool themselves. It samples a bite of zilla plant, the thornbush whose flowers can enshroud an entire valley in radiant purple during springtime in the Sinai. It munches on the plant. The strong hair on the camel's nose and its tough mouth and adept digestive system combine to allow it to eat thorns that sheep and goats cannot tolerate.

The caravan steps off in the traditional line formation, which is natural for the camels, as they travel this way even when moving as a group in the wild. They follow the course of the wadi, the riders rocking agreeably in their saddles.

Jacinta pulls the wilted date palm frond from the saddle strap and slowly fans it near Zane to keep the flies off him. His head turns side to side, taking in the smooth-rocked hills, pocked with caverns large and small.

They pass enormous slabs and boulders that the mountain had shed over the centuries. She points out to Zane etchings marked high on the smooth surfaces, carved by unknown peoples long ago. Loftier than the carvings and the mountain, bearded vultures ride the currents, without flapping a wing. She feels small amid it all.

As they enter a narrower section of the wadi, the padded feet of the camels flatten the crumbly vegetation, releasing the menthol scent from the baytheran and infusing it with the peachy smell of nigd plants. This rising dust powders the line in a natural perfume.

The gully flattens. Breaking into the open, the budding flowers from the comb-leaved mirr plants blotch the rolling landscape, speckling the tan with patches of brilliant yellow. Jacinta once saw the Bedu boil this plant and use the solution to cure a terrible rash on a cameleer's legs.

The Mamluk guards push out to the front, rear and flanks, steering their camels atop the heaving dunes on either side.

Swaying in the saddle, Zane tips to her arm, fast asleep. She pulls him snug, adjusting his headscarf so that it shades his eyes.

"Do not waste your camel time," her father used to say. She lets her mind roam.

She left Cairo this time without turning back. She has an inkling that she will never again see the mighty Nile or her family.

She runs her fingers through the thick hair on the camel's shoulder, its coat perfectly suited to help the animal retain water and protect it against the desert's extreme conditions. Who or what protects her and Zane where she goes? Nobody, nothing.

The camel's giant nostrils open and close. It blinks its long eyelashes. She recalls the gales on the trip to Hama, during which the camels completely closed their giant nostrils and long eyelashes to shield themselves against the wind and sand. She will have no safeguard of any kind when she arrives in Damascus.

She considers the camel, whom she calls "Lucky," and regards the scars that mark its face, welts from ancient fights. The bridge of the animal's forehead is chevroned with dark stripes where the bridle has cut in on past treks. She figures if the camel were a soldier, it would be a seasoned amir. Yet she feels sorry for it. Like her, the path behind it had not been comfortable. And the road ahead promises to be no easier, no less dangerous.

She rubs the animal's neck. If she were a camel, she, too, would have like scars upon her forehead. She has already outlasted nearly every other Egyptian she knows in her perilous trade. Some are permitted to quit, most seem to just vanish, likely killed on the job.

She never had much choice, regarding the direction of her life and the course of her work. Long ago, she resigned herself to fate. God's will. She controls nothing. Allah again pushes her eastward, always north and east to the next stage in this dangerous trade. Her camel nods its battle-scarred head on each step, as if agreeing with her thoughts.

She pats its neck. "Yes, my friend, you know."

Fate. Leander. Once again, orders from the sultanate oblige an intersection in her path and his. She met the Frank after the battle of Damietta in 1249, while she was working in the infirmary there. Her job of treating wounded troops was second to her primary task of listening to their chatter, her ear tuned to sounds of duplicity or self-service, foul-mouthing the sultan—yet also to the songs of praise toward their patron, al-Salih. Easy work.

She reported regularly to al-Salih over informal cups of tea, letting the sultan know which Mamluks she thought were the most devoted and who were deserving of higher rank and pay. Their business talks were brief and quickly switched into lighter topics of history and art. She often left their visits with a gifted book in hand.

Early on, she saw her covert information gathering as a means to serve Egypt. She felt important. How many young women were escorted by the guards to privately brief the sultan in his meeting chamber? It bothered her little, knowing that her father, Kaphiri, had suggested the arrangement as a means to gain influence with the sultan and command. Kaphiri could think of little else other than growing his business.

And Leander. So young and pure. So sharp. She found none more dedicated to al-Salih and his Bahri mates. She smiles, remembering their evening walks through Cairo, wading in the sea, sharing kibbeh and olives in the shade of a feathery tamarisk.

In all, she had known Leander about four years. Most of that time, she was working in the infirmary and he was away fighting King Louis' Crusaders. Perhaps the moments they spent together were so precious for that very reason. Flickers of joy amid so much death and destruction during the Seventh Crusade. So much sadness surrounding both of their designated paths.

Al-Salih had the Crusaders well in hand by midyear 1250. The realm grew muddled, however, after al-Salih's death, especially once Aybeg came to power. She tried to leave the trade to get away from Aybeg and his sharp-toothed advisors, who were cloying and constantly scheming. But the new sultan refused to let Jacinta take her leave.

From the start, Aybeg was preoccupied with ferreting out who was unfaithful to him. She knew if she quit or declined an assignment, he would make good on his promises to kill her and her family. She had no choice but to stay at Aybeg's behest.

And now Aybeg has been replaced with an equally brutal man in Qutuz. Although Qutuz is not yet sultan, he is the next tyrant imposing his will in Cairo.

Zane shifts in her arms. Above, a hawk breaks from the clouds and banks on high, looking down on the string of camels.

She imagines what the raptor sees. The snaking caravan slithering along the Trunk Road, gliding between the rippled sand mounds and protrusions of shadowy rock, leaving a subtle trail of upturned shingle behind it. The head of the serpent—the front camel puller and animal—are hardly leaders of the caravan, merely following the light impressions made by the camel pads of previous travelers. Mother and child, indistinguishable from the Bedu and packloads, are just two more lumps of tan on saddle frame. Just another link in the chain of beasts.

They trudge farther eastward into the wilderness, as if slowly drawn forward by the faint prints of the past. They slink toward days more of this windswept country, the snake obeying some preset bearing, perhaps prearranged by the Creator himself.

She unwraps the long scarf from around her shoulders with one hand and binds it loosely atop her head and across her face. Pitching in the saddle, her head bobs in time with the camel's. Fate and circumstance. Perhaps Allah brings her to Damascus for a reason. Perhaps He has a plan for her.

CHAPTER 21

Esel

Nablus

September 27, 1257

Esel, riding an Arabian bay, follows the clap of hooves to her front, her nephew on a fine gray mare, flanked by two stout bodyguards. Baybars steers right onto *Tariq Al'aswad*, one of the numerous east-west roads in Nablus, a Palestinian town four day's ride south of Damascus. This street name is one retained by the Arabs, but converted into their language, after the Muslims conquered the town in the seventh century.

Esel turns to the man riding beside her, Hamit, Baybars' "Amir of the Armor." She wonders if he also notices that of all the eastern routes through town, her nephew chose a street called "Lion's Way." Hamit shows no reaction, the thick-bearded Circassian either unable to read Arabic, like many of Baybar's men, or simply not making the connection.

This road's designation aptly conveys the manner in which her nephew, the new governor of the town, has conducted himself of late. "Brazen" is what the locals are labeling Baybars.

Esel supposes she played a role, even if only a minor one, in Baybars' decision to bring his growing army of three hundred here. Maybe her disclosure last summer of the treachery planned for the Bahri was the last straw for Baybars' relationship with al-Nasir. She calls to mind their talk, the night after they reunited.

> *Baybars shook his head. "So the best bowyer on the Kipchak steppe was made into a housekeeper—for an arms dealer?" He snickered at the irony, propping his beefy forearms atop the tiny desk in his tent.*
>
> *"If not for serving in that household, I would not have heard the prince's words that night," Esel said.*
>
> *He nodded.*
>
> *Esel grabbed his callused hand. "Al-Nasir has no desire to assist you in the taking of Cairo. He has no intention to provide the entire lot of agreed arms he promised, or to pay your men what is owed them. He runs out of gold. He thinks he can get away with just paying you and not your soldiers."*
>
> *Baybars looked to the ground, nodding at his own thoughts. "Well, he is wrong."*
>
> *Esel, frowned. "His hands are like a woman's. He would need two swings to cut a melon."*
>
> *Baybars smiled. "Al-Nasir may be of Saladin's blood, but he is not of Saladin's heart. He is more a waffling conniver than anything—and you are right—soft as a kitty." He looked about the scrolls on his desk. "Thanks for confirming what I suspected."*
>
> *He shook his head. "Al-Nasir's unfit to be the Prince of Damascus, much less sultan of the entire empire. His only utility for us lies in his coffers of gold and the horsemen in his citadels."*
>
> *"Yet too many of his dinars now go to the Mongols in tribute," she says, "which make him less able to field that army, much less supply yours."*
>
> *He sat back. "My loyalty lies with those Bahri Mamluks in my care, plus the Salihi, those Kipchak brothers stuck in Egypt.*

My aim is to free Cairo from the Muizziyya Mamluks. I just need more men and fresh kit. Between us, I do not care where this help comes from. But I will not dishonor my men here by accepting less than what was promised us."

He pulled a map of Palestine into the candlelight. "We knew there would come a time to leave Damascus. It has arrived, my Teyze. Time to take up al-Nasir on his gracious offer."

She looked at him curiously.

He smiled. "Now is when I will take governorship of Nablus and Jenin."

"This all sounds like a big job," she said.

"Yes." Baybars stared at the supports in his tents. "You risked much to bring me this information. Your life."

"The choice was an easy one," she said. "Once I learned where you were."

He rose from his chair and hugged her. Her ribs bent under his arms.

"I will leave. Will stay out of your way," she said. "I am pleased to have provided you this word, but. . ."

"Leave? By Allah! Never."

She straightened herself on the stool.

"You would be in danger. Plus, I need people whom I trust completely. That is you." He clutched her shoulders. "Not since I left your ger as a lad have I seen a bow as fine as those you made. These skills of yours must be put back to use."

She looked down at her knotted fingers and then up at him.

He shook his head and pointed to his temple. "Your knowledge, my Teyze. Not your hands."

Esel reins in behind Hamit. She figures that even without her warning, al-Nasir likely would have nudged Baybars from his Damascene camp to the prince's Palestinian territories—newly-won lands gotten in the hasty treaty brokered by the Caliph al-Mustasim last year between then Sultan Aybeg and al-Nasir.

With Baybars frustrated with the prince's dithering and al-Nasir weary of Baybars' insistence on striking Cairo —appeals made more adamantly since the murders of Aybeg and al-Durr—a split in the tenuous partnership was inevitable. While al-Nasir saw a war in Egypt as a violation of the Caliph's treaty, a dear expense, and a potential sapping of his valued military, Baybars saw only opportunity in Cairo and payback against Qutuz and the Muizziyya.

Yet even with his plan to rescue Egypt temporarily foiled, Baybars had no intention of settling into a leisurely life of governing the pair of Palestinian trading towns accorded him by al-Nasir of Damascus. On the way south, Baybars declared himself to another of al-Nasir's rivals, Prince al-Mughith Umar, Governor of Karak. Although al-Mughith knew nothing of Baybar's newfound allegiance to him.

Baybars then diverted to Jerusalem. There, he unsuccessfully attempted to persuade Kutuk, another Bahri amir installed as governor by al-Nasir, to join Baybars in supporting the Prince of Karak, with the ultimate aim of taking back Cairo. When Kutuk refused, the Bahri removed him, ravaging the stores in Jerusalem and a good portion of its treasury. With caravans of booty taken from the holy city, Baybars continued on to Gaza and did much of the same there.

While the population in Nablus saw these acts as horrendous, Esel saw Baybars and his Bahri as no different than the Kipchak raiders from her past, men who for generations looted goods and livestock from the sedentary Rus back in the old country. Just as the Kipchaks needed pots, metal tools, and rams to breed, so did Baybars' little army need food, goods, and kit to sustain itself.

Some may now call the Bahriyya freebooters, yet Esel would call them warriors of the steppe, fed up with al-Nasir's lies and his feeble leadership. Was the Bahri wrong to simply answer the call of their bloodline?

When their caravan arrived in Nablus four days ago, Baybars dug into his accumulated plunder and paid his troops what al-Nasir owed them. He now looks to better equip his force.

As the road narrows, their column forms a single file down the middle. She draws her shawl up to swaddle her face in its shadows. Their hoof clatter acts as a warning to the myriad of travelers, merchants, and shoppers. These people peel left and right to avoid them.

As they enter the bazaar, they lose the afternoon sun behind the mud-bricked buildings. The air thickens between the mud-slathered walls, tainted with the smoke of cooking fires. They clod past rickety stalls, the tables effusing the spicy scents of ground ginger and cinnamon and clove. They cantor by proprietors offering tomatoes, cucumbers, leeks, and peppers.

They slow. As the crowds grow heavier, so do the tables they pass, bountiful with mounds of plums in an array of purples and slanted bins of crimson-skinned pomegranates. Other vendors hawk melons, sabra fruit, passiflora, yellow dates, and dragon fruit.

Turks, Syrians, Greeks, and Seljuqs, cloaked in an assortment of long coats and robes, pack into alleys around the stalls. An indecipherable multitude of voices echoes between the walls. Men in sweaty turbans and cylindrical kalpaks, women beneath their hijabs—all haggling, dealing, sorting, cooking. The Muslims make ready to break their Ramadan fast, gathering goods for the big evening meal, *iftar*, served after sunset. From simmering pots emanate aromas dense with spice.

Esel eyes a young girl who tests the consistency of her jujube compote over a small fire, looking up from her steamy pot with dark eyes for confirmation from her mother. Esel's heart aches. The child reminds her of her little Saja and their shared times at the market and in the kitchen.

As they pass, Esel looks back over her shoulder until her jostled vision of the girl becomes obscured by a throng of buyers and sellers, the town folk funneling back into the temporary wake made by the riders.

The path widens again and turns to cobbles. Here, the vendor booths are sturdier. Peddlers sit on three-legged stools, swatting flies amid bolts of cloth, rugs, and shawls of every design and color.

Since the beginning of man, this place in northern Palestine has been about trade. Nablus lies in a thin valley between two large mountains, Mount Ebal and Mount Gerizim. This position set up Nablus as a natural junction for ancient trade routes: east-west, linking the Jordan valley to the seacoast and Egypt; north-south, connecting Damascus to Jerusalem.

Founded as Neapolis in 72 AD by Italian gentry, the city once touted a large hippodrome and fine amphitheater. In time, the trading town grew into one of the biggest Roman cities in the region. Situated only a two-day ride north of Jerusalem and a one-day ride east of the Mediterranean Sea, the bustling center acted like the hub of a wheel, collecting and then spinning off goods in all directions.

When the Arabs eventually took the city in the mid-seventh century, they kept the Roman street grid and allowed some of the Latins' buildings to stand. They tweaked the Flavian city's name to Nablus. Both traveler and local alike refer to the town as "Little Damascus" for its similarities to its big sister in Syria.

The riders pass a pair of giant Roman pillars and a set of stairs leading to a building that no longer exists, its large blocks long since taken by the inhabitants for use in other structures. More vendor stalls occupy the white-stoned floor that remains. The merchants pound anchor rings into stubborn cracks in the stone columns to hold up the corners of their tarped hooches.

The hoof clacks in front of her slow to a walk. She catches an errant scowl from a merchant she passes and guesses at his thoughts. "A woman on horseback? A dame in the entourage of the seldom-seen governor? A female pillager, soon to plunder the merchants' goods in Nablus, just as the Bahri did in Jerusalem and Gaza?"

She stares him down from atop her steed. He looks away, fear or awareness of her position—baffling as it must seem—likely getting the best of him.

Ahead, a line of carts curves around a bend in the road. Turbaned men meander about them, waiting. A vendor sees the approach of Baybars and his train, and directs two men to untarp the first load. He turns and looks up to the mounted Mamluks, with his hands crossed respectfully in front. "Good afternoon, amirs."

Baybars nods. The riders dismount and drop their reins. Their horses stand obediently.

"As ordered, we have your weapons," the merchant says in a Syrian accent. He reaches over the cart's side to unbundle the fleece packing material within. He pulls a sheathed sword from the cloth and presents it to Baybars with the grip cradled in the crook of his elbow, as if he were handing a newborn child to its mother.

Baybars draws the sword from its silver scabbard and rubs his thumb across the edge of the Damascene steel. Holding the blade up to his eyes, he admires the melded series of decorative bars crossing the blade, known as "Mohammad's Ladder."

He grins. Looking farther up the blade, he reads aloud the inscription, highlighted with gold damascening: "Strive hard in Jihad in the way of Allah, such a striving is due to Him. Al-Nasir Yusuf, Governor of Aleppo and Damascus."

Baybars furls his brow, then chuckles. "No truer words," he looks to a guard at his side. "Yet we have seen little evidence that the one who sanctioned the crafting of this weapon wishes to make much good on this verse."

The trader appears unaffected by the slight thrown against his ruler. He places one hand atop another across his heart. "You will find all the swords of identical quality."

"We will see," Baybars says. Putting the sun to his back, he runs his hand down ornately-flowered etchings on the flat of the wootz steel and places his other through the leather-woven strap. He stares at the ivory handle in his palm, brass rivets and a pommel coated in silver. He returns the sword to its scabbard and looks to his Amir of the Armor.

Hamit takes his senior's cue, accepting the scabbard from Baybars. Hamit turns to the Syrians. "Place the swords atop the packing. I will examine each." He tests the snugness of fit between the scabbard's locket and body. Sliding his hand down, he does the same at the tip of chape.

"And the bows?" Baybars asks.

"Yes, of course," a second vendor says, waving his younger assistant forward. The assistant sweeps his hand toward the low-walled carts lined up in a row. "In these six here," he says.

"My second armorer will inspect," Baybars says.

Esel walks up beside Baybars. Both merchants look at the short woman and then at one another confusedly.

She looks up to eye the elder Turk, the man in a colored turban, with a beard trimmed to a dark point. "You do not understand the governor's simple order? Pull back these camel hides and let us have a look at these bows."

CHAPTER 22

Esel

Nablus

September 27, 1257

The crowd in the souk starts to disperse, the locals making their way home to break their Ramadan fast with an evening meal. Esel ignores the rumble in her belly and leans her palms atop the first cart of bows she is to inspect.

"You are serious?" the older Turkish merchant asks Baybars. "You will have this woman conduct the inspection?"

"Does my demeanor imply I am jesting?" Baybars says. "She is my armorer. Let us get on with it." He takes a step forward.

Esel is not shocked by the merchants' reception. Fortunately, she has received just the opposite welcome from Baybars and his corps of Bahri. For the past four moons, Esel spent many days repairing damaged bows for the troops and assisting with the logistics of planning the Bahri's departure from their Damascus camp.

On Baybars' orders, she coordinated requisitions for new arms with Hamit, utilizing only the best contacts she could recall from Gamal's conversations. Told by Baybars to have all weapons transported to Nablus in early October, she knew her nephew would pay the vendors then. She never fathomed Baybars would use the coin taken from al-Nasir's coffers in Gaza and Jerusalem and then declare himself to al-Mughith of Karak, a prince who challenges al-Nasir's rule.

The Turk looks down, then over to his friend. This man shrugs his shoulders and begins digging through the dirty wool used to cushion the bows. He removes the first weapon, unties a cord, and flips open the flap of an oil cloth. He pulls out the c-shaped bow with its string hanging loose from one end.

"Please string them all and lay them atop the tarps," Esel says.

The Turks' jaws drop. "There are one hundred seventy-five of them."

"And once strung I will be able to assess their quality," she says. "If there is not enough space on the tarps, you can place the rest atop their oil cloths."

The Turks look to Baybars. "Is this necessary, my Amir?"

"You may consider her words as my own. We have not all day."

The senior Turk tightens his lips. "Very well."

The Turk summons four more men. The senior Turk sits on the road with his feet set against the grip of the bow. He pulls back each limb and holds, while his assistant places the twisted leather bowstrings on each tip. He looks up to the others who watch. "Will you watch me string them all?"

As the six Turks string bows, Esel picks up the first, its entire wood frame and sinew backing covered in a red lacquer. Gold-colored leaves and floral patterns accent the ruddy surfaces. The older Turk leaves the stringing to the other men.

"We covered our warriors' bows in birch bark or rawhide to protect the components from the weather—not flowered paint," Esel says. "Are these implements of war, or adornments for a prince's palace?"

The vendor scowls. Baybars laughs.

"With this coat of paint, I cannot identify the wood used for the frame. Ash?" she asks.

"Yes."

Her eyes go to the seams where segments of horn were spliced together. "Why did your bowyer not use longer and wider horn strips, to avoid so many joints?"

"They use the horn available to them," the Turk says.

"So they used scraps to save you coin," she says matter-of-factly.

She tilts the bow and looks closely along the entire edge, noticing where the lacquer sucks tight into the horn joints. She shakes her head, setting the weapon on the ground, perpendicular to the cart wheel.

She picks up another painted bow. She runs her fingernail along the wood limbs and the inner belly of horn. Her nail cuts through the lacquer, exposing the gap between these layers. She lays this one beside the other reject.

The younger Turk, exhausted from his bow-stringing exercise notices. "Woman, what are you doing?" He snatches the next bow from her.

"These are defective," she says calmly. "Which glue was used to bond the horn and wood?"

"Boiled horse tendon glue, of course," he says.

"Fish glue is also necessary." She shakes her head. "Your bowyers either used glue that was too thin, applied too little of it, or did not wind the cord tight enough to bind the bone to wood layers with enough force to squeeze the glue out the sides. These bows will only delaminate further."

He looks down at the seam as if noticing the defect for the first time.

"Seems an arms dealer would know these simplest of things," she says.

The young vendor storms off. Esel continues down the line, setting aside more painted bows after only seconds of examination. She knows each would eventually fall apart.

Arriving at the first unpainted bow, she holds it up to her eye. She looks down each limb, from tip to tip, turning the weapon from side to side, inspecting the thickness and width of the wood, horn, and sinew layers. She checks to see if each limb is of equal dimension in each layer of material. She sets the weapon down perpendicular to the wheel.

She picks up the next one and runs the back of the bow closely beneath her eyes, looking hard at the strands of stout sinew glued atop the wood. "Did they use rear leg or backstrap tendon for the sinew layers on all the bows?" she asks the elder merchant.

"I think so," he says apprehensively.

"I do not. I can see where the sinew was spliced, where they likely used the front legs, or tendons from smaller animals. Only deer and wild sheep sinew is acceptable. Applying one uncut piece that reaches grip to tip prevents weak spots."

She stands for a moment staring at him. "But a seller as long in the trade as you knows this." She runs her finger along a lean section of the bow. "And I can see where the same amount of sinew was not applied equally to each limb and the high spots were not rasped. This affects the bow's balance."

She picks up another. After eyeing it and finding it so far acceptable, she pulls two measuring reeds from her pocket.

The merchant looks to Baybars. "Please, the sun will be down soon. Those are not needed. Our craftsmen are skilled."

Baybars notes the beads of sweat on the merchant's brow. "If she has identified the need to measure, then it is necessary."

With the longer Cyprus reed, she measures from the center of the grip to midway down the lower limb, marking the spot on the rod with her nail. With the second, she gages the limb width and thickness. She flips the bow and does the same along the upper limb, comparing the dimensions at the identical point. She sets this bow down on the ground with the other discarded weapons.

"These bows would all shoot fine," the vendor says.

She stows her reeds. "Each limb must be of the same width and thickness along the entire length of the weapon, otherwise the bow will be unbalanced. I do not even have to draw this one to know it would not shoot straight enough to knock down a hare at thirty paces."

She scrutinizes a dozen more bows, drawing several a few inches at time to check for balance. She rejects more than half of the weapons: those which would not shoot straight or would fall apart in short order; those with misshapen horn tips; those with sinew strands drawn up into twists; those with horn that cracked during the drying process; those with various layers of unequal thickness or stiffness, and those with twists that could have been remedied by simple heat corrections or tillering.

"You can tell your men to stop stringing the rest of the weapons," she says. She turns to the Turk. "How many different hands made these bows?" she asks.

The merchant just stares at her.

"The weapons covered in paint were the worst of them, slathered in lacquer to cover the flaws. And they appear made by many bowyers, some with inadequate skills, probably in a rush."

The Turk takes a step closer. "These bows you set aside were constructed by some of the best bow makers in Anatolia. Little is wrong with them. Each weapon has its own personality."

Esel looks up to his face. "Well, then I would say these recurves have lazy, sloppy personalities."

He looks the other way.

She conjures her father's serious face, the look he would have after seeing these weapons. A similar disgust rises in her.

She addresses Baybars. "At least half of these bows appear to have been constructed by unsupervised novices. I have no confidence their craftsmen scored the horn and roughed the wood where the layers were joined. Who knows if they coated the splices with appropriate coats of sizing, before putting on the thicker glue coat? Or if the wood and bone layers were properly dried before tillering. I could go on, but in the end, most of these bows do not meet your standards. I suggest we reject them all."

The older Turk looks ill. He glares at her and then turns to Baybars. "You are very picky for troops receiving weapons as gifts from a prince."

"Gifts?" Baybars says. "I pay for them with silver earned by my men. Services rendered to al-Nasir." He steps closer. "And we will not fight with shoddy weapons. But what do you know about using the items you peddle?"

"I will not pretend to be a soldier, or a craftsman. My business is selling." The Turk smiles. He sees his assistant round the corner, beaming and nodding as he speaks to a foreign man. "And this I will do—with all of these bows." He opens his palm to the castoffs. "Others will find little wrong with them."

A Mongol with short legs, swathed in a long jacket and scaled armor, struts toward the carts. His black-braided hair falls about his cuirass. The Tartar's nose sits flat beneath narrow eyes. His skin is dark, his scant beard interrupted from cheek to chin by a wide scar. The right sleeve of his deel, the collared neck-to-ankle tunic favored by Mongol horsemen, is cut off at the elbow, where his arm had been severed. Despite this amputation, he swings his stump with the equal arrogance of his full left arm.

Watching the man, a shiver of fear moves through her. She bites her lip. "Mongol," she mumbles to herself.

On the steppe, the Black Tartars had always been a threatening presence, but one unseen by Esel's tower. The Mongols existed as mysterious warriors, mighty raiders, and enslavers of women and adolescents. Stories of pillage and rape pushed her Goker Kipchaks westward for years, trying to avoid an overwhelming power that could not be countered. It was they who shoved Esel's tower into that Anatolian snare. Here and now for her, the unidentifiable, unconquerable invaders take the form of this one, maimed soldier.

"You will sell to the enemy?" Baybars asks.

The Turk raises his chin. "The Mongols are not enemies here in Palestine. Al-Nasir Yusof has an understanding with these Tartars. You as his governor know this."

"Yes, we know al-Nasir submitted to the invaders," Baybars says. "The Prince of Damascus prefers the effortless solution, finds it comfortable to make allies with all of our common enemies. That is the easy remedy. For now."

The Turk shrugs his shoulders, watching the Mongol pick up one of the rejected bows. "The Mongol emissaries and purchasers go where they wish. Their coin spends as well as any Muslim's. Today, it appears they wish to buy bows," the Turk says, raising his eyebrows at Esel. "Good bows."

But Esel does not notice his slight, her eyes staying on the Tartar.

The Mongol feels her stare. He takes in their group, his eyes settling upon Esel, the sole female, as out of place at this bazaar as the one-armed Mongol.

A flame of vengeance burns deep inside her belly. She thinks of her tower. The ambush near the Rotten Sea, those events sixteen years past on the Orkapi narrow. She hisses at him. The Mongol seems to acknowledge her hate, perhaps recognizing her as a Kipchak. A yellow-toothed smile stretches the scar on his bearded chin.

Hamit, having completed his inspection of the swords, walks up to Baybars with the Syrian. "The workmanship with the swords is fine, but they bring only thirty-five of the sixty al-Nasir promised."

"And the two hundred and fifty jawshans—Kalid's lighter version—where are they?" Baybars asks after the agreed-upon cuirasses.

"No armor. We only brought those swords allowed by al-Nasir's amirs," the Syrian says.

"So the Syrians provided half the swords promised, none of the lamellar armor, and most of the bows from the Turks were of poor quality," Baybars says.

The merchants look to one another and then back at Baybars.

"We will purchase the weapons that were of acceptable workmanship. Perhaps Prince al-Mughith Umar, al-Nasir's foe in Karak, will provide better bows. And armor."

CHAPTER 23

Jacinta

Karak

November 9, 1257

Jacinta strolls the dirt-pathed marketplace of Karak, the Transjordan outpost, a half day's ride east of the Dead Sea. She wears a worn pack strapped upon her shoulders. Holding Zane's hand, she steps under the papyrus-roofed stand.

Leather bags of varying sizes hang on wooden pegs, as do thin-soled sandals on inclined racks. She nods a good morning to the young lady, who rises from her stool as Jacinta enters.

The lady winks at Zane. He buries his face shyly in his mother's dress.

Jacinta sorts through the largest of the satchels. "Where would I find the tanner's booth?"

The woman points down the south road. "Past the last of the mud huts. They do not let him work near here." She leans down to Zane and pinches her nose atop her hijab. Zane and the shop keeper giggle.

"Yes, of course. The smell," Jacinta says.

"If you prefer a bag of a different size, we have others at a booth on the next street over," she says, pointing east.

"Oh, thank you."

"Are you not the ginger lady?"

Jacinta smiles. "Yes."

"I recognized your boy. So cute, always so well-behaved."

Jacinta grins. Zane again turns away, hiding behind his mother's tiny body.

"My mother loves ginger," the merchant says, "especially in her winter tea."

Jacinta nods. "My mother, too. And she lays it heavily on her lentil curries—her favorite. The smell of fresh ginger reminds me of her. Deep down, I think that is why I choose to sell it. In a small way, it keeps her near us." A pang sets in her stomach as she thinks of the softhearted lady back in Cairo, possibly still ill. "You come to my booth and I will give you a very low price. A gift for your mother."

"That is kind of you."

"Well, I'd best keep moving," Jacinta says.

She and Zane take the south road.

Jacinta had met an Arab trader west of Gaza, as her caravan made its way to Damascus this past summer. The old man held twenty camels, loaded with ginger. He made a living buying directly from the Indian merchants at the Red Sea docks and caravanning the spice to Gaza and Cairo.

"I know every wadi, every dune from Abbasa to Gaza," the Arab chuckled. The trader had just lost a grandson and he paid special attention to Zane, the sole child at the oasis. She sensed the man's pity for her. A woman traveling alone. No husband to provide for her; no father for her son.

"People in Damascus might pay more for their ginger freshly ground," he said, smiling. "You should consider selling it that way there."

Knowing that she would need a cover soon, a fake occupation, she spent the subsequent rest stops gabbing with the shrewd merchant. She learned of his life on the silk path, the minutia of his trade, even how to properly grind the root and where to set her price. By the time they reached Gaza, she had purchased a camel load of ginger from the man, using the coin provided by Qutuz.

Once she arrived in Damascus, she rented a booth at the eastern souk and quickly realized that the thoughtful Arab had grossly undercharged her for the bulk spice. And, of course, the elderly man was right. When she pulled out the grinder that he had given her and offered the ginger as fresh-ground, she became a customer favorite. Without trying, she made extra silver. While making small talk with the locals, she pulled together shreds of knowledge on Baybars' doings and the whereabouts of his cadre. A good thing she earned the extra coin, as her mission dragged into an expensive and time-consuming ordeal.

In Damascus, her primary leads consisted of craftsmen, bladesmiths, and makers of lamellar armor. While the dealers would not disclose the identities of those for whom they crafted their blades and cuirasses, the smiths saw their earlier works in town, upon the Nasiriyya and Aziziyya. Most of the smiths and armorers figured that their wares were arming the swelling force of Bahri, who lingered on the periphery of Damascus.

She was hardly in Damascus one moon before learning that Baybars had abandoned his camp for Nablus in early September. She joined a caravan heading for that town, but the train was halted outside of Jerusalem when fellow travelers and refugees heading north warned that Baybars was sacking the holy city.

For two weeks, she sat mostly idle in the camp, knitting together bits and pieces of verifiable information and sifting through rumors on the "rogue Bahri." She learned from local herders that Baybars was thought to be headed for Gaza, his work in Jerusalem finished. She tried to seek passage there, yet the Bedu refused caravan travel during Ramadan, and few merchants were willing to risk their goods with Baybars' freebooters in the vicinity anyway. So she waited.

By the time she found a caravan headed for Gaza, she learned from a cameleer that Baybars had asserted his governorship in Nablus. She went there, buying another load of ginger and peddling it in the bustling town for most of October. After the Bahri skirmished with al-Nasir's forces on the edge of Nablus at end of the month, Baybars and his men escaped to Karak.

Well-received there by Prince al-Mughith, the Bahri's commander settled his regiment outside of the city. Just as with al-Nasir in Damascus, the Ayyubid Prince in Karak was happy to augment his force of horsemen with the elite Bahri, yet not so comfortable with Baybars' corps of Mamluks to let this wild pack of steppe dogs into his fortress.

She and Zane had little choice but to follow. They endured another eight days on camelback, arriving in Karak last week. She rented a small flat to live in and a booth in the bazaar. She resumed selling her remaining stock of ginger while attempting to learn more on Baybars and Leander.

In all, during the last four moons, she felt like a dog chasing her tail, her task made more difficult with a son in tow. So far, she succeeded mostly in traveling and honing her vending skills, being always one day late and one step behind the Bahri. She penned two dispatches to Qutuz in Cairo. These contained the Bahri's recent activity, yet negligible word on Baybars' future intent or the location of Leander, the amir's translator.

Vicegerent Qutuz was an impatient man. He would not be happy with her. Four months was the typical timeframe of other "ineffectives" being eliminated if they did not prove to be a capable source of intelligence. "The fourth moon is doom," her fellow spies always warned.

On the streets of Karak, she looks over her shoulder, watching for moles or assassins tasked with snuffing out the unproductive. She is not afraid to die. She only fears for what would happen to Zane without her. She squeezes his hand. He looks up and smiles.

"Hungry?" she asks.

He nods. She reaches into her pouch and hands him two dried dates.

They pass the last of the reed-thatched huts and catch the wind swirling the noxious scent of the tannery. Zane pulls up the neck of his tunic. They round the bend.

The aproned legs of three men appear beneath a mass of weathered camel skins. She ducks under the highest flap of camel skin.

The reek of gutted animals and buzzing flies fills the air. A brown dirt floor is littered with fur and scrapings of flesh. Three severed ox heads lie dripping, one's blue tongue sticking out sideways. Piles of skins sit chin-high in a corner, stacked dried and stiff, filthy with soil and gore. Other hides of fur in brown and tans and gray lie neatly bundled atop blackened tarps, their straps tied with clever rope handles atop them.

Zane hugs her leg.

Out of the wind, the stench of piss and dirty animals accentuates. Shallow-sided barrels hold piles of ox brain and urine, materials used to tan the hides. Rumpled leather protrudes from the rancid liquid. Skins hang both high and low, some turned gray from the salty alum, several stretched across tilted frames of stripped pine. Others flop wet over forked beams, dripping upon the dirt floor.

A man with a wrinkled neck bends over a tool that he cradles beneath his armpits. He scrapes the flesh from a hide, steadying the handle of the tool with one hand and pulling down on the skin with his other. He moves methodically, in a repeated bowing motion, dried muscle and fat curling from his scythe-shaped blade. He looks up, taking in her and then the boy. He goes back to his work.

Zane looks up to her with wide eyes.

A man completely hidden behind a hanging skin elbows it aside, exposing his workstation atop a small table. "What do you need?" he asks gruffly.

She slides her bag to her front, exposing the cracking hide and nearly worn strap. She looks down at it and then up at him with hopeful eyes.

He grimaces, signaling her over with a hairy finger.

They take a wide path around the ox heads and past two open bags of feces and a barrel of cedar oil. She stands opposite the man, who appears to be the boss. She holds the bag so he can see it, not wanting him to touch it with his filthy hands. He looks with squinted eyes, while absently pulling handfuls of matted hair from the hide secured atop his grungy table. It falls about his feet in a growing mound.

He looks up to her with an unanticipated softness in his eyes. "If the seam leather had not given way I could have resewed it for you and replaced the strap." He snatches the double-bladed fleshing tool from the table and begins hoeing the blade across the raw hide. "But the hide is too far gone. It might be best just to get another. I really only provide the tanned leather for the three families who make the bags. They have two booths in the souk. Easy to find."

Knowing how he would send her back to the booth she just left, she feigns disappointment. "Well, all right. Thank you for looking at it."

His eyes go back to his bench.

"Is your leather also used for saddles?" she asks.

He nods, wiping his wrist across his nose. "And quivers for arrows. Leather stitching and binding material for armor—for both horse and man."

"Have you sold to the Bahri, recently arrived here—Baybars?" she asks, getting to her reason for the visit.

He looks at her sideways. "Not the commander, but two of his Bahri came in with bridles needing repair and one man's cuirass."

"I only ask because I had a friend who served Baybars as a translator, a Frank. Leander was his name. I was just curious if he happened to come here. Was wondering if he was still alive."

"No Franj came here."

She nods. "I have a small booth where I sell ginger in the bazaar. If you happen to hear of this man, Leander, could you please let me know?"

He looks at her blankly.

She reaches into her bag and pulls out a single dinar, a gold piece. She hands it to him. "I am surely not a rich lady, but knowing of this Frank is important to me."

He rolls the coin in his fingers, then looks up to his two other workers to see if they notice. One sloshes a leather skin in the saltwater barrel, while the other remains engrossed in the hiss of his scraping blade across the hide. He slips the coin into his pocket. "I see this."

"And this conversation is just between you and me, right?" she whispers.

He lowers his voice. "Of course. This is nobody else's business."

CHAPTER 24

Esel

Outskirts of Karak

Nov 12, 1257

Esel takes three steps forward in the winding line beside three young Bahri, eighty paces from the entrance to the dining tent.

The young Mamluk nicknamed "The *Hoca*" (Teacher) points his finger at his red-haired mate. "We cannot be soldiers forever. I told you, her father has no son to carry on the business. It is not just cotton, he wants to trade in ivory, too. We had dinner one night. He needs a young, keen man to help him. I am that man." The Hoca thumbs his chest.

"Ivory," Kas, the older, third friend, says in his deep voice. "Remember Kadri, the big man? When he left the regiment, he worked for that ivory dealer from Ashmun. They went broke. Kadri is still broke."

"Yeah, now an old man working the fields," the redhead says. "You could be *that* man, Hoca—dumb, old, working a field, too."

Laughter from a Mamluk behind them who overhears. "The Hoca knows all!" The line accordions forward.

"Kadri got in with the wrong man," Hoca says. "Ivory is good when the prices are good. Ivory is good when you are with a smart merchant." He turns to draw Esel into their conversation.

"Ivory is good?" the redhead asks. "You think selling elephant tusk to the Franj so that it can be carved into statuettes of the Virgin Mary and crucifixes is good?"

The Hoca shrugs. "And combs and mirror backs. Infidel gold spends, too, my brother. Nothing wrong with planning for life after this." He points his chin at the slow-moving line stretching past two tents.

"Listen to him," Kas says. "All we needed in Nablus was another hundred cavalrymen and we would have taken al-Nasir." He glances to Esel. "Then Baybars might have been prince of Damascus. But all The Hoca can squawk about is leaving our leader another man short."

Esel grins, appreciating Kas' loyalty to her nephew and his positive take from their recent battle. After the Bahri sacked both Jerusalem and Gaza and then emptied the treasury in Nablus, al-Nasir of Damascus showed up on the outskirts of Nablus looking to bring his renegade subjects under control. Baybars was ready for him.

Yet once her nephew realized his force of three hundred fifty Mamluks was vastly outmanned, Esel understands that Baybars wisely led his Mamluks in retreat, saving his men for battle another day. But in an act of final boldness, before breaking contact, Baybars came close enough to the prince to cut down one of al-Nasir's standards. This boldness was not lost on the troops.

While the battle was brief and technically a loss, Baybars actually gained men, as more disgruntled Salihi from Cairo filed in to join the Bahri. By the time Baybars reached Karak, he pledged his support to the Ayyubid prince, al-Mughith Umar.

Since the fight, the Bahri have stayed in this camp, northwest of Karak, along the River Jordan.

"I am not looking to leave the service of our amir. I'm just looking down the road, that is all," Hoca says.

"Kadri was long in the tooth—it was time for him to go," Kas says. "You are still green. Seems you ought to be a little more thankful for your spot in the Bahri and not be thinking of ways to angle out."

Esel raises her eyebrows at Hoca.

"See, Esel is a wise woman. I am thinking she recognizes the difference between a good merchant and bad. Knows that a man must chart his own future. She appreciates a good relationship when she hears one," he says.

Their eyes turn to her, waiting for the grandmotherly advice that she is known to grant when asked.

"A good relationship," she says. "So far, all we have heard from you is about her father's business and what is in it for you." She rubs his shoulder. "Do you love the woman, or do you love her father's gold?" She winks at him and smiles.

The other men laugh. One elbows Hoca in the shoulder. "Yes, Esel knows."

"Of course I love her, Esel. That goes without saying."

"But you speak little of her. Marriage is about more than silver. It is about who you go home to when the campaign is ended."

Kas sighs. "Save your words, Esel. By the time the Bahri are done with him—by the time we get back to Cairo—her father will have not only started and sold that ivory business, he will also have three grandkids from that daughter—from another son-in-law."

More chortles.

The Hoca frowns, looks to the ground.

"You keep the faith. You keep your love for this girl," Esel says. "The stars know. Sometimes Allah preserves two people for the right time."

"And sometimes Allah needs infidels slayed," Kas says, nodding respectfully to Esel, then shaking his head at the young Mamluk. "Sometimes Allah needs men willing and able to wield steel against his enemies. Look where we are—so far from home." He opens his palm to the Jordan's blue water snaking past and the tan hills farther off. He sets his eyes on the youth. "You need to be thinking more of the task ahead and your brothers right now and less about a wife—and even less about silver."

A tap on her shoulder.

"Esel, Amir Baybars would like to speak with you," a guard says.

"We will save a goat leg for you," Hoca says.

"Thank you."

She heads to the center of camp, stopping at the largest tent among the fifty. She raps four times on the wooden frame above Baybars' tent flap.

"Enter."

A fire smolders in the center of the tent, the smoke drifting up toward the vented apex. Baybars sits at small table covered in maps and anchored at the corners by piles of dispatches. An empty cup of tea. A small candle burning. "Please sit, Teyze."

She sits across from him on the offered stool. "Keep this up and you will go blind in this dim light," she says.

He smiles. "Sorry to disturb your meal."

"No disruption. Some of the men said they would snatch me a little."

"I bet they will. They have grown quite fond of you the past five moons."

"Bowyers are often popular with the warriors."

"True. But it is more than that." He drops his quill on the desk, rubs his eyes. "My spies in town. They are on to a woman who has been snooping around Karak—and Nablus before that. She is following us and asking a lot of questions."

"A woman?" Esel asks.

Baybars nods. "She works a booth at the marketplace. Sells ginger." He looks Esel in the eye. "I need to know what she is up to. She could be an assassin, or could be leading others like her we do not know about. It would be good to know who hired her and how many others there are before we kill her."

Esel nods.

"She has been fairly careful. Shc likely works for al-Nasir, maybe Qutuz—I would expect such. But it would be good to know if al-Mughith is connected."

Esel understands her nephew's unease. Al-Mughith of Karak recently portioned a share of his treasury to Baybars in return for the Bahri leaving the service of al-Nasir of Damascus. Still, Baybars and Esel did not trust al-Mughith completely.

She senses that, while Baybars desires a new ally in his quest to oust Qutuz from Cairo, her nephew's expectations are also grounded in reality. Baybars knows that manipulation and plotting are often-used tools in the Ayyubid princes' kit. Her nephew will take from these royals what he can get.

It was no surprise to Esel that Baybars spent much of his newly-gotten gold on the armor and mounts for his men that al-Nasir had promised, but did not deliver. Each of Baybars' men now owns a baggage donkey, plus a new jawsan, first-rate chest armor. Those Bahri who once tended lame horses now ride healthy Arabian mares.

Baybars leans his elbows on his desk. "One of our spies confronted the tanner in Karak. The tanner admitted that this woman has been dredging him for information. He reckons this peddler lady is a spy. She even paid him to keep quiet."

Esel nods.

"Anyhow, this woman, Jacinta, will not be hard to find. She is at her booth most every day. I thought maybe you would have a chat with her."

"Me?" Esel asks.

"Yes."

"I understand an old woman is plenty expendable," she says, believing her words. "But there will be another battle, more bows to fix in the moons to come."

He shakes his head. "You are the least expendable. This is a job for a warrioress, not another mole. A woman with some predator intuition and snap judgment. We need to get this one right."

"I see," she says, the hunter in her pushing aside her initial tentativeness, the "wolf taker" part of her mind already mulling options to best engage this ginger-selling spy, this threat to her nephew and his band.

CHAPTER 25

Leander

Gilan Gharb Valley, western Persia

November 16, 1257

Leander sneaks along the grassy side of the finger, his bow at the ready. He trails his two teammates, their quivers and scabbards silenced with tufts of raw wool and leather wraps. They move along the most prominent of the goat trails that striate the steep wall, its foot-worn ledges interwoven like wrinkles on an old man's arm.

The Mamluks use the sharp banks to conceal themselves and dampen the little foot noise they make. Yesterday, they spotted Mongol observation posts both north and south of this place. Hence, twice Duyal's team has chosen this route eastward, the path located midway between the two enemy positions. Leander's eyes stay to the track, vigilant for sign of the round hooves or boot prints of the enemy.

Apparently, the Mongol leader, Hulegu, felt comfortable that he had the situation in Iran under control and left his headquarters in Hamadan, Persia, almost two moons ago.

Slowly, he made his way toward Mesopotamia, gathering up additional forces and equipment over each mile he made westward. As tasked by Amir Baybars, the scouting trio followed every inch of the Tartars' progress.

Hulegu halted last week, making camp in the valley on the opposite side of the ridge beneath which they now stalk. Each day since, additional Mongol units trickled down the Zagros Mountains into the wide basin as they finished their tasks of mopping up the last of the Assassin resistance—to the north in Alamut and northeast in Demavend.

Leander checks to ensure his leather scroll case is slung securely on his back, paranoid that the writings remain in his possession. For weeks, he and Duyal have recorded their observations of the invaders' gear and actions. The work was scribed in duplicate, in case one copy of the papyrus was damaged, or one man was captured.

They drop from the ridgeline to the ravine bottom, the draw snarled with hackberry and elm saplings. Duyal and Singer weave around boulders and bypass the thickest vegetation, following the natural drainage.

And fluid as water is how his Kipchak friends move. Singer steps noiselessly on the balls of his feet, his eyes focusing ahead and to his flanks, yet almost never down to his feet, which stay to the quieter pebbles and sand. Short and stocky, Singer is known throughout the Bahri as a good bird, a fighter one wants around when a clever solution is needed, or when things get ugly.

His real name is Halis. Somewhere along the line, his mates gave him the nickname "Singer," as the amir can often be overheard quietly humming or singing to himself the tunes from his nomadic past. His chants most often occur during the lulls in duty— or when events become chaotic—his way of both alleviating boredom and steadying his nerve when the arrows start to fly.

Orphaned when but a teenager, Singer cared for his young brother and sister for years. Singer speaks little of it, but the story goes that he would come down from his Ural Mountains hideouts at night to pilfer the occasional sheep from nearby towers when game was lean, or filch the odd pot, knife, or metal bridle from roving bands. When the Mongols later occupied Kipchak lands, he snatched their food and gear in the night. But mostly he hunted and trapped. His daily stalks to kill deer, antelope, marmot, and birds were his young family's primary means of survival.

Only last moon, Leander learned that both of Singer's siblings were clubbed to death by Mongol raiding parties when Singer was sixteen. Singer found them bludgeoned along a stream bank. The youngsters had been hunting ground that Singer had forbidden them to enter, land the Tartars had traveled back in the 1230s, while they were putting their heel to the last of the Kipchak tribes. His brother and sister were more like his children than his siblings. Their deaths still weigh heavily on Singer.

Shortly after his kin's demise, Singer walked into the Mongol camp with palms held forward. With his family dead and what remained of his tower scattered to the west, he had little choice but to join the enemy. An expert horseman and archer, he was quickly welcomed into the Tartar ranks, as were other Kipchak youth in his predicament.

Several moons later, after Kipchak rebels ambushed his new Mongol unit, Singer and two mates fled the Mongols. The three traveled south for weeks through unfriendly Christian territory and Turkish Anatolia before being taken in by al-Salih, then the prince of Hisn Kayfa, in the northern reaches of the empire.

At the citadel there, novices Duyal and Singer trained in the same class. They graduated and later fought together, blood brothers of the same Khushdash. Singer's competence, coupled with his experience in the Mongols' ways and his crude understanding of their language, made Singer an easy choice for Baybars on this mission.

Duyal and Singer plod ahead with three arrows staged between fingers on their draw hands, a broadhead nocked in their recurved bows. Their weapons are slightly smaller than the qaws, the heavier recurves used by Mamluks in battle, and are compact in the Turkish style, so ideal for the patrol work they have been conducting for the past year.

Over his shoulder, Leander carries his girl, Gamila, Arabic for "gorgeous woman." This crossbow has a butt carved from stout elm and composite bow staves crafted of wood, sinew, and yellowed horn, bonded by fish glue. His girl is little different from his father's, which hung above the mantle back home in the French Kingdom.

Gamila has a twin sister back in camp, Galina, Rus for "woman of serenity." Aside from his books—possibly destroyed by Qutuz, along with their fortress at Rawda Island in Cairo—the pair of crossbows are his only prized possessions. Both weapons were made in Genoa and purchased in Damascus in 1238, just before the Frank-Saracens treaty expired the following year and such trade was no longer allowed.

His father gave him both weapons in 1239, when Leander was but ten years old, a few months before the boy was sent away to serve as squire to the knights of his father's lord, Erard of Brienne Ramerupt. It was then that his father—also a crossbowman, who fought thirty-eight years ago against the Ayyubid alliance in the Fifth Crusade—taught Leander everything about the weapon. While his father lost an arm in battle, ending his career, the crossbow had been the one item that bonded them.

An air of melancholy surges through Leander as fragments of memories of the old country fill his mind. As a child, and then later as a page in France, he spent every spare moment stalking the hills and fields for fox and deer in Lord Erard's vast lands. He hid from the rangers, men paid to keep out poachers, and applied the shooting skills learned from his father and the instructors in Erard's castle. From the elder grooms and farmhands on the Erard's massive estate, the young Leander begged and pried for scouting and tracking advice until he excelled at all forms of hunting. He figures this pursuit of game likely kept him sane back then, it being his sole reprieve from the endless chores, religious services, and education within the castle walls.

He pats his crossbow. How easy it would have been to learn the stalk in Ramerupt, if Duyal and Singer had been his mates those twenty years past, if his comrades had been Frenchmen, not Kipchaks on the other end of the continent. He envisions the three of them as boys learning the stalk together in France on one of those autumn evenings, charging afield with weapons in hand. He grins, feeling fortunate to have these men in his life now.

Certainly only Leander's unusual aptitude in Arabic, Coptic Egyptian, French, English, Turkish—and even a few Kurdish strains—gives him this opportunity to work with Duyal and Singer, the best of the Bahri warriors from al-Salih's second generation of Royal Mamluks. Indeed, only his knowledge of these languages allowed his unlikely admission into the Bahriyya from the start.

Leander defected from the Crusaders in October of 1244, just northeast of Gaza, before a major battle known as "Harbiyya" to the Muslims, "La Forbie" to the Franks. He was only sixteen years old and serving as a translator in the service of Walter IV of Brienne, Count of Jaffa and Ascalon, in the Kingdom of Jerusalem. Translating during the pre-battle meeting just outside of La Forbie, Leander again beheld what was all too common—the leaders from each group of Crusaders fighting over plans and endless petty concerns, fueled by greed and ego.

On October 17th, Leander and two other interpreters were sent to the gates of La Forbie to demand the enemy's surrender, an act deemed benevolent by the Crusaders. In the Mamluks' eyes across from him that day, Leander saw only a sturdy determination to defend their homeland and a steadfast unity in their response. There, perhaps guided by the Almighty, he chucked his sword toward the Crusader line and gave himself over to the Mamluks.

"I wish to join the ranks of the Salihiyya, I wish to enroll with the Bahri," Leander said in their Turkish dialect that day, surrendering both of his bagged crossbows to the Mamluk amir in charge. Although spat upon and called a traitor by the Hospitaller accompanying him, Leander felt an unexplainable relief at that moment.

Leander shakes his head, thinking of the unlikelihood of it all. Why hadn't those Mamluk amirs executed him on the spot in La Forbie? Then al-Salih allowed him into the tibaq, where he somehow survived the four years of training in Cairo. He was lucky enough to be accepted into the Bahri, the most prestigious of the Mamluk regiments. His situation bordered on the impossible. It had all been fate.

"Sultan, I cannot deny that I am a defector, but I am no traitor," Leander said near the end of his questioning, the moment al-Salih decided Leander's destiny. "I feel there is a difference. Through my work as a translator, I was able to observe events in the Levant—at levels both high and low—long enough for the unsavory actions of my people to peck away at my soul."

Leander put his hand over his heart. "Before La Forbie, I could feel God summoning me, prodding me to make a change. And I heeded His call."

The sultan looked him over carefully. Eventually, he set his tired eyes hard upon Leander's. "A swift execution will be yours if I suspect even a speck of infidelity."

"I understand."

"You would serve me loyally?"

"Yes. Of course. Until the end."

CHAPTER 26

Leander

Gilan Gharb Valley, western Persia

November 16, 1257

They near the ridge, the vaulted spine of mountain to their east trimmed in dark bands of ancient sediment. Duyal lowers his right arm to his side three times in signal. Leander and Singer slow their pace, silently placing each step so as not to scuff a rock or snap a twig on their final downhill stretch.

The team has lived off the land the past few moons, moving from cave to cave, always staying a safe distance from the westward-encroaching Mongols. Low light was for reconnaissance; daylight for sleep and log writing; night for longer movements.

As the Mongol force grew and the team's proximity to the enemy shrunk, the Mamluks' scant assistance from the populace dried up. They often went to sleep hungry if Singer's traps and snares were empty, or when they spotted no game to shoot on their way back to camp. Two days ago, they snatched a stray sheep that had wandered from the giant Mongol flock. But dinner was mostly birds and the odd varmint. None complained, accustomed to such.

Leander stops to check their rear, his eyes probing the sharp outcroppings, boulders, and scrubland. All still.

At the hill bottom, they halt. Each man rotates his sword belt, so that his scabbard rests upon his buttocks. Leander slides his crossbow to his back. From the native grass and creepers about them, they refresh the plant material placed in their headbands and the wool loops that are sewn into the shoulders and backside of their cloaks. They pull silken covers over their faces, pale-colored pieces cut from their turbans and worn around their necks.

Duyal checks his men with a pensive squint and subtle nod, approving their camouflage efforts. With that affirmation, a familiar calm falls over Leander, one his mentor has instilled since their first action together, years ago in Damietta.

Duyal turns to confirm the location of the sun at their backs. They sneak toward a vegetated gap in the ridge. Near the top, the men sling their bows and tighten straps so that both weapons and quivers rest atop their shoulders. They crawl over the crest, amid the rock and grassy hummocks. On the forward side of the slope, they pause, taking in all about them.

In the expansive valley below, the Mongol camp bustles. Leander ignores it, concentrating on his commander, Duyal. The amir sweeps his hand slowly to direct both Singer and Leander to the bushes downslope. They low-crawl, each man inching toward the same bush he crawled into three days past. Together, these spots afford them a view along every sector of the basin.

Nestling into his cedar, Leander breathes a cautious sigh of relief. He turns to see that his brothers, too, have found their sanctuaries, the trio screened from Mongol eyes by the foliage about them and the blinding sun shining at their backs.

In the vast Gilan Gharb Valley below, droves of Tartars stretch across the lush flat. Over the past two weeks, the Mongol army has grown from one to fourteen *mingan*, nearly fourteen-thousand men. Leander begins to count the battalion standards, the colors of the enemy units. Thirty one. Hulegu's force has more than doubled in just days. The Mongols are now triple the size of the Egyptian army—that is, when Cairo's units were unified as one, her Mamluks not divided and scattered about the realm.

In one corner of the valley floor, flocks of sheep and goats graze. Abundant meat to feed the enemy. In the adjacent section, fully one third of the valley floor, thousands of stout ponies feed on the best of the vegetation, the lush grass nurtured by a late rainy season. Each Mongol brings three to four ponies, as success on the battlefield for a cavalry army requires fresh-legged remounts, vital in outmaneuvering foes.

Oxen-towed carts wobble their way down the rugged slope opposite them. Lashed in sections upon the wagon beds are a variety of catapult parts, those weapons previously employed to batter the Persians' mountain fortresses. At the bottom, Chinese engineers direct the serviceable pieces into columns of like machines, already staged. They point broken siege craft toward repair crews, who busy themselves fixing wheels and replacing frayed tension ropes and other components. A dozen more pieces have arrived since the last time the team counted. Leander drills into memory the quantity of each type.

From the northeast, camel loads also lurch their way downhill, carrying booty seized from the recently-conquered Assassins. From the south, incoming caravans stretch to the horizon—more camels loaded with food and materials to support the army's auxiliaries. Oxen pull burlap-covered carts, the trailers jostling arrows, spare wheels, sword blades, and every other imaginable implement of war. Leander is astounded by the abundance in the Mongol supply line. The invaders want for nothing.

Cream-colored felted shelters, Mongol gers, dot the periphery of the camp. The Black Tartars organize their hooches by individual *tumens*, corps of ten thousand men. Their lodgings form concentric circles, the khan's larger shelter placed in the center, like the carpel of some deadly flower. His soldiers' gers fill the perimeter rings like petals. Collectively, the gers decorate the gigantic field like a border of lethal daisies in a tidy garden of death.

In front of some gers wave the *sulde*, the Mongol spirit banners. Each copper-wrapped spike is ornamented with a thick clump of black horsehair and represents the bravest of warriors from the various units, both long and recently dead. The tufts of knotted ponytail catch an upsurge of wind and undulate as one. The hair from the dead warriors' ponies provides motivation and the spiritual presence of the deceased warriors for those living as another battle looms.

The opposite rim of stone stretches in tans and browns, north to south, as far as the eye can see. Above the rim, the last of the Zagros Mountains loom far to the east, the flat-topped crowns bejeweled with patches of snow. The distant pillars of eroded rock appear as rows of camel's teeth, brown and rounded and shadowed dark. At the camel's jawline, piles of scree mound in funnel-shaped formations, as if an assemblage of hour glasses concur that time has somehow expired. For whom? Leander wonders.

The team watches the Mongols' preparations through the late afternoon until the shadows creep midway up the facing ridge.

Leander thinks of Mother Cairo, its bountiful souk and river walks and white-blocked citadels. Some of his closest friends and their families are still there. He looks down, imagining the full force of the Tartars and the equipment below launched at the beautiful town.

He ponders if Qutuz has submitted to Mongol rule. Does the vicegerent have any idea about the existence of this valley of weapons and men that will likely be hurled against Cairo if he defies the Black Tartars? Surely Qutuz has no comprehension of how well-supplied the Mongols are.

Duyal has seen enough. He squeaks like a mouse, signaling the others that it is time to move out. They ease out of their bushes and slither over the peak. With the sun setting in their faces, they silently make their way back westward to camp, increasing their speed every hill away from the Mongol's valley.

Leander scopes the pathway. Last moon, he found a lost Mongol saddlebag on the trail. In the bag was dried meat, but also a tunic made from the finest grade of silk that Leander had ever seen.

Singer now wears the tunic. Identical undergarments were probably distributed to many warriors from the goods secured during the Mongol conquests in Northern China. The material dries almost instantly, keeping one warm in the desert cold and cool in the summer heat. Yet comfort is not the Tartars' primary reason for wearing the tunic. "This grade of silk is strong enough to follow an arrowhead into a man's body without tearing. A mate can then pull the arrow clean out without tearing flesh," Singer said.

Also in the Mongol's bag was a more sobering find—several gold coins, apparently souvenirs, newly-minted by the aged Syrian Prince of Mosul. The dinars bore Hulegu's name. The inscription read: "Lord of the World." Leander frets, knowing that at least one of the Syrian Princes closer to home has already decided who his new king will be.

Leander looks up from the ground.

Singer crouches, gazing northward. Duyal kneels, waiting for Leander to look his way. When he does, Duyal holds his fist to his front.

Leander halts. Duyal calmly points both fingers at his eyes, and then slowly moves his hand in a deliberate chopping movement, toward where Singer observes. He hand signals twelve hundred paces.

Two specs—Mongol watchmen, Leander assumes—move along an opposite finger just west of their position.

Duyal points over his shoulder to the draw below them. Leander nods. The three Mamluks sneak down the hill out of Mongol view and hearing.

"We will overtake them to the west, using the cover of this hill," Duyal says. "We will then sneak over and set up a hasty ambush." He points to Leander. "You will take out the one whom you assess to be the junior. Singer and I will snatch the senior."

They stay to the goat trail bottom, covering the ground quickly, silently.

Once well past the presumed progress of the Mongol watchmen, Duyal veers right toward a cluster of cedars choking a saddle in the ridge. His mates take a knee and turn to Leander.

Leander slips from under his crossbow's strap. He engages the trigger and moves the roller nut backward into firing position. The nut spring clicks its approval. He puts his boot through the stirrup at the weapon's tip. With knee braced outside the tiller, he pulls back the thick hemp, securing the string up and over the top of the roller nut.

Leander flips open his quiver. Figuring the Mongols are wearing armor, he pulls a square-headed bolt from the case, a tip known to pierce both hardened leather and metal scales. He loads it and then moves his right hand along the stock of his weapon, leaving it underneath the trigger assembly to act as a safety. He takes a deep breath. "Allah be with us." He pulls two more bolts from the quiver and stages them in his left hand.

They creep over where the cedars mark the crest and lie among the spent needles. No sign of the Tartars.

Duyal points to a flat rock midway down the slope. Leander nods.

Leander creeps to the large slab and lies upon its downward sloping face. He tries to force a calm in his breathing.

Where are the two Mongols? He worries that the pair increased their pace and passed farther west. Or perhaps they settled into an observation post back east among the rocks. Could the enemy have seen Duyal's team and be laying a trap of their own?

Low voices in the foreign tongue of enemy sound from the east. He sees nothing. Leander shifts his body to the right. He slips the hood over his head and orients his body toward the two shooting lanes offered. He drops his glove in a wide cranny and nestles the foregrip of his weapon on this rock cradle to stabilize it. He flips up his sight and slinks backward to better hide himself. He straightens one of the copper flights, the metal fletching on his loaded bolt, while his eyes search for the enemy.

Two figures emerge in the faint light, swathed in the black armor of the enemy. Both appear to be troopers. Maybe the first is older, more senior. The second looks at his feet as he clambers, carrying his strung recurve over his shoulder by the ear. Leander surmises that they should cross his front from right to left at one hundred fifty feet.

The Mongols stay their course. Closer they come. Leander moves his hand atop his weapon's worn trigger, where the surface is rubbed shiny-smooth. The enemy chat as they walk, as if strolling in the safety of their own camp.

Leander edges right to square himself on the best of his available shooting lanes. He settles in behind the stock of his weapon. When the two Mongols approach the opening, he puts the tip of the copper flight on the head of the second man. He waits until he can make out the rivets on the Tartar's cone-shaped helmet and the hardened leather piece that protects the Mongol's ears.

Leander grimaces, preferring frontal shots.

Concentrate. Concentrate. He sighs the air from his lungs, the flight now resting on the ear of the trailing man. He slowly squeezes the trigger device.

Twang. Thump.

The hissing missile strikes the Mongol just beneath the leather earpiece of his helmet. The Mongol drops in a heap.

The surviving man looks back as he hears the clump behind him and the clamor of his mate's bow upon the rocks.

Duyal rushes past Leander with Singer on his heels. The Mongol turns to see them. He runs back to the east along the bottom, with the Mamluks gaining. Leander kisses Gamila on the stock and sprints over to help, angling his pursuit to intercept him.

Duyal arrives first, tackling the Mongol and wrestling him to the ground. Singer snatches a fistful of dark hair and blurts some phrase in the Mongol's Altaic tongue. The squirming man shouts.

Singer drops to his butt and wraps an arm around the Mongol's throat. Singer squeezes the enemy's neck in the vee of his arm. Leander arrives as Duyal buries his armpit across the man's shins.

As rehearsed countless times, Leander digs into his pocket for his hide wraps and a leather glove.

The Mongol slumps, his eyes rolling to the back of his head. Leander pounces, pulling the Mongol's arms behind his back and cinching his hands at the wrists. Leander pries open the man's mouth and jams his glove deeply into the cavity. Singer binds the man's ankles.

Leander looks over his shoulder to ensure that the first Mongol he shot is truly dead. Leander looks up to his amir.

"Back over our hill," Duyal says.

Leander grabs the tied man under one armpit. Singer swoops under the other. They run uphill, the heels of their captive dragging behind them.

Halfway up the hill, the man begins moving his head side to side, slowly regaining consciousness. Duyal is ready for this. Singer and Leander push the squirming Tartar to the ground. Duyal punches the Mongol twice in the head, putting him out again.

Once over the crest, they dump the enemy behind a rock and pull him to a seated position against it. The Mongol flounders. Feeling his restraints, he seems resigned to the fact that he is powerless.

The Mongol's eyes flitter. Unable to breathe through his mouth with the glove wedged in it, he snorts through his nose. Blood runs from a slash above his eye.

The warrior is short, but thick in the shoulders and legs. His shoulder-length hair is oily. High-riding cheek bones are pronounced in his rounded face. He wears heavy wool pants and thick-soled riding boots. His Mongol overcoat bulges in the front with overlapping plates that are attached inside the thick cloth with rivets.

With a dagger in one hand, Duyal backhands the Mongol across the face. He turns to Singer. "Find out what unit he is with, how many bows each man carries, and how many more Mongols are coming from the east."

Singer translates. The Mongol eyes the trio warily. Duyal raises his blade and glares at the enemy. He slowly pulls the glove from the Mongol's mouth.

The Mongol swallows painfully. He croaks a hate-filled reply.

"He is with one of Hulegu's light cavalry tumens. He says each man has two bows. And before long there will be a hundred thousand horsemen like him pillaging this whole region."

"He lies," Leander says.

The Mongol leers at Leander, perhaps grasping the Frank's doubt. The Tartar hisses more in his gruff language, seeming to grow more assured as he speaks. His eyes go to their faces and the sword hanging on Duyal's hip.

"The infidel says we are dead men," Singer says. "They will send a patrol to find us when he and his friend do not report back. Says he knows we are Mamluks and that unless we submit, thousands of Mongols, all braver than we are, will kill our brothers, just like they did the Assassins."

Duyal leans forward. "Ask him if the Mongols in the black armor we saw last week in the valley were those of the Mongol Commander Baiju. And who were the Christians who rode with him?"

The Mongol speaks.

"He said it was Baiju with the Georgian vanguard," Singer says. "Thousands more from Georgia are coming, too. As Genghis Khan envisioned, the Mongols will rule all of the desert country, clear to the sea. The whole world."

The Mongol laughs, seeing the look on Leander's face.

"Ask when Hulegu plans to attack Syria and Egypt," Duyal says evenly.

Singer does so. The Mongol yells some obscenity and spits in Singer's face.

Leander lunges at the Tartar. He pins the man's head against the rock to his back in a tight grip on the nomad's throat.

The Mongol's eyes glass over. He smiles peacefully.

Duyal places his hand on Leander's forearm. Leander gradually releases.

The Mongol speaks solemnly, exposing small yellow teeth and dark gums as he utters the foreign words. He ends his dialogue with a sincere nodding of his head and a tilt of his chin in Duyal's direction.

"*Khangalttai*." ("Enough.") Singer says, looking away from the Mongol. "We will get no more from him."

"Where do they go next?" Leander asks.

"Baghdad."

Duyal and Singer exchange a glance.

The spiritual center of the Middle East. Leander considers whether or not the haughty caliph there will be wise enough to submit. His army is tiny compared to the enemy horde in the valley. Or might Muslim allies be on their way to save him?

"What else did he say?" Duyal asks.

"He said go ahead and kill him," Singer says. "He will die knowing his people will be victorious, unstoppable. The

Mongols will enjoy eating our Arabians. Our white coats will be soaked red in our own blood."

"Why did he nod at me?" Duyal asks.

Singer looks up to Duyal. "He said his father killed our fathers on the Kalka River Valley in 1223. And that a dozen years after, his tumen had their way with our Kipchak mothers and sisters."

Duyal springs from his knees as if shot from a catapult. He grabs the Mongol by the ears. He bangs the Tartar's head against the rock. The dull thump of skull on stone.

He rears back and slams the head more vigorously, the sound now reminiscent of the pumpkins Leander smashed upon rocks at his deer blinds in France. Singer and Leander step aside.

Duyal roars, his third hit splitting the Mongol's head in pieces. Gray matter splatters Duyal's forearms. He continues pounding until the skull becomes a mash of wet, folded meat. Soon, only Duyal's palms mash into the rock, the stone now slick with the Tartar's blood.

Leander rips his mentor backward. "No more! He is finished!"

Exhausted, Duyal falls back with the corpse in his lap, the mangled ears still firmly in his grip. He looks to his mates and then to the gore in his hands. He flings the Mongol aside and rises. "Go back over and fetch the other mongrel. We need to get him away from wherever their watch station was. Search him for anything useful."

He wipes a bloodied wrist across his chin. He kicks the dead man in the chest. "Dump him right here with his friend. The hyenas will have a feed tonight."

Leander and Singer unsheathe their swords and head north over the hill. In the crotch of the ridge, they stop and listen, their eyes to the darkening hills.

Detecting nothing, they move down the slope.

Leander looks back. "What exactly happened to Duyal's tower on the Volga?" Leander whispers.

"Slaughtered," Singer says. "The Tartars killed his parents and uncle. They raped his cousin. His younger brother was impressed into Mongol service like me. Most survivors of fighting age were sold into slavery."

They walk along in silence, aiming for the crumpled Tartar.

"Duyal never told us. I do not think any in his old amirate knew this."

"You do now," Singer says. "Duyal's situation is not unique among us."

"I know. Did Duyal witness this butchery?"

"No, his uncle made Duyal and his brother hide when the Mongols attacked."

"I cannot see Duyal obeying that command."

"I am sure he regrets it."

Leander sighs. "Well, doing so preserved him. One thirteen-year-old lad was not going to save their tribe."

Singer stops. He kicks the dead Mongol in the leg. He listens in the silence and looks closely atop the ridge. "At that age on the steppe, a boy is on the verge of becoming a warrior. In Duyal's eyes, he was already a man."

"But he was still a boy, just doing what he was told."

"I doubt you could convince him of that."

CHAPTER 27

Cenk

Cairo, Egypt

January 20, 1258

Cenk pushes open the door and stumbles across the stoop. He sheds his overcoat.

His wife and daughter turn from the basin, where they wash dishes by candlelight.

He grunts an incoherent greeting and they turn back to their work.

"You prepare a feed?" he slurs, grabbing a skin of wine from his rack and ceramic cup from a shelf. He takes both with him to the table.

"We have had our meal already," Fidan says, drying her hands. She keeps her back to him.

He pours a full cup and leans his elbows on the table. He runs his fingers through his greasy hair and beard.

She goes around the corner to the shelf beside her clay oven and tears him a chunk of barley loaf, placing it on his bronze plate. She stirs the black pot hanging over the smoldering coals and plops two scoops of *Molokhia*, traditional rabbit stew, onto the engraved metal. She smacks the ladle on the side of her kettle, dislodging the overcooked Jute stuck to the wood.

She pushes the dish in front of him. Standing at the table with her hands resting on her hips, his wife glares at his mug and then down at him in disgust. "You decided to come home tonight?"

He looks up through bushy eyebrows. "We worked into the evening yesterday. I stayed in my chamber at the citadel, knowing today would start early. I do not own my time anymore. Qutuz needed me."

Inci frowns and goes to her room.

Fidan watches her daughter leave. "You have said the same for over seven years now, since Mansura. Back then it was Aybeg and the invading Franj. Then the Bahri. Now, another enemy. You have a daughter who needs you, too."

He scowls. "Our empire is facing many threats. We are in dire circumstances."

"It is always dire circumstances. You keep drinking that wine and your health will be in dire circumstances, too."

He throws his cup at the fireplace. "Hold your words, insolent woman!"

While he has not struck her in more than ten years, he sees the fear from those days return to her face. She turns to the wine splattered across the face of her fireplace. She withdraws to the hearth and removes the kettle from its hook.

Eventually, she meets his eyes. "You have a family as well as your duty. We understand your obligations, but the other amirs come home to their wives and kids when not on campaign."

He stands, wobbling a little, catching himself on the back of the chair. "Some of the other amirs shirk their responsibilities. And none other than Tarkhan and I serve the vicegerent directly. Most amirs do not fully comprehend all that Egypt faces." He looks with regret to the pool of wine and broken clay in the corner of the hearth. He wishes he had not wasted his wine.

He sits and tries to slow his breath to calm his anger, a method learned from Aybeg to center himself before battle. Cenk found the breathing technique helpful a decade past in controlling his rage at home, perhaps saving his marriage then.

In time, he speaks with a forced civility. "I have served three sultans now. I am sure Qutuz will be the fourth. Aybeg's son, al-Mansur Ali," he grimaces. "All in the citadel know that the sixteen-year-old is not up to the task of ruling as sultan. Qutuz is running the empire. That means *I* am running the empire." He makes a fist. "Do you not understand? None of the prior sultans I have attended faced a greater challenge than Qutuz does now. None of them."

"But why do the heaviest of loads always seem to fall on your shoulders?"

He raises his palms. "I am a horseman. I am not even suited for this work. I do not ask for this."

"And neither do Inci and I." Her eyes beg.

Her constant demands on him are as a bellows to the furnace of anger in his gut.

Spoiled . . . selfish . . . bitch.

His anger rises from his belly. He feels the upsurge of heat to his neck. He grits his teeth and clenches and unclenches the fist of his sword hand. He tries to subdue the eruption that the wine and stress and frustration arouse.

He snarls. "I know, I know. I should have withdrawn from this service when I had the chance in 1250, once the Crusaders departed. Left these worries to others. We would be living by the sea with few cares. But things do not always work out as we plan."

"The promotion from Aybeg," she says meekly.

"I was ready to leave the life of a soldier. But when my sultan says I am needed. . ."

She shakes her head.

He fumes. "And how has this really affected you?" He stands.

Fidan takes a step back.

"You and Inci live in Cairo's best quarter. You have fine rugs and a kitchen the other women envy. Enough coin that you are never in need."

He softens for a moment at the thought of his murdered friend Aybeg, a blood brother from his Khushdash. "Before I brought you into my house, you were a miserable Kipchak slave, eating rats on the steppe," Cenk says. "In rags. Your tower destroyed, nothing to your name."

Fidan begins to weep.

He feels no sympathy for her distress. He walks around the table. "For years it has been my blood and my sweat that have given you this high living. You forget the pain of hunger and the fear of invaders arriving over the horizon."

He draws back to backhand her. She cowers, holding her hand across her eyes to shield against the cuff she expects.

"So now, with enemies threatening and your husband laboring by candlelight to plan another defense of Cairo, you somehow feel neglected?"

Mother of his child or no, Cenk glowers with revulsion at this needy woman. "Your drunkard of a husband, so inattentive of his wife, is one of the few amirs charged with formulating a design to save the empire. And an amir such as this should tolerate the mewling of a pampered woman?"

He pulls another wine skin from the rack. He takes a long drag from it, wiping a sleeve across his mouth. "Do you know that if Qutuz, Tarkhan, and I fail in our policy and its execution, that the Mongols will raze this home? What do you think the aggressors would do to your precious daughter?"

Fidan wipes a tear from her cheek and looks away.

"And after being raped, you will be slaughtered with the others. Or, if you are lucky, put back on the slave block. Or, if you flee beforehand, you will be living under a camelhide tent in the scrubland, wishing you were dead."

He puts his foot atop a chair. "Or, if the Mongols dither, it may well be Baybars and al-Mughith with his army from Transjordan here first. We were fortunate to have beaten them back from al-Salihiyya."

He paces. "They will be back. And how do you think Baybars would treat us Muizziyya and our families if he takes power? Think he has forgotten that we beheaded his old tutor, Aqtay?"

Inci is now standing behind a support beam just outside the kitchen, her eyes puffy and red.

He addresses his daughter with lifted chin. "And the Crusaders. They smile from their fortresses, enjoying the fact that Muslims kill Muslims—and that a gigantic Mongol army, led by Hulegu, a man with a Christian mother and thousands of Christian allies, approaches from the east. The Crusaders would love to swoop in and thrash whichever weakened army prevails."

He grinds his molars, his jaw muscles rippling the sides of his dark beard. "And while you coddled women concern yourselves with extra honey for your pantry and finer dishes to match those of the other wives, the Mongols trounce Mesopotamia. They likely put the caliph in Baghdad to the sword. This is how well the Mongols tolerate Islam!" He swings his hand, knocking the metal plate from the table.

Cenk turns back to his wife. "Where do you think the Mongols will go from there? And you hound me on the time I spend, on how hard I work, to save this city and the empire my patrons built?!"

He walks toward her with fists clenched.

Inci runs in, stands between them. "Leave her alone. She has done nothing to you!"

His daughter. Having been born and raised in complete placidity and the abundant serenity which is Cairo, perhaps her sins are at least understandable. She may be a gifted student, but she is just young and ignorant.

He closes his eyes and belches up a mouthful of sour bile. He swallows it slowly, allowing it to burn his throat, savoring the pain he knows he deserves.

He walks to the entry, grabs his cloak, opens the door, and buries his forehead on the edge of the timber until the drunkenness allows him to feel the delayed ache.

He speaks into the door, his words calm, but muffled. He recites a line Amir Turkmani used to say. "The world is composed mostly of useless sheep. Amid them, a few shepherds and herding dogs are tasked to lead and protect the mindless flock from the hungry wolves and jackals."

He lifts his head and leans his shoulder against the door. "I do not expect you two to fight the wolves, but Cairo does not need you distracting one of its guardians. She does not need you whipping the herd dogs."

Mother and daughter hold each other.

Cenk frowns. "Whether you realize it or not, Allah—not just the sultan—has entrusted me with this awful chore. Not just preserving our lands from the infidels, but also shielding His religion from the menace who attempts to diminish it."

He snatches his wineskin from the table and stares at the pathetic creatures before him. The room spins. He slams the door behind him.

CHAPTER 28

Leander

Baghdad, Mesopotamia

February 9, 1258

The Mongols are besieging Baghdad. The heart of ageless Mesopotamia bleeds; its soul mourns.

On blistered feet, Leander snakes between the ruins of half-buried foundation blocks, thatched roofs, and debris of every sort outside the walls near the *Kufa* Gate on the southwest edge of the city, in what was once the great business district there. He hurries, moving as swiftly and quietly as his feet will allow.

With the Mongols in firm control of every quarter outside of Baghdad's perimeter fortifications, Duyal leads his team toward the eastern ramparts. It is there that the Mongols now mass their forces for an attack to enter the city proper. And on this topic, Baybars was clear in his instructions, passed to the squad over a year ago in Damascus: "Do not linger in Persia. Anticipate the enemy's next move and stay in front of them. If the Mongols lay siege to Baghdad, you tally every man, each blade, every cart load. And log their capability—from counterweight trebuchets hurling giant block to the smallest catapult lobbing dead cats." Hence the trio of Mamluks makes their way to a place in the eastern sector where they might gain a view of the enemy and record the numbers of men and siege engines being assembled.

In the pale light, Leander looks up from his slippers to realize that he has again lost sight of the rounded pack on Singer's back. The familiar twinge of worry seeps through him.

A dark cloud covers the moon. Embers from the skeletons of charred shops and homes blot the landscape, pulsing in the dark. The bite of smoldering fumes stings his throat. Like a young boy unable to keep up with the long strides of his older brothers, Leander worries about becoming separated from his fellow Mamluks and getting lost in the murk with several enemy units still in the area. Hungry and tired, he curses himself for falling behind. He stumbles over a dead man's arm.

A haze of cloud sweeps past the waning crescent moon, still low on the eastern horizon. Remnants of vendor hooches reappear in the muted glow. Leander begins to jog, dodging rubble, bloated corpses bristling with arrows, and men with their turbaned heads lying where they fell from Mongol blades. He pants, drawing in and out of his lungs the smell of rotting flesh and shit from those misfortunate ones who were disemboweled by the Mongol attackers.

Formerly known as *Madīnat al-Salām*, Arabic for "City of Peace," Baghdad is now a city at war. Leander doubts Mesopotamia has ever been assaulted like this in its long history.

The Third Caliphate rulers—the descendants of Abbas, one of Mohammad's uncles—made Baghdad the capital of the Abbasid Caliphate. Home to the caliphs for over five hundred years, the royals selected the city's location because of its favorable links to trade routes, pleasant climate, proximity to water, and terrain suitable for fortification. Baghdad thrived, becoming fertile ground for culture and knowledge.

For centuries, riches from the Muslim world and beyond flooded into the four gates of "the round city." The border walls were spherical like a wagon wheel, with fine roads appearing as spokes. The caliphs poured their abundant gold into building schools, mosques, churches, and even public gardens.

Travelers visited Baghdad to soak in lavish baths and shop in bazaars overflowing with exotic goods. Merchandise spilled in from all directions, much of it on the back of camels, merging on the Khurasan Road, or floated in from both the Tigris and Euphrates rivers on papyrus-hulled skiffs and barges.

A visitor strolling down any of the ancient city's marketplaces found goods on silk-covered displays from as far away as China and India sitting beside wares from Armenia and Egypt. In many quarters outside the city gates, ornate fountains splayed water into clean pools, celebrating the splendid wealth and knowledge of the world's most impressive metropolis. Yet the bounty and splendor once found beyond the walls are now reduced to flames and wreckage by the Mongol invaders.

And who ultimately bears the responsibility for the carnage along Baghdad's fringes? Leander thinks one man: the caliph, al-Mustasim Billah, successor to the Prophet Mohammad. Known among the Mamluks to be a gutless man, al-Mustasim has ruled Baghdad for the past sixteen years with an ego that personifies the incredible capital he governs. Perhaps the Franj best described him as an Islamic blend of monarch and pope.

Yet while this thirty-seventh caliph remains the most influential secular ruler in the Muslim world and granted his religious legitimacy to the various rulers in the realm, the man wields little practical power in the Middle East. Known to care more about his poems and the soft life in the city than truly defending Islam, the caliph keeps only a small army and his city's walls have fallen into gross disrepair. The Abbasids' political power and military muscle are things of the distant past. The caliph is now mostly a figurehead, relevant only because he is an heir of Islamic orthodoxy and heads a city which has no rivals in cultural greatness. Or had, that is.

Duyal's team snatched a pair of departing emissaries last week. From the envoys, Leander discovered that years ago, the Great Khan, Mongke, insisted that in addition to the annual tribute al-Mustasim paid, the caliph was obliged to provide military support for the Mongol's approaching campaign in Persia. The Caliph ignored this request and Mongke's earlier call for the caliph to appear in person at the Mongol capital in Karakorum.

Once the mountain strongholds in Persia fell under Mongol heel, Mongke's brother, Hulegu, demanded al-Mustasim's unconditional surrender. The caliph also dismissed this mandate. Instead, al-Mustasim sought military support from al-Nasir of Damascus and the other princes in the realm. So far, these efforts to forge an alliance against the invaders have gone unanswered.

For twelve days now, Leander saw firsthand how Hulegu responded to the caliph's defiance of the Great Khan. Combing the city edges and hiding as close to the city's protective walls as was practical, Duyal's team surveyed Mongol tactics and equipment. They changed observation locations and attire each day. One day they wore the rags of a peasant, the next they were in the stolen garb of merchants.

For the sake of the mission, the Mamluks posed as Christians, Leander teaching Duyal and Singer verses from the bible to memorize and utter, when grilled by the enemy. Only luck, or perhaps Allah's will, allowed them to elude capture while posing in this fake status.

Yet always they wore the Christian crosses about their necks. These they pulled from under the tunics of dead Mesopotamians, civilians who were in the wrong place at the wrong time; people who did not know that displaying the symbol of their religion atop their garments would mark them as sheep to be spared. Leander was unsure if Hulegu pardoned Christians to appease his auxiliaries of the same faith, or because his mother and his favorite wife were Nestorian Christians. Perhaps both.

The topography presented a formidable and expected challenge. While Duyal's team had the mountain elevations in Persia to hide in and view from, the terrain surrounding Baghdad was an enormous alluvial plain, smooth as Bedouin flat bread.

Since first observing Hulegu's army three moons past in the Gilan Gharb Valley in Persia, Leander now saw that the Tartar army had swollen from fourteen thousand to over forty thousand. Another fifty thousand Armenians and Georgians, approaching from the northwest, joined them. While the Tigris and Euphrates had historically been effective obstacles, the Mongols and their allies moved easily across both rivers on a string of pontoon boat bridges.

On news of the Mongols' advance, most of the residents and merchants on the outskirts of Baghdad fled. As if planned by Hulegu himself, thousands of locals sought protection inside the high block walls. Soon the city was overfilled with refugees. "The Mongols did the same with the Rus settlements twenty years past, driving them like sheep into a pen," Singer said. "More Baghdadi civilians trapped inside the fortification means more mouths to feed and a speedy gobbling of limited stores. An otherwise long siege then turns into a short one. The Tartars do not need a fight to feel victorious. Conquest without a single mangonel deployed, or without a single arrow fired, is fine with them."

Mongol commanders mixed Armenian and Georgian envoys in among local shopkeepers and house matrons with children, and snuck these infiltrators through the gates. Their mission was to seek out Christians and other minorities and promise them their lives and other favors, in return for help in sowing division among the populace and divulging information on local defenses.

The scant defenses inside Baghdad's walls are all that the caliph has left. Engineers long ago built Baghdad's elaborate dike system to catch and disperse precious water from both the Tigris and Euphrates deltas while controlling the floods from the Tigris's tributaries to the north and east. When the caliph sent his army of twenty thousand cavalry to engage the enemy, the Mongol horde quickly destroyed much of the Tigris River dike system, which flooded the Muslim camp. Most of the caliph's soldiers fled or drowned. The Tartars advanced from both sides of the Tigris in the predawn darkness, sniping with accurate bowshot the Mesopotamians who resisted, and those floundering in the water.

With most of the caliph's army dead or scattered, the Mongols and their allies descended upon the four roads that ran toward the city center. Accustomed to open spaces and hating all structures other than the felt-walled gers of their steppe land, the invaders razed nearly every building outside the city bulwarks. They slashed at the vaulted arcades that lined the streets, ripping down by hand post-and-beam shade structures. Papyrus reed and mud-built huts outside the city walls were stomped by hooves.

For days, Leander and team watched the Tartars dismantle Baghdad's periphery. The Mongols stripped walls, streets, and canals of every stone and block. For the bigger slabs of rock, they attached grappling hooks to their oxen rigs. In two days, decorative bazaars that had served the people for ages were reduced to rubbish piles.

With metal bars and saws, the Mongols pried apart debris and cut wood to desired lengths, chucking this lumber into cart beds. When there were no more free oxen to pull the carts, the Tartars yoked captured Mesopotamians into eight-man teams, often whipping the locals into cooperation.

Towering date palms, precious trees nourished by the Baghdadis for centuries, were chopped down by axe. The Mongols cut some trunks to size, while they left other palms whole, harnessing them with chains to their camels.

This work was not the mindless destruction of barbarians, but rather the methodical work of ants. Late into the evenings, this material clapped and scraped and jumbled down the ancient roads. After clearing the outskirts' four main arteries, the Mongols then turned to the smaller roads that branched out from the primary streets, similarly disassembling the community squares and houses with the same machine-like efficiency. In two days, the once-gorgeous fringes of Baghdad were reduced to ruins.

Wagons filled with this material merged alongside carts loaded with artillery components. These groaned and jostled to each section of wall, where crews offloaded the payloads and quickly made the artillery pieces war-ready.

All the while, thousands of men dug an extensive ditch along the city's eastern wall, the section of fortification which the Mongol sappers and Chinese engineers had likely identified as the most vulnerable of the caliph's bulwarks, Leander reasoned. All day and night, one heard the clanks of shovels and picks on rock and the grunt of oxen hauling fill from the giant dugout to the earthen rampart they mounded on the Mesopotamian side.

With the ditch dug and the catapults ready, the Mongols began their bombardment. Dozens of catapults hurled projectile after projectile over the walls. The Tartars hollowed out the gathered palm trees, filled them with charcoal or fiery naft, and then launched the flaming hulks.

From inside the walls came the distant crash of rock through rooftops and the cries from residents. Soldiers atop the battlements futilely employed their smaller counter batteries, usually without the range needed to affect the aggressors.

Ceaselessly, for a dozen days and even through the dark of night, the Mongols besieged Baghdad. Only in the last half day has Leander seen a lull in the launching of projectiles. Especially on the west and north sides, the catapult crews went silent. A few waiting impatiently for more rocks and other projectiles to arrive from the mountain country, but most units moved eastward toward their primary objective on that side of the wall.

Leander catches sight of Singer just ahead, bounding over a toppled pillar, Duyal farther out front, both wearing carpenter's garb and the leather slippers of the locals. They push along with the ease and fluidity of the Tigris to their east, instinctively hopping over crumbled walls, their feet silently feeling their way over shards of timber and pounded stone.

Leander trips over a log and curses. How is that his friends, men now in their mid-thirties, can move with the fresh legs of novices, while the younger Leander often has to test his steps on this uneven terrain to avoid injury, and the clatter which might alert the enemy?

Having lived their entire childhoods on the inhospitable steppe, both Duyal and Singer hunted, trapped, and fished to survive. No ground slowed them—not slippery rocks, thick swamps, or snow-covered ridges. Back then, it was kill or go hungry. Return with meat for the people of their Kipchak towers or be thrashed—or worse, shunned by the older warriors.

His teammates rarely turn around to see if he is near, expecting the younger man to keep up. Leander harbors no resentment toward them for this. Their old culture made them as rugged and independent-minded as they are. Their behavior is probably a sign of the confidence they have in him, whether justified or not.

Prior to his time with these Kipchaks, Leander had thought himself a fine stalker, a competent hunter and tracker, and a man who could hump a heavy pack with the best of them. Back in France as a squire—and even as a young Bahri opposing King Louis' Crusaders with Duyal's Amirate Three—Leander never fell out of a trudge or lagged on a patrol. Yet after living and fighting alongside Singer and Duyal, always in challenging terrain, he now knows that proficiency in these areas is relative. Leander considers himself a hard man, but these steppe warriors, his adopted brothers, are harder still. Leander has attempted to cover his perceived inadequacies these past months by shouldering more than his share of the menial tasks.

Even his language skills, the primary reason he was chosen for this assignment, have been of marginal use recently. While Leander is helpful in translating the Mesopotamian Arabic and Kurdish spoken in the Jazira, he understands little of the Mongolian dialects spoken by the enemy. Singer picks up this deficiency, recalling much from his time serving the Black Tartars as a teenager.

Leander springs over a low wall, and again the gap between him and his teammates grows. Losing sight of his mates, he hops atop a wall and scans.

The distant whack of an axe on wood resounds somewhere in the southern district. Then the chink of hammer on splitting wedge into stone, closer to them in the north. Mongol work parties collect the last of the payload material nearby. Chinese voices in the distance. Some laughter. *Thump-whoosh.* The sound of a far-off catapult launched farther east.

"By Allah," he says. He has lost them. Singer and Duyal. Where are they? He takes what he hopes will be a more direct route to where his friends should reach, loping toward that intersection point. Approaching the wreckage of two adjoining homes, he hears a squeal. Perhaps he is mistaken. He halts.

"No, no!" A girl's voice? Male giggles and a jest cracked in the *Kartvelian* language of the Georgians.

Leander pushes aside his robe and slowly pulls his sword from its scabbard. Taking a wide course, he sneaks toward the voices. Closer, he quietly sheds his pack and crawls behind a short wall that bisects what remains of the mud-bricked homes. When only twenty paces from the scuffling, he takes a knee and listens.

"Get hold of her arms," the same Georgian voice says, laughing. "Turn her over. Pin her."

Leander slinks closer. He peeks above the wall.

A wide-shouldered man in tunic stands with his back to Leander, the man's trousers at his ankles. A young girls' white ass wriggles in the soldier's hands, her dress wadded under her armpits. Her torso is bent over at the waist atop an overturned table. The child claws at a smaller man on the other side of the table, a Georgian attempting to latch his arm about her head. Behind the soldiers, two broadswords lay atop their cuirasses.

Leander memorizes the ground from the wall to the men in one glimpse. He eases back down.

"By the time you restrain her, my scepter will be as limp as a spent tulip," the burly man chuckles.

Leander quietly vaults the wall and creeps behind the men, the Georgians' backs still to him. He cups his left hand over his right fist and swings his sword in stride at the nearest man.

The enemy's head bounces off the girl's back and thuds to the ground. Leander, with his sword raised again, elbows aside the headless goon. The other soldier releases his grasp on the child and looks up at Leander in horror. The child tumbles over the table edge and scrabbles away on hands and knees.

The Georgian's eyes flash to the sword lying atop his armor. Leander slashes diagonally across the man's collar bone. The man falls backward with a scream. As the soldier crumbles, Leander backswings across the man's neck and spins, looking for more enemy.

A shadow moves amid the rubble. Another Georgian? His comrades? His second hand goes back to the sword grip. Amid the gurgles from the dying rapist, Leander listens in the darkness. He eases back into a corner and waits. Perhaps it was nothing.

Convinced, he retrieves his pack and sits with his back against the wall. He calls to the girl.

"Come out. I will not hurt you. I am not the enemy," he says in the Arabic of the locals.

The girl peeks out from behind a slab of wood in the far corner. She looks at her fallen attackers with wide eyes and then to Leander's bloody weapon.

Leander sets aside his blade and sighs. "It is all right now. I will not hurt you. Why are you alone? Why did you not leave with the others?"

"My father is a scribe for the caliph," the girl says meekly. Maybe ten years old, she crawls out from behind the mass of wood. "Once the gates were closed, my parents could not come out." She straightens her dress that is torn at the neck.

"I am sorry," he says. She looks skinny. "When is the last time you ate?"

"Two days ago," she says.

Leander pulls a water skin and the last of his dried meat from his pack. He takes a swig of water and eats a small piece of meat. He squats. "Here," he pushes the food and drink to her. "It is good."

She shuffles forward in the dark. She brushes her hair from her swollen eyes and stands before him with both hands at her sides, her lip split and bleeding. Leander sits cross-legged across from her. "Go ahead," he says.

She sits on her knees a safe distance across from him and sips from his flask, her eyes never leaving him. She pulls a piece of meat from his pouch. "Thank you," she says, through a mouthful.

The crunch of stones under heel. Leander snatches his sword and stands to face those who approach. She runs back to her hiding place.

Once recognizing Singer and Duyal, Leander sits. "It is all right. They are my friends."

His mates eye the dead Georgians. The girl peeps around the edge of the slab and then stands before them.

Leander senses Duyal's impatience. Their mission is not to save little girls.

"I will not be long," Leander says. "Her father works for the caliph."

Duyal looks away.

Leander turns back to the child. "Before your parents were trapped inside, did they tell you what the caliph decided, what he told the Mongols?"

She looks at the Kipchaks and then back to the Frank. "My father said the caliph believed that God would not allow a horde of infidels to seize our city and that the people of Islam everywhere would rise and defend him, and us."

Duyal looks to Singer and shakes his head.

"Did your father tell you anything about the caliph's success in getting the other princes to join him?" Leander asks. "Do you know if Muslim reinforcements are coming here?"

"No," she says. "He does not tell me much about his work. Is not allowed to, I think."

"We understand."

Duyal motions with his thumb eastward. They must leave.

Leander stands. "Where will you go?" He asks her.

"I will wait for my parents to come out."

Leander feels pity for her. "Your parents would want you out of harm's way, would be pleased to know that you went far from here. Do you have friends or relatives away from the city?"

"My aunt lives west of here."

He rubs her shoulder. "I think your parents would be relieved to know that you went to this aunt. Things will likely get worse here, before they get better. You can come back to your mother and father when it is safer."

She looks up with sad eyes.

"We must go," Leander says. He ignores the grumble in his belly and shoves the pouch and flask toward her. "Here, ration it. Sorry I cannot help more."

She looks back to the dead Georgians and fights off the tears. "Thank you."

He shoulders his pack. "Allah be with you, treasured one."

CHAPTER 29

Leander

Baghdad

February 9, 1258

Leander pads through the mud, walking in Duyal's footsteps, Singer close behind him. They continue their eastward march, skirting the outside of Baghdad's southern wall in search of a secure place in one of the eastern quarters from which to observe the enemy.

The Mongol khans keep just enough artillery along the northern and western sections of wall to keep the Baghdadis' heads down on those parts of the two-mile wide city. The enemy has sent most of their mangonels, the smaller catapults that reinforced their larger counterweight trebuchets, to concentrate their fire on the eastern wall. It is near there that Duyal wishes to set up their next observation post.

The team moves unseen, the horns of a rising moon masked by clouds. They move quickly past the sprawl of ruin that was once the thriving *Baduraya* District, following the same two-tracked path that was recently churned to muck by the enemy's oxen pulling battle wagons and wheeled catapults.

The clank of hammer on steel echoes from quarters south and east. Leander tires of the racket. Under shade structures and lamp light, Chinese masons and locals pressed into service work day and night to split the more stubborn blocks and tall pillars from Baghdad's toppled structures into manageable sizes. Decorative columns, once erected to support majestic structures, are now cleaved to be loosed as missiles of demolition. The enemy focuses on acquiring denser payloads for their artillery—material that will not break apart upon contact with the fortification's sturdy walls.

Two groups of Mongols holler in the dark. The smack of punches landed.

Duyal raises his right arm with clenched fist. The trio freezes.

More enemy tussle in the next neighborhood.

Whistles pierce the dark. Five harsh blasts near them. The scrap ends gradually, some men now laughing. More cussing in the indecipherable language of the Chinese.

Duyal exhales in relief. Just another fistfight between catapult crews. He turns to his mates, the creases in his brow reflecting the burden of command. He chops a hand southward, signaling that he will steer them clear of the fracas.

These brawls erupt over the distribution of choice hunks of rubble, each trebuchet team eager to do its part in bringing down the city's buttresses. Hulegu's soldiers prove themselves keen to show the caliph what happens to vassals who rebel against the wishes of the Mongol khans. Baghdad's al-Mustasim is no less guilty in the enemies' eyes than is the Persian imam they pulverized just months earlier.

Duyal points east toward what the Baghdadi locals call the *Shabriya* Quarter, far off along the west bank of the mighty Tigris. A small mosque sits there, lonesome amid the wreckage, its characteristic minaret reaching toward the heavens in the distance.

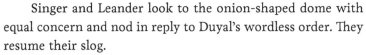

Singer and Leander look to the onion-shaped dome with equal concern and nod in reply to Duyal's wordless order. They resume their slog.

A northeastern breeze pushes thick smoke from the watchmen's fires into the team's faces, further evidence of more enemy occupying the eastern and southeastern districts. The smoke does little to cover the cloying stink of rot from dead Muslims, who were fighters and civilians alike. Festering gut piles from livestock lie scattered abundantly like excrement discharged from this giant army, this ravenous beast.

"*Belen baina*!" ("Ready!")

"*Neg ni! Khoyor! Gurav*!" ("One! Two! Three!")

These faint preparatory and executory commands from unseen Mongol crews on the lighter mangonels pierce the evening silence. Their shouts overlap from both the east and southeast. For days, the team has heard these same words over and over, the strange phrases about the only Mongolian Leander has learned.

A collective grunt from the Mongol crew. Leander does not require the light of day to understand the enemy's actions. Dozens of men launch their catapult into the night sky, the Black Tartars vigorously yanking downward in unison on the lanyards which dangle from the bracing arm of their traction trebuchets, powering the flight of their projectile.

The traction trebuchet is no more than a simple lever. The simultaneous tug from the crew rotates a sturdy swing arm set over a wooden axle, which heaves the payload from the sling on the opposite and longer end of the beam. Leander has counted over six dozen of these stationed around the walls of Baghdad.

Easy to operate and able to toss a variety of materials, these catapults can launch projectiles up to four hundred feet, depending on the catapult size, projectile type, and size of the crew. After some training from Chinese engineers, the Mongols are tasked with manning most of these smaller, less-complicated mangonels.

Whoosh. A payload flings into the darkness, whizzing through the night sky to batter the city walls.

Leander and his team continue toward the thickening smoke.

The groan of torsion ropes through block-and-tackle sing out in the murk. The creak of wooden beam on axle. Signature sounds of the Chinese loading one of their heavier pieces, the counterweight trebuchet.

"*Zhǔnbèi shū!*" ("Prepare to Loose!")

"*Shūsōng!*" ("Loose!")

A clink of metal on metal as the trigger device is released, followed by a heavy thump and the distinguishable roar of a large missile.

The crew working the counterweight trebuchets crank the winches which, aided by block-and-tackle, raise a stone-filled box. This heavy strongbox is attached to the shorter end of a beam. With this counterweight acting as stored energy, the Chinese then release this force via a trigger.

With its heavier beam and longer sling, this style of catapult flings bigger payloads farther than can the mangonels. A counterweight trebuchet throws large stones nearly eight hundred feet, often twice as far as the largest traction trebuchet can manage. This powerful seigecraft has one engineered purpose: to knock down fortress walls.

As this catapult's parts are under considerable pressure, operating one is dangerous work. Only a few men are needed to fire it, but the process is complicated and time-consuming. The crew must adjust the sling's release point to fine-tune the range and desired trajectory of the load. Leander has found that the Mongols leave the handling of these finicky catapults mostly to the artillery specialists, their Chinese allies.

The cloud breaks. The outline of the neighborhood mosque is now highlighted by moonlight. Leander eyes his team's destination. Its tower stands prominent and cylindrical, like a solitary tree that has somehow survived a violent hurricane. For some reason, the Mongols left only this mosque unscathed, yet Hulegu ordered all of the neighborhood churches saved.

Leander spots the tall basilica of one such cathedral across the Tigris. Only its cross-topped steeple breeches the horizon, defiant amid the obliteration. Its belfry appears similar to that of the cathedral of his old lord, Erard of Brienne, back home in the Kingdom of France.

Darkness sweeps across the landscape as clouds again blanket the sky, as if some invisible hand were tugging a giant curtain across the wasteland, leaving the Frank alone with his thoughts. Stifled memories from years on Erard's estate break free and flood into his mind.

When Leander was just a lowly squire in Ramerupt, he thought his French lord was a man second only to God Almighty in stature and honor. If Leander's father saw flaws in Erard, he said nothing of them. When Leander was ten years old—shortly after his mother died of the fever—his father sent him to serve at the noble's castle. There, Leander toiled as a vassal would and also received tutoring beneath the slate shingles of the castle's church.

He snorts. Erard. Time and perspective have permitted Leander to realize what the old geezer really was—nothing but a jealous man and a deficient social-climber from a minor branch of the Brienne family.

Lord Erard held no lands in Brienne and had little cause to take the name of "Brienne" for himself. His grandfather had truly ruled as Count of Brienne, but Erard was just Lord of Ramerupt, overseeing a domain that was modest compared to the possessions of more senior branches of the Brienne family. Lord Erard tried to enhance his prestige by referring to himself as "Erard of Brienne" and conveniently leaving out the humbler name of "Ramerupt."

Leander sensed that Erard yearned to be like his cousin, John, yet simply lacked his kin's stones and charisma. John ruled wide swathes of the Holy Land and married into wealth, while Erard proved himself to be just another petty Crusader.

Erard was a Franj without the battle skills and gumption to stay in the Levant. There, he might have won fame in combat and secured a fief where he could increase his prestige and fortune in God's land. Or, he might have died, receiving the ultimate Crusader glory as a martyr.

Having closed the distance to the mosque outside the eastern wall, Duyal takes a knee. Singer and Leander squat beside him.

"What do you think?" Duyal asks, surveying the top of the tower.

"Surely the pricks have someone up there," Leander says.

"For what—to watch their own attack?" Singer says. "To view the horizon for an approaching enemy whom they know will never arrive? The Mongols own the ground. They realize no Muslim army comes to rescue the city."

Duyal's lips purse. He rises and points them forward.

They circle the mosque, their eyes to the dark portals which disclose none of the open space inside the minaret. They approach the building from the east side.

Leander feels a tinge of unease. Something not quite right. A squad of Mongols could easily be hiding inside.

Duyal walks beneath the ornately-decorated stone archway. Then halts. Now concealed, he parts his cloak and draws his sword. His teammates do the same. Duyal pushes open the wrought iron gate just far enough to enter sideways.

They slip into the small courtyard and creep past the ablution fountain, where worshipers perform their ritual washing before prayer. The Mamluks stop before a pair of tall wooden doors left ajar, ancient and splintered, and engraved with Islamic verses. Duyal nudges them open with a creak. They enter the mosque.

The recessed blocks of the *mihrab*, the arched niche which positions the prayer-leader to face toward Mecca, sit undisturbed. As does the wooden *minbar*, the pulpit where the prayer leader delivers the Friday sermon.

Left of the minbar, Duyal finds the stone stairway leading to the minaret. He turns to Singer and opens his mouth as if to whisper.

Singer pops his chest and points his thumb back toward where they came.

Duyal nods. The pair are like husband and wife, knowing what the other is thinking and what the other will say, before words leave lips. Singer will cover the courtyard gate.

Duyal turns to Leander, his face quickly turning sober. "Assume we have company up there," he whispers.

"Aye," Leander says, firming his grasp on the grip of his sword. He takes a deep breath and falls in behind his amir. The two wind their way up the narrow passage, their steps noiseless upon the foot-worn stairs.

CHAPTER 30

Leander

Baghdad

February 9, 1258

Leander and Duyal slink up the minaret stairs. Rounding the last curve at the top, Duyal raises his blade and peers around the corner.

Leander grips his sword and grits his teeth in anticipation of a skirmish.

His commander steps forward at the crouch. Seeing nothing, he slowly lowers his weapon.

Leander closes his eyes and heaves a sigh. He follows Duyal into the circular chamber where during peaceful times, the muezzin chants his call to prayer, summoning believers to this mosque, outside of Baghdad's southeastern wall. They look through the latticed window, facing northeast. A bank of dark cloud still covers the moonlight at their backs.

The southwest catapults they passed have gone silent. Below, the sparks of a hundred small campfires dot the plain:

Mongol watchmen and squads just finishing their night stints lighting their cooking fires. The tiny blazes wave in the breeze.

Leander's thoughts return to the drafty cathedral of his past in Ramerupt. Those dozens of fluttering tapers, which lit the massive stone walls in Lord Erard's minster.

Another fleeting break in the clouds. His eyes return to the bell tower, the same church far across the Tigris that he spotted on their walk in. Bands of moonlight trundle across the shadowed flat for only seconds. Then the light is snuffed out like a candle by cloud.

He thumbs the cross hanging about his neck, his mind whirling back to a time spent under a similarly-fashioned spire back home when he was a Christian. He and twenty-four other pages, lads wearing the blue seal and yellow standing lion of their lord upon their chests, forced to sit on those cold pews, shivering.

Leander returns his blade to the scabbard and pulls his hands into the long arms of his worn tunic. He jams them under his pits in a useless attempt to ward off the biting chill.

The words of the priest, oft-repeated and impressionable upon the ears of ten-year-olds: "Keep thy faith strong and resolute throughout your life—and conduct thyself properly here—or dire consequences you will face upon death. Far, far below the earth."

The rippling flames from the pulpit wax light cast a ghoulish light across the abusive bastard's face as he described what would happen if the boys did not live a life acceptable to their Lord God—or more accurately, if the boys did not conform to the rules set by their keepers. The netherworld would be the young pages' terminus.

The reek of decaying bodies and vapors from Mongol fires linger in Leander's nostrils as he surveys the hellscape before them. Perhaps the priest was right. While Leander has somehow managed to stay above ground the last few months, Baghdad's devastated outskirts depict that ominous scene the priest foretold. If forced into a hell on earth, at least it is with the company of his brothers.

A drop of rain hits his head. Another. Leander looks up.

Drizzle pecks the roof. Heavier now, dripping in through the large gaps in the mud-slathered crown. Cracks, likely formed when an explosion rocked the town earlier. This, Leander figures, from Chinese sappers, diggers attempting to undermine the south and east walls with explosives from some unseen tunnel they burrowed.

Duyal pulls an oilskin from his pack. Leander finds a small bench along the opposite wall and sets it near the window, where the fewest trickles dribble upon the stone floor. They sit with the oilskin flopped atop their heads and shoulders, huddling in the dark. Only Leander shivers. The Kipchak appears unaffected, seemingly immune to misery, as always.

Beads of rainfall drum the roof and the skin over their heads, dampening the foreign voices and the occasional launching of distant catapults. The Mongols begin to shift their barrage of the wall farther east. The black cloud passes, replaced by a layer of thinning haze. The moonlight now gleams, gradually revealing the landscape outside the eastern wall below from left to right, as if Allah were slowly passing a glowing torch atop it.

The cream-colored gers of the invaders materialize, appearing as puffs of cotton in the eastern hills. Hundreds of shelters. The Mongol main camp. Rubble and moon-glimmered water materialize everywhere.

The distant residences, shops, and souks that once lined the *Nahr Buk* and *Kalwadha* Districts east of the Tigris are no more. The tops of the tallest date palms and jagged blocks from the ramparts of the old palace stick up like kelp and rock in a shallow ocean of desolation.

Shimmering water butts up to some sections of the city wall. The *Sarat* Canal, an essential component to the network of waterways that has drained the waters of the Euphrates into the Tigris for decades, is reduced to bits. Its ruins lie beneath the spread of river water. The *Basra* Gate, the southeast entrance to the city which normally opens to the Sarat waterway, stands with nearly half its massive blocks submerged.

The *Bassazim* and *Dajaj* Canals, whose elegant arches once graced the south and eastern parts of the round city are, too, underwater, their dikes at the Tigris destroyed by the invaders. In only three weeks, the Mongols have erased three hundred years of engineering work that long controlled the sister rivers' flows and irrigated the lands.

Where the flooding along the southeast wall ends, the encompassing ditch begins, its soil thrown high by the Mongols into a forbidding rampart. The defensive mangonels positioned atop the city walls by the Baghdadi defenders went silent days ago. Surely the caliph did not stock enough projectiles and repair parts to keep his catapults in action for the long term.

The breeze brings wisps of feathery cirrus cloud across the sky. The faintest glow of dawn begins to illuminate the east.

Hundreds of Mongol ponies emerge like spirits in the low light, hobbled mounts skip-jumping to feed in the short grass. The sounds of gear being staged and assembled under the cover of darkness can now be pinpointed to their individual workers.

Behind the dirt rampart, out of view of the Baghdadis, men erect nest and watchtower carts, wheeled assault covers, and wooden screens. Chinese engineers, with mallets and adze, repair damaged launching arms and rig other siege equipment.

A line of camels and ox-drawn carts approach on the westbound road that runs along the south side of the *Jafari* Canal, through the remains of the Nahr Buk District. The outline of a six-wheeled "cloud ladder" breaches the horizon, its hinged rungs halved during transit. Its armored compartment sways. Soon, the Mongols will erect the stowed ladder against the east wall and fill the windowed strongbox below with crossbowman, soldiers tasked with providing covering fire for those bold enough to scale the fortification.

Behind it, a "double hook cart" rambles, its pair of sickle-shaped claws reaching into the night like inverted hawk talons, outstretched to snatch an unsuspecting rodent. Shortly, the Chinese will deploy these hooks atop the fortification's blocks and whip a team of oxen into pulling the wall down.

"They bring forward the gear we saw them testing along the Persian border," Leander says.

"Aye," Duyal murmurs.

Two Mongol khans and their scribes stand at the road intersection just before the main bridge of boats on an outside bend of the Tigris. They direct the bigger loads over the crossing and keep appropriate spacing between all traffic. Before reaching the *Khorasan* Gate farther west, the carts meet more guides, who send the gear and catapult payloads to their desired positions along the deployment line, where the Mongols organize their forces for the assault.

Khans nearer the east wall point fingers and holler muffled orders. Brown-armored soldiers remove projectiles from large carts and load rock into slings. Mongol ants, constantly in motion, steadily at their duties.

Drivers of empty gear carts and unburdened camels exit the southern outskirts via the lower bridge. A cadre of flag-waving Mongols receives them, merging this one-way traffic with more unloaded wagons. Joined, this pack train grunts and stomps its way back eastward along the spoke that runs just north of the *Musa* Canal.

As darkness concedes to the coming daylight, Leander and Duyal scoot their bench back from the window, wary of the enemy catching sight of them. Leander pulls a papyrus sheet from his leather case. He finds a thin slab of wood leaning against the minaret's wall. He sets this across his thighs. Still able to peek over the ledge, he sketches the deployment of the Mongol forces and equipment, noting details and descriptions in small script.

Duyal slouches on the bench beside him and stares blankly ahead. While in Persia, his senior also recorded his observations on scroll, in case one version of their reports were damaged or captured. Yet since arriving in Mesopotamia, Duyal has shirked this important duty. Leander worries, unable to recall a time in years where his amir dodged any obligation.

"It is getting light. We must leave soon," Duyal says.

Leander stows his writing gear.

Bamboo shafts on oak stabilizers creak near the southeast wall. Dozens of ropes stretched to capacity squeal in multiple pitches. From the east, giant torsion pins wail in their brackets. These sounds of the siege engines drift in through the minaret window—a deadly conversation between lethal catapults. A chatty banter in the various languages of the mangonels, all conveying the identical message: pleasure in the destruction they produce and a rabid anticipation of the east wall's collapse.

A team of engineers take their positions on the splayed ropes suspended from the joined rods of their whirlwind trebuchet, the lines hanging like a mop of hair. These Mongols appear to Leander as light cavalry, temporarily tasked to the lightest of the mangonels. Following their Chinese leader's commands, they rotate their weapon on its pivot.

"Belen baina!"

"Neg ni! Khoyor! Gurav!"

The jagged rock soars from its sling, high over the wall. The Chinese artilleryman shakes his head. Apparently unhappy that his shot goes too far, he sends away two rope pullers to shorten the next pitch.

A hail from the men below. Leander looks in the direction where the Mongol heads are turning. Tartars nudge their mates, pointing at what just crests a hill along the westward moving traffic.

Five metal tubes mounted atop their wheeled frames lumber down the road.

Leander stands for a better view. He turns to his boss, who looks as if he had been drinking all night. Duyal shrugs his shoulders, apparently also having never seen such contraptions.

Mongols below rig oxen to the smaller wheeled trebuchets and pull these pieces out of the way. Farther north, soldiers haul date palm logs from a giant pile and butt them longwise behind the four-footed catapults. Men and oxen pull and push this artillery left and right along their makeshift roads, hastily making room for the more valuable gear approaching, the rising sun now glinting from the shiny barrels.

The Chinese engineers step up to receive each, the metal cylinders impressive—short- and long-barreled, all beefy in appearance. These are waved into their spaces along the line. Wooden kegs are brought up alongside them. The Chinese break open the casks and retrieve canvas bags from within. Some of these are carefully placed into the barrels.

"Brass tubes?" Leander asks.

"Must be. Maybe another form of 'eruptor'?"

"But bigger and wheeled?" Leander says, both men having heard of these new weapons, the outsized "firelances" of the Chinese, mounted on frames and filled with lead shot.

Men pushing handcarts arrive with rocks chiseled to fit neatly into the various tubes. A tarp is flopped aside to reveal another cart filled with steel balls. They wrangle one rock into the end of the barrel facing the fortification.

Soldiers back away from this first prepared weapon. Three Chinese remain and shift the cart to the left. They raise the barrel slightly, propping the metal up with shims. They chock the wheels. One pulls a short piece of hemp from his pouch and inserts it into a hole atop the closed end of the tube. Another man arrives with burning tinder. He touches the hemp with it and steps away.

Flame belches from the monster's maw, followed by a roar.

A blow from the concussion smacks Leander in the chest. Mud falls in plate-sized pieces from the roof. He covers his head. Does the tower sway? Could it come down?

A cheer from the troops below, muffled by the ringing in his ears.

As the powder settles, Leander sees the fear of a young boy on his amir's face, the first time he has ever seen anything resembling terror in Duyal. A similar dread fills the Frenchman.

Another shot bellows from the next cannon down the line. Leander feels the shudder of the explosion up through his feet, the air strangely pulled from his lungs. Mud and pebbles from the ceiling fall in clumps about his shoulders, speckling the floor.

A metal ball crashes into the eastern wall near its base just seconds later, crumbling the smooth block.

A cheer erupts from the enemy, louder than the last.

"By Allah." Duyal says, the anxiety on his face turning to rage.

"Those are no eruptors—how do those barrels not shatter from such an explosion?"

Neither Leander nor Duyal were strangers to naft, that oily liquid fire, nor to the variants of black powder used at war. Eight years ago, north of Cairo in Mansura, they fired naft-doused arrows at the Crusaders of King Louis during what they now call "The Seventh Crusade."

When the surviving Franj escaped the barricaded traps in town and scuttled north to their camp across the river, the Egyptian regulars shot firelances, which spit shrapnel from their bamboo barrels. Only the odd man carried one with a brass barrel. But those hand-held weapons of the Muslims' were a far cry from the size and destructive capability of what is before them now.

A shorter cannon, this one shaped like a vase, thunders and kicks.

A faint crash from inside Baghdad's walls. A curtain of smoke rises from the impact site.

"Bombs that throw smoke," Leander mumbles.

He imagines this arrangement of metal tubes being fired at the citadel in Cairo. He shudders. Feeling somebody watching him, he looks down and right. A Mongol points up to their minaret. His three mates nod. They converse for a short while and begin walking over to the mosque.

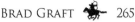

"We are spotted." Leander says. "Down to our right."

"We go," Duyal says.

They ease away from the window. Leander covers his scabbard with his cloak and unsheathes his dagger. He slips the weapon handle-first into his sleeve and reaches for the ceiling. Feeling the heel of the weapon strike his armpit, he clamps down on it. They scurry down the stairs.

"They are on us," Duyal says to Singer as they burst through the wooden doors to the courtyard. "Stick to the plan."

Duyal pulls a rope from his pack and tosses it over his shoulder. Singer pulls his dagger from the sheath and a scroll from his pack. They follow Duyal toward the wooden doors of the mosque.

The metal gate behind them bangs open. Four Mongols barge through the opening, swords bared, their leather-scaled armor squeaking on each step.

Two of them look young and narrow-waisted. Long hair spills from under their pointed helmets. Their braided beads click atop their cuirasses.

"Why you here?" a large-headed Mongol asks in broken Arabic.

Leander steps forward and smiles. He holds his cross away from his chest toward the enemy, showing the invaders they are Christians to be spared. "We are carpenters. We will turn this mosque into a church. The assignment came down to us from the *Catholikos Makikha*, after the patriarch's meeting with your khan."

The four Mongols exchange glances, none seeming to know of the meeting or recognize the Christian leader's name.

Leander opens his hand to the wooden doors, snatches the measuring rope from Duyal's shoulder. "We just finished deciding how many pews we must build and where they will go." And this man here," he thumbs to Singer. "He is very skilled.

The one who will craft the minbar into a proper pulpit. For the glory of God and Hulegu Khan."

"Why you up on tower?" the thick-tongued Mongol asks, pointing his sword tip in the direction of the minaret.

"We went up when we heard the explosions. We were giving thanks to our Lord for Him bringing the Mongol saviors from heaven to eliminate the heathens," Leander says.

"So you went up to pray?" the Mongol asks with raised lip.

"Of course," Leander says.

Their leader nods his head, seeming to believe. He sheathes his sword, prompting another of his men to do the same. Yet the oldest of them keeps his sword in fist, scowling. He blurts a few words in the Mongol language, assuming none of the strangers comprehend it. Perhaps this man does not believe Leander's account.

The large-headed Tartar shrugs his shoulders. He lifts his chin at the Mamluks and appears to offer his opinion otherwise. More words in the Mongol's Altaic tongue from the frowning man. The men eventually nod in agreement.

Another salvo from the cannon pounds the nearby city wall, a crashing of stone on stone that makes the ground tremble.

Their leader turns to Leander and smiles. He takes a few steps forward. "We do not care much about churches or Christians. But Hulegu Khan like, so we must also like."

The other Mongols come astride him. The apprehensive man moves his hand to his sword.

Singer comes forward with flopping scroll in hand. "Allow me to show you what we have planned," he says slowly in Arabic.

As the scowling man looks down, Singer lunges. His hidden dagger plunges into the old man's neck, the only unarmored area on his front side. The Mongol falls, gagging.

Leander releases his weapon from its clutch in his armpit. He catches the dagger in stride and charges the lead Mongol, bowling him over. He hits the man hard and fast with his blade, punching each lung. He finishes him by burying his blade deep in the man's neck. The Mongol falls limp.

He spins on his knees, dagger bared, prepared to defend his mates.

Duyal slits the throat of another, after having wrestled him to the ground. Singer, drops his dagger and struggles with the remaining young Mongol, who has his sword half out of the scabbard. Singer's bloody hand clutches the Mongol's exposed blade.

Leander slips behind this Mongol. Singer, aware of the coming assist, cinches the man's opposite arm at the bend of his elbow, giving Leander access to the Tartar's throat. Leander yanks the Tartar's braids and runs his dagger across the enemy's neck.

Duyal steps to the large-headed man, whose chest rises and falls rapidly. He slides his foot beneath the Mongol's neck to better expose his windpipe. And slices it through.

Leander looks past the wrought iron spikes. Seeing nothing, he snatches his pack and pulls a spare tunic from it. He kneels beside Singer.

"How bad?" Leander asks.

"It is nothing," Singer says calmly.

Leander takes Singer's wrist and turns it to expose the open gash across his palm. He wraps the tunic twice about Singer's hand, securing the wadded end tightly through the last wrap. "What did they say?"

Singer looks up from his wound. "That we lie. That we were probably spies, not Christians. The grumpy one said to remember that their commander gave them orders to kill anyone suspicious and that we were suspicious." He retrieves his dagger.

"We must go," Duyal says, dragging the large-headed Mongol by a single boot. He dumps him behind a tangle of shrubs beside the fountain. Leander grabs the two smaller men by the scruffs of their necks and hauls to them backward to the same hiding place. Duyal goes back for the last man.

Singer kicks a Mongol helmet under the vegetation.

Duyal eyes the area. “Slowly out. Reassembly point is the horse stable, in case we are separated.”

CHAPTER 31

Esel

Al-Karak

February 10, 1258

Nearing Karak, Esel studies the fortification ahead, the castle built atop a southern spur on the east-west running plateau. No wonder the locals call it *Hisn al Ghurab*, the Crow's Fortress. Three sides of the towering bastion are surrounded by natural ravines and steep ditches. She imagines attackers having to fight their way uphill, exposed to the defenders' arrowshot.

Built by the Crusaders more than a hundred years past, the stronghold was held by the Christians for only forty-six years and then snatched by Saladin's nephew in 1188. For the Muslims, its significance lies in its control over the caravan route between Damascus and Egypt and the pilgrimage route between Damascus and Mecca.

With a small basket strapped on her shoulder, Esel passes through the Jewish quarter and its well-kept cemetery. She approaches the city's gate and is nodded through with barely a glance from the three guards there, who recognize her.

She navigates through the tangle of winding lanes and their offshoot cul-de-sacs packed with nearly identical, two-story houses. She strolls alongside their interior courtyards, where children squeal in play and the woody aroma of cannabis wafts from terra cotta smoking bowls and the old men's calabash water pipes.

She rambles past the most prominent of the *medressas*, where some of Karak's brightest men study Islamic theology and law. Not far from here is the Friday Mosque, where most of the adult male population assembles for *juma*, the day of gathering, the most sacred day of worship.

The streets turn to heel-worn stone along bathhouse row, where the fragrance of spiced ghee and the tang of fish offal and dried snake skins emit from pastes molded around burning incense sticks. Nearing the souk, the main marketplace in Karak, she takes a deep breath, telling herself to relax.

This is just another hunt. A simple ambush, no different than back in her homeland. Just another wolf that needs killing.

Approaching the ginger monger's booth, Esel slows and looks up to the second and third floors of the mudbrick buildings on the left side of the street. She eyes the dark shadows inside the harem windows, the *mashrabiya*, rooms for the women. Supported by cantilevered beams and covered in ornate lattice, these rooms overlook the marketplace streets. Normally inside these home perches, Muslim women sit within earshot of the happenings on the street without having to wear their head covering or veil.

But not today. As her eyes go up to one harem window, a man's thumb slowly protrudes through the upper portion of the trellis, unnoticed by the throng below. Another thumb eases from the metal-gridded window of the next shaded mashrabiya she passes. Archers signaling that they are in their spots and prepared.

She stops directly across from the booth, shifting her basket to her other shoulder. Jacinta, the woman who hounds the locals for information on the Bahri's affairs, speaks with a customer. The ginger peddler laughs, touching the other woman's arm tenderly. This Jacinta does not look like a spy or assassin. But then a nice smile does not necessarily mean a harmless woman.

She turns to the stuccoed buildings across from her. Behind the wall on one flat roof, the upper limb of a bow rises. Another. More of Baybars' men noticing her glance and signing their readiness.

Two additional warriors, unseen by both her and the masses, huddle behind the elevated columns and higher awnings. One watches her through a crevice in the brick wall, the other via a gap in a canvas structure. Another Mamluk, dressed like a buyer, lurks at street level, his sword hidden beneath his robe.

She feels a moment of reassurance in the support, yet would prefer to be them—the shooters, the killers—in this wolf stand, not the bait. The soldiers' positions—elevated, or at least concealed in the ambusher's station—is more natural to her.

She shakes these thoughts from her mind and forces away the vison of herself as the lamb or wounded hare she used to stake in the high-grassed valleys of her past. She ignores the bawls and wails of the prey echoing in her mind, those sounds that were used to draw in the fanged prowlers of the steppe.

Her eyes go back to the booth, back to the she-wolf. Do the work. Execute the plan.

Baybars' guidance pounds in her head, "Trust your instincts. If you sense your life is in danger, or that she is an assassin working on her own, or just reckless, then signal. And we will dispatch her. If you think she would be of some use, spare her for questioning."

She approaches the stall with the confidence her nephew would expect.

Jacinta's boy sits under the slanted refuge, pulling fingers of peeled ginger root from a bag and lining them up neatly next to his mother's stone grinder. A cute lad, a good boy for helping his mother.

A pang twists her gut. For an instant, she hopes the boy will be spared. She then tries to will away this weakness in her thoughts. His mother is likely a predator who wishes to kill Baybars. Jacinta is no different than the pup-toting she-wolves that used to ravage her tower's flocks.

Many times during her summer hunts, she had called in and killed, not just the bitch, but also a string of three and four pups—adorable, fuzzy critters who would become prime killers themselves within six moons. Kill the she-wolf, the creator of more killers; kill the offspring. This business is nothing new to her. She sighs.

Jacinta is sorting ginger roots and looks up as Esel approaches.

"Good morning."

"Good morning. Could I just have just one thicker section of root?"

"Ground?"

"Yes, thank you."

She holds up a stout finger. "Good?"

Esel nods. "You have not been here long. Where are you from?"

"Originally, Cairo. You?"

"Damascus, originally the Kipchak steppe."

Jacinta nods, purses her lips. "Is your husband a Mamluk?"

Esel grins. "No, no. My husband is long dead. But I follow them. I wash the Bahri's uniforms."

Jacinta looks up from her grinder and briefly meets her eye. She nods, then looks past Esel's shoulder, surveying the crowd in a single glance.

"I have noticed that you, too, follow the Bahri. Why?"

Jacinta opens her palms. "Vendors must follow the silver. Baybars' buyers are known to pay a fair price to all in this bazaar. I have sold his men some ginger. As his army grows, I am hoping there will be more trades."

Esel nods. She tells herself to be like the bull. Do not dance around. "Is this the only reason you go to such trouble to follow them from Nablus to Karak? You ask a lot of questions to the people. You even pay some for information."

Jacinta again looks up from her work, first to the sellers hawking their charms and the women jostling for a closer look at the produce, then to the men unloading their spices from low-sided carts. Then back to Esel, where Jacinta holds Esel with the calm, sleepy eyes of a cheetah.

A twinge of fear runs up Esel's spine. This woman is feline, not canine. Unfamiliar quarry for Esel.

"It is not easy for a woman to be a merchant," Jacinta says. "She must know her regulars. Rent here is not cheap. It is not easy hiring camel pullers, or following Baybars' train. The Bahri move often."

"Let us stop the game. You are not who you say you are. You are not just a vendor. Who are you really? Who sent you?"

Jacinta sets her stone in the grinder basin. She looks to the merchants on each side, perhaps to see if they listen. Both are engaged with customers. Jacinta lowers her voice just above the din of the market. "Well, apparently we have this in common. You are more than a widow buying ginger for your evening meal of *mansaf*."

Esel takes a step forward. She looks to the boy, who now plays with a wooden ball, oblivious to the conversation. "What are you talking about?"

"You are the aunt of Baybars. An expert bowyer from his old tribe. The finest of hunters. You do not wash clothes, you buy arms. And now, you apparently hunt spies." Jacinta's gaze strays to the rooftop across from them. Possibly she has spotted an archer. Jacinta's eyes again find Esel's, locking dark, slanted, and confident upon her interrogator's.

Esel's heart races. This woman across from her is no novice, as Baybars warned. An insecurity fills her. Esel feels ill-equipped to deal with her. The hair rises on her neck. She takes a few breaths to compose herself. Esel leans across the table. "You'd best answer my questions."

"I think you may already know the answers. I am Jacinta. I have been a mole for twenty years, working at first directly for al-Salih, the Sultan of Cairo, and then Aybeg, and now Qutuz. I have been ordered to collect information on your nephew—an enemy of the empire."

Esel's eyes go wide. "You know I could have you killed for admitting this?"

"Of course," she says evenly.

"Why do you not lie? Or are you?" Esel asks.

"There is a time to mislead, a time to be straight. Now feels like the time to be straight. For both of us."

Esel swallows, a dryness now in her mouth. Remain collected, she tells herself. Pretend to be unafraid. "Yes, our words now will have great consequences."

Jacinta nods. "Qutuz and his amirs sought me out for this job. They saw my boy as a means to get close to Leander, one of Baybars' soldiers."

Esel's brow knits in concentration. She has heard of this man. "Leander, the Mamluk who speaks many languages, the interpreter?"

Jacinta's eyes brighten upon hearing his name. "You know him?"

"No."

Jacinta's smile turns wistful. "Well, we knew each other five years past in Cairo." Her face goes long. "Qutuz thought that if I tried to get close to Leander again, I would be able to learn the doings and intentions of Baybars."

Esel scowls. "The intentions of Baybars, or the location of Baybars, so your fellow assassins can kill him?"

"I am no killer. And the Muizziyya sent me alone. This is how much they regard my well-being," Jacinta says, tight-lipped. "I have no plan to kill Baybars or Leander. Sometimes one sent by the enemy is not truly a foe."

Esel looks at her suspiciously. She takes a step left to give the archers across the street a direct shot at Jacinta. A step closer to the table, where Esel could take cover if arrows begin to fly.

"So what are your intentions in al-Karak, Jacinta?"

She shakes her head. "I started the trip from Cairo not knowing my exact intentions, only knowing mine were not the same as Qutuz's. But as the weeks passed, I realized that I am only here for one reason."

"And what is that?"

"I wish to win back Leander's heart. When I think of anything more, emptiness fills me. My intent is for my boy to be raised with Leander's help."

Esel stares at her for a long while. "You expect me to believe this?"

"I have learned to expect nothing from anyone. All I can do now is tell you the truth. And my hopes."

Esel lifts her chin toward the lad, who still plays. "So this boy is Leander's issue?"

"Unfortunately not."

Esel scrunches her brow. "Then how could you expect Leander to help rear him?"

"Perhaps for the same reason that you helped look after Baybars, your sister's child."

Esel loses her breath for a moment. She feels a touch of perspiration on her upper lip. How does this woman know so much about her? Careful. Be careful. "If this is your boy, why did your family not help you with him at home in Cairo?"

Jacinta looks over to make sure her boy does not listen. "Zane is not of my blood," she whispers. "I have parents and a brother in Cairo. But my father is more concerned with the inheritance and how Zane might somehow take his coin one day."

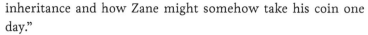

Jacinta looks down. "If I had not left, this child would have torn my family apart. And if I had not taken this mission, Qutuz may have killed my kin, or even my boy. He threatens such always."

Esel believes none of it.

Jacinta seems to read Esel's reaction. She meets Esel's eyes. "Zane's mother is of Egypt." she says. "But his father is a Kipchak."

Esel's heart sinks. The lad carries the blood of her people.

Jacinta gives a sad grin, likely reading Esel's response, sensing her softness on this topic. "Zane's father was a Mamluk murdered by Aybeg's thugs. They tracked him to Hama. I took care of Zane's ill mother until she died of the fever."

Jacinta shakes her head. "She had no family and few friends in Hama, so far from home. She pleaded with me to keep him out of the orphanages. I promised her I would take Zane as my own. And this is what I have done."

She looks to the smiling lad, who tosses the ball high into the air.

"You have thought of every detail in this story," Esel says.

"No. I have not thought enough about what comes next. I am risking everything on the hope that Leander will help me for love of the tribe. Surely you understand this?"

Esel's jaw tightens. Does this woman think her a fool?

Jacinta again seems to read her. "You have been around them, these Mamluks. Zane is the son of a brother Bahri. This means something to those of virtue." Her face softens. "And that is what Leander is. One of the best. One of pure heart."

Esel glares. "I heard that Leander is a Franj. There is no Kipchak blood in him. Or do you mean that Leander and this child's father are of the same Khushdash—that they were brothers from their initial training?"

Jacinta looks down. "No, I do not think so."

Esel looks at her sideways. "Seems you accept a big risk in thinking this Leander would take on this child out of the kindness of his heart, with no ties to blood or Khushdashiya," Esel says, squinting, assessing the obvious hole in Jacinta's account. "You know I can find Leander and check your story."

Jacinta's face remains placid. She sighs, as if the words already spoken were a heavy rock pushed from her chest. She stays silent. Her eyes glass with tears. "Leander is the finest man I have ever known. You can confirm my words. He knows how I feel about him."

"You know that if you are lying, you will die?" Esel says. "And I will personally assure it is a painful death. No matter where you go, the Bahri will find and kill you. I will find you."

Jacinta wipes her eyes.

Esel gnaws at the inside of her mouth. She worries that the warriors across the street may begin to think she is in trouble. Esel is veering from the plan. She places her left hand on her hip, the signal to "hold fire." She steps back to the right to block any broadside shot at Jacinta, in case a shooter misses her sign.

"Snatch or snuff," Baybars had said. "Act swiftly." Esel knows she takes too long to decide.

"I know how all of this sounds," Jacinta says.

"You have had lots of time to come up with this tale. Perhaps Qutuz's brutes even fabricated this story for you. Maybe Zane is just an urchin you plucked from an orphanage in Cairo." Esel gestures toward the gray hair peeking from under her head covering. "Do not think this granny soft or stupid." She looks deep into Jacinta's eyes in an attempt to detect any treachery, as Esel must resolve now.

"I doubt you are either."

"I do not care that you somehow learned that I tended Baybars as a lad. This does not make you and me kindred sisters. Does not make your account true. Spies make a living out of being clever storytellers. Good liars."

Jacinta nods. "I would be thinking the same as you. But what I told you is the truth, Esel. I came for Leander. No other reason."

She looks Esel squarely in the eyes. "I came east to fix a wrong I did him in the past." Her brow crinkles. "My only hope is that the passing years have melted Leander's ill will toward me. That he might forgive me and see my travel to these places and searching for him as evidence of my continued affection for him."

Esel clenches the edge of the table, her eyes momentarily to the lad. She lowers her voice. "Even if you tell the truth. This boy. He will not help your situation; he will only hurt you."

A resolve forms in Jacinta's face. A strength that surprises Esel. "I will honor my promise to the boy's mother, till the end. The boy is now mine, come fortune or ruin." Jacinta exhales. "Maybe I am wrong. Maybe I am crazy." Jacinta watches as Esel deliberates. "There were ways for me to have avoided this conversation with you. I chose to tell you the truth, because of who you are."

Esel snarls. "You have no idea who I am."

"Oh, I have an idea." Jacinta frowns, her eyes going back to the roof. "And you might want to make your move soon. Those men on the roof and the Mamluk you have pacing back and forth along the street. They grow anxious."

Esel's heart thumps in her chest. Her temples pound. Decide. Decide.

Jacinta turns toward her son and then back to Esel. She whispers. "Listen, I understand what it is like to be sent on a messy mission, having to execute bloodwork that you would rather not. Do what you must, my friend."

Esel's eyes again go wide. Can this woman read minds? Is she incredibly brave or insane? And "friend"—what is she talking about?

“Just do not let them harm the child. From one woman to another. From one surrogate mother to another. Please do not let anything happen to this child. He is a Kipchak, the son of a Bahri, no different than your own nephew.”

Esel raises her right hand and pats her head twice, her eyes staying on the lean-bodied cheetah.

Mamluks brush past each of her shoulders. A table is kicked aside. A woman at the next booth screams. Vendors on either side scramble. One merchant bunches the corners of the blanket where his jewelry sits, slings it over his shoulder, and runs. A wide gap in the crowd forms around the booth.

Disguised Mamluks force Jacinta’s arms behind her back. She stands tranquilly, mostly ignoring these men, her feline eyes affixed to Esel’s. Two men pat down Jacinta, while another keeps a sword pointed at her neck. She remains unaffected.

Zane rushes toward Jacinta, yet is intercepted. Another soldier arrives to assist. The lad kicks and yelps, as his wrists are secured with hemp.

Esel grabs the arm of a soldier, who manhandles the boy. “Easy, easy.”

The boy looks up at her with a scowl.

CHAPTER 32

Leander

Hit, Western Mesopotamia

February 16, 1258

Leander sleeps on a pile of palm fronds, his oilcloth atop him. Asleep beside him, Duyal begins to fidget.

The amir mumbles for a bit and then thrashes. "Run, run!" Duyal screams.

Leander throws aside the skin and rises with dagger in hand. He looks left and right, orienting himself in the low morning light.

Seeing nothing, the adrenalin surging through his body ebbs. He grabs the writhing Duyal by the shoulders and tries to shake him awake. Duyal fights him.

"Hey, you are just dreaming," Leander says.

Singer rushes in from his watch nearby with sword in hand.

Duyal sits up, his chest heaving.

"You all right?" Leander asks.

Duyal avoids eye contact. "I am fine."

"It is time anyhow. I can hear people starting to move nearby," Singer says.

Leander worries about his commander. He has been pulling too much of the watch duty for most of the last six days. When Leander tried to relieve him last night, Duyal said, "Go back to your mat. I cannot sleep anyway."

When his mentor does sleep, Leander has twice woken his friend from similar nightmares.

Leander gets to his feet and tightens his belt another notch. He is ravenous but has grown accustomed to being cold, tired, and hungry. Comfort is the last thing that occupies his mind.

Six days ago, Duyal decided that his team had completed gathering the intelligence that Baybars wanted. They had detailed information on the size and capability of the Mongol enemy, and notes and drawings on the Tartars' siegecraft, invaluable in mounting Cairo's defenses and those of her allies. Baybars specified that if Baghdad were to fall, they should return to him immediately.

After being rousted from their perch in the mosque, the team hid the first day in a cellar on the western edge of Baghdad. Staying off the roads and moving only in the dark, they spent the next night heading farther west. They bivouacked without a fire in a deep ravine far from the main road.

With more Mongol patrols roving the Jazira near the river crossings, Duyal's team spent the following day curled in the thick scrub, shuddering in the cold rain. For the past three days, they slept on the east bank of the Euphrates. Concealed among the thick palms, they searched for possible fording spots and waited for the flow of refugees they figured would stream westward once the caliph finally surrendered Baghdad. The team plans to blend in with the multitudes in the daylight, rather than risk being the few traveling at night.

Leander and Duyal stuff their bedding into packs. Leander grabs his crutch, a stout limb with a y-branch, and slings it over his shoulder.

They walk south on the stony path until just short of the King's Road, the main east-west route from Baghdad to the Jordan Valley. Leander reaches over his shoulder to feel the scrolls he has sewn into the back of his tunic, the stack of pages secured in a thin leathered sleeve. Duyal totes a leaner set.

Leander finds himself repeating this gesture every few moments. The habit is common with most cavalrymen—soldiers often pat their saddle scabbards and bow cases and quivers, constantly verifying that those things most valuable to them remain in their possession. These papyrus sheets are no less critical to Leander, representing not only months of work, but information that may help save the empire.

They must finish this last leg of their journey, this final part of their mission. They must return to Damascus, or find Baybars, wherever he is now. To get caught by the Mongols with these sheets in hand would mean an immediate execution, but worse, critical information would be lost to their commander.

"I will go first, then you two follow. Stay within each other's sight," Duyal says, with raised eyebrows.

Leander and Singer nod.

"Rally point is still the Bedu camp, the horse stable on the far side of the river." Duyal turns away.

Leander feels that lump again move into his stomach, the peculiar disquiet of a youngster soon to be left alone, mixed with a warrior's desire to be near enough his brothers to protect them. He knows he comes by this reaction honestly. It is a product of being so long within an arm's reach of his comrades and his constant worry for his mates' safety.

Leander clasps Duyal's forearm. His friend looks him in the eye, seeming to acknowledge that yet again they find themselves in another precarious moment where the situation forces them to separate, even if not for long.

Duyal steps off.

Leander exchanges a grip with Singer. Singer waits only seconds and continues down the path behind Duyal.

When Singer rounds the bend, Leander departs. He steps off on stiff legs, the soles of his slippers worn thin. Ahead, the clank of pots and stomp of hoof from the shuffling refugees becomes more distinct. The crack of whip on oxen. A dog barks.

Nearing the intersection, he flips up his hood and pretends to hobble, using the crutch. Like a tributary flowing into a main river, Leander merges with the current of Mesopotamian exiles coursing west.

Leander pushes his way forward to close the distance with his comrades. He eases alongside a woman with child, as if he travels with them. Dust churns across the path. The drone of hushed conversations and sounds of women calming their young. The barnyard stink of refugees sweating and unwashed.

Most here have departed the round city with no more than the clothes on their backs. Those with children clutch little hands tightly. Some push handcarts that are piled with foodstuffs, weary children, and whatever household implements they could gather on short notice. A boy wears sandals hastily cut from a pair of leather book covers. Leander catches Singer looking back to spot him.

They walk toward the big river.

Herders whip a string of cows into cooperation along the side of the road. A turbaned man in front of him trudges with a wooden cross in hand, a bent nail sticking from one end, where he likely ripped it from the wall of his home or another's. The man likely feigns his Christianity, his family's only defense against the infidel horde which could gallop up behind them at any moment.

Most are Muslims, token migrants purposely spared by the Mongols. The Black Tartars allow a few thousand Baghdadis to escape their wrath, not out of benevolence but so that survivors may spread the tales of Mongol slaughter to nearby towns. The Mongols know that warnings from exiles are better than words from any silver-tongued emissary at achieving early surrenders and avoiding the needless spilling of Mongol blood.

More people flood in at the next road junction from the north. Leander hears them before he sees them—distant wails and the piercing cries from two babies combine into a wretched melody. The dreary figures slog through the low light and join this river of misery.

The stream of refugees comes to an abrupt halt. Ahead, the mighty Euphrates intersects the road. Leander steps off the path for a look.

A long line forms on the nearside of the pontoon bridge crossing. Mongol guards traverse either side of the single-lane crossing. The Tartars prod the evacuees with their riding sticks like sheep, controlling the traffic across the planks. The soldiers ignore the women with children in tow, but seem to scrutinize the men.

The team has no choice but to cross. They would have already swum across the wide river, but Duyal did not wish to test their swimming skills against the river's width and deadly current, nor attempt to dodge the Mongol patrols who watch these open spaces. Not a single skiff could be found along the bank. The locals hid them ahead of the Mongol approach.

Once across, the trio plans to retrieve their mounts and gear on the west side, having paid some Bedouins to care for their horses last moon at a location about a half-day's walk from this bridge. While they paid the nomads well up front, Leander frets that this "tent" of Bedu might have sold the team's horses, or even eaten them. He hopes the nomads' respect for the animals' bloodlines might have kept them from this.

Leander shoves his way closer to where Singer and Duyal wait. He notices a veiled girl watching them, not far from where the Mongol soldiers work the riverbank. She releases a woman's hand and works her way toward them, searching the ground as if for something she may have lost.

She passes Duyal and Singer and stops beside Leander. She drops a button at his feet and bends down to sift through the dirt for it. Wiping it on her filthy dress, she stands beside him, facing where he came.

"I heard them speak," she whispers. "The guards hunt for a dozen men, you three among them. White-skinned spies, sham carpenters, who killed the Georgians and then the Mongol soldiers in the mosque. Go downriver. There is a ferry that just set up there."

Leander looks about him to see if anyone has heard her words. Singer watches them. She glances at Leander for just a moment. He winks.

Her eyes squint. A smile, he figures, hidden by veil. "Allah be with you, treasured one," she says, using the same words he spoke to her that night outside Baghdad amid the rubble of her destroyed home. She turns from him and continues her fake hunt along the roadside back toward her aunt.

Leander moves up beside Duyal. "The Mongols look for us. Follow me."

When the Mongol guards turn their backs, Leander slips into the thick sedge off the road. Duyal and Singer trail him into the reeds. When Leander confirms that his friends are behind him, he tries to put some distance between himself and the road, ducking beneath the tamarisk branches and pushing through the thick brush.

He stops and faces Duyal. "It was the girl we helped in Baghdad. The daughter of the scribe. She said the Mongols are on to us. She told me of another place to cross."

They push toward the riverbank, heading for an open space in the canopy. Downstream, a ferry crosses the river, attached to a stout rope. Behind it, a smaller skiff is poled by two men. The three slow their pace, Duyal now leading toward the anchor rope on the east shore, the barge's apparent landing spot.

Four families with a pair of oxen await the ferry. The boat noses up to the riverbank and the ferryman drops a rickety ramp. The Baghdadis drive their oxen onto the barge.

"May we come aboard?" Duyal asks the man with crossed arms.

"Not this trip. No more weight." He nods to the skiff coasting in downstream from him. "Ask them."

Duyal walks down the bank, muttering to himself. He wades up to his knees, catches the bow of the papyrus-hulled skiff, and helpfully drags it ashore. A slender Arab ferryman in front braces himself for the grounding. A burly man in the rear swooshes the muddy end of his pole in the water and lays it just inside the starboard gunwale beside another carved limb. He stretches and rubs his lower back.

"Can you take us across?" Duyal asks.

The big man in the back nods. "One hundred dirhams each."

"By Allah," Duyal says. "How about fifteen?"

The slender man in front leans on his pole. "We will do it for fifty each."

Duyal turns around to see that a middle-aged couple and another man have arrived. Duyal steps up into the bow. "You ill-treat the disadvantaged. Fifteen is more than fair. You take us all across for that, or I will soon hold both of your windpipes in my hand."

The bowman raises his eyebrows.

The big poler behind smiles. "So brave. Why didn't such a courageous man as you not stay and fight the Mongols?"

Leander steps between them, knowing his friend will make good on his threat. He pretends not to know Duyal. "Time spent haggling on price could be used in poling us across. You can see your line already grows," Leander says, nodding behind them. A family of six approaches in grubby clothes.

The thick-shouldered man scowls and shakes his head.

"Pay now, your price," the Mesopotamian in front says. "We go. Only six people."

Duyal's team, the husband and wife, and a dark-bearded refugee clamber aboard and pay the skinny Arab. The solitary man beside Leander is two coins short. He wears rags, and carries a small cross in his hand. Yet his boots peg him as a member of the Caliph's elite guard.

"Out," the poler says to this traveler.

Leander pulls two coins from his purse and gives them to the Arab in front.

"Thank you," the man says.

"You are a soldier?" Leander asks.

The bearded man follows Leander's eyes to his boots. "No, I pulled these from a dead one. I am just a herder—or was before my flock was eaten by the enemy. Why? Are you?"

"No, I am Zamir, a merchant from Egypt," Leander says. "I left Baghdad before the east wall fell. How bad was it?"

Duyal and Singer lean in for a better listen.

"The enemy was everywhere," the man says. "*Are* everywhere. The Mongols ruptured the wall with their cannon, then pulled the broken blocks down with their claw-handed machines. Once inside, they killed all in their path—men, children, women." He whimpers. "The city is theirs. I fear the entire Middle East is theirs."

"Oh dear Allah," Leander says dramatically, leaning his thigh against the gunwales to steady himself against the poler's shoves.

The shepherd in soldier's boots says, "I never thought I would live to see the day. Tens of thousands dead. So many innocents slain. Blood slicking the roads. The whole city butchered or put in chains." The man turns up his nose. "Only the Christians and Jews were spared. Or those pretending to be." He looks down at the cross protruding through his clenched fist. He jams it into his pocket.

"What of the Caliph?" Leander asks.

The old man's shoulders slump further. He looks up to Leander with wet eyes. "Dead. I heard from friends that he was rolled into a carpet and trampled by Hulegu's war horses."

Leander believes this. The Mongols have an aversion to shedding royal blood.

The man turns away, looks to the far bank.

"Those boots are not off a dead soldier, are they? They are yours," Leander says kindly. "You served the Caliph, did you not?"

The man looks down and wipes a fist across his face. His eyes go to the scars on Leander's hands. He lowers his voice. "I am as much a herder as you are a merchant."

Leander refuses to let the soldier's words shake him.

The soldier lowers his voice. "I spent a career in the cavalry, had seen plenty of fighting against large armies, but never against a foe like this."

Leander nods.

"I feel this is Allah punishing us. We have not obeyed His word. And now God has allowed this massive horde into the Holy Land." He closes his bloodshot eyes. His face goes long, as if he pictures it all again, replaying the terrible events in his mind. "Bloodthirsty. Endless waves of infidels, roaring through town, the devil's thunder in their hooves."

Duyal listens with no expression.

The soldier glares. "The Tartars poured hot oil into the ears and down the throats of defenders. My mates' heads were spiked atop the ramparts. Babies swung by their feet, their heads mashed against stone walls." His fist back to his eyes. "And I will be cursed with these sights and sounds and our unit's failure in stopping these demons for the rest of my days. I have earned the self-banishment I begin." He turns from Leander, slinging his small pack to the other shoulder.

Leander leaves the soldier to his own dark thoughts. The skiff lurches forward with the Arabs' coordinated thrusts. Surges of gray current lap against the reed hull.

"Where will you go?" Singer asks the man and wife alongside him, eyeing the heavy packs that burden the couple's shoulders.

"My wife has family near Homs. We will go there," he says, looking to her as if to reaffirm their intentions.

Singer eyes the corner of book cover protruding from the pack. "You are a lecturer?"

The husband looks down, "Of sorts. Did you live in the city?"

"No, I was just visiting for trade."

The husband nods. "I was a translator at the *Bayt al-Hikma*, the House of Wisdom. I translated texts from Portuguese and Spanish into Arabic. I also taught some at the libraries."

"Do those buildings still stand?" Singer asks.

The wife begins to cry, burying her head into her husband's shoulder.

He puts his arm around her. "I, uh, do not think any of the thirty-six libraries are still standing. The House of Wisdom is gone. Books on medicine and astronomy, ancient historical records. Gone. My entire life's work is ruined."

His wife tries to collect herself.

The husband rubs her back. "It was like the worst of dreams. The Tigris ran red from the blood of those killed and thrown into the river. And as we left, the river went to black—from the ink of countless books the Mongols tossed in while they pillaged. Books piling up. Books damming the river. Books floating everywhere, covering all of the water's surface."

The wife dabs a sleeve to dry her tears. "The mosques, the hospitals, the Hanbali School of Law. Save gold and livestock, the Mongols protected nothing, pardoned no one." She sobs. "Baghdad, the center of world learning, is now nothing but razed buildings and soggy pages."

"Books, buildings," the teacher says distantly. "Much more than that was lost. The infidels killed every philosopher and professor we knew. They raped. . . " He bites down on his bottom lip, his eyes watering. He looks to his wife. "How we escaped with our lives was a miracle. Dumb luck. Chance timing. We just stumbled out the Khorasan Gate, amid the confusion and slaughter."

The skiff glides to a stop on the western shore of the Euphrates, jarring the six riders.

CHAPTER 33

Cenk

Al-Salihiyya

March 26, 1258

Cenk stands in his stirrups, cupping his hand above his helmet visor. He strives to identify the array of distant cavalry on the battlefield. Hundreds of Egypt's best scuffle with those of the enemy under the Prince of Karak.

A haze rises above the galloping hoofs, marring the rose-colored horizon at al-Salihiyya. This rolling desert plain to his east has been the site of countless battles over the centuries—a place conducive to success for the tactics of mounted archers, a preferred battleground where Cairo's armies often chose to meet aggressors approaching Egypt from the Gaza Road.

Cenk picks out eight yellowish specks clustering on the north end of the plain. "There," he points at the Muizziyya's command flag. "I think Orhan has skirted their right flank."

"Are those our banners or Baybars'?" Tarkhan asks.

"I think they are al-Mughith's," Cenk says, referring to the Prince of Karak's cavalry.

"Why guess? Let us give heel and find out for sure," Qutuz says, turning his horse down the tapered rise. His squad of bodyguards follow.

"Vicegerent, please!" Cenk says. "Even with the Kurdish help, al-Mughith and the Bahri are outnumbered. I am sure Orhan has this under control."

Qutuz grimaces.

Tarkhan nods. "We beg that you stay. It will do the Muizziyya some good to know that you have faith in our commanders."

Qutuz shakes his head, the agony of not leading from the front seeming to grate at him.

"Worry not, my Amir," Tarkhan says, squinting into the rising sun. "Egypt will need you soon enough, when there are fifty Muslim regiments to command against the Mongol horde, not just a few amirates."

"He is right," Cenk says. "The last thing we need is for you to catch a stray arrow during a minor engagement. The Prince of Karak has no chance here."

Cenk believes this. Late last year, the Mongols ejected three thousand mounted warriors, the Shahrazur Kurds, from their homelands. Initially attempting to join al-Nasir of Damascus, these Kurds proved themselves to be greedy. When al-Nasir refused to grant them the silver and the iqta tax they desired, the Kurds headed south and joined al-Mughith's army in Transjordan.

With the additional cavalry, al-Mughith now seeks to rectify his loss on this same field, just four moons past. Cenk figures that Baybars was likely the impetus for the endeavor, the prod upon al-Mughith's ass. Regardless, the Prince of Karak's combined force is too small to achieve victory again today.

Cenk lifts his chin to a string of buttery-colored pennants, battle flags of the combatants, barely made out against the distant hills. These banners seem to glide above the bronzed powder, the soil on the valley floor churned from horse hoof. "There, on the rise. That red in the center is Baybars' colors. He flees." Cenk chuckles.

"Maybe with the rise of dawn, Baybars' courage has fallen off like a setting sun," Qutuz says.

"Or the rising sun provided him enough light to realize al-Mughith's troops scamper on contact—that they now leave him greatly outmanned," Tarkhan adds.

Cenk watches the banners drop over the farthest hill. The scarlet he sees in the center of the Bahri's banners is the red-lion of their deceased patron, the Sultan al-Salih.

He is annoyed at Baybars' audacity. The Bahri scoundrel continues to carry the pennant of their former patron. "By Allah, either way, Baybars retreats—that devil looks to be beaten again." Cenk grins at Qutuz.

They watch until the last of Qutuz's pursuing Mamluks disappear from view in a swirl of dust.

"The Bahri traveled far yesterday," Qutuz says. "Their horses will fatigue before ours. Our Muizziyya will soon return here. They may be with captured enemy. What shall we do if they bag some of Baybars' men this time?" He turns to his guards and motions them away so the trio can strategize in private. He looks to Tarkhan.

"Take them prisoner, but release them at some point, as we did here last November," Tarkhan says. "Maybe after putting them to the switch."

"Like misbehaving children or an unruly wife? You are not serious?" Cenk says.

"Of course," Tarkhan says. "Hulegu will soon be in Syria and full of confidence. Remember, my friend, I am still a Mongol. I know how they think. They will not stop their advance until they are making themselves drunk on *airag* up and down the Mediterranean coast. We cannot afford to kill any Muslim warriors, especially those most talented, fellow Mamluks."

"Fellow Mamluks? Is that who the Bahri are? Is that who the Salihi who snuck away from Cairo in the night to join Baybars are?" Cenk asks.

The Mongol shrugs. "Who else are they?"

"Enemy," Cenk growls. "Rival Mamluks, no different than those held by al-Nasir or al-Mughith." He removes his helmet and wipes his face. "The Salihi, who flew and joined Baybars, insult Qutuz. You are right that they are like spoiled brats, unappreciative of the pay and fiefs our vicegerent granted them. But we cannot treat them like children."

Qutuz raises his eyebrows.

"I understand," Tarkhan says. "But the Mongols are not on our doorstep with two thousand or twenty thousand warriors. They may have over sixty thousand, plus allies. We need every man, especially any who can ride a horse and shoot a bow."

Cenk grips his reins. "We do not need traitors."

"Baybars knows the Mongols are the common enemy. He may come around to join us in fighting them. For the sake of the empire, for the sake of Islam," Tarkhan says.

"Join us?" Cenk asks. "He has twice now tried to take Cairo with the help of al-Mughith, knowing full well the Mongol threat. And he pressured al-Nasir before that to do the same. Since leaving Cairo, Baybars has done nothing but whore himself out to Damascus and Karak."

"Since leaving Cairo, or since being driven from Cairo by us?" Tarkhan asks.

Cenk spits. "Al-Salih, Allah rest his soul, would see Baybars for what he is—a treasured son turned scamp. By the flames of hell, I would not doubt the next time we see Baybars on a battlefield, he will be riding beside Hulegu."

Qutuz nods, seemingly unhappy that his normally agreeable advisors make his decision a difficult one.

Tarkhan leans on his pommel. "Maybe, but we know one thing. If we want to discourage Baybars from returning to defend Cairo, then a fine way is to send him into the arms of the Mongol enemy by killing any Bahri or Salihi prisoners we catch today. Hate them if you wish, but Baybars has six hundred of the best fighters from here to the Urals, and three hundred of them Mamluks. This is no time for grudges. This is no time for pride."

Cenk turns to confirm that the guards are not listening. "It is not a matter of pride, it is a matter of deterrence," he says. "Go soft on Baybars and he will keep trying to take Egypt. Go easy on Salihi prisoners now and those Salihi loyal to us will see us as fainthearted and may leave us to join Baybars. The Bahri have already tripled in size in four years."

"And those Salihi who leave Cairo not only enlarge Baybars' forces, they diminish ours," Qutuz says.

Tarkhan stares at the horizon, which has gone blood red in the dirty sky, the light of the climbing sun beginning to spill over the mountainscape.

Cenk knows his mate has said his piece and will add little more. He straightens in the saddle and says to Tarkhan, "My friend, we must dishearten Baybars and the Bahri. We must truly punish any and all prisoners, not merely spank them over our knee."

Qutuz nods.

"We could bring the prisoners back with us to Cairo," Tarkhan says. "A few moons in the hole may be enough deterrence, enough punishment, for them to avoid taking part in another run on Cairo. That way we do not lose cavalry needed for later. Or once out of the hole, we let the sultan decide."

"Al-Mansur needs to know nothing of this. The decision is too big for a boy," Qutuz says, using his frequent description of Aybeg's adolescent heir, the youth who carries the title Sultan of Egypt.

Dust again mounts from the east, casting a dirty ring about the rising sun. A blanket of dark powder ascends from the stark plain, the brown cloud growing, lifting above the gleaming waves of heat. Troops inbound.

"Our Mamluks come," Cenk says. "We'd best decide a course soon."

Qutuz sighs. "We went easy on Baybars here last time, releasing prisoners, letting his friend, al-Alfi, go free. I would not doubt that al-Alfi commands troops against us again today."

Qutuz shakes his head. "Baybars and his amirs must learn or we may well lose the rest of our Salihi in Cairo to him." He turns to Tarkhan. "But you are right, too, my friend. We cannot be wasting our energy and resources fighting fellow Muslims, men we will need for the big fight to come."

Qutuz rocks in the saddle. "Know your enemy. Baybars is relentless. He will not stop until he has Cairo, or is dead. Mongols or no Mongols."

"Then maybe we need to try a little harder to make him dead," Cenk says. "Face it, Baybars is the source of our problem with the defying Ayyubid princes and Salihi in Cairo. He is why we are here—again—expending valuable stores."

They sit in silence for a few moments, watching from horseback as their faris approach.

Cenk turns to Qutuz. "Is Baybars any different from any of the scheming vassals who forever connived behind al-Salih's back when we were young men?"

"Not really," Qutuz says.

"Six years ago I had similar discussion with Aybeg." Cenk's eyes go soft, thinking of his friend. He looks to Tarkhan. "Then the nagging foe within our ranks was not Baybars, but his Bahri mentor, Aqtay."

"That day, I mentioned to Aybeg that when al-Salih and his father before him were faced with two or more enemies, they were adept at rendering one threat ineffective while they focused on the other. Like a spider—tangling one foe in a web of varying design, so all resources could be brought to bear upon the other. I recommended we do the same. Be like a spider."

Tarkhan peers quizzically at Cenk.

Cenk looks to Qutuz. "You will recall we ended up doing just that—imploring the caliph to make peace between Egypt and Damascus. This entangled al-Nasir in a web of diplomacy, and we could concentrate on Aqtay."

Cenk grins. "Our situation now reminds me of another fanged creature." He looks at Tarkhan. "Far south of here, spitting cobras are common. Right out of the egg, their hatchlings can shoot a stream of venom into your eye. The black bastards are born with this knack to blind you. They say stumbling upon a nest of young spitters is more dangerous than coming face-to-face with the biggest cobra here in Egypt."

Qutuz eyes the nearing dust cloud, his expression imploring Cenk to get to his point before his Muizziyya arrive.

Cenk smiles. "The good thing about little snakes is that you can still step on their heads and squash them."

"So you are saying Baybars and his three hundred Mamluks are but a nest of small snakes we might grind under foot?" Tarkhan asks.

"I am saying that Baybars needs to be squashed, but not before we maximize the use of his lethal venom to our utmost benefit."

Qutuz smiles. "Do not kill the little nest of snakes until we use them to strike the big snake."

Cenk grins. "That is it. If Tarkhan is right and Baybars offers to come back to Cairo to help us against the Mongols, then let us welcome him in. But let us keep the little snake busy and at a safe distance."

"So we are not forced into the trouble of trying to kill many snakes at the same time," Qutuz says.

"Yes," Cenk says. He again turns to Tarkhan. "This is what Sultan Aybeg did with Aqtay. Aybeg sent the Bahri's leader to Gaza to fight al-Nasir's men, with the hope of getting him killed."

"And such opportunities will surely present themselves for Baybars, too," Qutuz says.

Tarkhan nods. "Similar to what Genghis Khan did with the princes from every region he conquered on Mongolia's periphery—married his daughters to the most aspiring leaders of his new allies and then sent those men away to die in the most dangerous fights."

"And we cannot understate his success," Cenk says.

Qutuz agrees. "Pacifying Genghis' flanks, letting the princes die with honor in the eyes of their followers, eliminating threats to his rule."

The vicegerent strokes his beard. "When the time is right, we do everything possible to mend relations with Baybars and then divert the energies and ambitions of the small snake. Keep him away from Mother Cairo. Send the little spitter into the barren regions to attack the larger enemy."

Cenk smiles. "In hopes of his demise."

"But we get ahead of ourselves," Qutuz says, nodding to the dark mass that emerges from the desert. The black form materializes into horse and rider and then a column behind. The Muizziyya's banner flutters proudly at the front.

"Look in the middle of the formation. No stowed lances." Cenk nods.

"Prisoners," Tarkhan says.

A line of sixty captives comes into focus. Each is helmetless and sits atop his Arabian with his hands tied behind his back.

An amirate commander comes forward. He wipes the dust from his face. "Good morning, Vicegerent."

"Is it?" Qutuz asks.

"I believe so. We sent al-Mughith's fools spurring and managed to fetch a few of his allies," he smiles, nodding back to the captured men behind him.

Cenk picks out six men in the black armor of the Khwarizmians, nine Kurds in long coats, and thirteen Bedu, the dark-bearded men covered in the sheepskin wraps of their people. But his eyes linger on the remaining captives—a handful of Bahri Mamluks and two squads of Salihi, men recently arrived to Baybars' ranks.

"Well done," Qutuz says.

"Vicegerent, do you wish us to secure these men properly for transport back to Cairo?"

"Oh, that will not be necessary," Qutuz says.

Muizziyya helmets lift. Dusty faces look up from beneath visors at Qutuz. The captured, too, gaze with squinted eyes from beneath grungy turbans and dirty skullcaps, worn by the rival Mamluks.

Cenk turns to his boss. He knows what Qutuz will do. His mind roams to the Bashkir wilderness of his youth, when he and his father came upon a couple dozen sheep infected with "blackleg." The worst of the diseased were mottled with black patches. Others gimped on swollen legs. Some hopped with their bad legs raised off the snowy ground, their tails lifted in discomfort.

His father directed him to help pen the animals. And then without warning or mercy, his father waded into the enclosure and lopped the heads off the wailing livestock. "It is what needed to be done," his father said. "We must prevent this curse from spreading to the others."

Qutuz rides beside the column of prisoners. "You Kurds and Khwarizmians, you Bahri Mamluks—return to your units. Go home. Soon enough we will all face the invading hordes from the east."

A sigh of relief issues from these prisoners.

"As for the Salihi who deserted the Egyptian army," Qutuz nudges his horse forward to ride farther down the line of them. "Pull them from their horses and behead them."

CHAPTER 34

Jacinta

Karak

April 14, 1258

In the tawny light of late afternoon, Jacinta walks to the edge of the field adjacent to the Bahri's tent camp. Zane bounds ahead. He dashes between two hills and halts, waiting for his mother.

After being dragged in front of the Bahri's leader two months ago, Jacinta initially assumed a quick execution was impending. Instead, she was surprised to find that Esel had prepped the ground for her interrogation. Somehow Baybars seemed more interested in acquiring her assistance than proving her guilt.

"Why would you work for a man like Aybeg?" Baybars asked.

"I only intended to work for Sultan al-Salih," Jacinta said. "My father manages many of the canals northeast of Cairo. He knew al-Salih well and offered my services to him. Al-Salih eased me into the trade."

A beam spread across Baybars' face upon hearing his former patron's name. "What did our patron busy you with?"

"With al-Salih, the work was harmless," she said. "He tasked me mainly with listening to his troops in the infirmary. He only wanted to know which Mamluks I thought were his most dedicated." She grinned, thinking of her old friend. "He was like a grandfather to me."

"Aye, and a father to me." He appeared to recollect the man, one so beloved by his Mamluks. "Why did you not go back to your family when al-Salih died, when Aybeg took power?" he asked.

"In Aybeg's eyes, I was inherited property. He somehow thought I was a seasoned spy. My assignments from him grew more dangerous."

Baybars squinted in thought. "And why did you not sneak off?"

She looked him square in the eyes. "Aybeg threatened the lives of my family. I hated the man, but I had little choice but to do his work. It was the same with Qutuz."

"So you spied for the devil to save your family?"

She nods. "I guess I came to see myself as dispensable. I knew that if I were clever enough at the work, there was a chance of me escaping death. Not so for my parents and brother, who would be unable to escape Aybeg's throat slitters no matter where they went."

Baybars sat back and stared at her for several long moments. He looked down at her as would a boy with a stone in his hand, gawking at some injured creature. She knew that in this moment the big-shouldered man deliberated over whether or not he should crush the pathetic creature's head.

A calm fell upon her. The truth was rarely a burden to tell. She sat looking at him, mostly unworried about what next words the commander might utter.

"Would you consider working for me?" he asked.

"Do I have an alternative—aside from a blade across the back of my neck?" A wearied grin formed on her lips.

"Unlike Aybeg and Qutuz, I will not threaten you or your family, or this boy you have taken in," Baybars said. "Those who serve here do so in an environment of good spirit and mutual respect—and hard work."

She looked at him warily. The large man was handsome. The spot in his blue eye was curious to her.

He leaned across his cluttered table. "Work for me, instead of them. Those honest with me are treated well. You will find my word is good. Ask any here or those in town with whom I have dealt."

She sighed, resigned to more peril in the profession she loathed.

Baybars sat up straight. "Then again, for the last three moons you have already done plenty of asking about my undertakings." He chuckled.

Zane waits for his mother, his hands folded across his front. Jacinta reaches him, clutches his shoulder, and pauses for Esel to finish drawing her bow.

She releases her shot. The arrow drives into the center of the grass-filled target at forty paces.

Jacinta strolls to Esel. "I see our playing field has been converted into a shooting yard," Jacinta says. She points Zane in the opposite direction of the target. He runs off. "The commander's advisor must maintain her lethality." She smiles.

Esel huffs. "Maybe this is just the place where a tired old lady comes to get away from men—and maybe knock a little rust off her shooting skills."

"The infirmary was busy today, but some people do not care who is tired." Jacinta grins and points to Zane, who runs down a hill toward her carrying striated rocks in his hands.

He stops in front of Jacinta and presents his find.

"I am glad to see you have brought your young warrior with you," says Esel. "Thought I might see you two here again today. I have something for him."

Zane smiles, then looks down shyly.

"Cover your eyes, now," Esel says to Zane. She winks at Jacinta.

From her oilcloth bow case, Esel pulls a simple bow, one she quickly crafted from a single strip of juniper, and a quiver filled with blunt tips. She kneels before him with the gear. "All right. Open your eyes."

He drops the rocks from his hands. She hands him the weapon, the rough form of a lion engraved just above the handgrip.

Zane lets the unstrung bow sit in his open hands. He looks up at Esel with wide eyes.

"We will teach you how to shoot that properly this week," Esel says, taking it back from him and placing it back into the case.

He takes a step to run, but Jacinta intercepts him with one hand. She nods toward Esel.

"Thank you," he says. He snatches the rocks at his feet and runs off.

Esel aligns her feet and body to the target, pulls an arrow from her quiver, and places it in the raised leather nock on the string.

"Yakup from Amirate Two will recover?" Esel asks.

"He should. As ought the other six bedded in the first tent," Jacinta says. "I am glad the clash at al-Salihiyya was cut short. It could have been much worse. Few attendants and many wounded are a bad mix."

"Yes," Esel says. She raises her bow arm parallel to the ground and takes a breath. Sighting the target, she draws her bowstring and releases the nocked arrow in a single motion. Her arrow punches into the center of the target, beside three more. "Soon the caregiver will be in need of another line of work."

"I am sure your nephew will find another battlefield soon enough. Our cots will not be half-filled for long."

Esel nods.

"Back when your nephew first questioned me, I tried to convince him that I was also a good cook—that it is what bonded my mother and me," Jacinta says, a girlish twinkle forming in her eye as she thinks back to those comforting times.

Esel nocks another arrow and looks over, smiling. "Yes, a cook. But would that have been a good place for an unfamiliar spy whose dependability was still on trial? Baybars may have felt his new mole capable of slipping poison into the Bahri's gruel."

Jacinta chuckles. "So, instead, your nephew placed me near his wounded, where I had access to blades and bone cleavers?"

They both laugh.

"While I am sure the troops would appreciate your cooking, I think Baybars may consider you too valuable for that work," Esel says.

Jacinta's head drops. "Why is it that every Mamluk Amir I encounter feels me capable of more? This insight of theirs usually leads me into danger, or jobs in far-off places—or both."

"Baybars figures the Mongols camped in the pastures of Azerbaijan will approach Syria by way of Mayyafariquin and Amid."

Jacinta fears what will come from Esel's mouth next.

"He wants trusted eyes on the Tartars," Esel says.

"Trusted? Maybe your nephew is too quick to fully rely on a spy who only two moons ago was working for those most despised by the Bahri."

Esel lowers her bow. "No, I do not think so." She grins. "Baybars trusts me and my judgment. And I have developed a confidence in you."

Jacinta sighs. "So Baybars wishes to send me on a camel ride twenty days north to the Jazira?"

Esel tilts her head and shrugs one shoulder.

"Why would Baybars organize such?" Jacinta asks. "Would this not be a task already shouldered by the Prince of Karak or al-Nasir of Damascus? Both of these royals have plenty of gold to spend on emissaries who have the knack to spy while crossing the Jazira."

Esel frowns. "Since the loss in al-Salihiyya, Baybar's relationship with the al-Mughith of Karak has been . . . strained."

Jacinta nods.

"I do not think Baybars has faith in any words spoken by al-Mughith or al-Nasir," Esel says. "He does not feel either prince would tell him the truth about the situation with the Mongols—even if they could convince emissaries to go on such an assignment."

"So Baybars wishes to send me?"

Esel looks into Jacinta's cat eyes. "He believes word only from those he knows and sends personally."

"I know he is your nephew and how fond you are of him, but Baybars has but three hundred Mamluks, plus allies. Why does he act as if he is the one running the entire empire?"

Esel grins. "I think you probably know the reason. Baybars recognizes that if three hundred of the best will follow him into the unknowns of the desert for four years of misery and exile, then thirty thousand will also follow him from the steadiness and wealth of Cairo."

Jacinta looks at Zane. The boy inspects more rocks that he has neatly laid upon a slab.

"I know I may be partial, but to some men this sense of responsibility and ability to lead comes innately," Esel says. "Baybars has a few other emissaries out, moles sent to the north. But he needs someone who knows her way around Jazira and you have been there several times. The Tartars will suspect all fair-skinned, Turkish-speaking men of being Mamluks and spies. There will be Mongols in the marketplaces. With the right prompting, some might divulge their commanders' plans, when and where they might attack next."

Jacinta sighs. "I know, I know. My strength. And a dark-skinned woman with a child would be less suspicious." She watches Zane rearrange his stones, apprehensive at the thought of having to take him on another long journey into foreign lands. "Although from what I have heard, the Mongols do not care much for the ginger root I sell." Jacinta looks hopefully to Esel.

Esel smiles. "I am sure the Bahri would stock you with things the Mongols do buy."

"Of course. Maybe you are better suited for your nephew's task than I am, as who would expect an old lady spy? And we both know the Mongols are buyers of weapons. Who knows more about bows than you?"

Esel looses another arrow and chuckles. "I see now why Aybeg and Qutuz treated you so roughly. You are more than a little flippant."

"Both rudeness and politeness have gotten me nowhere."

Esel nocks another arrow. She draws, still smiling.

"Could you teach me to use that? You have just armed my boy. Perhaps I should know a thing or two about how to handle one."

They move closer to the target and Esel instructs Jacinta on the basics of stance, draw, and release.

Jacinta shoots several arrows, which splatter the edges of the target with inaccurate shots.

"Remember your falcon talons, my friend. Do not clasp the grip so tightly—that only introduces the left and right variability in your shots."

"There is more to this skill than one would think," Jacinta says.

"True for most things. My husband, Yagmur, had the most natural form I ever saw. The best warrior."

Jacinta releases another arrow. "When did you lose him?"

Esel stares at the target. "Seventeen years ago the Mongols drove my people west in flight from our homeland. The Tartars told our Kipchak khan, 'submit or die.' He chose to run instead. He convinced the tower that we could start a new life on the Tauric Peninsula."

Esel sighs and looks down. "So in the Sivash, the Turks who allowed our tower safe passage broke their word. They fell upon us, killing many and enslaving those who survived—Baybars and myself included. Yagmur was wounded, but recovered. The Mongols caught wind of his skill in leathercraft and spared him. I think his witnessing the end of our tower was his final curse. The death of his brothers and friends, the rape of our women. He took his own life the first chance he had. Bound in chains, he jumped overboard, rather than allowing himself to be put on the slave block. Drowned in the Black Sea."

"I am so sorry," Jacinta says.

"I have told few of this."

"It is very sad."

Esel nods. "It has been many years now." She looks over. "This man, Leander. He must also be something special for you to have done what you have this past year. How did you come across him?"

Jacinta sits. "Nine years ago, I met him at the infirmary in Cairo, where I was spying for the sultan then, al-Salih." She smiles, reflecting. "Never thought I would see that time as joyous. But amid the gore born from King Louis' invasion, I got to know Leander. I was nervous in his presence at first—he was a Crusader; I am a Muslim. Yet I learned to feel differently, admiring this striking man who had years before chosen to fight alongside my people, rather than against us."

"Hmm."

Jacinta rests the bow tip on her slipper. "Leander was wounded during the Crusader attack at Damietta and placed in my care. We had nice talks at his bedside. Once he recovered, we continued to see each other in town, whenever we could. Those were the best of times."

"Odd how the hardest spells can often produce the most fertile breeding ground for tenderness," Esel says.

Jacinta smiles forlornly. "I often wondered if the spark between us was because of the contrast. It was one of the few bright spots for us both, during a time of much loss and ruin in our lives."

"Why did you not marry?" Esel asks.

"My father would have none of it. He eventually forbade me from seeing Leander. My father refused to even utter his name, just called him 'the Franj.'"

"Could you not have left?"

"And I would have. But. . . "

"What?" Esel asks, her brow furled.

"This work of the mole. Eventually, or perhaps inevitably, it destroys people. Sometimes the spy, sometimes those spied upon—often both. Ripping apart bonds formed of legitimate affection."

Esel's look asks for more.

"The old sultan, Aybeg, along with Qutuz. They ensnared me," Jacinta says. "When tensions rose between the Mamluk regiments, after the death of al-Salih, Aybeg and the senior Salihi became paranoid. They deployed spies everywhere. Eventually, Aybeg decided to assassinate Bahri amirs and others he deemed valuable. Of course, you know Baybars' mentor, Aqtay, was killed then."

Esel nods.

"Well, Leander was on this list of important Bahri, too. He was vital because of his ability to interpret many languages. Aybeg and Qutuz tasked me with luring him into an eatery, where he would then be captured by hired Bedu. As always, Aybeg swore my family's death if I did not assist."

Esel shakes her head.

"On the night of the snatch, I wavered. I was seized with indecision. The Bedu assigned to detain Leander tried to kill him instead. Leander surely figured my hand was in this."

Esel. "Oh, child."

"There are regrets in life and then there are lapses in wisdom that can torture a person's soul. That night when the Bedu attempted to kill Leander is such for me. Unforgiveable."

"And you still hope this man will return to you?"

"It remains my wish. I have come this far to reclaim our affection. I shall not stop now."

Esel looks at the smattering of arrows on the target and then back to her friend. "You are not only a flippant one, but a stubborn one, too."

Jacinta smiles. "And unfortunately, a ditherer at the wrong times." She looks at her feet. "And I am the woman the leader of the Bahri wishes to send spying on the empire's most deadly enemy?" She fires an arrow, which hits closer to the center of the target.

"Better," Esel says. "Your release is smoothing. Your clutch on the grip has loosened. You just need some practice."

Zane returns with a fistful of purple flowers. He hands them to his mother.

"Lovely," Jacinta says.

"A charmer." Esel nods at the boy.

"Well, my name means hyacinth. He brings them to me whenever he finds them."

Esel smiles.

Jacinta carefully lays the flowers atop a rock. She shoots again, her arrow striking the right side of the target.

"Ehh," Esel gives a mock groan. "Well, I do not know exactly where Baybars will assign you, but I may try to steer you away from duty with his archers."

They laugh.

Jacinta hands Esel the bow and picks up her blooms. She smells them. "My mother used to tell me, 'Blossom where you are planted, my little flower.'" Her smile fades. The notion of another extended camel trek with Zane and a mission of spying on a dangerous enemy in unstable territories turns her apprehension to fear.

CHAPTER 35

Leander

Ghuta, southeast of Damascus

November 30, 1258

A squared-jawed Mamluk they call "Knuckles" stands before him. Leander rubs a piece of charcoal across the warrior's cheeks and forehead, eliminating the shine from his white face.

"Finally, a proper mission. I was getting a little tired of pilfering ebony and cedar wood, moon after moon," Knuckles says.

Leander shrugs. "I do not know. I was sort of growing fond of being the pursuer, instead of the pursued."

The trooper cracks a smile. "I suppose for you, filching strings of camels from a few guards is better than a year of nosing around in some far-off country, surrounded by Mongols."

"That, and since coming back, I cannot remember the last time I was hungry. If I would have known how well these camel tenders eat when I first came to the Levant, I might have rethought my line of work."

The Bahri laughs. "My mother would be saddened to know that her son has turned from Mamluk to brigand."

Leander grins. The young cavalryman's jest is not far from the truth. The Bahri's raid tonight outside of Damascus is the closest to a true military maneuver they have planned in more than a month. And for the past seven moons, they have been little more than freebooters. Since leaving Baghdad and rejoining the rest of Amirate Three, Duyal's unit has pillaged one caravan after another.

It started with goods in the *Ghaur* and the trade-rich coastal roads, belonging to al-Nasir Yusuf of Damascus. When the prince improved caravan security on the coast, Baybars shifted his Mamluks' efforts. For weeks more, they focused on other lightly guarded tracks in the prince's Syrian principalities. No spur of any trade route was safe from them. The Bahri drifted from road to road, like organized bees drifting from flower to flower.

Baybars was not stingy with the honey he had gathered. Stolen goods of no use to his army were sold to unscrupulous merchants in the backcountry. Baybars used this silver to buy the best mounts and weapons for his growing force. Those new arrivals from Cairo—more Salihi who left Qutuz—arrived to find fresh Arabians and new kit.

It was too easy. Al-Nasir's guards typically dropped their lances and swords as soon as they saw a red-lioned pennant. No merchant had the stomach to fight the Bahri Mamluks, no matter the value of their trade goods. Camel pullers began referring to the Bahriyya as *alshayatin albyd* (white devils), due to the abundance of silver and goods that the Mamluks seized.

Leander sees Baybars as an alley cat, a skilled mouser, a bright hunter always changing his locations. With his paw on al-Nasir's tail, the Bahri's leader bats around and toys with the prince—as well as with the merchants and traders whose tax coin was critical for maintaining Damascus.

Knuckles takes the charcoal from Leander and rubs the piece across the Frank's nose and cheeks. Leander's comrade is from Amirate Five, one of the nine "Amirates of Forty" in Baybars' regiment. The two men join Baybars, comprising the "command team."

Knuckles' only task on this coming mission will be to cover Baybars' back and ignite a firelance when Baybars signals the command to withdraw. While Leander holds the grade of Amir of Ten—qualifying him to lead a squad of Mamluks—the Frank's lethal reputation in close combat and his understanding of the Kurdish and Arabic spoken by the enemy are what places him at their commander's side tonight. He serves both as Baybars' second bodyguard and interpreter.

Singer and several other Mamluks also darken their faces, while the rest of the thirteen men hand-selected by Baybars string bows and stow spare daggers and light-headed maces on their belts and small packs.

All dress for speed and stealth, their armor limited to chainmail hauberks. They forego the heavier cuirass, the chest plate with its overlapping iron "lames" known to squeal on their leather bindings while on the move. The Mamluks also wear tight-fitting slippers, not noisy boots.

Knuckles lifts his chin toward Baybars, who prepares his war belt in solitude. "Look at him." Knuckles says. "Able to direct hundreds of Mamluks in formations stretching across the desert, plus handle a drove of fickle allies. But here he is, dirtying his hands on this little raid."

"He cannot help himself," Leander says. "He has to be where the fight is. It is his nature."

"Tsst. You would think those Ayyubid princes, men with Saladin's blood coursing through their veins, would be the ones to lead us against our real enemies."

"I think al-Nasir and al-Mughith used to drive Baybars mad," Leander says. "Sitting idly for years and wringing their hands like fishwives. Haggling among each other, worrying about the Muizziyya in Egypt, worrying about the Mongols, worrying about the Crusaders—but doing very little to actually counter these enemies."

"Aside from talking," Knuckles says mockingly. "And I suppose al-Nasir had pretty poems to write and walks in the garden that were more important to him than marshalling his force."

Leander rolls his eyes. He flings the charcoal and wipes his hands on his trousers.

"Since Gaza, I do not think Baybars worries much about the princes," Knuckles says.

Leander agrees. While Leander was with Amirate Three along the coast, the remaining Bahri raided the suburbs of Damascus last moon and then bolted to Palestine with the booty. The Syrian merchants howled in frustration.

Reluctant to take action, as always, al-Nasir eventually sent two thousand of his cavalry toward Baybars' base, near Gaza. Baybars surprised al-Nasir's Syrians, attacking with only six hundred horsemen, three quarters of those being Bedouin fighters, the *muqatila*.

Al-Nasir's troops initially overran both wings of Baybars' tiny force, but seventy Mamluks held the center with Baybars. These Bahri counterattacked, running al-Nasir's men from the field with their tails tucked between their cheeks. This victory increased Baybars' prestige among both friends and foes. Gaza, Hebron, and Nablus now bow to him.

Leander grins. "Baybars has done a job on al-Mughith and al-Nasir. He has exploited every sliver of advantage offered by either and kept the royals pitted against each other in the process. All while looting their caravans and collecting their gifts of arms, draining their treasuries. He has beaten them at their own ploys."

Knuckles smiles, engrossed in watching their leader don his gear.

On their own accord, by team, the Mamluks form a horseshoe around Baybars, a huddle of darkened faces, white eyes, and burly shoulders, barely visible in the night. Leander makes out the forms of Singer and Duyal standing alongside.

Baybars nods. "We will depart soon. Any final questions on our route, our plan?"

All remain silent, heads turning from man to man.

"Our lookouts should be at al-Nasir's camp now. If they see anything over the hill at al-Nasir's bivouac that would require a change to our plan, we will make those adjustments at the objective rally point."

The men nod.

"Flank guards, diversion-makers, kill team—anything at all?" Baybars looks to each team leader and then last to his own command team, Leander and Knuckles.

Leander shakes his head. How could they have questions? For three days the leaders organized and rehearsed every detail of this undertaking. Alternate routes and reassembly points. Backup plans and redundancy of critical gear. All of this has been considered and practiced. Leander looks near the command tent.

Baybars' terrain model of al-Nasir's camp lies obscured in the dark. The place where they scripted the maneuver. Mounds of contoured dirt simulate the rolling hills of the Ghuta—plus all of the outlying countryside, along Damascus' eastern and southern rim. Shrub branches stuck in the ground suggest thick cover. Heeled-in depressions represent water sources and streams. White pieces of canvas dot the mockup, showing the exact location of the tents of al-Nasir's Aziziyya Mamluks; brown pieces signify the one-man camel tents of his Syrian regulars. A single red piece denotes al-Nasir's royal pavilion—the objective—the place where the Prince of Damascus now camps in the Ghuta's oasis.

And this astute planning is not their only advantage here. Those gathered are some of the Bahri's best. Most have been in one of al-Nasir's camps before, while drilling with al-Nasir's

Mamluks years ago, when the relationship between Baybars and the Prince of Damascus was more genial. Firsthand, these troops have watched the times and frequency with which the prince's royal guard switched shifts.

"Keep always in the front of your mind my intent here, brothers. We make this raid to harass, disrupt, and demoralize al-Nasir. Fire more dissention in his ranks. That is it." He shrugs. "If we kill the weakling prince, that would only be a sweetener."

"Errr," the men grunt in the affirmative.

"We come to let the coward know that not only will we empty his merchants' panniers of valuables, we will also slit his throat in the night. Let his troops see him scared once again. Let more unrest be thrust upon the louse."

"Errr!"

Unrest, indeed. Baybars' moles reported endless bickering within al-Nasir's forces. The Bahri's raids and victory in Gaza have unsettled Damascus and threatened the prince's control of Palestine.

And since losing the support of the Shahrazur Kurds to the Prince of Karak, al-Nasir has grown paranoid. He required a renewed oath of loyalty from all his forces, yet his father's men, the Aziziyya, predictably balked. These Mamluks demanded larger fiefs and al-Nasir had no choice but to accede. With his capital exposed to attack, the royal set his camp outside the Damascene walls.

Baybars notices a troop looking skyward and mumbling a short prayer to himself. Others purse their lips.

"We have already snatched al-Nasir's jewels arriving from across the desert. Let us see if one of us might also hack off the pair that remain between his legs." Baybars wags a finger at them. "Yet do not waste much time looking there. My guess is that you may come up empty."

A roar of laughter from the men.

His smile eases to a frown. “Tonight we strike in the shadows. Tonight we exploit the momentum we have built.”

The men nod.

“But tonight we also keep our wits about us. We will sneak among al-Nasir’s thousands. All men bolder than he.” Baybars rests his hand upon Knuckles’ shoulder. “Upon my signal for withdrawal, we beat feet. Swift and orderly. We make this raid to sow chaos in al-Nasir’s ranks, not bury our brothers.”

He turns his head to eye each of them. “No casualties, no prisoners. And out before the full moon rises to expose us.”

CHAPTER 36

Leander

Ghuta, southeast of Damascus

November 30, 1258

Baybars walks up from the rear of the short column in the darkness, counting each man. Thirteen Bahri total. Satisfied, he steps off at the front of the staggered file, Leander behind him.

They head north. Baybars bobs and slides through the desert scrub, his long legs churning effortlessly. Leander recollects the alpha leopard he saw years past in the western desert, the muscular beast departing his high-limbed perch once the gazelles came near. With scarred head slunk between its shoulders, the predator closed on his quarry in the crouch, its curled tail lowered, its tip twitching in anticipation.

They reach the objective rally point, a safe distance from al-Nasir's camp. The men deploy into a hasty perimeter. Baybars' two lookouts rise from the prone. They have already put eyes on the bivouac and were lying here in wait, as designed.

Baybars receives their thumbs up, a signal that nothing has changed which would necessitate an alteration in plan.

Leander kneels beside Knuckles, who pulls a small blanket from his pack and digs in his pouch for his tinder kit and two sections of starter fuse. Knuckles drops to his butt and drapes the blanket over his head and shoulders. A clicking of stone sounds from under the cover. He emerges holding two fuses like coiled snakes, whorls of smoke emitting from each head. He hands a fuse to one of the diversion-makers, who joins his teammate. Knuckles slides the unlit end of the other up his sleeve, clamping the burning end between his middle fingers. He stows his blanket.

The diversion-makers remove the six pre-rigged firelances protruding from the tops of their packs. The men verify that the "slow matches" remain attached to the bottom of the bamboo tubes. They tighten the hemp lashings, which bind the explosive cylinders to their half lances on the opposite end of the spear from the pointed head, making it easier to shove them into the ground.

They nod their readiness to Baybars. He points them eastward and the two depart amid a sprinkling of shoulder pats from their mates, heading for the flatter side of al-Nasir's camp.

The remainder of the patrol, the flank guards and Duyal's kill team, wait for several minutes, listening intently for any sign of distress from the diversion team. Hearing nothing, Baybars stands, circles his finger in the air, and points to the ground, reminding them that this place will also serve as the withdrawal reassembly point. Leander notes the distinctive outline of the trees against the black sky in the clearing, orienting himself to this meeting place that he must find his way back to in the dark.

Baybars leads, stepping into a dry streambed. He slows the pace to a crawl, stopping intermittently to listen. The raspy screech of a desert owl breaks the night silence. A like reply from the north. A lizard scuttles from its wormwood cover. Leander sucks in the cold air and releases a swirl of frosty breath.

They stalk northward. Leander treads lightly, feeling for any loose rocks or branches beneath his slippers. They reach the concealment of a cluster of date palms. They take stock of their position and then turn slightly west, toward al-Nasir's side of camp.

Baybars' two lookouts stay to guard the patrol's rear, while the remaining men continue stalking westward. They move between stands of oak and clusters of pistachio, using the trees to mask their movement, the branches brushing silently against their trousers and the soft-clothed covering on their hauberks. Upon reaching the western edge of the Syrian camp, they inch their way closer to al-Nasir's pavilion. A chorus of snores emanates from between the lines of tents. Two enemy watchmen bicker nearby, the pair debating some petty topic.

Staying to the edge of the camp, the Bahri halt a short distance from the prince's extravagant marquee. Baybars pats the top of his head. The four flank guards creep up to a finger of higher ground. They spread out along the thick tufts of sawgrass, which afford cover atop the bump of elevation, yet also clear shots at both the prince's tent to their front and the unit's west flank behind them. The lead guard raises a thumb.

Baybars' men and the four Mamluks in Duyal's kill team sneak into position atop the hummock. They wait.

From the east side of camp, Leander sees three flashes of light, followed by concussive thumps as the diversion-makers deploy their firelances. Two more low explosions and shouts in Arabic ascend in the distance. A clatter of wings on nearby oak branches as the desert owls abandon their hunting perches.

Syrian voices rise in panic. Men pile out of their tents. Soldiers run eastward with lances and swords bared. A blurt of orders from their amirs. The last firelance detonates to the east.

Boom.

"Now," Baybars says, patting Duyal on the back. Duyal rises from his knee and creeps with his three men toward al-Nasir's tent, dagger in hand.

Baybars turns to Knuckles. "Be ready to light your fuses."

Knuckles pulls the two firelances from his pack and jams the spear tips into the sand, the lances pointing skyward. He eases more of the smoldering fuse from his sleeve.

The kill team moves to the north end of the rectangular tent, the side where al-Nasir is known to sleep. A Mamluk stabs the canvas and slices an arched entrance into the tent with his razor-sharp blade. Duyal leaps through the opening with the trio behind him. A woman inside screams. The sounds of a scuffle. A chair or table smashes. A man hollers in pain. The woman's shrieking voice stops abruptly.

Like ground squirrels flushed from their hole by a badger, men stumble out from al-Nasir's tent flap wearing only their tunics.

Baybars' flank guards rise amid the reeds. The twang of bow strings sing from up high. The whisp of a dozen arrows sizzle the air, as the Mamluks shoot from their overwatch position.

Arrows thwack into chests and torsos. The enemy slump to the ground.

Only grunts now from within the tent. In the distance, Leander can hear al-Nasir's amirs. They organize. Baybars begins to fidget.

Baybars looks to Knuckles. "Light it." Knuckles moves to his firelances and touches his starter fuse to the slow matches stubbed from the end of his tubes.

Boots pound the dusted earth. More Syrian soldiers run westward, perhaps having found the expended firelances on the east side of camp.

Baybars looks to the firelances, the slow match gone. Smoke twirls near the seated powder at the base of the bamboo. His primary signal devices appear to fail. He whistles loudly three times, his alternate indication for all men to withdraw from the objective area.

The game is up.

Two men from the kill team pop out from their hole in the tent. They hold their hands straight out from their bodies to prevent being skewered by the Mamluk flankers. Another Bahri follows.

These three scamper into the ravine out of sight. The flank guards, too, melt into the vegetation.

Leander hears more orders from al-Nasir's amirs in Arabic, closer now. He leans to Baybars. "They are on to our ruse. Troops are being ordered to come this way."

The north side of al-Nasir's tent collapses. Nothing moves under the heavy cloth, those inside possibly hiding under furniture or playing possum.

"Duyal is not out," Baybars says.

Leander sees one lump moving on the north end of the tent. He wonders if his friend continues the search for al-Nasir.

An uncomfortable tingle radiates from Leander's gut down to his fingertips. His amir is left exposed.

Boom.

Leander jumps. One of Knuckles' firelances explodes. A blast of flame showers the ground, followed by a burst of red exploding high in the air.

"Go, now!" Baybars says, turning from them.

Inbound enemy drop to the ground in clunks of shield and chainmail. Helmets topple from their heads as they take cover. Other Syrians retreat eastward.

One of al-Nasir's Mamluks walks the tent perimeter with sword in hand. He, too, sees the bump moving under the canvas. Duyal.

"Leave. I will get him," Leander tells Knuckles, pulling his dagger.

Leander runs to the north side of the tent, where he hopes to cross the enemy. That familiar rage swells. He embraces the bolstering inferno inside him, blessedly known to arrive before engaging any foe. The force seems to scald and then burn off the fear in his heart.

This frenzy sends him blissfully, perhaps ignorantly, forward. He will not let this bastard kill his friend.

He loses awareness of his feet and legs. Leander glides. As if watching his body from above, he stays his collision course with the soldier. He sees nothing but the visor and pointed shape of the Syrian helmet. Closer, closer.

The enemy, too, appears oblivious to anything but the lump under the tent. A blade tip protrudes, a man slashing his way out of the canvas. A chain-mailed arm reaches outside the canvas.

Leander arrives with a violent strike below the Syrian's jaw, delivered just as the soldier raises his sword. Leander feels his dagger plunge clear to its crossguard. He rips down on the blade, his force stopped by the chain mail armor at the man's neck.

His momentum knocks the Syrian atop the crumpled tent. The two roll, becoming a mass of tangled limbs. Duyal is out and pulls Leander to his feet. The enemy writhes in the dirt, blood spurting from his neck.

Duyal and Leander run into the thickest scrub. He shoves Duyal before him. "Faster."

Branches slap their faces. Buckthorn tears at their skin.

They break through the undergrowth and plow across the soft sand of a wadi, stumbling over protruding rocks. They circle toward the reassembly point.

The two burst into the clearing and fall in a pile, their chests heaving. A pair of Mamluk eyes look down. Thanks be to Allah. The reassembly point. Leander feels a tug on his hauberk. He fights his way to his knees, the sand cold against his palms.

Duyal lies sprawled.

"The prince escaped from his tent, my Amir," a Mamluk says to Duyal.

Duyal drops his forehead into the sand.

Baybars pushes aside Duyal's teammate. Their commander leans down to Duyal's ear. He whispers with chin jutted, "Disengage means disengage. We will talk on this later."

Baybars squints at the faint glow on the eastern horizon, the moon proclaiming its ascent. He turns to the others in the perimeter and chops his arm in the direction of their intended withdrawal southward.

CHAPTER 37

Esel

Karak Citadel

March 16, 1259

Esel props her elbows atop the backside of the parapet and gazes into the blustery twilight. Opposite the Karak Citadel, a faint crimson splatters the flat-topped mountains, their ancient peaks rounded, their drainages splotched in dark patches of brush. Tendrils of gray rain hang like a blowing curtain from the darkest of the clouds, obscuring the more distant mountains. She waits for the last of Baybars' soldiers to arrive at the fortification like a Kipchak mother frets until each of her sons are safe in their gers after their evening hunt.

In the low light, a flag in Ayyubid yellow materializes from the north. Horsemen, along the path below. As the column nears, Esel picks out the numeral three on their red-lioned pennant; a string of forty-six warriors behind it, straight-backed and dusted. She sighs in relief.

In punishment for Baybars' attempt on al-Nasir's life last November—plus the Bahri's raiding of the same prince's caravans for months—al-Nasir summoned his ally, al-Mansur of Hama. This royal pair assembled their armies and descended south toward Karak.

Venturing a day's ride north of Karak last week, Baybars and Prince al-Mughith of Karak found these challengers near Jericho. There, the Princes of Damascus and Hama dealt the Bahri and al-Mughith's undersized cavalry a quick defeat.

After the clash, Baybars fled the battlefield with several hundred of his men, taking sanctuary here in al-Mughith's bastion. Wishing to consolidate his forces, Baybars sent a runner north of Palestine with word for Amirates Three and Four, men who for months had plundered al-Nasir's caravans, to also return to Karak.

En route to the Karak Citadel, Baybars tasked the approaching Amirate Three to locate the whereabouts of al-Nasir's victorious army. Esel hopes the arriving Mamluks will report that the Prince of Damascus no longer lingers in Transjordan and that he has taken his troops home. She worries for the future of the Bahri and her nephew, as Baybars has managed to alienate every prince in the area.

The Bahri cross the northern bridge, their hoof clops resonating against the high stone face of the citadel. The pale talc of the country coats the legs of their Arabians, the dust tapering to a lighter tan up the riders' yellow trousers. Only the tops of their shoulders bear the washed-out red of their long coats, the men in their scarlet *qaba* of winter.

She takes the stairs, circling down the tight stone steps. She turns left down a vaulted passage, looking up at the thousands of hand-placed stones locked into the narrow overhead. A rat scurries past. She enters the northern courtyard where the troops now dismount their Arabians, handing their reins to eager *ghulams*, young slave boys.

While she has met most of the troops from Amirate Three over the past year, she has yet to come across the Franj, Leander. For moons, this soldier's knowledge of languages has made him a magnet for translating missions that pulled him away from the main body of Bahri. Baybars mentioned over dinner last night that their Frankish interpreter will be among the men returning today.

She catches the arm of a Mamluk who shuffles on sore legs. "Glad you are back safely," she says. "Is the translator, Leander, with you?"

Recognizing Esel as Baybars' aunt, he nods respectfully, his eyelashes crusted, his beard caked in a dirty powder. He points to a lanky Mamluk tending his horse.

This tall man leans his forehead against his mare's muzzle and scratches behind her ears. He whispers something to her before handing her off to the groom. "Stick to the hay if you would," he instructs. "The barley does not agree with her."

The ghulam nods. Leander pats the lad's back.

Esel smiles. He seems a good man, as Jacinta described.

He turns to leave.

"You are the soldier, Leander?" she asks.

"Yes."

She looks up at him. "I have heard much of you."

Leander regards her quizzically.

"Good things. Welcome to Karak."

He grins. "I wish it were under better circumstances. And you are. . .?"

"I am Esel, an armorer of sorts here."

He raises his dirty eyebrows and inclines his head. "Esel, the gifted bowyer. The huntress from the old country. The aunt of Amir Baybars. Oh yes, I have heard plenty. I am honored."

"When you are settled, could you come to the chamber off the eastern hall? I have something there for you," she says.

"Of course. Let me stow my gear and I will be there."

Leander tends to his kit as Esel returns to her quarters and gathers three of the best weapons that she has labored over for the past year.

She waits, seated at a table in the agreed-upon room, reading by candlelight a text on Muslim cavalry tactics given to her by Baybars.

A knock on the door.

"Please enter." Esel says, looking up from her book, a wooden cup of steaming tea in her hand.

"Ah, a reader," he says. "And a strategist."

She smiles. "Well, a reader I suppose, but nothing compared to what I have heard about your appetite for books." She slides a second mug to him.

He smiles. "Thank you."

"Did you find al-Nasir of Damascus?"

Leander scowls. "Yes, Amir Sedat is informing Baybars now. But it appears after Jericho that al-Nasir made his camp to the north in Birkat Ziza. And by the number of tents and lovely concubines with him, it appears he is planning to stay for a while."

"Not good," she says.

"He surely hates that so many Bahri have escaped him to come here. He likely schemes on how he can defeat us without lifting a sword or bloodying his men. Probably figures he can pressure al-Mughith to give us up to him."

She shakes her head. She stands and walks to a corner table, where she removes a beautiful crossbow and two recurves from their leather cases. "These, for you and your brothers, Duyal and Singer."

Leander looks down at the weapons, dumbfounded. His eyes stay on the crossbow. "Thank you. What is the occasion for gifts as fine as these?"

"Baybars asked me to build them for you last spring. He wanted to give you three something special. None of the teams he sent to watch the Mongols traveled as far or were as thorough in their reports as yours."

"That would be Amir Duyal's team. And truthfully, our effectiveness was mostly because of him," he says, his lips tightening, knowing that she likely has her nephew's ear.

She reckons that Leander is understandably displeased that Baybars relieved Duyal of his command of Amirate Three after the raid on al-Nasir's camp last fall.

"Well, Baybars saw that the most useful of the scrolls came from your hand."

He lightens, his eyes going back to the table. "May I?"

He picks up one of the recurved bows and turns it sideways to inspect its laminated layers. His jawline sets hard beneath eyes both thoughtful and perceptive. "Beautiful. Both amirs will, of course, come to thank you in person."

Esel smiles. It is no wonder Jacinta fell for this Leander.

His eyebrows tighten, "I know Amir Duyal well. He will be respectful, but may not accept the weapon. He may say that if Baybars wishes to provide a gift, he would rather it be his old command. So take no offense. Duyal has not been himself."

"Well, my usefulness to Amir Baybars lies in the getting of quality weapons for his men. I surely have no say in who commands which amirate. I know you are fond of Duyal."

He picks up the crossbow. He rubs his hand up the tiller and inspects the composite staves. He works the trigger. "By Allah."

"It is my first. I heard that you have a pair of crossbows that were made in Genoa. I thought you could use a new one made for shorter ranges."

"My girls are over twenty years old and have so many replacement parts from so many places that I can hardly say they are Genoese anymore. I thank you."

She smiles. "You mention twenty years ago. I came to know Duyal's older brother, Gozde, during that same time. He spent two moons with my Kipchak tower in the steppe country. He was on a recon mission for his prince, similar to your undertaking. The Mongols were moving through my people's lands, even then."

"I heard that. He was injured and your people brought him back to health, if my memory serves?"

"While driving sheep with my husband, Baybars found Gozde hiding after an attack by a Mongol patrol. My nephew was but a lad."

Leander shakes his head, smiles.

"We had never seen a Mamluk before. Gozde was strange to us. Stuck with arrows and close to dead. We took him home. One of our women nursed him back to health. Near the end of his recovery, Baybars took to Gozde, following him like a pup. The two were nearly inseparable for more than a month. Gozde taught the youth how to use a lance and a sword, and greatly improved the boy's archery skills. Gozde was probably the spark that put Baybars on the path to becoming a Mamluk."

He lays the crossbow upon its case. "Gozde, the Ribbon of Valor winner. Oh, how the world can get so very small."

"My point is that Baybars had a special connection to Gozde. And Baybars transferred his affection to Duyal after Gozde's death in battle. Baybars still carries the ivory thumb ring given to him by Gozde as a child, one of Baybars' few prized possessions. So I am sure the decision to relieve Duyal of command was not an easy one."

"I understand. Duyal did not show the discipline and restraint expected of an amir that day." Leander sighs. "There is a reason Baybars leads the Bahri."

She tilts her head.

Leander strokes his blond beard. "I do not say this to soften you up, in hopes that you will persuade Baybars to restore Duyal. But only one man stepped up to lead the fragmented Bahri in 1254, after we fled Aybeg's Muizziyya across the Sinai. Baybars."

She nods.

"I—we—would follow him anywhere. But you have to understand that Amir Duyal was my first and primary mentor. If Gozde was like a big brother to Baybars, then Duyal is such to me."

Leander looks to Esel's book and the stub of a candle flickering beside it. "I bare my heart to a woman I just met. My gibbering burns valuable tallow and wastes your reading time."

"No, I can read anytime. I appreciate this conversation." She smiles, looks down.

He goes to the table and cases the bows. "I thank you again." He stows the crossbow and hefts the cases across his shoulder.

She must get to her chief purpose in getting Leander alone. "Before you go. I have another thing to discuss with you."

He pauses, the three bags still atop his shoulder, and sits on the table corner.

"I have made friends with a young woman here. She knows you."

He raises his eyebrows.

"Jacinta, the woman you knew in Cairo ten years ago. She knows you serve Baybars and has come across the desert to see you."

Leander slips the bow cases from his shoulder. He gawks at the wall of jagged stone behind her head, his jaw agape. In time, he meets her eyes. "Jacinta is here? In Karak?"

"Yes."

He stands. "Do you know that she is a spy?"

"Yes."

He nods his head. "My friend, please listen. You are in grave danger. This woman is very clever, very deceptive. Very good at the infiltrator role she plays."

Esel feels a twinge of worry run down her spine. In the back of her mind, she wonders if Jacinta has fabricated her story. She wonders if their recent conversations, seemingly effortless and sincere, were also faked by her new friend.

Perhaps their budding friendship is entirely contrived. But surely Jacinta's passion when speaking of Leander was not pretended.

Esel shakes off her doubt. "I believe Jacinta came all the way from Cairo because of her love for you."

A twinge of anguish crosses his face. "Trouble follows this woman. She mesmerizes. She is an expert at misleading and devising stories. I know, I fell for her myself." He shakes his head. "She is here for business, not affection."

"She is here for you."

"If she is here for me, it is to get to something, or someone else through me—like to harm your nephew."

Esel's stomach goes queasy. She again begins to question her judgment, begins to question the validity of her new friend Jacinta. She stares at him.

"She is probably working for Qutuz or the boy sultan in Egypt," Leander says.

"She was. We netted her. Baybars and several other amirs questioned her at length. She is working with us now."

"Us?" He sits down again. "That work, those decisions, are well above my lowly grade. But I am telling you—do not trust her. She fooled me completely. Baybars needs to know that this woman is dangerous."

Esel makes a decision. "I trust her. And please, listen to yourself. A man who once wore the Crusader enemy's heraldry. A man who switched sides and was also interviewed many years back by the Sultan al-Salih and his amirs, and made to explain the purity of his intentions. A man who was given another chance, based on his word alone."

Leander looks away. He then nods in agreement. "I cannot rebuff my track to the Bahri. But it is not the same."

"Is it not? Men and women both have changes of heart. Both good and bad people make mistakes. For some it may take years, but often the good ones eventually come around to righting the wrongs that eat their souls. This a powerful motivation."

He looks into her eyes. "Yes. But I am not convinced she is good. While working for Aybeg, she set me up for an assassin's blade. And she nearly got it done."

Esel can tell Leander will hear no more discussion. He thumbs to the weapons on the table behind him. "I cannot thank you enough for these gifts. From the hands of an expert artisan."

"You and your team earned them." She clutches his callused hands. "Look, Jacinta left her family, risked her life in betraying Qutuz, and traveled long tracks of desert for no other reason than to speak with you and make things right. You owe her at least that chance."

He withdrew his hands from Esel's embrace. "I do not owe her anything. That same ploy she took part in five years after we met, which I narrowly evaded—it left other good men murdered in Cairo. There is Mamluk blood on her hands. If I owe her something, it is a blade across the throat."

Esel feels a tinge of sadness for Jacinta. Her friend stands no chance of winning back this man.

He appears to sense her melancholy. "Listen, we just lost three good men last week in Jericho. Hulegu Khan's son, Yoshmut, has been laying siege to Mayyafariqin for six months now. The route from Azerbaijan to the Jazira will soon be wide open for the Mongols. The Tartars may be down into Damascus—perhaps Cairo—before we know it."

He reaches for the cases. "And al-Nasir is only a two-day ride away from here. He probably hopes to chuck all the Bahri into prison for raiding his stores and caravans these last few moons. Al-Mughith is weak enough, in forces and character, to lose his nerve and surrender us. I—we—have enough complications right now. I surely do not need her in my life again on top of it."

He goes softer, looks up to the stone ceiling. “I can tell that you mean well. You are one of those good people that you mention.” He smiles, his eyes meet hers again. “But please, Esel. Remember who I serve. Your nephew. I need to keep my attention and dedication to the job at hand. For the Bahri’s road ahead looks more than a little daunting.”

CHAPTER 38

Cenk

Cairo palace

November 16, 1259

Cenk follows Tarkhan and Qutuz across the courtyard to a side passage. A squad of Muizziyya follow closely behind, their scaled armor squeaking in time with the clonk of bootheels on stone.

They reach the Sultan al-Mansur's quarters.

"We have matters to discuss with the sultan," Qutuz says to the pair of young Salihi guards. The fourteen troopers deploy abreast in two offset ranks behind the vicegerent and his amirs.

"The sultan is with a merchant, Vicegerent. He asked to be left undisturbed," the lead guard says, his eyes not on Qutuz or his counselors, but on the formation of soldiers to their rear. Both of the sultan's guards lock their long-handled axes across their bodies, their stances at the ready.

"Step aside," Qutuz says.

They grip their weapons tighter.

Qutuz shakes his head. "Obasi. Wade," Qutuz says in a fatherly voice. "Listen, Cenk and I watched you both arrive here by cart, years ago—ragged boys from the steppe, no different than we were. We witnessed you develop the skills of the faris and become good Mamluks. Egypt needs you both for the coming fight. She does not need you lying in a pool of blood here, after a needless scrap."

A look of resolve remains on the faces of both guards.

"Be wise now. You are both bound by oath and duty to give your life in order to protect the sultan. But your first obligation is the defense of Mother Egypt."

Cenk sighs. He attempts to be patient. He advised the vicegerent against this expected parleying with the Salihi. "Tell the sultan's guards to lower their axes or prepare to die," was Cenk's guidance.

But to his credit, Qutuz, wishing to be a diplomat, waved off this counsel. Qutuz knows the report of his conduct and words here will spread like fire to the entire Egyptian army and to every merchant and mother in Cairo's streets. He wishes his message of unification to be clear from the outset, before he speaks to the masses at Friday Prayer.

Hence, the vicegerent does not now see himself negotiating with these two guards, but rather convincing the entire regiment of wavering Salihi to stay put in Cairo and stay loyal to him. Qutuz does not bargain with this pair of common soldiers—he demonstrates to the entire army that he is the one ordained to protect the frightened people of Egypt and beyond. He alone is worthy to be sultan during these worrisome times.

Qutuz points to the western gate. "An emissary of al-Nasir of Damascus just arrived. I am sure he wishes to discuss a course of action against the Mongols on behalf of his prince." Obasi nods.

Qutuz fingers clench into a fist. "Lay down your weapons. I will not let Cairo's fate rest in the hands of a seventeen-year-old sultan who has barely sprouted whiskers. I have no intent to kill al-Mansur, only to detain him."

Wade lowers his axe.

Qutuz nods. He looks to Obasi. "Your Commander of the Guard is away hunting with his amirs. Assuming he is cooperative like you two, I will have no reason to harm them either."

Obasi lays his axe on the stone.

Qutuz steps forward and places his hand on Obasi's shoulder. "Good, my son. The survival of Egypt is bigger than protecting some unqualified inheritor to the throne. You have done the right thing, believe me."

Obasi looks down.

"Sultan al-Mansur is the son of Aybeg. Cenk and I not only served Aybeg loyally when he was sultan, we also shed sweat and blood with him within the ranks, when we were your age. By Allah, Aybeg is of our Khushdash. We will not kill the son of our own blood brother. There is no shame here for you."

Qutuz steps past the guards and into the royal chamber. Cenk, Tarkhan, and the Muizziyya follow.

The lad Al-Mansur, cloaked in a robe woven with golden thread, sits across from the vendor, the royal staff leaning against his thin arms.

"What are you doing?" the sultan asks. "I said no interruptions. Leave."

"Do not worry, where you are going there will be few interruptions." Qutuz looks to his troops. "Seize him."

Two Muizziyya grab the sultan by each arm and lift him from his high-backed seat. Al-Mansur does not struggle.

Qutuz eyes the merchant and points to the door. "Go."

The vendor steals to a small gap between the edge of the Mamluks' formation and the stone wall. He darts from the room.

"Get your hands off me, or you will soon have no hands!" al-Mansur tells the soldiers.

"That is not going to happen," Qutuz says.

Al-Mansur stiffens. “I am your sultan, and you will order these men to release me, Vicegerent.”

“I will not.”

Cenk tires of the theatrics. “Take the lad to the north gate,” he says to the squad leader. “A cart awaits.”

Al-Mansur winces at the soldiers’ grip on him. “Each man here,” al-Mansur points a roaming finger to all, “commits an offense punishable by death.”

“The only one here deserving of a death sentence is you.” Qutuz strolls toward the sultan. “Even once you knew the Mongols held Baghdad, plus all of al-Nasir Yusof’s possessions east of the Euphrates, you freed little coin for us to prepare for war.”

The sultan looks away.

Qutuz walks closer. “And even after learning that the Prince of Mosul, a traitor, now besieges Amid, and that Hulegu’s supply lines through the Jazira will soon be clear, you haggle with these merchants for weeks, instead of directing all of Cairo’s resources to the coming fight with Hulegu’s army.”

“Without more tax revenue from the merchants, there is no gold for a campaign,” the boy-sultan whines.

“Tsst. The sellers need to be told to pay, not bartered with. There will be no merchants, no buildings, no Egyptians if we do not stop the Tartars before they reach Cairo. Gold is the least of our problems. We told you this. The empire’s Syrian principalities and Cairo will be Hulegu’s next target. We now have little time to prepare.”

“You will be crucified for this,” the sultan says.

Qutuz raises a lip in disgust. “Death by Mongol sword will likely be the fate of us all, if bold action is not taken in the next few hours, the next few days. And you are not the man for such a job.”

The sultan looks at him, openmouthed.

“You will be taken to the safety of Damietta,” Qutuz says. “One step from the sea, where you can board a ship and depart if the Mongols get that far. We do this for your own good. We do this as a sign of devotion to your departed father."

"You do this as a sign of your selfishness. You use the Mongols as an excuse to seize power. And one day you will pay for it with your life."

Qutuz snorts. "My life!" He looks to Cenk, who glares at the adolescent.

The vicegerent steps in front of the boy sultan. "If Allah provides us with the miracle we need to defeat the Mongol scourge, I will bring you back from Damietta and we will see how the populace responds to the dreadful charges against you."

Qutuz looks to the soldiers about him. "All standing here, except you, will either be martyrs or living heroes. If we are the warriors who save Damascus and Cairo, do you think anyone will listen to a word from you, a kept boy?"

Qutuz thumbs toward the door.

The Muizziyya drag the sultan into the passage as would a teacher haul an unruly child.

They reach the north gate.

Sitting in the back of a cart is al-Mansur's mother and his younger brother, both tied about the wrists and ankles. A supply cart and a squad of mounted Mamluks bring up the rear.

Al-Mansur refuses help into the wagon. The Muizziyya jump aboard and secure restraints upon him.

"You will suffer for your duplicity, your traitorous ploy," his mother hisses at Qutuz.

"Woman, you should view my *ploy* as generous charity for your family."

Qutuz looks up the hill toward the palace and back to the mother. "Tonight I will sleep much better, knowing that Cairo's strategy to counter the Mongol foe will be fashioned by me, your new sultan, and my counselors—and not your son."

Qutuz points the driver northward.

CHAPTER 39

Esel

Southwest of Gaza

February 9, 1260

Esel leans against a tent pole in the lee of the surging wind, the gusts rocking her to and fro. She watches the hooch of the highest-ranking Shahrazuriyya Amir across camp.

The tent flap flops open and a dark-skinned guard turns his face from the gale. He holds open the fluttering camel hide. Out walks the first of the deserters from the Prince of Damascus' army, an amir from the Nasiriyya, al-Nasir's own Mamluks. Two Kurdish amirs from the Shahrazuriyya follow, trailed closely by al-Nasir's brother, al-Zahir Ghazi.

Esel frowns, saddened that Baybars and his Bahri have ended up with this lot of malcontents. Her nephew chose to bolt with these rebels for the safety of the Gazan hinterlands just several days past.

For over two years she has listened to her nephew's frustration with the Princes of Damascus and Karak, regarding their collective timidity in dealing with both Qutuz of Cairo and the

Mongols. Unsatisfied with the headship of either prince, Baybars responded by bouncing back and forth between the two royals, playing each against the other for years.

Esel eventually grew weary of Baybars' flip-flopping. A man's first oath of allegiance to a ruler ought be his last. Plus, what did a man have once his word was tarnished?

"My Aunt, I stayed loyal to my first patron until his death, a good man, the Sultan al-Salih," Baybars had told her. "Devotion to al-Salih was my only obligation. Now, the only vow worth honoring is to my men—a promise to rebuild our island citadel in Cairo, torn down by Aybeg, and fit them with the best kit and horses possible. If the Princes of Damascus and Karak wish to apply their gold toward these ends—all the better."

Esel reluctantly acceded to his logic. Yet she feels now that Baybars has been pulled by the recent tide of unfortunate events, sucked into the undertow caused by the opportunists in this encampment.

Last spring, the Prince of Damascus camped with his army for moons, just north of Karak, pressuring Prince al-Mughith to turn over the Bahri raiders who had looted al-Nasir's caravans. Sensing the Prince of Karak was to capitulate, Baybars slipped from the citadel there with most of his men, offering his services once more to al-Nasir, who remarkably took the Bahri back with him to Damascus.

Esel reckons the Prince of Damascus is a pitiful man—so short of troops and so void of courage that he would welcome any skilled outfit who owns the bravery needed to protect him from the Tartars, even men who attempted to slit his throat in the night, as the Bahri had done just over a year past.

Allied yet again with al-Nasir, the Bahri sat idle in Syria for several months, while the prince dawdled with his Kurdish advisors on what should be done to counter the Mongols' encroachment. Fed up with the indecision, last moon, al-Nasir's brother, al Zahir, and the Nasiriyya connived an overthrow.

Failing in their attempt to assassinate Prince al-Nasir, the renegades were compelled to flee Damascus.

Troubled by possible repercussions to come for his past association with the would-be murderers and his own assassination attempt on al-Nasir, Baybars led his Bahri across Palestine with these rogues. Reaching their old camp in Gaza, they found three thousand of the Shahrazuriyya Kurds camped at the oasis here, the same soldiers who had also bartered their loyalty between the princedoms of Karak and Damascus last year.

A cold squall whips across the barren desert, swirling the sand. Esel wraps the hijab about her face and buries her chin into the wool collar of her robe.

Blasts of wind beat the tent flap, as if angrily rousting the last of the meeting's attendants from within Shahrazuriyya Amir' quarters. Baybars exits with another of his amirs.

The pair tromp through the sand toward their shelters. Her nephew's pace is labored, his head down in thought. Baybars ducks into his own tent.

She retreats into her little tent and boils a pot of tea. She pockets a handful of dried yogurt curds. She pours the tea into a hardened leather vessel and then stuffs it, plus two wooden cups, into her small pack. She slings it over her shoulder.

The sun dips. She goes to Baybars' hooch, the wind fluttering the unit pennants and billowing the sides of the tents, the outfits as identifiable by their shelters' coverings as by the hue of their banners. She knocks four times on Baybars' tent frame, alerting him that it is her.

"Enter," he barks through the gale.

He lowers a map that he reads by candlelight and looks up with tired eyes. He smiles as she set the cups upon his small table.

"Forever the aunt," he says, leaning back.

She pours him a cup of tea and slides three of the hard curds across the table. She sits. "You look spent. Too important for sleep?" she asks.

"No, but I still cannot seem to catch much."

The tent poles creak in the wind. Hemp guy lines moan under their strain.

"What came of the discussion?"

"No accord. No higher purpose. Most of them cannot see past the bulge in their purses. At least when we were freebooting in al-Nasir's lands, there was some principle behind it."

She raises an eyebrow.

"We used the gold and swag to feed our troops and upgrade their weapons and mounts. Ultimately, for the good of Cairo, for the good of Islam."

She smiles and places a curd in her mouth.

"But this lot of rascals, here. Al-Nasir's brother, al-Zahir. . ." Baybars shakes his head and takes a sip of tea. "Why these men elected him the supposed new prince of Damascus, I will never understand," he says. "Although soon the city will be turned to rubble, once the Tartars are done with it."

Esel's thoughts flash to Saja, the young daughter of her old masters Gamal and Rashida. She bears the overfed arms merchant and his pampered wife no love, but her attachment to the child has never waned. She hopes the parents are wise enough to leave the city before the Mongols attack.

"I tried to convince al-Zahir to ally with Egypt and the rest of Syria to fight the Mongols, but he will not commit—to anything," says Baybars. "Vacillating must be a shared trait in their family. With no direction, these amirs talk about marauding caravans of all things—even with the Black Tartars bearing down on Damascus and Cairo." He sighs. "But with the Shahrazuriyya being so numerous here, their wishes carry the most weight."

"And what are their wishes?"

"They wish to attack the Egyptian force Qutuz sends to assist al-Nasir."

Esel stops chewing the curd.

"Egypt honors her alliance with Prince al-Nasir," he says. "Apparently, Kurdish scouts have spotted hundreds of

Muizziyya and Salihi heading east through the Sinai to safeguard Damascus. As much as I would like to see Qutuz's force ambushed, what sense does it make to take part in this? Bloody my men against some of our former brothers in the Salihi, while damaging both armies before a coming fight with the Mongols? Just to get into the Muizziyya's baggage train?"

She nods.

"Omer, one of the Nasiriyya amirs, pulled me aside last night and proposed our two units ally with the Mongols." He props his elbows upon his table. "I cannot help but consider this. Even with Syria's and Egypt's armies combined, the Mongols will still have us nearly ten men to one. Or more. And the Tartars' supply caravans stretch here to Mongolia, nearly unbroken. Our chances look grim."

A pain crosses his face. "And every fool knows it is better to ally with the Mongols early on, or face how they handle dissenters."

She tries to remain calm. Visions of that fateful day nineteen years past at the Sivash come pouring into her mind like the wreaking tides on the Rotten Sea there. Their Kipchak tower, pushed into the Turkmen's noose by the encroaching Tartars. The slaughter and rape of their people. She remembers the lad Baybars being torn from her arms that day by one of the Turks who betrayed her people.

She recalls the Turkish brute stripping the young Baybars of his knife and tinder kit, prized gear handed down from his father. The traitors then pushed her nephew into a pen with the other teenage boys, the Turks' most profitable commodity seized from the Goker Kipchaks that day.

"Need I remind you of our peoples' suffering? The agony caused by the Mongols? Have you forgotten being shoved into that coop?"

"I remember, Teyze," he says.

A burst of wind billows the side wall of the tent like a sail. The squall diminishes, leaving the hide pulsing gently, like the beat of a heart.

"If you ally yourself and your troops with the Mongols now, the spirits of our ancestors will haunt you for the remainder of your days," she admonishes.

He scowls. "At the Sivash, we were attacked by Turkmen, not Mongols. And as our khan used to say, 'Grievous times call for brazen strokes.' I have nearly four hundred Bahri warriors relying on me to do the right thing."

"Yes, the *right* thing."

"Nothing is straightforward anymore," he says. "The Black Tartars are not Kipchaks, but they live as closely to the way we did on the steppe as any. Like us, they do not put foot to ground if they can help it. They live atop ponies like we used to."

She is unconvinced of his argument.

"The *Yasa*, their law system, is similar to our tribal decrees," he says. "By Allah, we surely have more in common with the Mongols than the soft-handed Ayyubid princes who have ruled us here for decades."

Esel recoils. "You attempt to rationalize. The Mongols destroyed our tower and hundreds more like ours," she says, firmly.

He raises both palms. "And for years, Kipchaks killed many Tartars everywhere along the steppe. Those dead Mongol soldiers had families back home, too. There have always been losers and victors in war, but never innocence—on either side."

She stares through him.

"How can any leader not consider joining forces with the likely victor?" he asks. "My men stand the best chance of surviving this conflict as part of the Mongol army, not as its opposition. It would be heartening, for once, to shield my Bahri behind a massive force, rather than always being outmanned. And to deal with Mongol khans, fighters who may gather that I am the sensible choice to rule Cairo, under their banner."

He waits for her response, but she says nothing.

He leans back. "I understand how you feel. But the Mongols are herders, hunters, and warriors first. For five years I have tried to persuade these Syrian princes to help me take back Cairo—all of it a waste of time, treasure, and blood. The Mongols have boundless supplies and an aggressive outlook that matches mine. So am I wrong to prefer the approaching enemy to Qutuz, or to the dithering princes in Syria?"

She feels the blood pulse thump against her temple. "Yes."

"I think the Mongols would rather band with me, too, than any prince from Saladin's diluted bloodline. Once the Mongols take Cairo, they will hang Qutuz's head from the gate. My biggest obstacle to Egypt's rule would then be gone."

She glowers, wadding a fist of robe into her hand.

He collects his thoughts. "This is not the Kipchak steppe, my Aunt. What Mongke Khan has sent from Karakorum is no raiding party, no reconnaissance in force. Hulegu's Army of the Right is here—the largest horde we will ever lay eyes upon. They have already crossed the Euphrates and secured their rear. Who will stop their march to Cairo?"

He stands, paces with hands behind his back. "Hulegu's son, Yoshmut, has already taken Manbij and Tall Bashir on the west bank of the Euphrates—and this he did with only a fraction of their army. Syria is wide open to them. Who knows if Aleppo's prince will even fight?"

Baybars looks to the peak of his tent. "The Princes of Homs and Hama grovel to the Mongols. And last month, al-Nasir had thousands of Kurds, Turcoman—even the Persians—at his gate. They begged him to lead them in Jihad against the infidels. Naturally, at this momentous time, the Prince of Damascus was again seized with fear and indecisiveness."

He shakes his head. "After just dodging another assassination attempt, al-Nasir will be as fretful as a lost ewe with jackals encircling. He will trust no one. He will have no mind to mount a successful defense of Damascus."

"Well then, it appears we Kipchaks are again doomed," Esel says with condescension. "Once more at the mercy of the Black Tartars. So why do you pace about and lose sleep? You just said you have the same mentality as the Tartar enemy and another strong amir in Omer, who also wishes to join these Mongolian *brothers* of yours. You appear to have it sorted. You know your course."

She stands and put the cups and jug into her pack.

"Hmmph," he snorts.

She feigns bewilderment. "Of course, I am but an old woman, an escaped house slave, not a tested khan with an understanding of the complexities of warfare in these lands. So help me past my confusion."

Baybars looks at the ground, as he did when he was a boy and his aunt began a lecture.

"You served Sultan al-Salih for years," she says. "In Cairo, you were his slave while a youth in the tibaq. But after graduation from the barracks school, your bondage to the Ayyubid ended. You earned your place to serve this prince, but were also free to leave. True?"

"True. So?"

"So once manumitted, you were no captive, but instead a young warrior who made a choice. You stayed to serve a man you respected—out of duty and commitment to this royal who had bettered you and your station." Her eyes drill into his.

"Yes. But there is no man I wish to follow now."

"Yes, no other man to follow. So, now at the height of your martial ability and with the command of hundreds, you choose to not only back those undeserving, but to bend knee to them, to become their slave?"

He says nothing, like a chastised lad who acknowledges his guilt.

"You do not contemplate allying with the Tartars out of respect for their nomadic way of life," she says. "You merely ponder reasons that would justify you cowering at their feet."

He sits up straighter.

"I never pictured you as a vassal. A Mongol's dog." She shrugs. "But do what you must, amir—for your men, for your purse."

"I will be no man's dog," he says.

She turns her back to him. Grasping the tent flat flap, she looks back. "Not that I would be of any great loss to you, but the day you join the Mongol invaders is the day that I leave your company."

Esel walks to the edge of camp, the wind still swirling. She sits on a smooth-faced rock and wraps her arms about her shins. She finds the winter archer in the sky, her eyes staying to the sweep of the huntsman's bow.

She turns her gaze to the north star, beneath which she pictures the lands between the Black and Caspian Seas, her homeland lying frozen and dormant and ruled by Mongol keepers from the Golden Horde.

She looks back to Baybars' hooch and shakes her head.

CHAPTER 40

Eșel

Southwest of Gaza

February 9, 1260

A desert squall tussles Esel's hair. Seated on a rock, she looks back to Baybars' tent and sighs.

She envisions the gales rattling seedlets of grass on the Kipchak steppe, the spikelets clutching stubbornly to their stems across the pitching and plunging hills of her homeland. A crust of snow yokes the countless hollow shoots in winter's collar, their roots asleep beneath the ground, yearning for spring's pardon.

The wind hisses among the stalks, unheard on her native ground. Just whispers. Muted appeals made from the grasslands, like shushed pleas from her kindred tribesmen now living as subjects in that open country, where generations of Kipchaks once roamed freely.

She pushes the curls from her face and rises from where she sits at the periphery of the soldiers' bivouac. She takes in one last look at the stars and heads back to the warmth of her tent.

A shimmer of moonlight illumes the smoke emitted from vents atop the scattered shelters. The steady gale catches these palls, hurling the smoke sidelong across the stark desert in dissipating streaks. She lowers her head against the wind.

Hoofbeats sound from the east. The Mamluk rider springs from his mount and hastily ties his Arabian to a boulder. He converses with the watchman and pulls a cylindrical case from his saddle bag. Another dispatch. He goes to the entrance of Baybars' hooch. He knocks and hands Baybars the tube.

Esel enters her tent. She stokes her fire, lights a candle, and prepares for sleep.

Four knocks sound on her tent frame. She pulls aside the flap of hide.

Baybars raises his chin, his brow furled. "Teyze, let me in for just a moment. I have something to discuss with you."

She pulls a stool for him and sits upon her cot across from him. He hands her the scroll. "Read this."

She recognizes Jacinta's handwriting.

> *28 January, 1260. In Aleppo. This city is lost to Mongol siege. I witnessed the third day of widespread slaughter and pillage by Hulegu's full force.*
>
> *This from a reliable source, a khan's wife: Mongke, the Great Khan, is dead. He passed of illness while fighting in the Song Kingdom last August. I believe that Hulegu plans to leave Syria this coming spring with up to 90,000 men. This he does to support his brother, Kublai, against the other brother, Ariq Boke, for succession. Mongke's widow and sons support Ariq.*
>
> *I sense a growing mistrust between the two Mongol factions. Possible in-fighting to come for territory held by both sides. Mongol unity is no longer to be assumed.*
>
> *Despite this, the Mongols maintain their conviction. They plan to take Cairo. Command of the Army of the Right may soon fall to Hulegu's son, Kitbugha, with a much-reduced force.*

Hulegu's concern is less the prowess of the Mamluks of Egypt, but sufficient grass and fodder to support their large herds of ponies as they move through Palestine and the Sinai. Also the threat to their rear from Ariq Boke's Golden Family, north of the Black Sea. From J.

"Jacinta must have followed the Mongols west from the Jazira. Diverted to Aleppo on her own initiative. Somehow this khan's wife confided in her," Esel says.

"Can you verify that this message came from her quill?"

"Yes, it is her writing." Esel says.

"It came sealed with the imprint of her ring in the wax, as she and I agreed. Can we trust her written words? If she still works for Qutuz as well, then she would have reason to mislead us."

"I do not think she would do that," Esel says.

He nods. "I feel like this may be from the hand of Allah—the Great Khan's death. Mongol infighting. The timing is auspicious."

Esel squints in thought. "Qutuz in Cairo and the other Syrian princes—would they have this information?"

"Maybe not yet. Any benefit that comes in knowing this will not last long. Emissaries and spies would be riding back to their princes with similar messages right now."

"But Qutuz would not know yet."

"I doubt it." Baybars reads the scroll once more. "We must tell no one."

She nods.

He takes a knee and carefully lays the sheet onto her fire.

She watches the dark spot form in the center of the papyrus and then burst into flame. Soon the dry fibers are consumed by the blaze. They watch until the page curls into unreadable embers.

"Perhaps the Mongols are no longer such an unconquerable force," Esel says.

"Perhaps. For now. That is if Hulegu actually does leave for Mongolia, or if he diverts units to secure won territories throughout their empire. Even the grassland in Azerbaijan, where he would pass and likely camp, was once his cousins' land. It would be sensible for him to post men there now, thinning his attacking force."

"You said the Shahrazuriyya urged you to join them on their planned foray in the Sinai?"

Baybars nods, grimacing. "They feel that if their strike on the Muizziyya is successful, they could potentially continue on to Cairo with the empire void of its best horsemen."

"Even with some of Qutuz's cavalry gone, would not taking Cairo require an assault against the citadel?"

Baybars looks up from the smoking ash. "Yes. Impossible with the few thousand men here and no siege engines. Pure folly, I know."

She looks to her candle, the last of the wick burning steadily. "Which is easier, knocking on a door and then walking in invited, or busting the entrance down with a battle axe and fighting your way forward?"

"Walking in, of course."

"Do you think beating down Cairo's door is the way you will come to lead Egypt?" she asks.

Baybars leans back on his stool and crosses his arms.

"In my mind, for you to be successful, the Egyptians must unlatch Cairo's gates for you. True victory can only come through a bloodless entry."

"What do you mean by 'true victory?'"

"I mean bringing the Egyptians to heel without creating mass hatred in the process."

"But you forget that Qutuz is sultan and he delights in bloodshed. He will give up nothing without a fight to the death."

"Perhaps," she says. "But what if there were an opportunity for you to enter Cairo without a struggle and then walk down its streets with dignity as one of its key protectors? A man seen by the people as one whose heart was with them all along. The empire is desperate for a worthy leader right now. Let them see you are this man."

Baybars shakes his head. "Once the citadel guards see my face and the red-lion upon my banner, I would be full of crossbow bolts before I reached the gate."

"Yet what if you came palms forward, bearing an urgent message—not in Cairo, but first in the Sinai?" she asks. "A message which, if heeded, could literally save thousands of Egypt's best from deception and potential slaughter?"

Baybars strokes his beard, the thick growth clear down his neck.

"If you warned Egypt's force of this coming attack by the Shahrazuriyya, at a time when Cairo was thinly guarded and with the Tartars on the doorstep, I believe your past attempts on Egypt would not be forgiven by Qutuz, but perhaps they would at least be set aside."

He tilts his head in thought. "But once I warned the Muizziyya and Salihi in the Sinai, I would have little choice but to return to Cairo and join Qutuz. My men and I would be at the mercy of the scoundrel who killed my mentor, Aqtay."

"But Qutuz would realize that you just helped save his virgin sultanate. And the empire will be in need of many good troops, especially Mamluks. The sultan will not be looking for a reason to deny any unit willing to fight. 'The enemy of my enemy is my ally,' you always said."

She tries to read him. "Let Egypt see your face. Let the people know that you have returned to save your land and join its fellow protectors, not attack them. Then, once you do great things during the coming battle against the Mongols, you will be in a better position to lead Cairo one day."

"I do not know," Baybars says. He laces his hands atop his head. "Then again, Qutuz is known to lead from the front. Who knows if he will survive combat against the Mongols?

And if I happen to stay alive through it, then at least I would be in position to fill the void."

"Yes," says Esel. "And by preventing this coming ambush in the Sinai, you will also preserve some—maybe all—of the Kurdish attackers, as well. More Muslim cavalry needed to defend Egypt. The Kurds will not be happy with you. But when the time comes, they will answer a true call to Jihad."

Esel can see Baybars is not completely convinced. "What other choice do you really have?" she asks. "If you do not assist Qutuz in stopping the Mongols, will there be much of an Egypt left to rule? Qutuz is not al-Nasir. He will defend Cairo until the end. Will you just sit and watch the city's destruction? Or worse, ally with a reduced Mongol army and take part in the siege?"

She grabs his hand. "You said before that this is not the Kipchak steppe. But your circumstances are little different than when we were on the run there, fleeing the approach of the same Mongol enemy. Our people then were just looking to be led by the right man, just as the empire here is now. Do you remember Civan, the warrior from our tower?"

His brow rumples. "Yes."

"When the Mongols came in force to our homeland, do you recall eavesdropping on that conversation between Civan and me? You heard his plans to become a mercenary for the Bulgarian alliance against the Latins. I belittled him that day for choosing to fight for coin, rather than staying to defend our people and land."

He nods and his eyes crinkle. "My teyze forgets nothing, not even me hiding and listening outside her felt walls twenty years past."

"Do you remember what you told me that day, after I confronted you? What you said you would do to save our people from the Mongols back then, if you were in charge?"

"I do," he says, straight-lipped.

She dredges up that cold day on the steppe, the discussion between her and Baybars, once Civan departed her ger.

> *"Will we always be on the run, trying to stay one step ahead of the Mongols?" Baybars asked, the adolescent removing his wool cap.*
>
> *"I do not know," Esel said. "I just know this is our land and we must do all we can to stay on it. If not for us, then for those who come after us."*
>
> *"Running and hiding like rabbits is not the way Kipchaks were meant to live," he said. "Nor is living under Mongol bootheel."*
>
> *She slathered more fish glue upon the tendon shreds and spread it in along the maple bow frame with her fingers. "No. Our khan and the elders have made hard choices. Choices to preserve the tower."*
>
> *She glanced up from her work. "But you heard what Civan said. I am afraid some of his words are true—the confederation of towers has fragmented. And the more we run, the more our Kipchak warriors follow the coin west. And there they will stay."*
>
> *Baybars looked at the finished bows hanging from her ger frame.*
>
> *She looked up from her work and saw him inspecting the bows. Imagining himself as a grown warrior, she suspected. "What would you do if you were khan?"*
>
> *"There must be more towers who also do not wish to live this way," he said. "I would ride and talk with their khans, convince them to join our ranks, and bring strength back to the confederation. I would train them to be better warriors, not only on the bow, but also with the lance and sword."*
>
> *She grinned. "You have spent too much time with the Mamluk, Gozde."*
>
> *"I think Civan and the others would have been wise to spend some time with Gozde, too. Gozde said his warriors are*

not afraid of the Mongols. He was on our lands only to watch the enemy, so that Egypt's soldiers would know better how to defeat the Tartars. What if all the Kipchak warriors everywhere were skilled at the drills you and he taught me?"

She looked at him sadly as she combed a strand of tendon.

He again eyed her finished bows hanging above his head. "What if we could shoot better than the Mongols—all of us carrying bows of the quality you make? Even with fewer warriors, could we not win with more skill, a good plan, and superior weapons?"

"And if you could not find enough Kipchaks sharing your vision, then what?" she asked.

"Then I would go south with whatever warriors would follow me—not west. I would find Gozde and his Mamluk brothers. Join these men of our blood, who have not lost hope." He gazed at the felt walls. "And when the Mongols were defeated, I would come back north and give the steppe back to our people, so the Kipchak children could live as those before us have."

She nodded, lowering her head to her work, letting the curls cover her face to hide the mist that had gone to her eyes.

Esel lifts her chin to Baybars. "My Nephew, maybe this is your chance to make true on those old words."

PART 3

ARMA-GEDDON COMETH

"Demons mustered all the kings and their armies into one place. It is known in the Hebrew language as Armageddon."

—Revelation 16:9

CHAPTER 41

Cenk

Cairo

June 28, 1260

From his seat in the sultan's meeting hall, Cenk makes out the silhouettes of Qutuz's guards and the three Mongol envoys they escort down the half-lit corridor. The Muizziyya ushers are a full head taller than the Mongols, who walk bowlegged from a life atop their thick-legged ponies.

Approaching the entrance, the Mongol profiles strut. Cenk craves a jug of *bouza*, Egyptian beer.

Two more of the sultan's Mamluks intercept the approaching entourage with crossed battle axes.

"Let them in," Qutuz says.

The three Tartars enter, stepping into the full light: one middle-aged man and two nomads of prime fighting age. The older man leads. Under narrow eyes, his cheeks ride high, full as ripe plums. He is slightly taller than his comrades, his chest stout. A graying mustache covers his upper lip, which he holds in a scowl as he scans the ornate arches, lavish draperies, and carved stone walls of the palace. A younger emissary beside him snorts disdainfully at the intricately-painted ceiling and golden sconces that adorn the tables.

Cenk has a good idea what goes through these Mongols' minds. The Tartars probably figure that the rulers of Egypt were men of the steppe like themselves decades ago, but if the Mamluks now live in an opulent stone house such as this, they surely have picked up the soft ways of city people. The Mongols will expect Cairo's soldiers to be no different than their wealthy Ayyubid counterparts in Hama, Damascus, and Aleppo.

Cenk surmises that to the Mongols, Cairo is just another city filled with clean-handed merchants, veiled women, and inferior combatants—a breeding pen of weakness. The sultan's palace is just another giant-blocked house to be crushed by the Black Tartars, men who soldier now, but will eventually return to their rugged existence of hunting and herding on the Mongolian plains once this campaign is finished.

Typically, Muslim emissaries summoning Egypt's ruler would be garbed in full dress uniform—or more likely, the elegant robes of dignitaries—so as not to insult the sultan. Such diplomats have few practical skills of the faris, the cavalryman, save the ability to further their prince's agendas and speak the language of both factions.

But today, Hulegu sends warriors, men with road powder dusting their native long coats, the uppers of their riding boots rubbed dark from stirrup leather. Their heavy scaled armor shows signs of wear, yet is well-maintained, the plates of their cuirasses recently coated in a thin layer of oil.

Cenk has no way of knowing their skill level, but the men before him are not frauds. Cenk figures the pair of younger men command at least ten squads, forming a company of one hundred—what the Mongols call a *zagun*. Perhaps the older man leads a battalion of one thousand, the mingan, as fellow advisor Tarkhan once did.

Hulegu Khan does what Cenk would do if in his position: show as well as tell Qutuz and his counselors what will soon arrive. Hardened warriors who will tear down your walls and kill your people, if Egypt does not capitulate now.

Cenk returns a black look to the Mongol leader. He hates them only because they are the enemy. His own skin color and body shape is similar to theirs. Aside from their facial features, they are little different from the Bashkir hunter and herdsman that Cenk once was.

The Mongols approach the table. Qutuz, Cenk, and Tarkhan rise. They nod their greetings and Qutuz offers the chairs across from them. Servants arrive with trays of fruit, silver pots, and cups. The Mongols courteously refuse both the seats and food. The invaders come to deliver a message, not to make small talk or drink tea like friends.

One Mongol cannot take his eyes from Tarkhan. The Mongol smirks and shakes his head. He is seemingly surprised and disgusted with this traitor from his own bloodline in the Egyptian court.

"I am Yul," their leader says as he unrolls a scroll, "emissary to the great Hulegu Khan. He has directed me to communicate this message."

Yul reads in fluent Turkish. "From the King of Kings in the East and West, the mighty Khan. In your name O God, You who laid out the earth and raised up the skies. Let al-Malik al-Muzaffar Qutuz, who is of the race of Mamluks, who fled before our swords into this country, who enjoyed its comforts and then killed its rulers, let him, as well as the amirs of his state and the people of his realms, in Egypt and in the adjoining countries, know that we are the army of God on His Earth. He created us from His wrath and urged us against those who incurred His anger. In all lands, there are examples to admonish you and to deter you from challenging our resolve. Be warned by the fate of others and hand over your power to us, before the veil is torn and you are regretful. For we do not pity those who weep, nor are we tender to those who complain."

The sultan clutches the arms of his chair, the blood gone from his knuckles.

Yul's eyes go back to the weathered script, a sureness rising in his voice as he continues. "And what land will shelter you? What road save you? What country protect you? You have no deliverance from our swords, no escape from the terror of our arms. Our horses are swift in pursuit, our arrows piercing, our swords like thunderbolts, our hearts like rock, our numbers like sand. Fortresses cannot withstand us, armies are of no avail in fighting us. Your prayers against us will not be heard."

Cenk sits up straighter in his chair. The message insults Egypt and Qutuz. Dispatches between rulers were known to be cordial, regardless of the circumstances. The Mamluk command knew the Tartar missive would demand submission to Mongol rule, but Cenk did not anticipate slights such as these.

"Those who make war against us are sorry," the graying Mongols reads on. "Those who seek our protection are safe. If you submit to our orders and conditions, then your rights and duties are the same as ours. If you resist, you will be destroyed. Do not, therefore, defeat yourselves with your own hands."

The tartar looks up to take in the reactions from Qutuz and his two advisors. Cenk gives Yul the stink eye.

The Mongol resumes. "Do not debate long. Hasten to give us an answer, before the fires of war flare up and throw their sparks upon you. Then you will find no dignity, no comfort, no protector, no sanctuary. You will suffer at our hands the most fearful calamity and your land will be empty of you. By writing to you, we have dealt equitably with you and have awakened you by warning."

Yul sets the scroll upon the table. His fellow envoys wait with hands behind their backs for Qutuz's reply. The guards, advisors, and servants look to Qutuz.

The sultan tries to keep the stone face of a composed royal, but Qutuz cannot hide the fire of rage burning in his eyes. "We have learned that most of the Mongol army has gone to eastern Anatolia. Hulegu has only twelve thousand men left, under his son, Kitbugha. Are these the 'numbers like sand' that Hulegu writes of in his message?"

The Mongol bristles. "Your fellow princes in Aleppo, Damascus, and throughout Palestine have provided little match against any number of Mongols in battle. If our khan has need for more troops, they will surely be called upon."

Qutuz's eyes bounce from Mongol to Mongol, trying to read his adversaries. "But what if our scouts reported that Hulegu and his army ride northeast, not southwest. From his base in Akhlat it would take your khan more than twenty days to get here. Or these ponies of yours that you say are 'swift in pursuit'—do they have magic wings to fly Hulegu's warriors across the desert?"

Two Mongols remain expressionless. Yet the youngest among them purses his lips, possibly hiding his uneasiness.

The sultan picks up on this cue of anxiousness. "What a shame it would be if we got the best of Kitbugha's men in Palestine, before Hulegu's reserve arrived."

Yul glares. He steps forward. "You have heard Hulegu's demands. What is your answer, Sultan of Egypt?"

"You have traveled far. Please, do not be in a hurry to leave," Qutuz says. "Envoys are known to be good talkers and agreeable to communicate their leader's position in great detail to gain advantage for the one they serve. I have only a question or two more."

The graying man crosses his fists upon the front of his armor and raises his chin.

"Does Hulegu leaving a small force here have something to do with his army not having enough fodder to feed his great herd of ponies?" Qutuz asks. "Perhaps the Syrian campaign has taken too long and depleted all of the pastures?"

Cenk looks to the sultan, shocked that Qutuz would disclose Egypt's knowledge of this to the enemy.

Qutuz feigns compassion. "And now the dry season is upon us. How will you ever feed the flocks of sheep and goats necessary to sustain a hundred thousand men—or even thirty thousand?"

Another Tartar nods to his leader for permission and steps forward. "You forget we now hold the stores of every prince in your kingdom, including al-Nasir of Damascus. We have a mountain of grain for our ponies and thousands of camels to haul it. We have booted every herder from Syria with animals that might compete for graze land."

Qutuz nods. "Very clever. What about water? Both men and beasts must drink much during a desert summer, yes? We discovered when you Tartars visited us on the Kipchak steppe, twenty years back, that you preferred to campaign in the cold. I hope Kitbugha's men pack salve for the heat rash on their asses."

Qutuz looks to Cenk in wordless acknowledgement of his advisor's work the past several months. Cenk's reconnaissance teams in Homs and Hama related that the Orontes River's flows had dropped nearly tenfold this month. This drainage is now but a depleted water source through the heart of Syria, one essential for any large invading army.

The emissaries sneer. "This is no time or place for joking, Sultan," the younger Mongol says. "We were instructed to convey Hulegu Khan's dispatch and receive a direct answer." He looks to Yul. "We will only stay and listen to your prattle for so long."

Qutuz tilts his head. Perhaps the Mongol annoyance he detects is birthed in these logistical truths. Maybe the Mongols are fretful about their current situation.

"Our supply lines are secure from the Mediterranean Sea clear to our capital in Karakorum," Yul says. "We want for little. Do not be fooled that grass and water and supplies make for good reasons to resist us."

"Hmm, I see," Qutuz says. "But it appears there are others who may also resist Hulegu's grand army since the Great Khan Mongke's death. Like those of Hulegu's brother, Ariq Boke. Would this man be why your khan left in such a hurry with so many of his warriors?

"No," Yul says, glaring.

"What else could make a commander ride away from great swathes of territory that took him four years of toil and fighting to secure—and with the job so close to finished? Would Hulegu's departure have anything to do with his need to get back to Mongolia to back his brother, Kublai, against this other brother, Ariq?"

Again Cenk glances to the sultan, wishing Qutuz would quit divulging what they had learned. The Mongols stare at the sultan tightlipped.

The younger Mongol crosses his arms. "It is you slaves here who fight among yourselves. And there is endless backbiting between the princes in your other Muslim kingdoms. We have great harmony within the Mongol empire, even with Mongke's death. We are one people." He nods in disgust at Tarkhan. "'People of the felt walls.' You Mamluks, you king slayers, cannot say the same. We have plenty of men and common desire to destroy Cairo with ease. You'd best answer now, Sultan."

Cenk scrutinizes the hands, feet, and facial features of each Tartar. Yul rubs his thumb. The youngest Mongol shifts his weight from foot to foot. Cenk grins.

Qutuz shakes his head in bogus empathy. "A pity these Mongol brothers cannot get along. Their grandfather would be very disappointed. Then again, your great Genghis Khan raised sons who were enemies, too. This time, maybe a true Mongol war between brothers is brewing, especially with Berke Khan being a Muslim and you heathen bastards having killed so many innocent Muslims down here?"

Qutuz looks to Cenk. "If you were Hulegu, would you not be a little uncomfortable wondering if the Golden Horde to your rear might attempt to ally with fellow Muslims in Cairo? Kipchak men born on the same lands that Berke's Golden Family holds? And what if we Mamluks were to also ally with Christian Kingdoms on the coast, since the infidel Crusaders have not quite embraced the Mongols as their brother Christians?"

Cenk raises his eyebrows and looks to the ceiling in pretend contemplation. "Well, yes, my Sultan. If I were Hulegu, I might have some worry on these counts."

Yul presses his palms together. "We have come only out of munificence to prevent the needless bloodshed of thousands of your people. You do recognize that your only real allies have been rendered ineffective? Every Syrian prince is under our rule or on the run. We have surrounded the Frankish kingdoms on the coast. Only Cairo remains. Let us go back to Kitbugha with good word for both Egypt and the Mongols—that we have a cooperative sultanate on the Nile. Your answer?"

"Yes, cooperative, of course," Qutuz says. "When you arrive, I shall personally swing open the gate and welcome you in. You can sleep with my wife, and you," he points a finger at the youngest Mongol, "may have my daughters."

The younger Mongols look at each other in confusion.

"I think we have his reply," Yul says sternly, comprehending Qutuz's mockery. "You will not submit and you choose to face the consequences, correct, Sultan? This is the message you wish to give our khan?"

The sultan stands. He approaches the Mongols and looks down at each. "It will be very difficult for you three to deliver any dispatch to that wolf khan of yours with your heads detached."

Cenk's eyes grow large. Tarkhan looks to the ground, grimacing. The sultan and his two counselors had agreed to reject Mongol subjugation, not to slaying the emissaries.

"Sultan," Tarkhan says. "Respectfully, could we share words with you for just a moment?"

Qutuz holds up his hand, shushing his Mongol advisor.

The envoys look at Qutuz with a steady calm. Yul speaks. "I am Hulegu's cousin. Kill me and these two, and you will be tortured mercilessly. Your entire city will be stomped beneath our horses' hooves. There will be no clemency for anyone here. Your women and children will be put to the sword."

"This sounds most dreadful," Qutuz murmurs. "Well, the good thing for you and your friends is that you will have a great view of this butchery, as your heads will be hung atop the Zuwayla Gate."

The sultan looks to Cenk. "But I feel confident that their skulls will go black and leathered without their dry eye sockets ever witnessing a single Mongol setting a foot in Cairo."

"You are mad," the gray-mustached Tartar says.

Qutuz turns to his guards. "Take them to the horse market. Have them halved, then beheaded. Spike their gourds atop the gate, eyes facing northeast toward where Hulegu and their thousands of brothers departed."

CHAPTER 42

Leander
Rafah Oasis
July 1, 1260

A column of forty-six horses clop the hard pack. The jangle of their tack is lost in the open sky, muted in the broad expanse of the desert. A murky dust hangs on the northern horizon.

Leander digs the sand from his ears, lingering grit from the gale that whipped across the flats this morning. Singer rides beside him, shaking the sand from a glove.

The *khamsin* season, the fifty days of windstorms that plague the Sinai each spring, ended two moons past. Yet today's storm hit with similar ferocity. While they had warning of the tempest's northern advance—a bloody tint in the southern sky—the Mamluks from Amirate Three were in no position to evade it.

Taking shelter in the lee of a stony outcrop, the Bahri tightened their turbans with wraps across their faces and necks and knotted their reins about their forearms. Within moments, the scorching heat transformed into a whipping southern wind. They hunkered behind the rock all morning, horse and soldier taking the blasts of windswept sand in concert. When the squall passed, the Mamluks remounted and resumed their trek deeper into Palestine.

That they are again far from home and sent to observe the encroaching Mongol enemy is no surprise to Leander. If there was perilous reconnoitering work to be done in the hinterlands, it seemed to find Leander and his mates.

Last spring, the Bahriyya left the company of al-Nasir's brother, al-Zahir Ghazi, and his band of rogues at their camp outside Gaza. They headed west toward Cairo on the *Via Maris*, the coastal route through the Sinai. Two days into their journey, Leander and his Bahri came upon Qutuz's Muizziyya.

The contending regiments quickly drew into battle formations. With the units facing each other on that desolate flat, Baybars stripped the weapons from his saddle and advanced alone, palms forward, to meet with the Muizziyya Amirs. He warned them of the ambush being set ahead by al-Zahir's erratic allies, the Shahrazuriyya Kurds, and also of the unlikelihood of al-Nasir garnering the will and troops necessary to defend Damascus from the coming Mongol invasion. The Muizziyya clasped arms with Baybars.

Baybars then waved his men forward. "We wish to return home and defend Mother Cairo from the infidel hordes," Baybars said.

The short-limbed Muizziyya Amir they call *Timsah*, Turkish for crocodile, crinkled his brow. "You are serious?"

"Very," Baybars said. "If Qutuz knew of the planned treachery and al-Nasir's cowardice, he would desire his Mamluks to return to Egypt at once."

Timsah laughed. "Yes, of course. But what would the sultan say to us Muizziyya if we returned riding alongside the Bahriyya he chased out of Cairo?"

Baybars had anticipated the response. "I do not know what Qutuz might say, but he surely knows that much has changed in those seven years since we left. And in the last six moons, the sultanate he now rules has fallen into grave danger."

Timsah nodded. "By Allah."

The amirs sat their horses, eying each other.

Baybars spoke first. "Timsah, at one time our two regiments shared the name Salihiyya, joined under Sultan al-Salih. With the Mongol banner soon to be flying over all of Syria, I cannot see Qutuz being angry with you for bringing your old brothers home to protect Cairo against a common enemy."

Timsah pulled the head of his Arabian back west toward Cairo. "Yes, all has changed. Let us go, then, old comrade."

Together, the rivals took up the road for Egypt.

Having been notified by a runner of the two approaching units, Qutuz stood atop Cairo's southern gate to welcome the Bahri. The Sultan appeared delighted to reclaim the experienced amirs and additional cavalry, even if they had once been his bitter adversaries. That day, Qutuz granted Baybars a promotion and a generous iqta of fertile wheat fields northeast of Cairo.

In return, Baybars provided the sultan with reports on their common enemy, drawn from intelligence on the Mongols collected by Leander and his mates, plus that gathered from their commander's other roving patrols over the past several months. While appreciative of the information, the sultan followed the standoffish etiquette learned from the Ayyubid princes in Damascus and Karak. Qutuz sent the aggressive Baybars and his troops away from his citadel walls, pushing the Bahri to Qalyub, north of Cairo.

After a short stay in Qalyub, the sultan tasked Baybars with putting eyes on the Mongol outpost near Gaza. Baybars passed the mission to Amirate Three, charging them to confirm the foe's numbers and disposition in Palestine. Once finished, the unit were to bypass Gaza and seek the Crusader leadership in the Kingdom of Jerusalem. There, they would reach out a hand in alliance to the Franj, or at least pave the way for a safe passage north for the entire Egyptian Army, where the bulk of the Mongol enemy still looms.

With Leander's ability to speak the language of the Franj, and his background serving the Brienne family, the sultan directed Leander to seek out John, Count of Brienne. Baybars and Leander learned from Qutuz's spies that John had left his estate in Cyprus to assess the Mongol threat and possibly help with preparations in Acre, the Crusader's capital.

Leander dreads the possible reunion with the kin of his former French lord. Leander was serving John's father, Walter IV, prior to the Battle of La Forbie when Leander parted ways with the Franj. John would remember that Leander abandoned Walter for a chance to earn his station with the Mamluk enemy.

Although, what does it matter now? The Crusaders and Mamluks may soon fight alongside one another against a shared enemy. And in the end, Leander cares little how the Franj view him. John of Brienne epitomized why Leander left the Franj in the first place. While he never met the man, Leander certainly knew the type.

John skirted his duties in the County of Brienne, preferring the comfort of life on Cyprus with his mother's family over his responsibilities in the French Kingdom, or enduring the dusty hardness and hazards in the other Crusader Kingdoms. If John comes to Acre, it is probably because his trade in copper and ivory have dried up. Since the Mongol's arrival in Syria, exchange in all of Outremer's ports on the Mediterranean have suffered. If John is in Palestine, Leander will find him and carry out his obligation to Baybars.

The Mongol Khan, Kitbugha, recently established posts in Gaza and Nablus to prevent just this sort of interaction between the Crusaders and the Mamluks. The garrisons acted as a wedge between the Christian and Muslim armies, two opposing forces that might conspire against Mongol designs in the Levant. Amirate Three plans to split this wedge. First, by assessing the

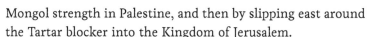

Mongol strength in Palestine, and then by slipping east around the Tartar blocker into the Kingdom of Jerusalem.

Leander reaches across his Arabian's head and pulls away the sandy crust from below her eyes.

Last spring, his old gray, Luna, had stopped eating. The mare weakened until she could no longer stand. Having endured unspeakable trials with Luna for years—from combat in Damietta and Mansura to the Bahri's epic bolt across the Sinai after Amir Aqtay's murder—Leander gutted through the terrible chore of putting his horse out of her misery near Damascus.

There, Baybars presented Leander with a three-year old roan from prime al-Bahrayan stock. Matching the color of sand, his new mare is perfectly camouflaged. Black from the knees down, the horse appears to have just frolicked in a mudhole.

And such conduct would match her jovial temperament. Leander named his new girl *San*, or "Glory" in Turkish, as his Arabian is inclined to prance and arch her dark-maned neck playfully. But she knows when it is work time. He has grown fond of his spirited girl, the two having worked out most of their differences over the last few weeks.

He shoos the pestering flies which are relentless in their attempts to enter San's nose and ears. They burrow at the corners of Leander's mouth, digging through his thick beard. He reaches into the bowl of his turban and strokes with a forefinger the scaly back of the chameleon that he caught earlier. The lizards are cherished creatures on these trips. Grasping the turban silk with pincer-like toes, the chameleons snatch flies from the Mamluks' heads with their projectile tongues.

Beneath the cloudless sky, they travel the *Karb el Sultani*, the King's Highway, eastward. Russet-tinted monoliths protrude from the beige flatscape ahead like enormous piles of horse dung, rounded and crevassed and stacked in tilted segments. Farther ahead, the road bends south into an unseen corner at a canyon. From this crook in the path, three figures upon camels emerge from the dark rock, their forms highlighted against the sand mounds.

As the trio of camel riders bob closer, they reveal themselves like ghosts from the distant past. The men's faces are sun-marred hide, their long beards as gray as Damascene steel. Strapped to their camels' flanks are the original helmets of the Salihiyya: domes of hardened leather coated with shiny layers of red and black lacquer. Embossed on each side of the head armor is the lioned heraldry of the past Sultan, al-Salih Ayyubid, Leander's first patron.

They wear yellow summer trousers and old-style long coats, the white qaba of summer. Hooped cuirasses sit strapped to the back of their camels like rib-boned skeletons from some extinct creature. This type of leather armor was abandoned more than three decades past in favor of the current lamellar version, the former known to snag a shooter's bowstrings.

These jawshans and the chainmail strapped beside them brand the former Mamluks as al-Salih's original cadre of Mamluks, men long past their useful service. The story goes that al-Salih purchased these first five hundred when his then sultan father, al-Kamil, went away on campaign and left the ambitious Prince al-Salih in charge of Cairo.

Recognizing their archaic attire, Leander stows his lance along with the others. Duyal eases to the back of the cluster and sits his horse alone.

Sedat, Amirate Three's leader, clomps forward upon the rock-strewn path. "By Allah, Salihiyya warriors fit for battle," he says, as if he has known them for years.

The old men smile, one through lips misshapen by a poorly-healed slash wound earned decades past. The Mamluk with the traditional amir's purse moves forward. "We have sold ourselves and God has bought us," he said, rephrasing a well-known passage from the Koran.

"Err!" The Mamluks bark in approval. Leander follows Sedat's men, who circle the camel riders, nodding and smiling. They inspect the Salihiyya, pointing to their weapons and kit and shaking their heads in amazement, as if the dust-covered relics were living exhibit pieces.

Sedat beams. "You bring fire to your brothers' hearts."

"Looked to us like somebody truly has brought the fire," the old amir says. "The pastures were burned the whole way here—and we hear north, clear past Hebron."

"That was us."

The old man squints.

"Well, other Mamluk units, my Amir," Sedat says. "The Tartar enemy uses many remounts. The sultan wishes to see how well the Mongol pony herds thrive in the sand and summer scorch, with no grass along their route south."

"Hmm," the old man says. "For once we were glad to have been on the back of camels and not our Arabians."

Sedat nods to the train of camels behind his Mamluks, loads of fodder strapped to their sides. "We brought more feed than normal and are taking our journey in short bites to save the horses. So you took the western fork in the road from Shawbak?"

"Yes."

"Where do you go?"

"Cairo, of course. The easy life of pensioned men in Shawbak has not suited us." His mates nod. "Since it seemed that al-Mughith of Karak would not be fighting the infidels, we figured heading west to do our part in protecting Mother Egypt would be most pleasing to Allah," he says, patting the cane shaft of his lance.

The Mamluks grunt. Sedat grins.

"We reckoned with another Mamluk as sultan, the royal might receive three of his kind with a little fight left in them." He turns to his friends and grins. "Even if we are a little long in the tooth."

Snickers from the young men.

"You are Qutuz's Royal Mamluks?" the old amir asks.

Faces go serious.

"No, we are Bahri, under Amir Baybars," says Sedat.

"Ah, the new River Island Regiment. We heard."

"Not so new anymore," Sedat says, smiling politely.

"The sultan sent you out here alone?"

"Well, Qutuz stashed the rest of Baybars' four hundred Mamluks at the Qalyub outpost."

The old man smiles. "Where does Baybars send you?" he asks.

"I must not say, my friend," Sedat says.

The three men nod. Leander figures the old salts already have an idea.

"Was there water at the oasis in Rafah?" Sedat asks.

"Plenty. And no one is there."

The old man's camel yowls, causing several others to roar. "Well, we all know who has the last word on these rides." He smiles, rubbing his camel's neck. "The ladies say it is time to move along."

Several from Amirate Three move up to grasp arms with the elder Mamluks, the young troopers standing in their stirrups to reach the camel riders' outstretched hands. Leander and others nod the stoic trio a farewell.

Their ancient leader turns in his saddle, his dark eyes set warm into the leather seams of his face. "Allah's blessings. See you back in Cairo," he says, with one hand raised. The three lurch westward.

Duyal has paid the old men no attention. Wrinkles etch the corners of his eyes; bags swoop below them. He faces eastward, his shoulder propped against the standard, whose metal base he lodged between the rocks at his horse's hooves. Several scales on his cuirass are set crooked, one is loose. The dust charitably hides the unfaded spot on his war belt where his amir's purse once hung. His eyes are set upon on the wide country ahead and a darkness pouring across the swelling hills and dunes beneath the shifting clouds.

As he observes his old mentor, a sadness returns to Leander's heart. Baybars leaves the forty men of Amirate Three temporarily under the control of Duyal's former Amirate Leader, Sedat. Having led the amirate for many moons during Duyal's absence in the east, Sedat was Baybars' logical choice.

The broad-shouldered Sedat refused the billet unless he could keep Duyal in the unit. Unwilling to demote Duyal to Squad Leader, Sedat made Duyal a Guidon, a position often left unfilled in many units. Duyal carries the unit's banner. He is responsible for no one but himself. He acts as a utility man for the Amirate Leader, one assigned odd jobs.

The designation and Duyal's current situation is atypical. Usually an Amir of One Hundred, such as Baybars, would send a relieved Amir of Forty as far from his old unit as possible. Yet Baybars did not. Perhaps, the Bahri's commander hopes Duyal will revert to his old self. Perhaps Baybars knows that, while Duyal deserved to lose his command, he is too talented to pull from the field.

Sedat kept Duyal in the unit as a signal of loyalty and friendship. The Amirate Commander and Amirate Leader positions were often kidded about as being similar to that of husband and wife. Maybe Sedat knows that Duyal would be lost outside the unit.

The wind blows the amirate's pennant over Duyal's shoulder. He snatches the point and holds it, securing the yellow background and red numeral three across his back. The banner covers him like a cloak. Leander finds this apt—his friend literally wearing the colors of the amirate, which has been his only treasure and pride for years.

Duyal senses Leander watching. He turns and winks. The familiar lump of woe churns in Leander's stomach. Leander goes to him. They exchange grins, Duyal's short and forced through sun-cracked lips.

Duyal looks around to confirm that nobody else hears him critique the commander. "We need to get through that canyon before we lose our light," Duyal says.

Leander nods. "At least the old Salihiyya saw no one there."

"Aye," Duyal says.

As if his old subordinate had heard, Sedat points the unit to the steep country.

CHAPTER 43

Leander

Rafah Oasis

July 1, 1260

Sedat waves his farewell to the old Salihiyya Mamluks and moves to the front of the formation. They head east for the water hole at the Rafah Oasis, en route to assess the disposition of enemy Mongol forces, last reported at an outpost near Gaza.

Leander touches his calves to San's flanks. She settles into her familiar sway.

He rides near the front of the column with Singer and Zeki, his fellow translators on this patrol. Zeki—Baybars' most trusted staff amir and an Amir of Forty—is under-tasked, leading only their small section of interpreters. Yet the old salt is needed, since Zeki is conversational in most languages of this dusty land. Leander and Singer are also detached from their regular units, due to their fluency with the Franj and Mongol tongues, respectively.

Zeki takes in the breadth of the desolate country with his usual broad grin. Rumor is that Zeki angles for command of Amirate Three. On this mission, Baybars allows Zeki an early look at the unit in operation. While Leander wants to hate Zeki for desiring to command Duyal's amirate, he cannot bring himself to it.

Zeki's disposition is that of a likable workhorse. Unmarried, distinguished for his refusal to accept any duty that would take him off the back of his mount and known for his fondness for wine, Zeki is said to have spent more time in the field during his twenty-five years in service than any other amir in the Bahri.

Zeki is so accustomed to living in the scrub and sleeping outside that when he does snooze in the barracks, he is notorious for relieving himself in the middle of the night by taking three drunken steps from his cot and pissing wherever he may be—sometimes on the stone floor of the barracks, too often upon another amir in the adjacent cot.

Nearing Rafah, Sedat sends four Bahri ahead to ride the high ground on either side.

As they enter a water hole that is also a choke point, the remaining Mamluks do not wait for Sedat's coming order—they know what to do. The Bahri spread into a staggered file and unlash their strung bows from their saddles. Laying the weapons atop their thighs, they pull arrows from saddle quivers, staging the projectiles between fingers on their draw hands. Leander loads a bolt into his crossbow on the move, while steering San away from the young *esparto* she desires off-path. The clumps of grass grow more abundant the closer they get to the oasis.

Entering the thicker underbrush, the extended file condenses into a tighter line. They drop into a wadi, the sand sculpted in lazy curves by the wind. The lead riders splash through the first trickle of water. Leander forces a dry swallow. He looks forward to filling his flasks.

As they enter the steep-walled canyon, date palms fringe the eastern horizon, a sign of the oasis proper. The men sit up straighter in their saddles, knowing a break is soon coming.

Leander notices a sayal tree with a branch freshly hewn close to the trunk. A mound of sand, recently disturbed, maybe raked by hand. Another. Fresh prints, where the old Salihiyya's camels passed down the road. Up the hill, a light sweeping of palm fronds against the sand? Dried leaves looking as if placed there by hand, not naturally fallen.

A hiss of arrows rains down from the southern hillside. Sun glints off helmet and whetted steel. Round faces with dark, stringy beards. A dozen Mongols shoot from horseback, exposing only their head and chest armor above the crest. Other archers appear on foot, leaning against the flanks of their ponies to steady their shots.

More incoming arrows. A Mamluk to Leander's rear yelps. A horse screams.

Adrenalin surges through Leander's limbs. The enemy knew they were coming. They let the old men pass unmolested so as not to alert the bigger trophy.

No man has to think. Mamluks nearest the enemy return fire. Leander pulls San behind a sprawling tamarisk while trying to acquire a target. Singer follows. Arrows whiz overhead, some shattering upon impact on the rough cairns nearby.

The initial burst of arrow fire diminishes. Mongols drop behind the reverse slope, surprised by the rapidity of the Bahri response.

"Enemy right. Enemy right!" Sedat shouts, pointing in the direction of the now-concealed foe.

Most Mamluks do not hear the command, or have already begun to execute what their amirate calls "direct action for enemy right." As practiced countless times in drill, men from Second and Fourth Squads peel back, disperse, and re-form into a broad line facing the enemy. Those with clear avenues shoot on the move to keep the Mongols' heads down.

"Spread out!" Squad leaders bellow.

Soon this newly-set formation of Bahri archers produce a steady hail of arrows directed at the elevated Tartars, those enemy who have repositioned or resupplied with arrows.

Jumbled commands in Mongolian and Turkish echo from the stone walls as both sides adjust to the fire they receive. First and Third Squads push their Arabians toward the enemy, firing as they ride.

A Mongol "short stick," an arrow shorter than arm's length, slips through the tangle of branches, the steel head snagging Leander's coat sleeve. He snatches it midshaft and snaps it at the hafting. He chucks it fiercely to the dirt, leaving the stub of shaft and barbed head imbedded in the fabric.

More arrows plow into the bush, slowed or stuck in the branches by the four feathers in the enemy's fletching.

Zeki moves up. Singer moves closer beside him, where the thickest limbs provide a semblance of cover. With a pause in enemy fire, Singer moves to a gap in the branches and shoots his fist of arrows in only seconds. He ignores the projectiles that sail over his head and whiff the sand below him. A Mongol tumbles down the hill across from them.

Words from Leander's archery master years ago ring in his head. "We call it 'shower shooting.' Even a single squad of Mamluks can put hundreds of arrows into enemy ranks in seconds, causing most enemy to flee. It is about rate of fire, overwhelming the infidel bastards with arrows on target."

This is what the Bahri now accomplish. Fortunately, the enemy does not execute this Mamluk tactic, as well. These Tartars do not stage arrows in both draw and bow hands. Nor have they mastered the "finger dance" as Leander's brothers have, manipulating the arrows between their fingers so they can fire an arrow every two seconds. Most of these Mongols pull a single arrow from the quiver on each shot, or labor to fire from several arrows staged in their bow hands only.

The Mongols again duck behind the ridge.

Sedat smells the tide of their skirmish shifting. He knows they must attack through the ambush. Staying pinned in this Mongol "slaughter zone"—the place where the Mongols have concentrated their men and weapons—is not an option. He draws his sword. "First and Third assault through!"

"Forward," Zeki says evenly, almost as if spoken in conversation.

Leander gives heel. The three join the other men who push their Arabians up the hillside, lances deployed, some with swords in hand. San thrashes in the loose talus, churning the gravel on each upward lunge. Up his girl climbs, huffing on each lurch.

"Left, left!"

A scattering of spiked globes top the crest both north and south. Thirty or more additional helmets. The Mamluks hesitate. More Mongol waves behind this first?

Black-armored Tartars pour over the hilltop, many with tack fashioned crudely from thick hemp. The Mongols lean back in their wooden saddles, holding up the heads of their ponies to keep their mounts from stumbling in the loose rock. Their stallions' untrimmed manes flow about the beasts' shoulders, their eyes white and wild. Some men hold swords high, others fire their recurves from the saddle.

The plunk of bowstrings and sizzle of arrows fill the air. More horses squeal. An Arabian slides down the bank with its rider.

Leander raises his crossbow and takes aim at a Mongol. He looses a bolt. It strikes the Mongol square in the chest.

"They are everywhere," Singer says.

Other Mongols now emerge from the scrub farther north.

Sedat sees them, too. He spins his horse. Mongols on foot sneak rock to rock, attempting to get behind the Mamluks. More Bahri push their Arabians up the bank, their hoof strikes dislodging flows of scree. It cascades down the hill in slow tumbling waves.

Mongol teams, with timbers in hand, loose boulders down the slope. A large one bounces down the hill at the massing cavalrymen.

Sedat sees they are greatly outnumbered. "Disengage, disengage!" he hollers, riding up and down the base of the hill. Zeki's interpreters turn their mounts and follow the others down the hill.

Second and Fourth Squads open their ranks, while shooting, allowing First and Third Squads to ride through. When the last rider enters their line, they pull the heads of their horses back toward the western narrow from where they came.

First and Third Squads slow when they reach just east of the funnel-shaped opening. They rein in and form a crescent formation across the front of the sheltered bottleneck.

They turn back to the east and sit their horses, firing a steady barrage of arrows at the growing horde of enemy that pursue their Mamluk brothers. One by one, these Bahri flip empty quivers across their backs and begin firing arrows from their larger saddle quivers.

"Go, go, go!" Sedat yells, as men from Second and Fourth Squads gallop past him and through First Squad's line. The troopers in curved formation keep a constant stream of missiles on the enemy, shooting around their own comrades. Sedat heads back east to direct the last of his escaping troops.

The Mamluks attempt to use this steeper terrain to their advantage. Here, much of the Tartar bowshot down from the tops will be blocked by jagged outcroppings on high and thicker vegetation below. The Mongols will have little choice but to chase the Bahri westward across the flat ground, endeavoring to skewer the fleeing Muslims before the Bahri break from the canyon and take flight into the open ground to the west, where the Mamluks' Arabians can outrun the Mongols' short-legged ponies.

Leander halts San between two Mamluks from First Squad and loads another bolt. He brings the crossbow to his shoulder, releases a breath, and aims at a Mongol who rides straight in. He slowly depresses the tickler.

As the string is released, he feels the knock of lath against his shoulder. His bolt hits low and right, sticking the pony's shoulder. The animal's front leg buckles, sending the rider overtop. Another Mamluk sends two arrows into the downed man's back.

An enemy projectile slams into the stock of Leander's weapon. The impact throws the butt of the crossbow into his unarmored ribcage like a wild punch. Leander braces his forearm upon the pommel to regain his breath.

Sedat returns from the west. "Third is out. Back through the narrow. Go."

First Squad wheel their steeds behind Sedat. Leander and Singer follow Sedat and Zeki westward to the throat of the funnel, where only six horses can pass abreast, the hills on both north and south steep and choked with goat brush. Half of Second Squad awaits them, their six bows raised to the high ground, where they pluck the Mongols who hide amid the ledges above them.

While out of the slaughter zone, they must still exit this adjacent high country, before more Mongols shift west and occupy more of this area on foot.

Duyal brings up the last of the riders with him. He reins in, while the others continue through the gap and into the wadi. Duyal appears unruffled. He calmly stages four arrows in both his draw and bow hands. He twists the nocks, until they are all parallel with his bowstring.

Five more Mamluks depart, leaving just the three of them.

Duyal turns to Singer and Leander. "Go," he says quietly.

Singer ignores him, taking aim at the first Mongol to rush the bottleneck.

The head of Singer's arrow pierces the Mongol's chest armor.

Singer draws again, this time drilling an arrow into the open mouth of a Mongol horseman. The enemy is flung backward as if he had ridden into a strung rope.

Singer stages two more arrows in his draw hand, his torso erect. His predator eyes scan both left and right.

Leander presses his trigger and shifts the roller nut backward into its firing position. The nut spring on the weapon gifted from Esel will not click into place. He adjusts it back and forth, his eyes forward to the gap.

Three Mongols plow in.

"Left two mine," Duyal says.

He draws and shoots twice in speedy succession.

Both Mongols fall, the arrows striking each man in the neck, the only area void of both scaled armor and chain mail. Singer drops the third attacker.

Leander jerks on the trigger and wiggles the roller nut. He looks down, realizing that the strike from the Mongol broadhead has knocked the roller nut askew.

Duyal snatches Singer's second quiver from his saddle, leaving Singer with only a handful of arrows left in his shoulder quiver.

"What are you doing?" Singer says.

"Git!" Duyal says, dumping both his empty quivers to the ground. He flops Singer's quiver strap over his cantle, opposite Singer.

"Horseshit," Singer says, firing another arrow.

Duyal shoots at a Tartar moving across the gap. He misses. He smacks Singer's horse on the ass with his bow. "I will be right behind you."

Singer leaves, looking back for them to follow.

Leander continues to struggle with his damaged weapon. He grows frustrated, clawing at the roller nut.

"Git!" Duyal shouts at Leander. "It is buggered. You will be of no use here."

"I am staying," Leander says, dropping his crossbow to the ground. He looks to Duyal's saddle for a spare recurve. Seeing none, Leander draws his sword. He will make this stand with

Duyal and buy the amirate the precious moments it needs to reach safety.

"You are nothing but a sitting target. I will not command it again," Duyal says, his face having gone hard, his eyes searching for another Mongol.

Leander has seen this look before during times when the talking is done and his mentor's mind is made up.

Seeing another Tartar from the corner of his eye, Duyal shoots across his body, felling this rider from the saddle.

He nocks another arrow and half draws his bow. "I will not be long," Duyal says flatly, a grim resignation of death upon his face.

Leander looks to the high ground and then behind them. No enemy. He pulls his reins hard right and gives San both heels. He dips behind his horse's neck and crashes through a wall of shrubbery. Once spit out upon the road, he puts San to the gallop. He glances rearward.

No Duyal.

Topping a mound, Leander reins in and looks behind.

Mongol ponies now clog the passage, one dragging its fallen rider back and forth across Duyal's front. His commander fires arrows as quickly as his eyes acquire enemy. The Tartar dead and wounded act as an expedient barrier for the lone defender.

Leander turns his horse toward the narrow. Some force, some power other than fear, keeps him from giving heel. He must leave his friend as ordered. This is what Duyal wants. To depart this earth while defending his Amirate Three.

Leander looks up to the waves of cirrus cloud with watered eyes. "Allah forgive me! Allah receive him!"

He turns back west and gallops toward his fleeing amirate.

CHAPTER 44

Cenk

Salihiyya

August 2, 1260

Cenk strides the west side of the Muslim camp at Salihiyya, a three-day ride southeast of Cairo. He makes for the assembly area in the center of the massive encampment. Looking behind him, he slips between the Bedouins' shelters, their hooches sun-bleached and freckled with curling patches of hide.

Half-hidden from Muslim eyes, he lifts the skin of koumis, fermented mare's milk, bought from the Turkmen here. Sucking the liquid about his teeth, he savors the sour taste and familiar buzz.

He wipes his chin and looks heavenward to the cloudless sky. "Allah, help us this day."

The Muslims will soon wage war on the unconquerable Mongols. The only unknowns are where this combat will take place and how many in this camp full of hesitant participants will be on hand when the fighting commences.

He corks his skin, flips it to his back, and continues walking, nodding the occasional greeting to the senior amirs from the various units. He passes the Kurds' round-walled shelters and the dark-leathered tents where the Turkmen bed.

Their women tend children. Some stoke crackling fires. Others hang clothes on drooping lines stretched between tent poles. A few young boys clack sticks together, make-believe swords, chasing each other around the lick of flames. Pairs of Bedouin women stake out their "Damascus hides," the overlapping camel skins these nomads have sheltered beneath for centuries.

Cenk works his way to the periphery of the great assemblage of warriors, men ordered to meet now about the wooden platform they built so as to better see and hear the Sultan of Egypt speak. The air is thick with the smell of leather, smoke, and sweat. Hoots of laughter interject the drone of indecipherable languages, like cracks of lightning amid some dreaded rumble of distant thunder. These countless, splintered dialects—Kurdish, Turkish, Arabic—mash into Cenk's aching head.

How these twelve thousand stand in this one place is a miracle from Allah. The eight thousand men from the Egyptian army almost refused to leave Cairo. They followed their sultan out of the citadel only after Qutuz rode unaccompanied through the gate, saying to them, "I will go fight the Mongols alone. He who chooses the Holy War can follow."

Cenk feels the accumulation of the remaining four thousand troops to augment the main army, plus supplies to feed and equip this massive force, was an incredible achievement. Since Qutuz slayed the Mongol envoys last moon, Egypt had done little else but prepare for war.

The sultan ordered grains confiscated far and wide, plus two thirds of all local herds slaughtered. If Cenk's mobs saw an untended sheep or goat, they snatched it. Soon, slabs of drying meat hung from the ramparts of Cairo's citadels and the windows of amirs' homes like bloody shutters.

Day and night, Qutuz and his advisors met with merchants, princes, and amirs. Armies from across the realm straggled into Egypt.

First into Cairo was the rabble from Damascus. This past spring, al-Nasir departed his great city to make an alliance with Egypt. He assigned a small garrison to his citadel there, but left the town defenseless. In return for al-Nasir's neglect, the locals climbed atop Damascus' walls to give their prince a fitting farewell. They jeered, spit, and threw sandals at al-Nasir and his absconders as they left.

When he reached Gaza, al-Nasir reunited with his traitorous brother, al-Zahir. Somehow, they mended their brotherly differences and al-Nasir again inherited al-Zahir's motley collection of wayward fighters: the hardened Shahrazuri Kurds, al-Mansur II's cavalry from Haṃa, and the Nasiriyya, al-Nasir's personal Mamluks. The latter had betrayed their patron repeatedly for years—stranding their prince on battlefields, abandoning al-Nasir for Egypt's Sultan Aybeg, and most recently snubbing their patron for the prince's brother, al-Zahir.

Toward Cairo this collection of malcontents rode. Forever a dawdler and growing more fearful of Qutuz the closer he came to the city, al-Nasir eventually lost his nerve a day's ride from this bivouac. He worried about the Mongols to his rear and the vicious Qutuz to his front. Flustered, al-Nasir turned back east into the Sinai with a tiny escort, abandoning his soldiers who wished to join the Egyptians against the Mongols.

All the while, disgruntled Mongol soldiers, the Wafidiyya, also knocked on Cairo's door, drifting in by the dozens, looking to defect. Tarkhan engaged these men of his blood who had endured injustices under Hulegu or Kitbugha. Cenk's friend welcomed the resentful Tartars into the Egyptian ranks, telling all that he was an example of how decently they would be treated in their new home if they would only partake in the coming fight.

Khwarazmians, Kurds, Turkmen, and stray Syrian cavalry—remnants of units bested by the Mongols, but still with some fight in them—descended upon Cairo like locusts. These troops were willing—for now—to help keep sovereign the last major city in the Egyptian empire. They were welcomed like kinfolk, properly equipped and folded in among their countrymen for use as auxiliaries in the Egyptian Army.

At times, the sultan stood outside the citadel walls in the sweltering heat, with his guards and an entourage of interpreters welcoming these new allies, directing them to food and water. Bedu *goums*, "tents" of the roving nomads inhabited by those linked by blood and marriage, arrived in droves. Some evenings, Qutuz spoke at mosques in his hoarse voice attempting to sooth the anxious crowds, assuring the civilians of their protection.

Qutuz offered stipends to those Mamluks and Egyptian regulars of reasonable health whose period of service had expired. Packs of ancient Mamluks arrived at the gates unsolicited—relics in their forties and even sixties, decrepit men with missing fingers, hands, and feet. Those unable to fight, yet adept at logistics, were taken in to help acquire supplies and organize caravan loads.

All instruction at the hippodrome ceased. Novices in the tibaq, regardless of where they were in the indoctrination process, were spread to Mamluk units, where they trained on any field not covered by the Nile during the flooding season. These lads wore sun-dulled coats of mail and shouldered barely-serviceable kit from the schools. The commander of the training regiment became a glorified innkeeper for the burgeoning army, erecting tarp shelters and cots in his hippodrome.

The welcome was granted not just to freemen or slave soldiers and novices in good standing. Mamluks discharged with a lesser degree of respectability, the *Battal*, were also beckoned.

They arrived like ragged villains in the night, on the back of the same donkeys which the sultanate had provided them upon their release from service. Eventually, those Mamluks banished from Egypt for every imaginable offense were recalled.

Even Mamluks locked in the citadel dungeons from as far away as Alexandria were patted on the backs and granted amnesty for nearly any crime, if they would honor one pledge—fight. Qutuz's missive to these outcasts was clear: join in the coming battle and you remain in Mother Egypt's grateful bosom forever. Most captives jumped at the chance, if not for the opportunity to redeem themselves in the sultan's eyes, then for the religious obligations they felt.

In addition to each soldier's monthly pay, Qutuz insisted on providing a hefty *nafaqa*, a pre-campaign lump sum payment, for all. And how was this behemoth of an army funded? Qutuz ordered the treasury of every principality drained. He also levied a hefty war tax on Cairo's populace. His gamble to lock horns with the Mongols was absolute. If there was a backup plan, Cenk knew nothing of it.

Opportunity for diplomacy with the enemy was extinguished with the Mongol emissaries' final breaths last month. Qutuz quipped to Cenk, "Why would I spare a dinar to hand over saved gold to the Mongols, when we could have used the coin to kill more of them?" Amirs did not stash their shares of this gold but put them to use in purchasing additional camels and Arabians, and filling shortfalls in their men's kits.

Cenk reaches the constructed platform. He looks down the line of Royal Mamluks who guard the makeshift stage. The white-coated Muizziyya brandish long axes and their eyes scan the ranks for sign of agitators.

Cenk nods to Tarkhan, who waits for him. The Mongol looks at Cenk with measuring eyes, assessing his friend's sobriety, wondering what level of assistance Cenk will require this day. Tarkhan returns a grin, but then straightens his posture and purses his lips, looking over Cenk's shoulder.

Cenk turns to the arriving Qutuz. "Assembled as ordered, my Sultan."

Qutuz climbs the six rungs of the ladder and strides to the front edge of the stand, closest to the troops. Cenk follows him, moving gingerly up the ladder like the old man he is becoming. Tarkhan trails behind him, and the pair ease to the back of platform. They lock their hands to their fronts at the same instant. Their eyes focus on the sultan's back, and then beyond him a multitude of rugged faces. Cenk feels a racing in his heart.

Men in robes of the nomad stand beside those in long coats and countless varieties of chainmail. A splattering of creams and grays and yellows and dark browns. Groups of Bedouin in their sweaty turbans butt up to factions wearing the pointed helmets of the Syrian cavalry. In the back, young Turkmen stand upon their saddled horses with crossed arms. Farther out, Bedu sit atop strings of camels.

A gradual hush falls over the assemblage.

"I am a sultan, yes. But I am a soldier first," Qutuz declares in a voice strong enough to carry. "And one with ears. I have overheard your murmurings in camp, your quiet discussions over meals. Since the Mongols have not come to meet us on our preferred ground here as we wished, some of you wish to go home. Some doubt we can beat the mighty Tartar enemy on any field."

The assembly goes silent.

"We will beat them." Qutuz delivers this line slowly, one word at a time. "Let me tell you how."

A mumbling spreads in the crowd.

"We do the opposite of the Syrian princes who holed up their forces behind stone walls. Instead, we do what good cavalry does—seek out the enemy and bring the fight to him."

Louder mutterings from the men, as runners along the edges pass Qutuz's words up the formation. The sultan pauses to allow his words to filter back and inward.

"We will force the Mongols onto terrain of our choosing. Instead of sitting here waiting for them like a bunch of old women, we will meet them with a punch to their mouths. They have not experienced that!"

Nods from a few men here and there in the crowd. One or two noisy cheers.

Qutuz strengthens his voice and sends it out over the heads of his men. "Catapults? Siege defense? Bah! We are cavalry on the move. Strike! Move! Strike again!"

More nods and more cheers.

Cenk sighs. His boss speaks the truth, yet his advisors agreed that his Muslim army should come this far southeast of Cairo to give the Egyptians a place to fall back to—a secondary position behind the city walls and inside the citadel within them. Even as the sultan speaks, men at the fortress assemble defensive engines and gather payloads for the catapults. Qutuz knows they may well end up on the wrong end of a siege.

Qutuz continues. "'But Sultan,' you say. 'We ride to face a foe who has never been beaten on any battlefield.' Horseshit! The army we face is inferior to ours in both numbers and ability." He grins confidently. "Hulegu has taken most of his men and equipment to the grasslands of Anatolia."

More grumbling from the throng.

"Hulegu's north flank is vulnerable to Ariq Boke's Golden Horde—and the horde are Muslims like we are.

"We know this land. The Mongols do not!" He shouts to the throngs. "There is not enough grass and water to feed their remounts once they push farther south." Qutuz again waits for his words to be passed back to those who cannot hear.

Some Syrians who live in that barren country nod.

"Our animals are watered and well-fed. The Mongols fight atop thirsty, hungry ponies. You saw the ash from our fires on your travels here. We burned the grass along the paths the Tartars must take. Kitbugha Khan's men travel through a dry, blackened land void of feed."

A roar from the men in the front ranks.

Cenk looks to Tarkhan in recognition. The judicious Mongol's words to Qutuz last moon had nudged the sultan in the right direction.

> *"It is the Mongol's way to not bother with fodder for their horses," Tarkhan said to Qutuz and Cenk. "Just as when you were boys on the Kipchak steppe. Nomads in summer trust what the earth has afforded. Where the ground is fertile, they go and stay. Where the terrain is infertile, they do not go."*
>
> *"Aye," Cenk said.*
>
> *Tarkhan met Qutuz's eyes. "And even if the Mongols wanted to bring fodder, there are not enough available camels in the entire Levant to carry the amount they need. Four, five ponies per man eat much. If we burn the pastures from here to Hebron, by the time the enemy reaches Egypt, Hulegu's men will be dying of thirst and their ponies will be scattered dead across the Sinai."*

"The young Kitbugha," Qutuz continues, his voice rising, "commands only ten or fifteen thousand men. Too few to beat us. He is distracted. His army is busy beating down the anti-Christian revolt in Damascus. He is spread too thin. When it counts, we will have more men than they do, not fewer!"

Qutuz paces as his words filter to the rear. More nods in the crowd.

"And not only are we more numerous than the enemy, we are also better trained and equipped!"

Cenk agrees. Qutuz does not embellish. The Black Tartars are mostly part-time soldiers, like the Rus armies the Kipchaks and Bashkirs saw on the steppe lands of their childhoods. The Mongols are herders pulled from their livestock to fight, armed with weapons and mounts often inferior to those of this army.

Men begin to cheer, the verve moving rearward like an accordion. Tongues click in approval.

"Need I remind you just who this enemy is? They are the sons of whores who killed your families and plowed your wives and daughters! They destroyed your cities and stole every animal and material possession you and your people had!"

The crowd roars. They stomp their feet on the earth in booming approbation.

Qutuz stoops down to the Mamluks nearest the stage, his fists tucked to his sides as a diving hawk folds his wings in descent. "And we Mamluks raised on the Kipchak steppe!" he levels a pointed finger at them. "These Mongols murdered our kin, disbanded our towers, and slaughtered our livestock! Thousands sold into slavery like sheep!"

Mamluks in the front shout in accord of the past wrongs done them by the foe. Tears fill the eyes of the oldest, men who remember the Mongol invasions of the Kipchak steppe land twenty-five years past.

"Vengeance, my brothers!" Qutuz bellows.

Mamluks from all regiments raise their fists. More clenched knuckles ascend as the word is passed back to Syrians and Arabs, too.

"For decades, we have enjoyed the treasures of our Mother Egypt. Her life—our lives—are now at stake. Will you turn and run? Will you let the Mongols ride into Cairo and enslave your children and rape your women? Will you let them burn our mosques and take our lands?"

He paces. "Will you kneel and pray and hope away the Mongols, as the caliph tried from inside his walls in Baghdad? The enemy seeks to destroy Mecca and Medina and all our holy places! Never has so much of the land of Islam been under the rule of infidels."

He draws his sword. "Will you embrace the fight—wherever it may be?" He holds the weapon in his open palm, letting the sun highlight the Damascene steel. "Will you go forth to defend the Holy Land from hordes of non-believers and bloodthirsty pagans? What would Mohammad wish from us?"

Sultan Qutuz raises his sword high.

Cheers from the men, the gathered army growing louder. Cenk glances to Tarkhan. The Mongol, too, is astounded. Qutuz, their former peer turned sultan has made one army out of this pastiche of men gathered from many places and mixed faiths.

"Allahu Akbar!" the assembly thunders in response. "God is great!"

Tears stream down the men's faces. Soldiers embrace roughly, swearing oaths to each other. Men clasp their Muslim brothers' forearms—Arabs, Kurds, and rival Mamluks.

Qutuz turns from the warriors. His face is flushed, his turban soaked in sweat. He looks to Cenk with a hint of relief on his face.

CHAPTER 45

Esel

Mount Carmel, near Haifa

September 2, 1260

From the shade of a terebinth tree, Esel observes two Syrian infantrymen chatting under a crude lean-to. The soldiers face the sun-browned coastal plain south of Haifa at the edge of a string of forty dozen horses they guard. These grazing Arabians are just a small cut from the bulk of the herd, animals which speckle the better grass farther west and north in the Plain of Acre for miles.

Esel reckons that if not for her nephew and his Bahri, the horses and men of the Muslim army would not be in the Kingdom of Jerusalem at all. Without the work of Baybars' vanguard, the sultan would not have had a safe road along which to bring his gathered force northeast to Acre from its camp in Salihiyya, just outside of Cairo.

Much had happened since last spring when Baybars took Esel's advice to leave the camp of al-Nasir's brother, al-Zahir Ghazi, west of Gaza. In the Sinai, her nephew alerted Qutuz's

Mamluks of the treachery planned against them, foiling the Shahrazuriyya Kurds' scheme to attack the sultan's Muizziyya, soldiers en route to support the defense of Damascus.

Outwardly, Qutuz seemed grateful for the forewarning. In Cairo, the sultan was quick to freshen the Bahri's kit and fill their purses. Baybars also received an unexpected appointment from Qutuz—the future governorship of Aleppo. Of course, Baybars' assignment to this significant post was only valid if Egypt and the Bahri checked the Mongol advance.

With Aleppo in his hands, Baybars could grow the city's treasury, expand his army, and provide his Bahri amirs with abundant fiefs. The sultan offered a city now in ruins from Tartar attack, but Baybars would rebuild this Syrian principality, which trailed only Cairo and Damascus in importance.

But since this pledge of Aleppo, Qutuz has also assigned Baybars' Mamluks something much less desirable—the most dangerous of the Muslim army's missions thus far. Two months past, an overwhelming Mongol force ambushed Amirate Three's scouting patrol near Gaza. There, the Mongols wounded several Mamluks and killed eight, including Gozde's younger brother, the beloved Amir Duyal.

Thirsty to exact revenge upon the Mongols, Baybars gladly accepted Qutuz's follow-on orders last moon to bring his entire regiment to Palestine from Cairo. His vanguard quickly reduced the Tartar outpost commanded by the Mongol Khan Baydara. The Bahri then reoccupied Gaza, removing the Mongol blocker between the Egyptian and Christian camps.

Upon receiving word that the western fringe of Palestine was secured, Qutuz brought the Egyptian army east across the Sinai and linked with Baybars in Gaza. The sultan sent Baybars north, tasking his nimble unit of seven hundred with luring the Mongols south from their bivouac on the Plain of Biqa. This sizeable valley east of Beirut was the farthest point southwest on the main route to Egypt, where decent pastureland and water could be had in summer.

Esel stayed in the Muslim camp repairing weapons with Qutuz's armorers. For weeks she fretted, listening for the courier's hooves to arrive with word on Baybars' skirmishes south of Damascus. Even though the sultan ordered her nephew to engage and then break contact with the enemy at all times, in order to gradually entice the enemy into following, this brought Esel no solace.

While Baybars drew Kitbugha's force of eleven thousand south toward the Sea of Galilee, the sultan sent envoys north to Acre. Qutuz requested secure passage for his army through the Kingdom of Jerusalem and extended an offer of alliance with the Franj against the Mongol enemy.

The Crusaders granted the Muslims use of the coastal route into Syria. This was no small thing. The coastal route was the only practical track with adequate water during the drought season. Unlike their Christian brothers just north in Antioch and Tripoli, the knights in the Kingdom of Jerusalem saw their Muslim neighbors as a more manageable opponent than the Tartars and a vital trade partner.

Yet, the barons in Acre ultimately chose neutrality. After all, in these Crusaders' eyes, the Mamluks were still infidels. Flush with any type of victory over the Tartars, the Muslims may well turn their swords against their new Christian "allies."

Qutuz was not disappointed with the arrangement. In addition to permitting unmolested access through Christian territories, the Franj delivered vital provisions and allowed the sultan's army to camp along the twenty-mile long Plain of Acre. Perhaps more importantly, Qutuz now had his rear flank covered, allowing him to concentrate his full attention on the Black Tartars to his north. If the Mongol Khan Kitbugha made a southward dash to attack Egypt, the Mamluks could strike inland from the coastal road at the Tartar supply caravans.

The Mongols are now estimated to be a two-day ride from the broad Jezreel Valley. This flat basin, just southeast of Acre, is where the sultan wishes to engage Kitbugha. Esel figures only the gods know if the enemy will oblige.

Fortunately, Qutuz pulled Baybars' vanguard back into Acre two days ago to lick their wounds in camp. Tonight the Bahri will stage with Qutuz's main force on the south side of the Mount Carmel range, out of the Mongol scouts' view.

Esel eyes a pair of hobbled donkeys who have made their way behind the far-off watchmen, along with a few horses. The guards are oblivious to her presence. Engrossed in their conversation, they have not turned around once since she arrived.

She had a dream two nights past. In it, her friend, Jacinta, was in a small boat, paddling wildly upstream in a wide river. While Esel hovered above the water helplessly, Mongol soldiers oared two massive galleys toward Jacinta. Once within bow range, the Tartars began shooting at her. The dream ended with Jacinta ducking behind the gunwales, screaming out for help. Esel awoke in a sweat.

She cannot let go of the nightmare. She feels it a premonition, a sign that her friend who spies on the Mongols to the north may be in trouble. With the bulk of the Tartars now near, she is compelled to find Jacinta and bring her back to the safety of Acre.

She takes a deep breath and shoulders her saddlebag, stuffed with pears she picked from an orchard just south. A bridle lies atop the load. She clutches a small bow, made by her hand, and a quiver of arrows. She slings her water skin and leaves the concealment of the shade for the donkeys.

Reaching the healthier of the two beasts, she lays down her gear and strokes the donkey's forelock. She speaks softly to him. When he is comfortable with her, she loosens the girth strap holding the blanket atop his back. She slides her strung bow and quiver under the leather banding just above the animal's ribs. She tightens the strap enough to hold the bow in place, but allowing her the ability to remove it with little effort.

She pulls an oversized horse blanket off the swale-backed brute next to him and flops it over the younger donkey, covering the weapon. With an eye to the guards, she slips the headpiece over his ears and flops her saddle bag across the donkey's withers. She removes the hobble. The guards remain unaware of her presence as she leads the animal southward toward the tree line.

Will the guards turn around and stop her? Known among many in the Muslim camp as Baybars' aunt, none would likely prevent her from using the animal. Yet she would rather not have to explain who she is and where she goes.

Cresting a mound, she grabs the donkey's mane and slides atop his back. She enters the bush line, her path choked with spiny broom and spent Greek sage. She rides beneath the canopy of a blooming carob tree, its tiny florets the shade of Mamluk scarlet. The locals call loaves made of carob "poor man's bread," as the underprivileged here grind the ripened beans from the tree into a crude flour. The bread is a symbol of humility.

Humility, meekness. Esel supposes there is a time and place to embrace these parts of one's makeup, but now is not one of them. With Jacinta possibly unaware of the Mongol enemy's proximity—and maybe in harm's way—Esel must call forth her courage and boldness today. Superstitious, she leaves the earthy fragrance of the spiked blooms for the shade of a gnarled oak, so as to preclude the carob's scent of timidity from entering her nostrils and subconsciously leading her back toward the safety of camp.

Hidden there, she dismounts to tighten the buckles on the throat lash and cheek pieces of the bridle. She lifts the blanket and checks that she is able to pull out her bow with ease.

She mounts and gives the animal some calf. The donkey stays with his ears pinned back.

"I know, you do not want to leave your friends," she whispers. "You should not be going. We both should not be going."

Last night, Baybars had directed her to stay in Acre.

"Were you able to get a message to Jacinta?" Esel asked.

"No," Baybars said flatly.

"So Jacinta is not aware how close the Mongols are now."

"It is her job to send word to Acre once the enemy closes on Galilee. She will be safe at that bazaar on the Jordan. Moles know when and how to disappear. She is the least of my worries."

He seemed to read the concern on her face. "Do not get any ideas. Please stay in Acre until the whole thing is over. You have already done more than your share of duty."

She knows her nephew only wished to shelter her in the rear. She had agreed to his quasi-order. But like a mother who knows best, she now disregards his appeal.

She talks to the donkey, while rubbing his neck. She digs in her heels. He moves forward halfheartedly.

She stays on the south slope of lower Mount Carmel, weaving between the oaks and tall bushes. She rides until well out of sight of the guards to the north and the Muslim camp to the west, on the reverse slope of the lower mountain range. She drops down to a goat trail and follows it eastward, the trail meandering between the rolling foothills.

Mount Tabor materializes to her northeast, the scrub-dotted crag growing in stature among the smoky hills of Nazareth. She approaches the Great Trunk Road, its path bisecting the flat at Megiddo. Qutuz's forces took this major route northward from Gaza into the lands of the Franj, just days ago.

The donkey's ears stand straight up. He halts and looks back in the direction of his mate and the herd of Arabians. Able to hear what Esel does not—possibly a distress bray of his companion—he honks mournfully in response.

"Please. I will bring you back to your donkey comrade in due time," she tells the beast, scratching behind his ears.

The jack will not budge. He continues his wretched song.

She tries to speak over his noise. "You think you are the only one with a heavy heart? Everything I have touched in the last half year has turned to shit." She believes this. Since convincing Baybars to ally with Qutuz, the sultan has treated her nephew and his men like expendable decoys.

The donkey looks away.

"I would ignore me, too," she mumbles. Surely Qutuz wants Baybars dead. He has put Baybars in every conceivable position of danger to achieve this. Should Baybars be killed, Qutuz will be spared the threat of having a rival as governor of Aleppo.

She kneads the base of the donkey's mane. No doubt Qutuz will saddle Baybars' vanguard with the rotten duty of drawing Kitbugha's army the rest of the way into the Jezreel Valley. She looks back toward Acre. "I should have known my nephew was right about Qutuz."

The donkey's bray turns sorrowful.

"Why do I bother divulging my fears and doubts to a thick-skulled beast like you? Even you care not." She feels that she has contributed to imperiling the entire Bahri—some like grandsons to her—along with Jacinta, whom she persuaded to spy on the closing enemy.

She rubs his neck, his bristled fur flicking dust with each stroke. This does nothing to quell his crooning.

"Come now. We only go a little farther—to the marketplace."

She sits him a long while, speaking quietly of nothing to him. When the donkey calms, they continue eastward, Esel pitching atop the beast.

"Maybe you are the smart one between us. Maybe you can sense that the Tartars come again now to ruin my tribe, as they did when I was young."

He fights her steer. She tugs his head back on course.

"Maybe you and I are one and the same. Willful. I think you know that I will be looking for a chance to put a few arrows into the yellow demons. How could I not? It is they who slaughtered my people and ended Kipchak rule on the steppe."

He dips his head, yanking the leather in her hands. She regrets choosing the bitless bridle. "Are you afraid to hide in the scrub and help me pluck the odd Tartar? Are you going to cry or help me? You think the Mongols would really suspect a stubborn old woman on a stubborn old donkey like you?"

She crosses the two shallow forks of a feeble tributary that feeds the Kishon River. "I have unfinished business with these Black Tartars. But first we must warn my friend. I can feel she is in danger."

She pushes southeast across the rock-strewn hills of short grass, toward the lowest of the rising hills in the Gilboa ridge.

To the south, hundreds of camels and their pullers sleep under the trees and shade created by the steeper draws. These distant Bedouin pay her no attention.

The Bedu hide and wait for darkness to come. Baybars had explained the nomads' orders to her. Tonight, the Bedouin will slip north to the Jezreel spring and fill the leather water bladders secured to their saddle horns. They will then spray water from slices cut from the corners of their giant sacks, moistening the dusty grass in the giant horseshoe-shaped flat on the west end of Gilboa, behind the great mountain and out of Tartar view.

This is where Qutuz plans to hide the bulk of his forces; from here, the sultan will spring his trap. The Bedu's only mission is to free the entire staging area of powdery silt which might reveal the army's hideaway.

The ground steepens. She heads for the lowest saddle. She climbs and descends the south-stretching fingers of the ridge, continuing eastward south of Beit Shean to the Jordan River, its flow cutting south from the Sea of Galilee.

At the ford east of the marketplace, she splashes into the stream. She stops to let the donkey drink. She crosses and halts on the eastern bank, scanning the small bazaar. Two Arabs approach her on foot, one carrying a staff. She rounds her back to appear frail.

"What it is you are selling?" one asks.

"I have some fruit," she says, in a feeble voice.

She lifts the flap on her saddlebag and pulls out two ripe pears. She hands one to each man. "My gratitude for you allowing a grandmother to earn a few coins to help feed her family."

They point her toward the market.

She continues into the sparse bazaar, half the booths shaded by sunbaked hides or tattered linen. Only a few locals peruse the stalls. A vendor swishes a branch to drive off the flies from the last of the cured tilapia she sells, the skin having gone dark and dry.

"I sell these cheap," the woman says, waving Esel in.

Esel smiles politely and continues past a barrel seller and a fly-covered sheep carcass, twisting in the breeze. She passes crates of melon and a booth where parents and child lie snoring, sprawled beside stacks of burlap wraps. A slab of apricot paste lies flat upon a pair of overlapping palm fronds. A staple for the poor here, the fruit roll looks like a hunk of peeled flesh.

Esel seeks Jacinta and Zane, yet cannot locate them.

Little wonder. No bustle of business here. Few southbound travelers means few sources for Jacinta to query for information on the Mongol force's composition and location. Esel wonders if her friend set up in another bazaar farther north, closer to the enemy, similar to what she did in Aleppo.

Esel meets the stare of a woman selling blankets; the woman looks away. An old man across the pathway offers a selection of carved ebony pieces and necklaces under a papyrus reed awning. He wears a patch over one eye and gapes at her with his other. He picks his teeth.

Under a tree on the eastern edge of the market, Esel slides off the donkey, her knees and back aching. She removes her saddlebag. Setting it on the ground, she opens the flaps and rolls some of the fruit out onto the leather so the pears are visible to the scattering of women, both Muslim and white-skinned Franj, who browse the goods and gather their dinner-time supplies.

Four Mongols in the black-scaled leather of light cavalry make the turn in the road. They walk down the street toward the market, one eating an apple. She forces herself to be calm and leans against the donkey to pull a rock from her slipper. Look normal. Just be a vendor, she thinks.

The inbound Mongols swagger, two of them with thumbs locked atop their thick war belts. Attired in chest armor and the long deel worn by their kind, the warriors survey the booths. They wear no helmets, just their odd felt hats with three flaps tied up to the crown of their heads.

Esel scrutinizes the oldest of them. His dark beard is cleaved by a thick swath of pink scar tissue. Grimy braids hang below his cap. Somehow she recognizes him. Impossible.

The Mongol studies trinkets on a tilted display and then struts along to catch his mates. His eyes go to her and the donkey. As he turns, she notices the cut-and-sewn sleeve on the right arm of his coat. He has but one arm. She remembers the haughty swing of his stub.

Her heart begins to hammer. He is the same arms purchaser she saw at the souk in Nablus, nearly three years past. She recalls the Mongol scowling at her there, this one-armed enemy of the empire as out of place at that weapons trade as Esel, a woman arms dealer.

Esel's stomach turns. She looks away. He will not recall, much less recognize her.

His eyebrows tighten. She adjusts the fruit on the ground, pulling a few more from the bag. She takes a bite out of a pear and pats the donkey's shoulder, pretending to casually observe the stands.

A tightness fills her chest as her eyes come back across him. He has stopped in the path. He gazes at her. She should have worn a full niqab to better conceal her face. His eyes grow wide.

"*Tuunlig av!*" the Mongol screams, pointing her out to his mates. "Tuunlig av!"

She turns and runs.

To the river. She spits out the fruit and sprints across the open space to the thicker brush. She turns west into the heavy growth of reeds along the Jordan's bank.

A thumping of boot stomps trail her, perhaps only two men, one of them pulling away. The squeak of armor closes.

She wills her legs to move faster.

She plunges into a ravine, the papyrus whipping her face. Go. Push through it.

The crash of toppled cane only steps behind her now. He moves swiftly. She tumbles into the river, her shin smashing against a rock. She is rapidly to her feet, her legs churning against the current.

The young Mongol jumps from the bank and lands with his knee to her back.

Pain on the backside of her ribs. The air leaves her lungs.

Water fills her nose. The sensation of being stuck in the depths of a cistern. The swoosh of his movements in water. The grate of his boot heel scraping gravel on stone. The hum of passing current.

She brawls underwater, yet the man presses her right cheek against the stony bottom with one sturdy paw. She punches and claws at his forearm, her nail scrapes having no impact upon on his sleeve and thick-skinned hands. She thrashes her legs.

Her strength begins to fade. Soon, her arms do little more than grope his. She gasps for a breath, sucking in water. She chokes, fighting the strong hand with the last of her ability. Her arms fall limp.

This is how it will end. She opens her eyes. Light shines through the river, forming a crown of light at the surface. Grains of floating sand nestle between the rocks. The purr of stream over rock. She is no longer frightened. The form of a man enters the column of light and becomes centered in its nimbus. Is it her husband? She smiles. Yagmur will take her to the Great Sky.

Her neck wrenches backward. A stab of pain on the back of her head. Her scalp.

The Mongol drags her to shore by the hair, dumping her on the muddy bank. She struggles to take a breath. She turns upon her side. Her belly convulses and she vomits on her arm. She coughs.

In time, she looks into the sun at the dark figure looming above her. He grips a sword. She closes her eyes. "Kill me, just kill me," she thinks.

When she looks up again, the silhouettes of three men block the sky. A voice blurts something in their thick tongue. They confer.

The one-armed Mongol arrives. He drops her bow across her hips. "Forget this?" he says in rough Turkish. "Bowyers, agents of enemy, should know better."

CHAPTER 46

Leander

Mt. Carmel staging area

September 3, 1260

To the comforting sound of his horse ripping grass and chewing, Leander loops a leather strap through the last buckle on his left gaiter, working only by feel in the dark. Securing his right gaiter, he stands and rubs San's muzzle.

A sickle of new moon sets prominently in the clear sky, the yellow arch perched atop Mt. Carmel. He recalls a dog-eared book in Erard's castle. In it, the story of the Byzantine emperor adopting this same waxing crescent as the symbol of their city, before the Anatolian center became Constantinople. The ruler chose the emblem in honor of an epic battle won on the first day of some lunar month, when the Roman forces defeated the Goths. Leander prays this same slice of moon brings Egypt victory in their forthcoming contest.

That Leander and his mates remain alive to see this day is astounding in itself. Allah's mercy, he figures. Qutuz, of course, has showed the Bahri none of God's benevolence. After the

Bahri lost eight men at the Mongol ambush near Gaza last July, the sultan did not pull Baybars' unit back to reorganize. Perhaps thinking the Bahriyya accustomed to ambuscades and being outnumbered—and certainly seeing them as dispensable—Qutuz instead sent the Bahri north to bait the Mongols down from Damascus.

The Bahri disengaged the enemy in three quick-hitting encounters over the summer and lost a dozen more Mamluks. And as desired by Qutuz, Baybars' faris gradually enticed Kitbugha's army of eleven thousand southward.

Yesterday, the sultan's lookouts spotted the enemy bivouacked just north of the Sea of Galilee. Now, one more time, the Bahri must lure the enemy just a little farther southward. On this occasion, they must not fail. Qutuz's plan centers on Baybars' regiment tempting the enemy into the huge basin to their east.

In the scant moonshine, the vague outlines of the Bahri and their mounts in the assembly area appear like wandering specters in the dim glow, dull apparitions of some ill-starred army, slain generations past, forced to again take the field in repentance for their grave sins.

Leander loosely secures his belt and attaches the baldric to the suspension loops midway down his scabbard. He reaches his arms to the sky, freeing the right amount of chain mail above his beltline, a measure to retain his mobility in the hauberk. He cinches his belt, locking it into the same worn notch. He feels for the second sword in his saddle scabbard. He pats his crossbow and double-checks his assortment of heavy-headed bolts, those used for penetrating armor and felling horses.

Around him, hundreds of Bahri Mamluks prepare similarly for battle, their sounds intensified in the blackness: the creaks and groans of armor and saddle straps being tightened, the grunt of men sliding lamellar jawshans over torsos, and the clunk of breast armor being strapped to the chests of horses. Murmurings from hushed chats mingle with the tinkling of harnesses, the clank of bamboo lance shafts, and the hiss of steel gliding into scabbards. Nervous Arabians snort their realization of what soon comes.

Leander works the wrinkles from the *qayah*, the satin skull cap, atop his head. He puts his nose to the headband and webbing of the Italian helmet provided by Baybars last year. He breathes in the earthy aroma of sweat-worn leather before placing it upon his head.

The musty smell brings him back to endless hours of training, broken bones and compresses held atop oozing slash wounds, screaming instructors and mentors expertly wielding lance and sword, and *Mu'allim* offering stern words of wisdom from their hippodrome's raked grounds in Cairo. His self-assurance was forged in sweat and years of daily training, which he knows the Mongols do not share.

Even if his mates are better trained, Leander wonders how of many of his friends will still die here. Will this be the last time that he shoulders Mamluk armor?

He strokes San's withers, pondering the Mongol horde he saw three years past preparing in the Gilan Gharb Valley just after their Persian victories—the enemy was so numerous and well-supplied. The Tartars' string of conquests since then creeps into his mind like a spreading fog, fouling any sense of optimism he can muster.

Leander slides his arm through the grip straps of his tur shield, its rounded face wrapped in dyed leather, the Ayyubid red lion snarling dead center amid the mustard yellow. An orb of rivets bond hide to wood, encircling the bronze boss. Etched inside every hardened-leather bowl is the same inscription that has adorned the Bahri shields for at least a dozen years: "Defender of the faith." This dedication is made in unending homage to al-Salih, the last sultan to command all of Egypt's loyalty.

Homage. An emptiness fills him. He touches the black armband at the base of his bicep, the same worn by every

Mamluk in Duyal's former amirate. Those from Amirate Three wear the emblem in tribute to their leader who died near Gaza. Duyal was posthumously decorated with a Ribbon of Valor, like his older brother, Gozde.

Prior to every previous battle, Leander had Duyal's composed presence to bolster him. No more. He recalls the day they buried his idol south of Gaza.

> *The day after the ambush, Amirate Three returned to the same canyon near the Rafah Oasis. Singer and Leander entered where the wadi constricted, the remainder of the amirate having scoured the high ground and thick country ahead for any lingering enemy.*
>
> *Singer pointed, tight-lipped, to a large rock to their front. A white figure with yellow trousers lay atop. They halted their horses, neither wishing to see their dead mate up close.*
>
> *Singer dismounted slowly and tied his mount on a sayal limb. Leander did the same. They unstrapped shovels from their saddles and walked to him.*
>
> *Duyal rested with his arms atop his chest, crossed over his strung bow. His face still wore its determination from the fight. Darkened blood encrusted his coat. The Mongols had cut flush each of the six arrows that riddled his body. The dry weather and shaded gorge had preserved him and the animals had not yet come to feed upon their friend.*
>
> *"They put our brother atop the stone to honor him in their own way," Singer said.*
>
> *"Aye," Leander said. He lowered his head against the rock and fought back the tears. Singer hummed a Kipchak death song.*
>
> *They stood a while in silence.*
>
> *"Let us get on with it," Singer said, unsheathing his knife.*
>
> *They cut Duyal's leather neck guard from his jawshan and removed his gaiters, stowing this kit in their saddlebags. They dug a hole and then lifted Duyal from the flat stone, his stiff*

arms enfolded about the bow he shot so capably. The Mongols, too, wished for this warrior to go underground with his weapon, armed in the afterlife.

They buried him on the edge of the wadi amid a patch of knapweed. The purple flowers drooped in the heat, as if sharing the diggers' grief. The bloom's pineapple-shaped bladders swelled, like sacks filled with teardrops. Tears to be shed for Duyal, the best man among them.

Singer stands with his back to Leander, snugging the worn leather billet strap on his saddle. Attached to the back of Singer's cuirass is Duyal's old neck guard, stained and weather-beaten. While Leander cannot see Duyal's favorite passage in Turkish script etched upon the neck armor, Leander murmurs the words he learned by rote: "And be not weak-hearted in the pursuit of the enemy."

Leander looks down to his gaiters, once worn by Amir Duyal, for the continuation of the verse. Down the length of the left gaiter: "If you suffer pain, then surely they too suffer pain as you suffer pain." Down his right: "And you hope from Allah what they do not hope; Allah is knowing and wise."

The faint bawl of sheep and bleat of goats float on the breeze from the west, snapping him from his thoughts. The Bedu herdsmen execute Qutuz's plan in moving their livestock closer to the western slope of Mt. Carmel. The ruse begins. Hundreds of shepherds begin shifting thousands of animals.

By the time the sun breaks the eastern horizon, the resultant dust will simulate the movement of the Muslim main body behind the mountain. Leander looks to the northern hills, wondering if moving the livestock will fool the Mongols, who will surely be watching from afar once the sun rises. The rest of Qutuz's army, nearly eleven thousand strong, departed in the middle of the night for their true staging area, a half-day's ride southeast.

The plaintive howl of an ivory olifant calls the troops to assemble. Baybars stands atop a cart. The amirs gather nearest him, their respective Mamluks packing close behind. The farthest of the men mount their horses to catch a glimpse.

Their commander bellows. "There are few times when seven hundred and twenty-four men can make history. Never have Islam and its people been so threatened. Yet have faith; rarely have so many jihadis been gathered in one place to counter the menace."

Baybars looks about him, sensing the tenseness among his men. "Some of you know that the Franj enjoy hanging their thieves from a loop tossed over a tree branch. Such is little different than what Amir Qutuz has in store for the Mongols." He nods his head. "Yet while Qutuz, the hangman, waits from behind the refuge of Gilboa Mountain with his gallows tree rigged and ready, we again are the lowly scamps who must lead the Mongols' heads into the Mamluk noose."

His soldiers look on somber-faced in the dim moonlight.

Baybars springs from the cart and mounts his gray, the Arabian looking in the moon's gleam as if she is cast in silver. He looks eastward and forces a grin. "But have heart, my brothers! If we get caught with Qutuz's noose about our necks along with the Tartars, then at least Allah will enjoy watching his Bahri dancing in the air together, before we meet him in paradise."

"Err!" The men blurt a dark chuckle and then turn silently away to finish preparing.

Leander nods, not because of Baybars' humor, nor his clever comparison of Qutuz's tactical snare to a hangman's rope, but rather because the Bahri's commander still refuses to call Qutuz "sultan." Instead, Baybars refers to his rival by Qutuz's old military title, "amir." Baybars does not hide the fact that he, too, worries of a Qutuz doublecross, if and when the Bahri can entice the Mongols into the Mamluk slaughter zone at Gilboa.

Baybars' face turns back to stone. "Now is the time. The time is at hand. Simply do as we have designed and rehearsed."

Their work ahead is indeed as straightforward as Baybars states. But Qutuz's battle plan is both basic and intricate—basic in concept, yet intricate in the coordination required to hide and then maneuver such a great number of troops. The disclosure of any element of the attacking force is likely to spoil the surprise.

Baybars and his vanguard comprise Qutuz's "Carrot Element," or what many of the Bahri have nicknamed the "Ass-Wipe Element," as it is clear to all that the sultan sees them as expendable. Their mission is to find the Mongols in the vicinity of Galilee and draw the Mongols southwest into the wide valley at Ayn Julut, where Qutuz's main body waits.

Qutuz's main army—the "Strike Element," as he called it in his order—plans to hide on the reverse slope of the Gilboa Highlands. When the Mongol enemy is spread out and exposed on the wide Jezreel Valley, the sultan will then attack from the south.

Will the feigned retreat maneuver fool the Mongols, warriors of the steppe themselves, fighters whose forefathers used the same trick for generations? Only Allah knows.

Leander watches Baybars give final instruction to his amirs. Leander wonders how many of the soldiers recognize that the brevity and content of Baybars' words echo those of Saladin the Great in his speech to his amirs before the Ayyubid founder's victory at the Horns of Hittin, just a two-day ride northeast from this spot.

Baybars is no fool. He is a man who understands not only human nature, but also history. Undoubtedly, their commander grasps the resemblance between what lies ahead for the Bahri today and what Saladin faced at Hittin seventy-three years ago. Here near Ayn Julut, just as before at nearby Hittin, the downside of failure could not be higher. And the combatants on each side are once again of nearly identical size and perhaps unified in their cause for only a limited time. And just as at Hittin, the Muslims lay a trap.

At Hittin in the summer of 1187, Saladin's men faked an assault on the Franj citadel in Tiberias. Ignoring wise counsel to the contrary, King Guy of Jerusalem listened to Reynald of Chatillon—plus the Hospitallers' and Templars' arrogant hawks, who pressured Guy to attack. Guy moved twelve thousand Franj east from Sepphoris.

As Guy's Franj trudged from Sepphoris to Tiberias, they found the waterholes and streambeds dry. Saladin's archers fell upon the Christians from every direction, killing hundreds. Dying of thirst, fresh water from the Sea of Galilee became the Crusaders' revised objective. The problem: between the Franj and the big lake was Saladin's army in a great plain.

At night, Saladin slipped a force behind the Crusaders, blocking the Franj retreat westward. The next day, surrounded by enemy and mad with thirst, the Crusaders rushed for the lake and were cut down by Muslim lance and sword in droves. The Muslims set fire to the grass, blowing smoke into the Crusaders' faces.

Assailed by thirst, firestorms, and the heart of the Muslim army, the Crusaders lost thousands more, as well as the True Cross, on which they claimed the Messiah was crucified. These Christian disasters at Hittin, plus the massive crusader defeat at La Forbie, resulted in manpower losses the Crusaders have yet to recover from.

Manpower. Leander shakes his head. The Mongols have no such worry. Even in the midst of a messy struggle between his brothers for the rule of the Mongol empire, Hulegu still has an army of over eighty thousand in Anatolia, which he could unleash upon Egypt at any moment. Allah help them.

Leander's hand returns to the mourning strip atop his coat sleeve. Beneath the armband and chainmail, he bears a lateral welt across the base of his biceps. Twelve years ago, standing in a circle of newly-graduated Mamluk youths, he took a dagger from the novice beside him and sliced his own skin at the bend in each arm. He stood proudly in this grisly ring, hinged at the dripping elbows with his brothers in training, the ritual binding them as blood brothers, *ikhwa.*

The black band on his coat and rope of scar tissue underneath it embody Duyal's spirit and the support of his brothers in arms who still live. He must call forth the strength provided by both when his courage is soon summoned. Whether or not God favors the Mamluks here today, Leander must do as Saladin's men did those decades ago: fight the invader with all he is worth.

CHAPTER 47

Esel

East of Beit Shean

September 3, 1260

Esel watches the stars fade in the low morning light. She shivers, her backside soaked from the spongy ground, her skin rubbed raw at the ankles and wrists where the rope binds her. The hemp runs to knotted wraps at four tamarisk trees, splaying her limbs wide. Acrid smoke from the watchman's fire stings her eyes and belabors her breath.

Her face wears scratches and reddish bruises from the scrape of branches during her fleeing and the smack of Tartar knuckles after her capture. Each pump of her heart pulses a throb to the singed flesh on her chest, where last night her Mongol captors thought red-hot steel might compel her answers.

> *The one-armed Mongol rested against the running end of his rope, which looped midway up the tamarisk trunk and attached to Esel's left wrist. Seated, his mates likewise secured Esel's legs*

at the ankles. The fourth man had tied his rope to another tree while he stoked their fire.

The one-armed leader nodded to this fourth Mongol. The young Tartar pulled his sword blade from the smoldering coals and rose, smoke curling from his blackened steel as he walked over. He took a knee beside Esel's shoulder and eyed his commander.

She clenched her lips, the scent of hot metal filling her nostrils.

"Your silence not save Egyptians. Where Baybars, where Qutuz army?" the leader asked in his broken Turkish.

"I came north on the King's Highway from Karak. I saw no soldiers," Esel lied, looking straight into his eyes. She would not betray her nephew or disclose Egypt's plan.

The one-armed soldier took another gulp of wine from his flask. He shook his head, tightened the rope about the tree, and pointed at the blade. The two Mongols holding the ropes secured to her legs pulled them taut.

Esel wrangled to get free. The three soldiers gave one last tug, immobilizing her.

The young Tartar laid the flat of the blade across her chest.

The sound of sizzling meat. A surge of agonizing pain. The smell of burning linen, mixed with flesh. She opened her mouth wide as if to scream, but refused to utter a sound. She arched her back, digging the back of her head into the soil.

The trooper removed the steel with her buttery flesh attached. Expressionless, he looked to his senior.

The one-armed Mongol drained his jug and wiped a sleeve across his dripping beard. "Tell me!"

She looked away, a dull ache on her breast.

"She talk if we set the blade to her face," the man holding the rope at her right leg said.

Her interrogator chucked his empty flask, striking Esel in the face. He struggled to his feet. He spat on her. He picked up his jug and walked toward the wine cask they had gotten from the souk. "Thick-skulled bitch care nothing of fist or fire."

The Mongol holding the blade shrugged his shoulders.

When the one-armed Tartar refilled his flask and walked to the river, the older of them cinched his rope end to the tree trunk. "Secure your ties. We drink."

The Tartar watchman glances at her disinterestedly and yawns. He whittles to stay awake.

When the last stars have dwindled in the cobalt sky, titmice begin chirping riverside from the safety of their oaken roosts. When the watchman's three comrades stir beneath their deel covers, the bowlegged Mongol rises wearily and rekindles the blaze. He fills his pot at the river and sets it amid the glowing coals.

The one-armed Mongol flings aside his long coat. While unable to comprehend their language, she has pegged him as perhaps a former commander, shifted to the duty of outfitting the army after losing his arm in some battle. A bitter man.

He props himself up to his only elbow and peers at her with bloodshot eyes. He glares as if just now recalling her existence. Bleary-eyed, the other two men sit up, one holding his head.

Esel is dumbfounded that her four captors have allowed her to live this long and baffled that the Mongols halted their interrogation and torture of her last night. Their commander had turned to drinking once the sun set, as if this was his custom, no matter the task at hand. The other troopers seemed to know his habit. Following his lead, they soon were drunk, too, and she was ignored.

The sun tops the horizon. She broods on their temperament this morning.

The one-armed man rises and begins assembling his gear with great care, stowing it in the packs strapped to his hobbled horse. When finished, he walks to her. "You talk more today," he says, his teeth looking sharp enough to cut hide.

She closes her eyes.

Once packed, the Mongols sit on a pair of half-rotted logs facing opposite directions like bedded deer. They eat the pears from her saddlebag with scarcely a word passing between them. Done with their meal, the commander points a stubby thumb toward her. They rise.

As they approach her, Esel's heart races. She calls to mind the countless marmots she trapped during her youth on the steppe. The jubilation felt when coming upon the furred quarry. Meat for the tower's children; fur for their mittens. Now in her fear, she feels pity for those captive creatures, animals making their last, frantic attempts at escape from her snares as she drew near.

Each Mongol returns to the same rope he manned last night. They untie the stretched running ends of the four ropes from the nearby tree trunks.

Esel whimpers as the pressure is released from her wrists and feet. Pain surges to her knees and elbows and wrists and shoulders. She chastens herself for revealing any feebleness to them.

She looks to the closest tree and notices one wrap is left about the rope-scarred trunk. She trembles. They are not done with her.

Her shivering grows in intensity. Her chest heaves. Three Mongols wind the hemp about their fists and look to the leader.

He runs the rope behind his back and holds it with his only hand. "*Tatakh*," he says, his ass only three feet from her shoulder. She turns her head, sickened to again be smelling his sour rank.

The men dig in their heels and haul their ropes.

The hemp rasps across the scarred bark. Their tight lines groan that same wretched song. Her shoulder blades lift from the ground. A bite of pain as the blisters upon her chest stretch and open. She grinds her molars as the ache in her joints sets in. She tries to control her breathing, yet is unable. She sucks the smoky air in fast, shallow breaths.

Just as last night, she refuses to cry out. She will tell them nothing but the same lies. Whether they believe her words as truth or become irate with her falsehoods, she cares little. She hopes only that the Tartars will kill her soon.

She tries to detach from the agony, her mind spinning images from the old country—snow-blanketed meadowlands and fall festivals and bows gifted to friends. She pictures the Respectable Woman's serene face and broad shoulders. "A great woman doing man's work," the old Kipchaks had said of the sculpture's namesake. If the Gods had chosen her to also take up the work of men, she must now take the agony as lightly as the statue.

She mumbles a prayer to the Respectable Woman, asking the goddess for a dignified death, one fit for the huntress she once was.

"You now speak truth. How many Muslim? Where Baybars and Qutuz army?" the one-armed Mongol demands.

"I told you," she says. "I am just a bowyer. I am nothing. They tell me nothing. I heard that Qutuz and Baybars quarreled. I think Qutuz went back to Cairo. Only Baybars is in the big valley with his vanguard."

"Untruths!" The commander nods to the others. They lean into their ropes. The squeak of tightening hemp. Her buttocks rise from the ground. She groans. "Endure," she tells herself.

They hold this position for what seems like hours, their commander repeating the same questions. She says nothing.

She begins to see spots in the puffs of cloud. Half-delirious, she murmurs to her dead husband, Yagmur. "I will soon join you, my dear."

"I join you, my dear," their leader mocks in her tone. He hurls a barb at one of the men in their native tongue. The others chuckle. This man eyes her spread legs.

They release their grip on the ropes, leaving her sprawled on the earth. They loosely re-tie their ends to the trunks.

The one-armed Mongol brushes the dirt from his pants. He looks down at her and shakes his head. He again blurts something to them in their language and then squats beside her. "Stupid woman." He removes his knife from its sheath. "You know where Mamluk Qutuz is."

She turns from him.

He grabs her hair and twists her curls until her head faces him. "Tell truth now, or die." He flicks his knife across her left cheek.

A dribble of blood trickles down her cheek and into her ear.

He grazes the knife across her forehead with a backhand motion. "Tell me!"

Esel mumbles another prayer to the Respectable Woman, begging her to end this soon.

The Mongol stands with hand on hip for several moments, perhaps thinking of what he might do next to loosen her lips. Eventually, he opens his palm to where she lies, as if inviting forward the troop he teased earlier. The commander walks away with two others behind him.

The remaining Mongol waits for the men to walk only a few steps. He drops his trousers. He nudges between her legs and lifts her tunic.

"I like," she says, blinking the blood from her eyes.

He raises a lip skeptically. He tries to probe her. Esel moans. When he bends closer to her, she smashes her forehead into his nose.

He falls back, holding his face.

Dazed, the Mongol rolls to his ass and sits dumbfounded with his trousers about his feet, feeling for the break in his nasal bone. Blood trickles into his thin mustache. The other Mongols turn and laugh. She feels the welt forming on her brow.

An arrow smacks into the rapist's unarmored chest. Esel's eyes go wide.

The soldier looks at her as a child would. He grasps the shaft with one hand and studies the fletching, as if assessing how it appeared. He tips backward.

More zips of arrow fire come from the nearby scrub.

Another smack of iron head into flesh. The one-armed Mongol tries to pull a shaft from his neck. Two more "whops" as arrowheads lodge into meat. She cranes her neck in a useless effort to see who has been hit. She writhes against the ties on her wrists and ankles. Another thump of arrow on aim.

"Baybars," she says. The Respectable Woman's spirit somehow sent her nephew to find her.

Esel looks side to side. Seeing nothing, she wriggles to look behind.

Movement in the shrubbery there. A Mongol groans, another cries out. One crawls away into a thicket.

Esel flails against the slackened ropes with all of her might. She cringes as a dark form arrives from above her head. The figure straddles her arm and begins sawing at the knot on Esel's left wrist.

Esel looks into the blinding sunrise at her rescuer. A gray tunic with collar up and a filthy Turkish hat. Esel recognizes the bow lying on the ground as one made from her own hand. A quiver of arrows. Another rope goes limp at her ankle. When Esel's limbs are free, the shooter turns and looks down.

The warrior's deep-brown eyes skirt the environs. A veiled face, with clear-skinned cheekbones exposed. Esel's jaw drops.

Jacinta. Why would Baybars' Mamluks allow her to join them? Esel looks for the archers. She sees no one. Jacinta is alone.

A wet slap across Esel's bloody face. "Get up! Get up!" Jacinta says, nocking another arrow. She shoots from the kneeling position.

Her arrow plows harmlessly into the scrub.

Jacinta reaches out with her free hand and grabs Esel under the arm.

Esel rolls to her knees, but her legs feel as if knives poke at her hips and ankles. She wills herself to stand.

"Hurry!" Jacinta says. She grasps Esel's elbow and pushes her forward.

Esel limps into the brush line.

Jacinta forces a dagger into Esel's hand. "We must leave. I missed one, he is..."

A Mongol leaps from behind a white poplar and tackles Jacinta, a broken arrow sticking from his side. Jacinta rolls away. She springs to her feet. The Tartar lurches. Jacinta raises her bow with two hands and parries the man's knife jabs.

Esel flings herself atop the Mongol's back. In a fury, she stabs at his neck, her shoulders throbbing, her arms working at half strength. She sinks the blade into flesh twice. He shucks her off, swipes his blade, and misses.

She lands on her side with a yelp.

Esel struggles to her feet and again rushes the enemy. Using her momentum, she plunges the dagger deep into his right lung. A surge of adrenalin emboldens her. She opens her palm to flatten the entry of her knife-edge. She sticks the man repeatedly, feeling the slender blade glide between the bastard's ribs on each thrust. She jams her knee against his torso and twists the weapon as she withdraws it with both hands.

The Tartar rolls from Jacinta, dropping his knife.

Esel falls upon him with a primal howl, thrashing and goring recklessly. When he no longer resists, she pulls on his beaded locks and rips the dagger across his throat.

She staggers to her feet, her face slathered in blood and sweat. Jacinta lies unmoving. Esel slips the wet dagger into her waistline and picks up the bow and quiver from the ground. She turns, looking for others still alive.

She nocks an arrow and walks around the thickest of the willows, where she last saw the other Mongols. She hears a scrabble of boot on pebbles. She waits for a moment and then widens her arc of pursuit to intersect where the noise goes.

Blood on the rocks. Treading lightly on the balls of her feet, she follows the crimson trail, the globs transitioning to a smear on the dirt. She raises her weapon and half draws. She peers through the leaves over the three-feathered fletching.

The one-armed Mongol crawls away on all fours, his tunic saturated. She drops the bow and springs atop his back, pinning him with both knees. Grabbing a fist of his knotted hair, she wrenches his head up. "To hell you go," she says, with dagger in hand.

Esel tears across his neck brusquely, cutting so deep she hits spine. Blood gushes to the stones like a horse pissing. She works up enough spittle to shoot a bloody gob on the back of his nearly-severed head.

She retrieves her bow and slings it on her back. She steps over the other Mongol corpses riddled with her friend's arrows. She watches for any rise and fall in their chests, kicking each in the head as she moves along. She returns to Jacinta.

She drops to her knees beside her friend. Blood saturates Jacinta's tunic. Esel snatches the veil from her face. "My child, my precious child."

"They dead?" Jacinta asks.

"Yes, yes."

Jacinta hugs her with one arm. "I am all right. We go."

Esel holds Jacinta in place and lifts her friend's tunic. Two wide punctures leak from Jacinta's abdomen.

Esel winces. "We need to dress these first."

Jacinta tries to get up. Esel puts a hand on her shoulder to restrain her.

Esel goes to one of the Mongol's saddlebags. Finding a clean tunic, she cuts several pieces from the silken cloth. She kneels over one of the dead Mongols and slashes at the back of his deel, detaching a section of heavy cloth from his long coat. She rolls him over to expose his belt buckle. She tugs the belt loose.

She packs Jacinta's wounds with clean silk. She lays the thicker cloth across the dressed punctures and snugs the belt around her friend's waist to apply pressure.

Esel shakes her head, unsatisfied with her work. She walks to where the Mongol ponies are tied in the shade. She removes the hobbles from the two fittest animals, a bay and a white-spotted chestnut. She leads the ponies to her friend. "Are you able to ride?"

"I must." Jacinta tries to move, but recoils.

Esel helps Jacinta to her feet. Her friend takes one uneasy step toward the pony.

Esel looks to the northwest, where a far-off haze above Ayn Julut floats downwind. The battle begins on the great plain. "We need to get north where there will be help to better tend those wounds."

Jacinta nods. She takes the reins from Esel, grabs the cantle, and attempts to place her foot in the stirrup. She cannot. Esel squats under Jacinta's raised leg and eases her into the saddle.

Jacinta wraps her arm across the Mongol's belt, her head down.

Esel runs back to another Mongol corpse. She unbuttons his deel and frees his arms from the sleeves. She doubles the long coat into a makeshift pad. She snatches a lead from where the ponies were tied.

She places the deel atop the cantle, flopping the excess upon the pony's neck. She ties the lead to Jacinta's reins. "I will guide him. Slowly. You lean forward on the coat and wrap your hands around his neck."

Jacinta nods.

Just ahead of them, east of Megiddo, is the great plain of Armageddon, the place where Esel recalls the holy men say the fight to end all fights will befall. Esel must bring her friend there, somehow avoiding the battle while finding the rear-guard, where the surgeons tend wounded Muslims.

CHAPTER 48

Leander

Ayn Julut

September 3, 1260

Leaving the Bahri's staging area in the valley on the south side of Mount Carmel, the Mamluks merge into a staggered column. Leander and Singer fall in behind Baybars, a crescent of moon drawing their pale shadows long and slender upon the ground. The Muslim army's vanguard passes through stands of juniper into a horse pasture with the grasses grazed fetlock-high. They slip around the south side of Lower Carmel and follow the Great Trunk Road north.

Upon the flat-topped mound to their front, moonlight contours the ancient ruins of Megiddo. The tumbled relics are all that remains of this once strategically vital city. Centuries ago, Megiddo sprawled across the northern reaches of Lower Carmel and into the broad Jezreel Valley. The old palace and the granaries and temple—their most impressive stones long since stripped for construction of other buildings—now sit as monuments to the metropolis built to guard this narrow pass on the most important route linking Egypt with Mesopotamia and Anatolia.

Roughly translated in Hebrew as "place of crowds," Megiddo is more widely known by its Greek derivative: Armageddon. The Bahri tread over the ground where it is prophesied that armies will gather one day for the battle of all battles. Both the Christian Book of Revelation and the Islamic Hadith declare this site as the place where the world ends.

As they enter the grassy opening of the Megiddo Valley, dozens of Mamluks begin to pray in their saddles. While all seven hundred had joined earlier for Morning Prayer, perhaps the significance of the place—and the foe they will soon face—does indeed justify further supplication.

Leander supposes that today is not likely the end for all of man. But like those brothers chanting with their foreheads buried in their horses' manes, he also wonders if this could be the last sunrise for many of the Bahriyya.

Once in the middle of the grassland, Baybars nudges his horse eastward, where the black horizon starts to lighten. A northeast wind blows their trailing dust toward the cream-colored walls and dark crevasses of Mount Carmel's blocky ridge behind them. With a wordless hand signal, Baybars tasks the front, rear, and flank guards. These security elements break from the formation at the canter, staying within sight of the main body.

Leander's mare snorts a response to a horse in the ranks and then settles into her head-bobbing walk. The men in the cavalry column are left to their own thoughts, contemplating the fight to come amid the cadence of light-footed Arabians and the sounds of hooves swishing the grass. Flankers push out to their perimeters as the morning sky transitions from indigo to azure.

When the pastel overhead begins to bleed the color of red wine, they arrive where the land widens into the Valley of Jezreel. Centered in this vale, they cross through the crumbled-block remnants of the like-named city, hulks of rock scattered in tangles of weed and grass.

The word "Jezreel" is from the Hebrew for "God sows." Leander surmises that if God sowed the grass in this valley, then the shoots have grown lush from the blood spilled in battle here by generations of His lowly subjects nourishing the soil.

He watches San's hooves thump the dry ground, picturing the bones and armor and weapons of the Israelites, Midianites, Amalekites, and the Philistines that lie centuries-deep underground—unseen markers of battles won and lost for epochs on this historic Plain of Esdraelon. He wonders what history of the future God has already written and how the next chapter will be played out today, or tomorrow, on this infamous ground.

Whatever happens, at least Egypt carries the battle to the Mongols, rather than sitting back to take it on the nose, as did the rest of Syria. This flat terrain suits the strengths of the Muslim cavalry, even if the Tartars feel it befits them.

The Mamluks travel here unmolested, though few see more than a smidgen of good will in the Kingdom of Jerusalem allowing Qutuz's army to cross their lands to meet the common enemy. Nor do the "neutral" Franj show a speck of solidarity in supplying the Muslim war machine. The Crusaders hedge, as always, making every strategic decision with the primary goal of preserving their scant armies.

If the Mongols had not recently sacked the Christian port of Sidon—a justified response to Christian raids into Tartar-held lands west of Damascus—the Crusaders in this region might have allied with the Mongols, rather than providing this tepid support to Egypt's army. Although plenty of Mongols are Christians, including Kitbugha, the Franj cannot bring themselves to view the Tartars as God-sent liberators of the Christian Holy Land. To the Franj, the Mongols are just another strain of blood-drinking barbarian, not kindred men of the faith.

The sun breaks the horizon, shifting the meadow from gray to gilded bronze. To the cavalry's rear, powder rousted from the Bedu's flocks roils behind the southern tip of the Carmel range, rising like smoke from a smoldering fire.

Moreh Hill stands across the basin to their northeast. Will the Mongol scouts laid up there be fooled into thinking that Baybars' forces are merely the vanguard and that this stirring behind Mount Carmel is Qutuz assembling his army of thousands? Will those Tartar lookouts send runners to Kitbugha, who is somewhere farther northeast, alerting him of such? Hopefully.

To the northwest, the morning light paints the distant Mountains of Gilead, the east-west running hills of Galilee. Nestled in these slopes is the little town of Nazareth. Leander finds it ironic that the potential survival of Islam will be fought only a short ride from Jesus' boyhood home; just north of there lies Sepphoris, the birthplace of the Virgin Mary.

From his point on a rise, Leander stands in his stirrups and looks back. The column behind him takes on the menacing presence of a muscular snake—skinned in reflective steel, slinking through the grasslands.

They clomp along Jezreel spring, where wildflowers choke the slough in whites and pinks, contrasting with the immense span of sunbaked grass in the adjoining valley. They skirt the nearby headwaters of the Harod River, its course also traceable by the tapering green-brown along its banks. Its flow swells as they push eastward.

By mid-morning, the heat is upon them. Baybars stays to the south bank, eventually halting to let the horses drink from the river and sample the greens along the edge. His amirs ensure that half of the column remains mounted and ready.

When it is his turn, Leander leads San to the river. She sucks in the clear water, while he dunks both of his flasks. He removes his helmet and cap for only an instant, splashing cold water on his face and dumping some atop his head. He guzzles a full skin and then refills it.

They continue, crossing the face of Gilboa Mountain on their right. No man turns his head in this direction. Baybars instructed them earlier that Mongol eyes will somehow be watching them from somewhere. The vanguard must not disclose where Qutuz's main body hides and where the Muslim snare has been set. Keeping his head straight ahead, Leander strains his eyes to peer south.

Qutuz's main force, nearly nine thousand "strikers," supposedly conceal themselves on the backside of the entire ridgeline. The sultan's design is to stash one third of his force within "the horseshoe," the similarly-shaped basin on the south side of the Gilboa Highlands. Every draw, every ravine, east from there is to hold more troops, the reverse slope of the long rim being used to mask the Egyptian army's movement and sound from the valley opposite it.

Leander tries to pick out friendly scouts beneath the pines, or hidden in the clusters of juniper on the north face. He sees nothing. No dust rises from the opposite side of the mountain. Of course, the Bahri should not hear a horse nicker or see any sign of life, as Qutuz bade every man in his command to stay put and silent, under the threat of severe penalty.

Leander stews. Maybe the army is not there. Did Qutuz continue south in the night and was his real plan all along to leave Baybars' tiny vanguard exposed to the Mongol horde? If so, the Bahriyya, the "Carrot" in the planned maneuver, are dead men. Or if Qutuz is behind the mountain, will he let the Bahri be overrun and slain by the Tartars in the valley before he orders his strikers to attack the Mongols?

To Baybars' front, the amirate on point security returns at the gallop. They pull up just short of the vanguard. These men face eastward in a hasty crescent, their bows strung and at the ready. Once his men are in place, their amir continues to Baybars' banner.

The amir cannot disguise his alarm. "The Mongols ride south down the King's Highway. They begin to cross the Jordan on the north side of the Harod."

"Their vanguard?" Baybars asks.

"No, my Amir. All of them."

A lump sets in Leander's gut. Singer scans the northeastern skyline. Apparently the Bahri's luring over the past week has tempted, or perhaps sufficiently angered, Kitbugha.

The Mongol Khan comes.

Baybars glances to the southern sky. He tries to mask his unease. The late morning sun has not shifted far enough south above Gilboa for his liking. Forcing the Mongols to fight Qutuz's attackers with the sun's glare in their eyes is critical to the Muslim plan.

Their commander seems to shed this concern. He can control only his Bahri, not the movement of celestial orbs. He rides to the column's flank, his gray prancing without his urging, knowing that all eyes are upon her. Baybars raises his bow.

The cavalrymen take his cue mutely. They cinch down arm guards and tighten straps. Strung bows are pulled from rear cantles and thumb rings are slipped onto fingers. They nock arrows. Palms down, each man reaches his draw hand into his saddle quiver and extracts four more projectiles simultaneously between his fingers.

A tad shorter than the archers' arms and fletched with only three light feathers, these arrows are built for distance, not accuracy. For the first volley, the Bahri will sacrifice some precision for longer shots in barrages fired to harass, disrupt, and spread fear among the Tartars.

They rotate the arrow nocks until all are parallel to their bow strings. They make ready to execute the "finger dance," enabling the Bahri to shoot an arrow every second and a half.

The Mamluks dip their bow hands back into their quivers, removing another four arrows in the web of their paws. These are heavier, longer arrows with more fletching for closer shots taken from the gallop—those volleys requiring accuracy and greater penetration.

Some faris pick shafts with notches cut perpendicular to the arrowhead— arrows crafted to separate ribs. Other cavalrymen prepare square arrows constructed to penetrate armor, aware of the improvements in Mongol breastplates.

Mamluks arrange projectiles of alternating design in various orders, giving the shooters flexibility in employing a variety of deadly tips against specific targets. Forever seeking dark humor, amirates have assigned the originators' names to some of the wider-used combinations—Mads' Mix, Kaapo's Rib-Splitter, and Bandi's Blend.

Leander unfastens his crossbow, Galina, from his saddle, leaving her twin sister stowed. He regrets chucking his third weapon during the ambush at Gaza, the fine crossbow given to him by the bow maker, Esel. While the weapon was damaged, it sickens him knowing that some Mongol carries her now. But the wood stock had blocked an enemy arrow that would have otherwise cleaved his ribs. Her crossbow likely saved his life that day. Perhaps the weapon's loss is fitting, as he would have always associated the weapon's malfunction with Duyal's death.

He lays Galina across his thigh and thumbs her nut to confirm it is locked. Looking eastward, he steps into the stirrup, grasps the thick hemp on either side of it and pulls it back, latching the string up and over the top of the roller nut. He slides his hand around her stock, leaving it underneath the trigger assembly, his only safety. He loads a square-headed bolt topped with copper flights, an "armor spike," as the Franj crossbowmen in Ramerupt often called them.

Baybars pushes out their flankers and places the remainder of his troops into a single-walled wedge across the broad valley, the point of the formation marking northeast toward the expected contact with the Mongols. On signal, his pennant snaps and the Turkish drummers move forward into the protected belly of the configuration, pounding their felt-tipped beaters upon the leather heads at their horses' sides.

The thumps of the kettledrums bounce off the walls of Gilboa to the south, the hammering gradually lost in the wide expanse northward. Thick-shouldered players riding camels soon join. They bang upon the bigger drums strapped to the sides of their long-legged beasts. A heavy gonging emanates from their skins, the deeper pitch shuddering the ground like tremors before some terrible earthquake.

The multi-pitched Arabian horns drone their death wail. If Baybars and Kitbugha were champions, circling each other in some grappling match, Baybars now waves the Khan in. "We are right here. Come and get us."

The Bahri's angled formation plows the brown grass amid the clamor, the pointed mass of leather and steel appearing as if silently riding a hidden undercurrent toward the enemy. The Mamluks ride centered between pommel and cantle—backs straight, palms facing heaven, feet balanced in the stirrups, and heels down.

Each possesses what the Bahri call *libaqa*, or exceptional horsemanship. Knowledge of the great enemy's presence will not alter their distinguished appearance, or otherwise put these horsemen sloppy in their seats. The four willow shafts extending from each man's hands appear like giant fingers—their armor-piercing crescents, prongs, and traditional points splayed like lethal claws.

Baybars again looks up to the sun's location. He signals to slow their pace.

Singer quietly hums, his head subtly rocking. The droning beat likely rebirths a herder's melody from his Kipchak past. He methodically rubs his fingers over the arched tail of the scorpion embossed into his silver arm guards. His bow hand mindlessly clicks the four arrow shafts between his knuckles.

The blades of the formation carve their way past Beit She-an, the old Roman town, the place where the Bible says King

Saul and his sons were hung from the city walls. The current inhabitants of the town have abandoned their white-domed huts. The merchandise stalls sit bare, buckets turned upside down. The shutters on their mud-slathered shops are latched shut.

The Bahri wedge glides closer to the River Jordan. They pass Roman pillars sticking up like crooked tombstones from the grass, some in parallel lines, marking a ghostly path where cobbled roads once stretched five hundred years past.

The winds shift and now come from due east. The Bahri's Arabians lift their noses to taste the new air. Ear tips rise. Flopped ears transform into furry bowls, elongated and swiveling eastward toward where the unseen ponies of the enemy are detected. Lazily held tails now swish up and down and side to side in equine anticipation.

Hooves stomp. Several Arabians rear. Warriors curse. Others mumble comforting words to calm their anxious steeds.

Leander's horse arches her neck, snuffles, and begins shaking her head, like a tired man clearing the cobwebs after a midday nap. Leander leans forward to her ear and deceives the female most precious to him. "We are all right, San. We are all right."

CHAPTER 49

Leander

Ayn Julut

September 3, 1260

The northeastern wind returns, shifting the Mongol army's scent away from the Bahri's Arabians. The horses calm, again settling Baybars' wedge formation of seven hundred Mamluks into an advancing hulk of clomping hooves and jangling bridles.

The morning sun has burned off the last of the dew from the grass in the basin. Spider webs strung between the tall blades are coated with dust from the passing cavalry.

Men blow between their fingers, an attempt to dry where their pre-positioned arrow shafts contact sweaty skin. Helmets turn left and right, each Bahri monitoring the eastern horizon for sign of the enemy they know is near.

Leander tilts up his bronze visor and wipes the perspiration from his brow. He drops his head and closes his stinging eyes. When he opens them, he faces Singer's horse.

The mare's eyes go wide and white. She flares her nostrils and snorts. Goosebumps form along Leander's arms. He knows what the horse sees, even before the Mongol roar explodes across the valley, before the two-noted whine of the Arabian horns exclaim the Mongol's presence and Baybars' order to come forward into a line formation.

The enemy reveals himself gradually over a shallow crest in the valley—a growing front of black forms upon horseback and foot, perhaps fifteen hundred paces away. Sunbeams steal through a gap in the cloud, emblazoning the enemy's standards in reds and blues and yellows. These dart across the field, seeming to pull the dark-armored units into position like iron shavings around the pole of a magnet. Leander tightens his hold on the grip straps of his tur shield and his weapon's tiller. Oh, dear Allah.

Baybars moves to the tip of the Mamluk wedge. He ignores the enemy, concentrating on keeping his horsemen in the center at the walk, directing the left and right flanks to step up their pace to the trot. These wings now act as leaves on a massive hinge, flapping open at the formation's pivot, until parallel to the enemy.

The Bahri close on the Mongols while tightening their dispersion between riders on the move. In only seconds, the line of Tartars to their east doubles in span. Thousands of metal spines and tufts of horsehair—some dyed red—look as if they sprouted from the crowns of their fire-hardened leather and banded steel helmets. From this distance, their faces appear undistinguished—a mingling of browns and yellows, black facial hair dappled upon most chins.

Sitting their ponies, the Tartars howl again. Their wail sounds like a calling one would expect to ring out from the underworld, the hell of *Jahannam* described in the Koran. They clang their swords and lances upon their shields. This clatter reverberates through the valley.

A few Mamluks quail in their saddles. Some bawl at the Mongols their insults and challenges. Singer rocks to and fro, his head thrown back, intoning skyward some ancient Kipchak war hymn. Barks of profanity mix with calls to Allah for strength and cunning.

A thinly whiskered Bahri sits in trousers darkened at the crotch, piss dripping from his saddle leather. This Mamluk, and others likewise shaken, are not ridiculed by their mates. The faris bolster the courage of their fellows with words of encouragement. Several Bahri fight to restrain their warhorses from charging ahead, the mounts more eager to do battle than their riders. Baybars pushes forward calmly, his attention given only to his amirs and their alignment of the formation.

When the Bahri are within seven hundred paces of the Mongols, Leander picks out the heavy cavalry in the enemy center, their ponies fitted with rawhide armor from knee to throat, a thin plate of iron protecting their animals' foreheads. These heavy horsemen tote knobby-headed maces and lances—twelve-footers fitted with hooks.

Short-handled battle axes and coiled ropes adorn the saddles of the Mongol "flankers," the few light horsemen positioned at each tail of their line. In their shield hands, the flankers clutch fistfuls of short javelins, making their shields appear as malevolent porcupines. The Bahri know that most of these lighter units will comprise the Tartars' second rank, preserved behind the heavier-armored units until the khans call them forth for their greater mobility and quickness.

Every mounted Tartar clutches a recurved bow, with another cased across his horse's rump. Quivers hang from enemy shoulders and saddles, the mouths of these bristling with fletched willow. Scimitars with blades curved into a menacing leer hang at many riders' sides.

San prances, shaking her head. Leander pats her neck. The dust thickens in his nose. He lays a finger alongside and blows a gob of dark snot from each nostril.

The red-crossed pennons from the Kingdom of Georgia emerge on the enemy's right, allies willingly employed since the siege of Baghdad. Sections of their mailed infantryman carry halberds, axe blades topped with a spike mounted on a six-foot-long shaft, a "thorn" on the back side of the axe blade for grappling mounted combatants. Others wear teardrop-shaped shields on their left hips.

Sunlight gleams from their crescent-shaped axe heads and wide-brimmed "kettle hats." Mustering beside the infantry are Georgian crossbowmen in soft armor, their padded tunics colored white with the red cross of Saint George upon their breasts.

The Mongol line gradually compresses in width until no light can be seen between horses. The Tartar front now matches the Mamluks' single rank in breadth.

When the Bahriyya are about six hundred paces from the enemy line, Baybars turns to Leander. "You agree that we are still over a hundred paces from the range of those Georgian crossbows?"

"Yes, my Amir," Leander says, eying the limbs of the weapons, plus the small pulley blocks and the double spanning hooks dangling from their archers' thick belts. Such devices, he knows, are required to load the weapons that likely have a draw power of at least three hundred pounds, throwing their bolts farther than most recurved bows.

The Georgian archers attach the pulley blocks atop the pegs on the back of their crossbow stocks. The men bend to hook the metal claws of their spanning hooks on to the strings of their crossbows, stepping their right feet into the bows' stirrups.

At the signal of one who must be the captain of these archers, the soldiers stand upright as one, loading their weapons. They seat bolts in the center of their strings.

"Up!" Baybars commands. The order is passed down the line. Leander raises his shield with the others. As the line goes silent, Leander's breaths amplify against his temporary sanctuary of stretched hide.

The enemy raise their weapons to the sky. The air carries the sound of another muffled order from the Georgians. The metallic click of a hundred triggers travels across the basin, followed immediately by the communal knock of released bowstaves.

A flurry of bolts hurls toward the Bahri.

The deadly hail of projectiles land about the Bahri in *whiffs* and *pops*, and *pings*. Foot-long bolts plummet into the tall grass about them and thump into the thick hide of their shields and horse armor. A missile skewers one horseman's thigh to his saddle. Arabians crumple with their riders unstruck. These men accept offered hands and are pulled up and behind other horsemen.

A bolt pierces the hide of Leander's shield, dinging his helmet top like a cuff to the head. He snatches the maple shaft and pulls the three-feathered bolt violently through his shield leather. He chucks the shaft to the ground.

About them, shields look like pin cushions. Once seeing that both Leander and Baybars beside him are uninjured, Singer flashes Leander a somber half-grin from beneath his bowl.

Their commander's shield remains stowed on his saddle. "Align!" Baybars shouts, his glimpses alternating between each side of their advancing front as his amirs redress the line, closing the gaps made by the fallen. His eyes flit to their adversary every few paces as he gauges the Bahri's distance from the Mongols.

When his Mamluks are just under five hundred paces—a range where Baybars recognizes his troops' bowshot can reach the enemy with modest effectiveness, yet where fire from most of the Mongol recurves should fall short—Baybars turns to his Bahri who carries the unit guidon. "Raise it."

The red-lioned pennant snaps erect. Mamluk flags rise in response from units on Baybars' right and left. The Bahri aim their composite bows above the horizon and loose a shower of arrows. Leander fires his crossbow and reloads.

The Bahri projectiles arc away with the twang of bowstrings and the hiss of fletches. While the arrows are aimed to kill, Baybars directs this volley with the primary intent to harass and provoke. Like stings from a small hive of overaggressive bees, the Mamluks will be satisfied in agitating the mighty Mongol bear enough to make him follow.

The Bahri's shafts cross midflight with the next fusillade of missiles shot from the Georgians. Copper vanes from enemy bolts tick the fletching on some of the Bahri's arrows in passing. A few bolts collide, dropping shafts like wounded birds from the sky. In only seconds, one arrow after another sweeps across the sky in elegant curves as the Bahri shoot the four arrows staged between fingers on their draw hands.

With Mamluk faces and chests exposed, some men take enemy shafts into the face and chest and arms. One Bahri takes a bolt through the eye, the iron warhead showing itself out the back of his neck. Another tumbles unharmed from his mortally wounded mount, only to be staked to the ground by a trio of enemy shafts.

Bolts thud into scaled plates and impale the Bahri's shoulders. Hollered curses and groans from comrades down the line. More soldiers tip from their Arabians. Some of those men who lost horses earlier jump atop these abandoned mounts. Up and down the front, men snap the hardwood chutes that they cannot pull free.

The Mongols remain shielded behind their varied bowls of wicker, bronze, and basswood, only their helmet spikes and horsehair tassels exposed over their shields' rims. Bahri shafts splinter on the metal shield faces and rain atop men and beasts.

Horses shriek. Almost a hundred struck Tartars tumble from their ponies. The Bahri roar in approbation.

When the barrage ceases, the Mongols, too, dislodge arrows stuck in their wooden shields and those broadheads not fully buried in their jointed leg armor and that of their ponies.

Baybars eases his mount ahead of the formation, his head turning left and right, the guidon watching his every move. Their commander pulls his horse's nose toward the enemy and throws his arm forward. He will not give the Mongols time to fully recover, nor his men another instant to think. Wordlessly and personally, Baybars leads their charge.

The guidon beside him flips his pennant downward, catching the butt end of the shank in his armpit.

For an instant, time slows. The Ayyubid yellow unfurls from its bamboo shaft like a falcon unfolding its wings before departing its perch for located quarry. The guidon's spiked tip is revealed. A wink of sunlight reflects from its point.

His mind absent for a split moment, Leander's eyes stay to this glint, the tiny spark trained on the Mongol throng—men unbeaten in this dusty land, warriors who have yet to experience any serious impediment to asserting their will in the Levant, or anywhere else they have ventured.

The turf erupts with the pound of galloping Arabians. A primitive yowl from his fellow Mamluks shatters the air. Leander steers San beside the guidon. Singer comes up on his right, the ground thundering with the tattoo of hoofbeats.

Enemy arrowshot hums and buzzes overhead. A soldier to his left falls from his mount. More Bahri are knocked from their horses. Leander grits his teeth, refusing to look back.

The Tartars level their pike tips at the Muslims, the Mongol banners snapping to a halt, being held parallel to the ground. The enemy horde assails. The cry of opposing armies fuses with the rumble of charging horse. A homogenous din resounds.

Mamluk eyes stay to their amirs. When the Tartars are but ninety paces, yellow banners flip up. The Bahriyya loose a flurry of the longer-shafted arrows from their bow hands, at the gallop.

The Mongols who raise their bows in reply become prime targets for successive shots from the faris, the Bahri competing for the enemy's unshielded armpits and ribcages. Mamluk barbs land with the distinguishable *pop* and *whap* of arrowheads penetrating lungs and flesh.

Soldiers drop on both sides. Ponies crumble, rolling atop their riders. The screams of men and agonizing squeals of wounded horses interject within the tumult of churning earth. A murk swirls about them as both sides rein in, both wishing to engage the other with bowshot, not steel.

A cloud of soot stirs thicker in the north. Baybars' eyes are already on it. The Mongol's right wing ventures to sweep the Mamluk left and end the skirmish before it hardly begins.

Leander rubs the grime from his eyes. A young-faced Mongol materializes from the powdery haze. Their eyes lock. Trepidation fills the enemy's face, the Tartar more boy than man. Quickly assessing the range, Leander takes aim with his crossbow, before the youth can raise his recurve. Placing the copper fins on the black chest of the enemy, Leander slowly depresses the trigger.

His bolt sticks the Mongol center-chest, the impact throwing the Tartar off his mount. The foe lands on his back with a clang, the bolt's spiraled flights protruding from the Mongol's armor like a brooch worn on a French nobleman's cloak.

Some Mongols to their front turn away from the torrent of projectiles, seemingly astonished by the well-aimed volume of fire produced by so few men. Most Mongols appear capable of shooting but one arrow in the time the typical Bahri shoots three or four.

Both armies peel left and right amid the incoming missiles. Units reassemble. Leander uses the lull to load another bolt into his crossbow. Through the fine powder, he watches Singer employ the finger dance, nocking and shooting arrows with his usual dexterity.

Mongol khans snap their orders in the thick tongue of their people. Soon, the entire Tartar first wave filters back through a second line which comes forward with full quivers. Khans near the Mamluk's southern flank begin to shift their squads inboard. The enemy attempts to envelope the smaller Mamluk vanguard.

Baybars remains collected. "Out!" he hollers.

The guidon circles his standard repeatedly. This gesture is replicated by the flag bearers in each amirate. Muslim horns reinforce the signal, blasting the repetitive flat tone, directing the vanguard to withdraw and execute the scheme to draw the Mongols across the northern face of Gilboa.

Leander and Singer fall in behind Baybars. The Bahri turn their steeds west. Leander eyes Mount Gilboa, the ridge feeling distant, unreachable.

Projectiles shrill overhead. Leander ducks. The enemy launches signal arrows, missiles with holes drilled into bronze inserts and snugged to the base of their arrowheads. These whistling shafts now fill the air, directing the Tartar units to follow. The Mongols take the bait. The pursuit begins.

As rehearsed for days on the plains of Acre, the Bahri look to their rear with contrived distress on their faces to sell the retreat to the enemy, a tactic used by generations of their Kipchak and Circassian kin on the steppe. The Bahri are outnumbered at least ten to one; Leander reckons the fright on many faces appears genuine. Mamluks shoot arrows to the rear in the classic form of the steppe archer—this "Parthian shot" named after the ancient Persians, yet used by every nomadic fighter for ages.

Singer comes alongside Leander and the two kick their mounts to a gallop. Leander feels San flinch. He looks down. The fletching of a Mongol arrow flaps in San's left rear leg, just below her armor.

Farther back, he sees several wounded on the ground being swarmed by mounted Mongol at odds of three to one. A horseman whose Arabian has gone lame is pulled from his mount by the hooked end of a Tartar's lance. A hollowness fills Leander. They lose Bahri brothers. Yet Baybars' orders were clear: "Halt for no one. Get to Gilboa. The mission comes before any single man."

San takes another arrow, this one absorbed by the padded armor across her rump. Leander snarls at the Bodkin-styled head, most of the tapered spike visible. He hugs her neck, focusing on the drumming of her hooves, the four-part beat of her gallop.

He wishes he could do something, anything, to make her work easier. He concentrates on collecting himself at her high point and being feather-light at her bottom. His girl stays strong, ignoring the wagging shafts on her thigh and croup and the occasional whisper of arrows passing their ears.

He peeks around her neck, picking the best of the ground to travel, guiding her slightly left toward Gilboa. He stays to her neck, her cadenced breaths fetching him a semblance of comfort.

One breath, one stride. She paces herself, seeming to know this is the race of her life, their lives. They put some distance between themselves and the pursuing enemy.

Singer drops from Leander's peripheral vision. Leander turns to see a whirl of dust and a tangle of hooves. A white-patched belly flips over. He reins in. Baybars glances over his shoulder to view Singer sprawled on the grass. Their commander follows his own guidance and continues his westward gallop.

Leander pictures Duyal's face in the narrows, the last time he saw his mentor alive near Gaza. He refuses to leave the last of his close friends on another battlefield in harm's way. He will gladly take the flogging, or a worse punishment to come, for breaking Baybars' command. He circles back for Singer.

Bahri fly past, either side of him. Heads turn. Crinkled brows and pursed lips. Fleeting looks of pity, maybe sadness—those expressions one would see on the faces of a passing funeral. His comrades watch a dead man riding; a brave fool endeavoring to fetch his mate, who is equally as good as dead.

The last of the Bahri decoys sail past. Suddenly, Leander is without the company of brothers, save his friend before him who struggles to free himself from his stirrups. Farther away, perhaps a quarter mile from him, a scattered front of Mongol steel and leather and sod-tossing hooves. Tartar purveyors of death, in pursuit.

The first wave of Mongols bears down, more units stacked behind them. A fear, greater than any he has ever known, grips Leander. He digs his heels in deeper, angling San directly at Singer. He closes the distance on his friend, assessing how long they have before the Mongols will be swarming them.

At perhaps three hundred paces from Singer, a pair of Tartar horsemen race to be the first to reach him. One pulls a throwing dart from his shield hand. He holds the weapon palm up to his side, in preparation for launch. The other Mongol nocks an arrow at the gallop.

Singer has risen to his hands and knees. His horse limps, her front leg shattered and flopping grotesquely.

Leander knows he must lighten his load. At the gallop, he releases the lance from his saddle, letting it drop it to the dirt. He taps the pommel at his hip to confirm the sword remains in his possession. He then reaches down and dumps the second blade from his saddle scabbard. He unties the leather case of his spare crossbow attached to his cantle, the weapon given to him by his father decades past. He lets the precious gift tumble behind him without a second thought. He sheds a water skin. His eyes bounce between Singer and the pair of Mongols. He questions if he will make it to his mate in time.

Singer rises unsteadily to his feet and struggles to catch his reins. A Mongol arrow plows into the grass. Another.

Leander aims his crossbow at the Mongol archer. He shoots, knowing immediately that he pulled the shot right.

The bolt misses over the Tąrtar's left shoulder. This Mongol slows and quarters away. Unfazed, the other light cavalryman continues his direct course, raising his javelin for the throw.

Singer lurches, snatching his Arabian. He pulls his strung bow from the saddle case, the weapon somehow unbroken. He shoulders the quiver and quickly nocks an arrow, while setting his feet for the coming shot.

Singer aims and releases a missile at the javelineer, sticking the man in the left shoulder. Singer looks with regret at his horse's broken limb.

Leander swoops in from behind him. "Leave her. Up!" He reaches down and lifts him onto San's back.

CHAPTER 50

Leander

Ayn Julut

September 3, 1260

Eyeing the approaching pair of Mongols, Leander grasps Singer's forearm and lifts. His friend swings atop San's rump, sliding up behind the cantle with his bow held out and away. When Leander feels him grasp the shoulder strap on his cuirass, he whirls San westward and brings her up to the gallop.

A third Mongol archer breaks from the horde to join in the hunt. Another wolf smelling blood; another enemy anticipating Leander's Arabian to soon tire with the second rider upon her back.

Singer discards broken arrows from his quiver, those crushed during his horse's fall. Finding two "shorts" intact, he squeezes the cantle between his knees, turns rearward, and draws his bow. Timing San's up and down rhythm, Singer fires at the closest Tartar when he feels her hooves leave the ground.

His first arrow soars over the rider's shoulder; his second plows into the pony's chest armor. The Mongol drops back with the others.

Another Tartar raises his weapon in response and looses an arrow. Singer squares himself to protect his friend. The dart arrives with a *smack* into Singer's jawsan. Singer wiggles the unseated barb from between lamellar scales.

Leander looks back.

"We are good," Singer says, flinging the arrow and tucking behind him.

San pulls farther from the Tartars and closer to the hundreds of Bahri who push west across the Jezreel Valley, their dust trails wafting toward the Gilboa highlands ahead. With the reins held to her neck and Leander's heels tucked high, San needs neither crop nor whip to sustain her gallop. His Arabian seems cognizant that her speed alone keeps them alive.

The short-limbed ponies behind them are no match for the swiftness and endurance of the Mamluks' horses. The Arabians' longer legs, lean muscle structure, and knack of preserving energy combine to widen the gap between the pursuers and prey.

Following Baybars' lead, the Bahri now mask their efforts to slow their horses, pretending to whip the Arabians' hindquarters, while softly reining in. Their commander wishes to keep the Mongols at about four hundred paces, out of effective bow range, yet close enough to keep the Tartars following them into the slaughter zone at Gilboa where Qutuz awaits with his main body.

The Bahri's slackening pace allows Leander to close with his comrades, some of them bloodied and bearing crossbow bolts and Mongol arrows in their shoulders and backs. The two Mongols who have been in hot pursuit appear to realize their chance to finish the stray riders is lost. They slow to join the Mongol first wave.

Leander spots Baybars' gray and his guidon, the colors now wrapped about the bamboo shaft to make their leader's position less obvious to the enemy. Leander reins San toward Baybars as they reach the eastern crook of Gilboa, where pine and juniper-covered fingers of land extend to the south and east.

They continue at the gallop westward for three more miles. When the Bahri hurtle past the yellowed grass and hard chalk cliffs of Mount Gilboa, they begin merging into two files behind Baybars, their horses still at the run. The first wave of Mongols behind them slows, perhaps smelling something rotten in the works. Thousands of Tartars extend across the front of Gilboa, their follow-on waves now butting up to the lead elements.

As the highlands taper into the gentler grade on the west end of the ridge, incoming arrow shafts flare in the sunlight from the southern uplands.

"Down," Leander says, turning to Singer.

Leander flattens himself upon San's neck. He turns away, half expecting to hear the dull thumps and bites of Muslim arrows entering his body as the sultan orders his army to slay the rival Bahri now, before the Muslim main force engages the Mongols.

Yet he feels only Singer pressed over him. He looks to their rear.

None of his Bahri mates in the formation take arrows or fall from their horses. Farther east, some Mongol chasers turn back, several with arrows stuck in their horses' rumps. One Tartar, with an arrow lodged in his shoulder, runs on foot toward some sparse cover. He is cut down by three more shafts only twenty steps from his downed horse.

Leander dips his head, allowing his visor to block some of the late morning glare atop Gilboa. Dark figures move downhill in the shadows and between the scrub pines and spindly bushes. Cavalry sitting their horses shoot one arrow after another at the Mongol enemy. Soon a shower of arrows is pouring into the Mongol foe. The devils have stepped squarely into the Egyptian snare.

The Mongols take arrows to their chests and legs. Most turn their ponies to escape, exposing their unarmored backs to accurate fire. Many of these men tip from their mounts, dozens dragged and stomped and crushed beneath their ponies' hooves.

Tartar mounts stumble with ten and thirty missiles protruding from their armor. Other animals writhe upon the bloody grass, some with dead riders still caught in the stirrups. Never has Leander seen so many arrows hitting such a large force at once.

With the mass of the Tartar army just past the bluffs of Gilboa—the center of Qutuz's trap—hundreds of Muslim warriors now descend from the foothills both east and west of the sun-bleached cliffs. More jihadis breach the tops with the sun to their backs, some looking as if they are enshrined in golden halos.

Leander cannot believe that he and Singer still live. He looks heavenward. "Thanks be to Allah," he murmurs as Baybars slows to the trot and starts his southward climb through the shrubs toward the staging area. With their role as bait fulfilled, the Bahri will now step aside and let Qutuz's army perform its duty.

Leander feels the adrenalin leaving his body like a curling wave that has crashed into the beach and now calmly withdraws into the sea. Exposed in the openness for so long, he is grateful for Gilboa's vegetative cover and the friendly archers that now traverse her slopes on foot.

The Hebrew word "Gilboa" means "water bursting from the rock." Leander muses that while water has not gushed from this mountain's stone in ages, today the rock is blessed to be surging with holy warriors. Amirates flow down the entire span of the ridge, boiling with determination to slay the Mongol invaders who steal their lands and endanger their religion.

As the grade steepens, Baybars follows a goat trail, slackening their pace to the walk. The shouts and whistles and blows from hundreds of winded Arabians mix with the clack of bony hoof on rock. Midway up the hill, Baybars moves off the path to assess the condition of his regiment as they pass.

Several men clomp by with vulture-feathered arrows flaring from their backs and shoulders. One Bahri with a jagged shaft impaled through both cheeks peers back into the valley, east where retreating enemy units bump into those arriving at the gallop to free their comrades from the Muslim noose.

Other Mamluks slump over their horses' necks. Two in blood-soaked chain mail sprawl helmetless across their saddles. Led by mates, crimson drips clear to their Arabians' hocks. Perhaps an eighth of the Bahri is wounded or killed, most casualties borne from the bolts of Georgian crossbowmen at the outset.

Men pat their treasured mares, the horses' nostrils expanding and contracting, their summer coats lathered in sweat, their hoof clops landing heavy with fatigue as they climb. Soldiers nod to mates as they head for the protection of the reverse slope, astounded they cheated death in playing rabbit to the wolves. Others outright guffaw, perhaps darkly amused at the improbability of so many of them surviving.

Baybars signals to Zeki and Anis, his most senior Amirs of Forty, as they pass. These men fall out of the column either side of him. Leander and Singer move away.

Baybars turns to Zeki. "Tend to our wounded and dead. Consolidate the amirates into full units. Resupply quickly—we must be ready to depart on command. Quivers and water skins filled. Go."

The amirs nod their affirmation and assume lead of the columns.

Seeing a break in the formation, Leander attempts to join his comrades.

"Not yet," Baybars says.

Leander backs his horse. He expects a berating from his commander once the last troops are out of earshot, a scolding for disregarding Baybars' order in turning back to recover Singer while on the run.

Singer slides from San's rump and empties his quiver into the grass. He selects three salvageable arrows from the shattered bits. Baybars hands him a fistful from his stash.

Of his own volition, Singer makes his bow ready and stands covering Baybars' back. His head pivots left and right as thirty paces on either side, Qutuz's Muizziyya eye the battered Mamluks while reining in their aggressive mounts on the way downhill. Singer acts to deter opportunists in the Muizziyya's rank from any ingenuous treachery against the Bahri's commander. Nearby, more horse soldiers—Halqa and black-flagged units from the Wafidiyya, the Mongol deserters gathered in Cairo—join to comprise the Muslim center.

To the west, ordered columns of Egyptian cavalry and Khwarazmian horsemen, regulars and allies who marry up to become Qutuz's left, filter smartly past the Mamluks. When these mounted troops reach the flatter ground in the plain, they put their horses to the gallop, following their amirs' pennants to their position on the northern stretch of the formation.

Amid the booming of hooves and shouts from the amirs farther east, more units of the sultan's army descend through the trees and gentler slopes—al-Nasir of Syria's fickle Nasiriyya, the yellow-trousered Shahrazuriyya Kurds, and al-Mansur's cavalry from Hama. These men stay to the hill bottom, forming Qutuz's right wing. The sultan intends to hold this shaky collection of units in place by cramming them between loyal amirates of the Muizziyya on their left and the towering uplands on their right.

The Bahri files move opposite the main body, serpentining up and around steep-faced draws, where patches of giant fennel reach above their heads. The plant's name is derived from the Latin *ferire*, meaning "to strike." Over the years, Leander watched dwellers in the Kingdom of Jerusalem use the browning stalks to discipline their children. Perhaps now, with the

Mongols facing the entire Muslim Army, the Tartars, too, will finally take their whipping like belligerent children.

Two by two, the Bahri disappear over the rounded hilltop. The amirs make for the Horseshoe, the staging area that units from Qutuz's army just departed. Behind the shelter of the great mountain, the Mamluks will reorganize and resupply.

Baybars scans the broad plain below them.

The late morning breeze has died off. The hoof strikes from hundreds of charging warhorses spread a floating dust about the valley floor. A scattering of Mongol deserters squirt from the mayhem, fleeing to the north.

At the base of the slope below, the Mongol khans are well aware of their predicament. Those caught in the open now endeavor to regroup their men out of Muslim bow range. They send rearward those Tartars unnerved by arrow fire, plus entire units who ride spent ponies. They usher forward cavalry on fresher mounts, follow-on waves of soldiers who preserved their animals by covering the ten-mile pursuit at a slower pace.

Other khans push dozens of men up the Gilboan slopes, futile attempts at quelling the deadly volley that persists. Some desperate Tartars jump from their mounts. Crouched, they sprint from dead pony to dead pony, diving behind the carcasses amid a deluge of arrows in their attempts to get closer to the archers above.

Two and three Mongols cower behind some of the dead animals that litter the hill bottom. Men fight for the modest refuge provided. Others refuse to go any farther. Several crawl into the ponies' groins, lifting muscled thighs atop their shoulders to protect them from the missiles that plunge into the flesh and ground about them. When the bravest, or craziest, of the enemy rise to run southward, they become easy targets, their chest armor slathered red in horse blood.

Most Tartars stay on their ponies, zigzagging their way within bowshot, shooting from the saddle. These attackers must look straight into the sun to acquire the Muslim archers concealed behind countless trees and darkened crevices afforded by the mountain.

Some Mongols tote injured mates behind their high-backed saddles. Dozens of the enemy hold their eyes, their vision spoiled from staring too long into the brightness when picking out rival bowmen. Several of these dismount, cowering behind ponies that collect arrow shafts on the uphill side of their leather shells.

Those blinded riders who have managed to break from the slaughter zone give up their reins to comrades and clutch fistfuls of horse mane to keep from tipping. These incapacitated riders are guided eastward at the canter.

On the west side of the great valley, Qutuz's amirs push their men north across the field, taking advantage of the enemy's disarray to fan out into the open plain. Small unit leaders restrain their troops from assailing the reeling enemy at once. The horsemen rapidly deploy into a north-south battle line, keen to properly exploit the tactical surprise and gain the right flank of the Tartar horde.

The follow-on wave of jihadis slink behind the first. The behemoth compresses into a single unit, closing ranks, all the while wheeling northeast like a giant scythe cutting across the grassland.

"Keep near me going forward," Baybars says, his eyes to Leander and Singer. "I must know immediately what comes from the mouths of the locals and Mongols."

"Yes, my Amir," Leander and Singer say, nearly in unison.

"We would have been disadvantaged had we lost you two back there," Baybars says. His attention returns to the battlefield.

Through the churning grime in the valley, the sunlight bounces from Mamluk bronze and steel like sparks off a smith's hammer. A single yellow pennant materializes from the stirring powder. The old banner of Aybeg's Muizziyya at the Muslim center. These cavalrymen pour arrow fire into the enemy units that still attempt to reconfigure.

Left and right of the Mamluks, more Ayyubid banners flutter across breaks in the thickening murk. Both Muslim flanks tighten, heartened by the unwavering Muizziyya. These amirates close on the Mongols with lances deployed.

Farther east, reassembled Mongols near the Gilboan cliffs come abreast, parallel to the Muslims. More Tartar *zaguns*, one hundred-man units, fall in behind. Mongol flags drop; pike tips point westward. The enemy horsemen charge.

Inside one hundred paces, both forces launch a hail of arrows through the dusty screen between them. A melded shriek from Arabians and ponies. Mounts buckle at the knee, sending riders overhead. Both lines disappear into the whirling brown cloud that now cloaks the valley. Leander finds he is unable to distinguish between friend and foe.

The deathly clang of saber on shield echoes across the basin, the warriors forced into employing steel in close quarters. This clamor overtakes the animals' screams. The cries and bellows of men fighting and dying. Singer drops his head in prayer.

Baybars eyes the sultan's banner on the western edge of the ridgeline. Four amirates from Qutuz's Royal Mamluks wait in reserve. The sultan watches from somewhere on this high ground, certainly eager to lead his best men at just the right moment to the ground he dubbed "salient" in his order, that which would show itself as advantageous during the fight. Yet what terrain could he identify as critical in this plain, shrouded as it is in choking powder?

"The air has turned thick as soup," Baybars says. "To join the fray now would mean us fighting almost blind, as likely stuck by friendly arrow as Mongol shaft."

"Allah knows when this haze might dispel, my Amir," Leander says.

The Prince of Homs' guidon breaks from the Tartar line far to the northeast, only half-obscured in the mire. Behind it, al-Ashraf's cavalrymen spur northward.

"Look!" Singer says, pointing. "Their lances are stowed, my Amir. Al-Ashraf of Homs ditches their Mongol ally. He exposes the enemy left."

They watch until the Prince of Homs' men become specks on the smoky horizon.

"By Allah," Baybars says. He looks to the knob where the sultan's yellow-shielded amirates stand their horses. They make no movement for the valley.

Baybars shakes his head. "Qutuz will exploit that breach in the Mongol line soon enough. He has more men than he needs. We must get to the Mongol rear, get to their remounts, before they all escape to the north."

The sultan made it clear in his order that after resupplying, the Bahri would come to Gilboa's north slope and stay there until summoned by Qutuz's runner. Tasked to function as the sultan's "force in reserve," Baybars' Mamluks were to be committed to the field only at the time and place of Qutuz's choosing, depending on how the battle unfolded.

Baybars seems to read Leander's concern. He lifts his chin toward Qutuz's banner. "He will not need us here. God has given us these"—he points to his eyes—"and this"—he points to his temple—"for His holy warriors to resolve how best to slay the aggressors in His lands."

Singer cracks a grin.

Baybars turns his horse. He gives a parting look to the Jezreel Valley, which has become a mass of roiling dirt and thundering hooves. Their visibility is gone. "Time is vital, my brothers. Allah would want us acting decisively, not passively waiting for permission to dispatch the infidels who threaten His faith."

"Yes, my Amir," Leander says.

"We have put the enemy in Amir Qutuz's lap," Baybars says. "Now he can push them back into ours."

Baybars' repeated exclamations of his intent rings in Leander's head: "Destroy the Mongol enemy and his means to fight."

Baybars moves past them. He speaks without looking back. "Quickly, to the south slope. Get Singer a horse. Fill your skins. We will give Kitbugha's Mongols another surprise, this time upon their rear flank."

Singer jumps atop San. They ride to the hilltop.

In the Horseshoe below, litter teams bring the last of the Bahri injured to clusters of women who wash the men's wounds from shallow basins and apply dressings. Ghulams, slave boys, reach into wide-mouthed barrels to replenish quivers with arrows. They strap lances to saddles.

Water bearers refill flasks and skins from bladders strapped to their camels' sides. Surgeons of the royal stables patch and inspect the Arabians' legs and hooves, sorting out those animals gone lame from those able to carry on. Bedouin grooms pull saddles from seriously injured horses and place them atop fresh steeds brought forward from the pastures to the southwest.

Tired Bahri hunker in the shade made from their horses, stuffing hard tack and dried meat into their mouths. They shoot glimpses to Baybars, who already briefs Zeki and Anis at the bottom.

Singer wipes the sweat from his face. "Thanks back there."

Leander turns.

Singer looks him in the eye, the lines of his face etched in filth. "For pulling me from that scrape."

Leander holds his gaze on Singer's face. The Kipchak is accustomed to being the savior of distressed siblings and battlemates, not the one being rescued.

Leander grins and turns back forward. He sighs. "No words needed, my brother. It won't be last of this battle."

CHAPTER 51

Leander

Beit Shean

September 3, 1260

Amir Baybars leads his dual columns of Bahriyya toward the west bank of the River Jordan. Ahead, four robed Arabs hack at a tangle of Cyprus cane with *falchions*, their single-edged blades crude like a machete, but curved like a sword. Evenly spaced behind them, three men and two boys face the tall reeds with Muslim lances and Mongol swords held unnaturally in their hands. One boy wears an oversized Mongol cuirass that covers him to his shins, the shoulder flaps reaching below his elbows. A Kurdish helmet streaked in blood rides high atop an old man's turban.

After his vanguard lured the Mongol army westward in chase to the Muslim ambush at Ayn Julut, Baybars was quick in refitting his Bahriyya on the back side of Gilboa. With the sun still high, the Bahri departed the Horseshoe staging area with six hundred twenty-four of their original seven hundred Mamluks. They entrusted their wounded to the surgeons and women at the Horseshoe, while their dead still lay unburied upon the Jezreel Valley.

Baybars posted a chain of riders along Gilboa's crest before he led the Bahri east behind the reverse slope. For hours, these scouts sent runners to inform Baybars about as much as they could see of the evolving battle taking place on the great plain to their north, as most of the field remained clouded in dust.

The Bahri lookouts were unaware that Qutuz did not commit his Mamluk reserves at the Muslim right flank as Baybars had anticipated, at the void created in the Mongol line where the Prince al-Ashraf of Homs had defected. Instead, the sultan personally brought his Muizziyya to the weakened Egyptian left, where the Mongols broke through and attempted to flank the Muslim army. Yet Baybars correctly predicted the outcome: the sultan's counterattack broke the Mongols' momentum, sending the Mongol commander Kitbugha and his men galloping east toward the old Roman city of Beit Shean.

Baybars continued his course, secreted behind the long Gilboan ridge, patiently searching for the right place and time to intercept the enemy—the position where he could thrust a killing blow at the Tartars, the spot where his Bahri could most effectively prevent the enemy from gaining access to their remounts and slay the fleeing Tartars before they escaped north.

East of Ayn Julut, near Beit Shean, Baybars found the Kurdish cavalry, Bedouin, and Turcoman archers routing some of the Mongols who had absconded. Staged last evening behind these easternmost hills and observing the enemy retreating across their front this afternoon, these Jihadis in Qutuz's reserve did not wait for the Sultan's order to attack. They descended upon the scurrying Mongols.

At the approach of Turks and Kurds, frightened pony tenders in the Tartar rearguard jumped on fresh remounts intended for the returning Mongol waves. These grooms bolted to the northeast, leaving thousands of remounts unguarded and hundreds of Tartars to the west at Ayn Julut stranded on tired, thirsty horses.

The Bahri joined the Turks in picking off the last of the Mongols hiding in the outskirts of Beit Shean. When the area was clear of enemy, the Kurds and Turks pushed northwest to attack the high ground at Moreh Hill, where a few hundred Mongol holdouts remained. Figuring this enemy would soon be surrounded and pinned in place, Baybars led his cavalry several miles east, looking for greater concentrations of fleeing enemy.

Baybars halts the staggered file twenty paces from where the Arabs chop at the thick reeds. He turns to Leander. "Ask them how many enemy they have seen and in what direction the Mongols fled."

Leander draws his sword and rides with two attendants up to the group of armed Muslims. He inquires in the locals' strain of Arabic.

A hunchbacked man lays down his falchion and steps forward. He looks up to Leander, squinting into the sun. He points west toward Beit Shean. "Jihadis came from behind the hills and attacked the invaders. The Mongol devils flushed like starlings."

Flapping his arms and making wild gestures, the man explains how the Turcoman, Kurds, and camel-mounted Bedu charged from their hiding spots and attacked the escaping Tartars, some fighting pillar-to-pillar on the north-leading road.

Leander sheathes his sword. The round-backed Arab gestures toward his weapon, describing how he and the other locals snatched them from the belts of three dead Tartars, along with lances dropped by the pursuing Kurds.

Leander lowers his palms in a calming motion for the Arab to settle. "Yes, we know this. Where did the Mongols go? How many have you seen?"

The man points excitedly to the reeds farther north and south. "Hundreds in every direction. They hide in the reeds! We hew the cane to drive the Mongols out—to kill the infidels."

Leander shakes his head at the madness in their ambition.

The second and third men nod their affirmation. "More of them north," one says.

Leander leaves the hunchback babbling. He tells Baybars what he has learned.

Baybars nods his appreciation to the locals and turns his horse away from them. He thinks for only a few moments and then signals for his surviving sixteen amirs to approach.

Squads of Bahri troopers watch the amirs, some anticipating the coming mission. Men begin buckling the saddle straps that holds their lances and rearranging arrows in their quivers, recognizing their steel-tipped bamboo spears will see no action here.

When the amirs have circled him, Baybars turns to Amir Zeki. "Spread Amirates One through Ten north on both sides of the river as far north as possible, concentrating your shooters where the reed grows heaviest. Ensure each amirate stays within sight of one another—with units upstream, downstream, and across the river."

Baybars lifts his chin to confirm the afternoon northwesterly that picks up. "Once you have the area covered, set fire to the reeds. We will let the wind fan the flames and push the Mongols out to our bowshot. Here is our rally point. Send a runner if at any time the enemy becomes numerous."

"Yes, my Amir," Zeki says.

Baybars turns to the remaining leaders. "Amir Anis, you will do the same with Amirates Twelve through Sixteen south from here. Bring Leander as your interpreter. Amirate Eleven will stay here with me as a reserve."

The amirs acknowledge their orders with a bow of their heads and turn their mounts back toward their men.

Baybars calls to his parting amirs with a final order. "Leave the Tartars no holes for escape. When done here, we will move north toward the big lake. We now fight daylight as well as the Mongols, my brothers. We must not let their survivors scamper north to Damascus in the darkness. Dispatch them now and we avoid a fight later with a reinvigorated foe. Go!" He backs his gray away.

Once informed by their amirs, the Mamluk amirates head north and south, trotting to their stations.

Leander falls in behind Amir Anis. As they make their way south upon the rolling high ground on the west bank, Anis assigns his five "Amirs of Forty" to various-sized sectors based on the terrain and volume of cane to be burned in each area.

When the last amirate is tasked, Leander moves to a hilltop with Anis, along with a squad of security from Amirate Sixteen.

Gray smoke lifts from the north. Mamluks near them ride down to the densest of the dry reeds with flint and steel. Anis strokes his dusted beard, his eyes narrowing, the large man seeming to be constantly figuring, regardless of how little sleep or nourishment he has had.

"Does not take our commander long to map a plan, eh?" Anis says.

"No, my Amir," Leander says. "And Baybars seems often to be thinking not just one step ahead, but three."

Anis give a nod of affirmation, never taking his eyes from the terrain in front of him.

Smoke churns in the reeds below. The wind stiffens, acting like a bellows upon the flames. To the north, billows of smoke rise in steady belches, drifting southward. The sun drops to two fists above the horizon. Out front, the amirate commander holds his men at one hundred paces from the River Jordan, a range where he feels his Mamluks can outshoot any Mongol archers who come out of the thickets aggressively.

Smolder filters through the unburned reeds to the south. A Mongol spurts from the cane on foot. Several more Tartars hightail northwest, heading for the rolling hills. One crawls out from the high stalks with a blackened face, his leather armor curled from what has become a streamside oven.

Waiting Mamluks close within fifty paces and skewer the evaders as they take only a few steps into the open country. Several Mongols run shrub-to-shrub, shooting the last of their arrows at the Mamluks. But the enemy missiles fall short. The Bahri pursue these, shooting them down like scampering hares.

Across the river, where the smoky haze churns heaviest, Tartars dash from the scrub with mouths covered in rags. Having shed their helmets and cuirasses, they sprint eastward uphill, with swords bared. Baybars' Mamluks drill these stumbling men with arrows.

Drawn by the burning, more locals arrive on the road from the south—merchants, schoolboys, and herders. Armed with clubs and herding staffs, these volunteers gather behind the Mamluks from Amirate Sixteen, emboldened by seeing the invaders routed.

Leander feels underutilized, reminiscent of uninspiring hunts he was forced to join in his Frankish homeland. From within their camouflaged stands he would doze off, waiting for the "quarry pushers" to roust deer from their havens toward royal hunters, the barons hiding along both sides of the funneling dale.

He considers asking Anis if he can join the amirate below, but he knows the answer. He is needed more as an interpreter than a slinger of bolts.

"Could the Tartars have predicted this?" Leander asks him.

"If you mean taking this thrashing," the amir says, "then I doubt it."

"I mean could the Tartars have ever guessed that the same Kipchak urchins, rounded up by the Mongols in youth and sold to the princes for years, would be the men down the road to halt their black tide from rolling across the entire realm?"

Anis looks to him contemplatively. "Probably not. But on the whole, we are far from halting much of anything. Black tide to us is unfulfilled destiny for them."

Anis' stare becomes lost in the outlying fires for a short time. "Hulegu still has the bulk of his army to the far north.

And if the sultan managed to skewer Kitbugha Khan today, we urchins may soon face Hulegu's wrath for killing one of the great khan's favorites."

Leander nods grimly.

The fire to their north now rages, the gusts whipping the blaze. Behind them, the sun rests just over one fist above the horizon—an eye of burnt orange gazing through a murky curtain.

Unarmed Mongols now scurry from the reeds like mice from a burning hay pile. The Bahri have stowed their bows. Almost leisurely at the canter, Mamluks approach the scampering Mongols from behind. They lean from their saddles and behead the enemy with sweeping backhand sword strokes. Mimicking exercises practiced in the hippodromes for years, some men flip their blades from hand to hand, tilting left, then right, to decapitate Tartars who attempt to run and creep through the grass.

Despite the gore and his hate of butchery, Leander admires the elegance in his comrades' death work—man and horse laboring in unison to eliminate not just infidels, but invaders who eyed the Mamluks' beloved Cairo as their final objective.

Shepherds with pitchfork and staff fall upon the odd Tartars who have managed to slink their way unseen farther west. Groups of three and four men club these soldiers to death, some using the lion-headed maces recovered from the field. Lads brawl to be the first at the corpses. Smiling youth run off with belts and boots and coins pulled from bloody pockets.

Dark clouds scuttle in from the north. The banks of the winding Jordan to their north have become a roaring inferno. Like a pair of fiery serpents slithering on either side of the river, the twisting fire consumes the dry reeds as far as the eye can see. Licks of flame ascend the yellow-grassed hills. Never has Leander seen a fire so large.

Leander and the squad of Mamluk security follow Anis higher, occupying the next rise to the west.

The wind swirls, pushing walls of smoke across them. Leander pulls a silken scarf across his face. Ash floats like snow flurries, sticking to San's mane and his chain-mailed kazaghand. The flakes and smell of smoke take Leander back to long winters on his French nobleman's estate; the drafty castle, enormous fireplaces, and tang of bitter oak; his time as a squire serving Lord Erard's knights in Ramerupt.

The smoke thickens. He coughs from the fetid vapors. He dumps some water from his skin upon the scarf. He closes his eyes and lowers his head, reflecting on his old life in that old world. When the wind shifts, his eyes return to the snaking flares. His mind roams to other countrymen, the Crusader ghosts from a generation past who met an end similar to the Mongols here, just north at Hittin.

Anis, too, must discern the connection. These hills east of Armageddon now burn like those did at the Horns of Hittin seventy-three years ago. And just as the Christians made a desperate retreat toward the Sea of Galilee in 1187, so did these Mongols withdraw to the apparent safety of the water today. While the thirsting Franj never made it to the big lake during that epic battle of their Third Crusade, the Mongols here managed to reach the River Jordan. Yet the stream's vegetated refuge will not save them.

Here, as at Hittin, when the enemy was at its most fatigued and parched, the Muslims gave them hell's fire. Just as hundreds of Crusaders were forced to breathe in smoke and face the conflagrations set by Saladin, so must the ravaged Mongol deserters now endure the same from the hand of Baybars—or perhaps Allah.

The firestorms from both the north and south begin to drop in ferocity. The sun touches the horizon; the sky turns to a somber gray. Wind-tumbled embers pulse in time with the gusts, contrasting against the meandering strips of char that border both sides of the river.

Anis' brow crinkles in concern, his attention focused to the south. Leander follows his eyes.

A rider approaches on a Mongol chestnut, a giant white spot across the pony's shoulder. The Mamluk squad has already begun to deploy in a semi-circle around Leander and Anis. Leander loads a bolt.

Acknowledging the Mamluks' disposition, the rider slows to a walk, arms out, palms forward. What Leander thought was a small turbaned man is a scarfed woman.

Anis walks his horse to the front of the formation. "Esel," he says, surprised to see his commander's aunt. "By Allah, are you all right?" He glances at her pony, undoubtedly pilfered from the enemy's herd, but his eyes stay to her face.

Esel advances. The skin exposed above her scarf is a mask of dried crimson. The neck of her tunic is bloodstained. Yellowed puss encrusts her bosom. The bottom of her garment looks cut away. "I am fine," she says, "most of this blood is not mine."

"You need those cuts dressed. That chest wound," Anis says, shaking his head. "I will send you back to the Horseshoe with three escorts. We—"

Esel shakes her head, out of selflessness or perhaps sensing that the amir offers to waste the resources of these valuable men only because she is the aunt of his superior. "No, no. Thank you. But how far away are the nurses?" she asks.

"Some may be moving east from the staging area by now. We may be able to get you to them at dark," Anis says.

Esel's face goes long. She says nothing, staring through them. A melancholy seems to fill her. "I care little of my treatment," she says. "The Mongols must remain our focus."

She looks down at the blood stains on her tunic. "An Arab just south of here beckoned me. I could not understand him. I think he was trying to deliver information about the enemy." She looks to Leander.

Anis turns to the Frank. “Go with her. If you do not find us here when your task is done, I will be farther north on this same side.”

“Yes, my Amir,” Leander says.

“Afterward, we then get you to the rear,” Anis says, looking to Esel.

Leander turns San’s head to follow Esel, who already heads south.

CHAPTER 52

Jacinta

Beit Shean

September 3, 1260

Lying under the boughs of a pine where Esel had secreted her, Jacinta presses her palms hard against the belly wounds the Mongol had inflicted. She attempts to control her breathing and put her mind off the pain that intensifies in her stomach. She struggles to an elbow.

Blood saturates her garments from breasts to thigh. Her hands are sticky from holding the improvised dressing. Her abdomen swells with what she knows must be her own lifeblood. She eases herself back down.

This morning, she and Esel had ridden about two hours north from the riverside where the Mongols had wounded Jacinta and Esel had opened her one-armed captor's windpipe, before the pain in Jacinta's stomach became unbearable. She could no longer stay in the saddle.

It mattered not. By early afternoon Mongol deserters from the main battle began trickling in from the west. The first riders splashed across the Jordan and never looked back, taking the road north at the gallop toward Damascus. When the masses arrived north of Beit Shean, the Tartars were greeted by hundreds of shrieking Turks and Kurds, plus Bedouin on camel—warriors assaulting north from the concealment of the hills.

Esel and Jacinta hid their ponies and withdrew to a stand of young pine on a ridge over the Jordan. With no lemon juice or boiled wine, twice Esel cleaned Jacinta's punctures with water and her own urine. Esel cut pieces from the hem of her tunic to repack the wounds. This remedy was inadequate and did little to stop the bleeding.

When Esel crept to the edge of their cover and saw the Bahriyya's yellow pennants in the distance, her spirits rose. "We are not doomed," she said. "The Bahri will make short work of the enemy, and their battle train will follow with supplies to treat your wounds."

Soon the reeds downhill were rustling both up and downstream. Moans and distant hisses sounded in the gruff speech of the Mongol enemy. The women huddled together, Esel seated with one of their last arrows nocked in the bow.

Hiding for hours, Jacinta's condition worsened. A fever set in. When they smelled smoke, Esel again snuck to the fringe of the pine grove and peered westward. She returned with another hint of optimism in her voice.

"I see the Bahri again on the far hills. I must get you help now. I will be right back. I promise." Esel grasped Jacinta's shoulder.

"Do not risk it," Jacinta whispered. "Let me pass here. Stay hidden until the enemy leaves."

Esel darted off. Soon after, Jacinta heard the thump of pony hooves as her friend made for the higher country to the northwest.

Jacinta folds her hands atop the Mongol belt that binds her wounds. She hopes the Tartars did not find Esel, once her friend exposed herself on the treeless slopes.

She thinks of her mother and father and brother, when they were younger. Those were the happiest of times for them, before her mother became ill and prior to Jacinta working for the Sultan al-Salih.

Another wave of nausea comes and passes. She grabs a handful of gravel in each hand and squeezes it until the ache in her stomach passes.

Block it out. Think of the good times. The beach in Damietta. Chatting with her mother in their kitchen while prepping the savory ingredients for fattah, meat simmering in their seasoned pot. Her mother's giggle—always genuine and delivered regularly for little reason, the woman as good-natured as any she had known. Surely her mother has passed by now. Jacinta will see her soon, Allah willing.

She wonders what she should have done differently in this life. Not much. Nothing that can be fixed now. She is thankful to have never lived like her aunt in Cairo. She is happy to not have subjected her mother to more family disgrace, as her mother's sister had done.

Jacinta's mother rapped on the weathered planks.

Jacinta grasped her mother's hand and looked up at the warped door. It cracked open. Sad eyes above the niqab peered through the opening. No smile hidden behind the wrinkled veil.

"We made fattah for you, Sister," her mother said, looking at the linen-covered basket in her hand. "I thought you might like some."

"Oh, thank you, dear," Jacinta's aunt said. The same gray dress. The same stain across the lower hem. Her aunt looked down at Jacinta with no expression. No invitation to come in.

"Do you need anything else?" her mother asked.

"I am fine. Thanks for this."

The sister accepted the basket of fattah and closed the door slowly.

They went down the stoop and walked home upon the cobblestones.

"Why does your sister live alone? Why does she never let us inside to visit?" Jacinta asked.

Her mother grimaced, seeming to have expected that one day her young daughter would ask these difficult questions.

Her mother started to speak and then shook her head, as if changing her mind. "My sister dishonored the family when she was a young woman." She looked up to the clouding sky. "Life is rarely tidy, my little flower. Auntie gave birth to her second child from a man other than her husband."

Those visits to her aunt were always the same. While her mother said nothing more of this calamity, Jacinta's aunt apparently never recovered from the shame of disgracing her family. The aunt eventually shunned everyone, once her husband and son left her. All of this sadness, even though the baby daughter from the other man had been snatched up, once off the teat, and taken to wherever those hooded women took the unwanted back then.

Jacinta feels a wetness on her buttocks. She rolls over to see she is lying in a puddle of her own blood. Her heart labors. She imagines it striking fiercely against her sternum. She looks down at her belly. It distends further. This is not the kind of place she wished to die. Alone. She prays for Esel's safety.

She envisions her own son's face and smiles. She pictures Zane shooting arrows and running between the tents and vendor stalls, always making the most of wherever she dragged him throughout his young life. He will be fine. Esel will care for him. "Breathe for him. Fight for him. Endure as you did at his birth," she tells herself.

The child's face morphs into Leander's. She smiles, remembering the boyish grin on the Mamluk's face and the best of their times together. Their walks on the beaches and the riverfront strolls through Cairo.

She stares at the boughs of pine branches and the darkening clouds between them. How delicate their needles. How perfectly formed by Allah's grace. How pretty the color of them, contrasting with the sky. Why did she have to be in this kind of condition in order for her to observe and enjoy their simple beauty?

A dizziness fills her head. Shivering, she curls into herself like a babe in its cradle. Her skin has gone cold and clammy. She fights off the desire to sleep. She shakes a foot continuously to stay awake and imagines pine twigs from the branches above holding her eyelids open.

Hoof clops awaken her. Two horses, she thinks. Esel must be bringing some help. She hears the footsteps crunching the rocky soil. They halt.

The man stops in his tracks, and turns angrily toward Esel. "What is this? An Arab, you say? With information on the Mongol enemy?"

Jacinta thinks she recognizes the voice. It could not be.

A hushed response from Esel.

The footsteps walk away. Jacinta cannot hear their argument.

Again she fights to stay awake, but her eyelids grow heavy.

When Jacinta opens her eyes, she finds Esel knelt over her, tenderly brushing the hair from her face. Esel looks over her shoulder to the warrior standing with his arms akimbo and rises to make way for him.

Leander kneels beside Jacinta. She looks up at him. His face is filthy with soot; his eyes are drawn from a lack of sleep. He looks older, hardened from these years away from Egypt.

"How is that you are here?" Jacinta says to Leander. "Do you not have enemy to kill? Or do you come here to put your worst foe out of her misery?" She forces a grin.

He looks over his shoulder to where Esel must be. He is not amused. "Esel lied to get me here. But if she has become friends with you, I would expect no different."

Jacinta's stomach hurts too much to feel sadness. "Well, as long as you are here, may we talk? Methinks I have few words left, so I will stick with only the truth."

His lips draw tight as he looks to her abdomen. "I am sorry for your wounds. I do not wish for you to die." He looks with irritation at Esel. "Listen, her nephew requires my services. I have brothers relying on me. I must—"

"I understand. Just give me just a few moments, as I may not have more."

He looks at her with a touch of sorrow in his eyes.

"Do you remember our nights on the dunes together, in each other's arms those many years ago?"

"Ah yes, let me recall," Leander says with his brow furrowed. "Was that before or after you tried to have my throat slit?"

She swallows. "I have a son."

"An adopted one from your time in Hama. Mert's boy. I have heard."

Her breath labored, she whispers. "Not the son of Mert. The boy is our son. His name is Zane."

Leander shakes his head slowly, in denial. "The lad is too young to be mine. And I have heard his skin is quite dark."

"He is the child of your blood and mine. I left for Hama that following January, not even three months pregnant. No one knew."

He looks away.

"It is the truth," she says. "Your son was born the twenty-fourth of July, 1254. When my belly began swelling, I convinced them that I was ill, as I had been treating those stricken with the fever. The mullahs isolated me—away from the mosque and infirmary in Hama. I confided in only one woman, who aided me. She delivered Zane. Your son."

Leander turns. He gazes at the orange streaks upon the western horizon. He moves beside her and drops to his buttocks. He dumps his helmet and wads the filthy skull cap into his hand.

"Is this another lie?" he asks in a voice softened.

"No. I have told people that Zane is five years old. But he is six, small for his age."

He looks over his shoulder with questioning eyes to where Esel stands.

"I have labored at many a deathbed," Jacinta says, her voice weakening. "I have found mortality to be a strong truth serum. On my soul, the child is ours."

"So why did you not come and tell me? Why would you keep this a secret?"

"Many reasons. I did not want to hurt my mother. She was ill and did not need the shame of a grandchild born out of wedlock."

The tightness around his eyes begins to allay. His hands, which had been clenched as fists, unclench. He takes one of her hands.

"And I wished for us to be together out of affection for one another, not because of any obligation you had to me or to your faith in teaching this child God's way," she says. "I left Cairo and my family for you. For us."

"But your lies. You have always lied," he says.

"When my assignments required it. For Egypt." She shivers and looks to the dark clouds above as her vision darkens around the edges, more than can be accounted for by the shadows of approaching night. "I know how this sounds. And I have spent a career setting snares. But just as often, I have spent a life stumbling into others' traps."

"Traps," he says.

"My father seeking to trap me into marriages to benefit his business. Trapped by him into spying for al-Salih. Trapped by Aybeg and Qutuz into dangerous work through their death threats against my family. Too young and overwhelmed to counter their pressures, I took part in trapping you in Cairo that night—the gravest error of my life. But I refused for Zane to be bait in a snare set for you."

Leander unbuckles his sword belt and cradles her head in his lap. He places his hand on her belly.

She smiles. The Frank touches where their child came from and from which her life now drains. "I wanted you to come back to me willingly, once you saw my devotion. I came across the desert only for you—and to bring you your son. I swear this. I beg your forgiveness. For my weakness in being pulled into Aybeg's ploy that night."

She tells him the truth. "The boy is our gift from Allah. Zane is what I wanted for us since the first day I met you. I swear this. Zane is our merged spirits." She smiles through the pain.

A single tear rolls down Leander's nose. She reaches up and lays her hand on his cheek, her belly blood mingling with the grime on his face. She wipes his tear with her finger.

A dark horizon appears closer with each blink of her eyes. She struggles to breathe, just as she had witnessed in the infirmary with so many soldiers and the old people that she cared for at the end. She knows it is coming. Finish your words to him, she tells herself. She reaches out her hand. He grasps it.

She squeezes his knuckles tightly. He leans over and carefully hugs her, his face wet upon hers. She breathes in his scent, savors it. He kisses her cheek.

"Stay alive," she says. "I hope you will take part in raising him."

He nods. His lips move, he says something, but she cannot hear him. She watches him watch her. Esel has joined the pair, her hand on Leander's shoulder. She begins to weep. The expressions of those watching the dying.

Jacinta tries to tell him that everything will be all right, that few people are blessed to be so content at their end. But her mouth will not speak. His wet eyes go wide.

She thinks of the twigs holding her eyelids open and tries to keep them that way. A blackness comes in from the edge of her vision, closing in, slowly. Closing.

Leander sets her hands across her chest, a smear of bloody mud left upon his armor. He wipes a tear from his eye and presses his moistened fingers on her tunic, atop her heart.

CHAPTER 53

Esel

East of al-Salihiyya
October 24, 1260

Esel seats a dagger in its pocket of her boot and pushes open the flap of her tent. A horn of moon emerges waxy-gold from the distant mountainscape, as if an ibex in her Kipchak country lifts his head from behind a crag.

She picks out the last of the dwindling stars in the Great Sky. Since childhood, she has cherished those lofty gems that vanish each day at sunrise with no commotion, only to make their blessed appearance again on the other side of the heavens at twilight with equal tranquility. The ache returns to her heart. She thinks of Jacinta, the composed warrioress, the only woman whom Esel may ever call friend. Esel prays the time until the two are reunited feels as short as the duration between star sightings.

The rolling hills of al-Salihiyya stretch before her, laced with hooches tinted mauve by the early dawn. The tents shelter only Qutuz's vanguard, Mamluks from all three regiments, and several units of Egyptian regulars, just a fraction of the army assembled last moon at Ayn Julut. Once Kitbugha's horde was beaten and most of the Mongol-assigned governors abandoned their posts in the Syrian cities, Qutuz sent the remainder of his large army home—the Turkmen, the Kurds, and the cavalry from Hama.

Yesterday, Qutuz received the pigeon message he was waiting for. Cairo is nearly finished with its preparations for the reception of its victorious sultan and his local troops. Qutuz stopped the column here, only a two-day ride from Cairo, ordering the army to camp for two nights. He waits for the main body of the Egyptian army to finish their crossing of the Sinai and will then allow his entire force a respite to freshen their kit and groom their mounts, while giving the city's officials extra time to organize for the procession.

On the west side of camp last night, hoots and lighthearted yarns resonated from the campfires of Qutuz's Muizziyya and some of the Salihi. And since their great victory at Ayn Julut last moon, these Mamluks most loyal to the sultan have grown accustomed to such levity.

Once their fighting ended upon the Jezreel Plain, Qutuz's men did little more than trail the Bahri Mamluks' path of destruction northward through the scorched Jordan River valley. South of the Sea of Galilee, they passed scatterings of Mongol corpses, some burned to a crisp, all stripped of valuables by the locals and then left to the crows and jackals. Baybars had taken it upon himself to push his regiment north of the big lake into Syria, exploiting Egypt's success by hunting and slaying pockets of enemy resistance, lest the Tartars reorganize and strike again in force.

Of course, news of the Egyptian victory preceded Qutuz's arrival into Damascus. There, Muslims responded to the Mongol defeat with rioting against the minorities holding power. Given control under the Tartar occupation, the Christians ruled the city for the first time in six hundred years. For months, the

Christians desecrated the holy precincts with wine and music, turning even the revered Umayyad Mosque into a church.

Predictably, Qutuz's Mamluks were in no hurry to put out the burning churches, or halt the pillaging of Christian homes and murders. Jewish and Muslim collaborators in Damascus fared little better. Within two days, the sultan's forces restored order.

For several weeks, Qutuz and his men occupied the Damascus citadel. The sultan personally set about tidying the Mamluk house. He took Syrian fiefs from the Kurdish Qaymariyya and assigned them to his own amirs. Now, not only do the Muizziyya return home as the triumphant saviors of Islam, but also as rich men. More importantly, from the fortress, Qutuz quickly asserted his authority over the entirety of Syria. The sultan confirmed and reassigned governorships to all of the Syrian principalities, places dominated by the kin of Saladin for generations.

Esel will never forget Baybars' visit to her hooch south of Damascus. The Bahri had just returned from weeks in the north, pursuing the broken Mongol enemy. Her nephew came to her fresh after a discussion with Qutuz.

A knock. Esel opened the door. Her nephew stood with dark rings beneath his eyes.

She threw her arms around him. "You live."

"You recover from your injuries?" he asked, eying the scars on her face.

"I am fine. When do you go to Aleppo?"

He looked down. "We will not be."

She tried to detect a sign of a jest. She saw none. "Will not be?"

Baybars shook his head. "While we chased the Mongol devils clear to Homs, Amir Qutuz spent his days doling out the offices. He handed Aleppo to al-Muzaffar."

"Al-Muzaffar? He is not a Kipchak," she said.

"Or a Mamluk—not even an Ayyubid of Saladin's blood. He is the son of a Seljuq slave."

Esel shook her head. "Qutuz promised you Aleppo if you helped defeat the Tartars. You could have done no more toward this end."

"Not all oaths are kept, my Teyze," he said, grimacing.

"What about Damascus?" She had heard al-Nasir was dead, slain by Hulegu once the khan learned of Kitbugha's loss at Ayn Julut. A fitting end, she felt, as the former Prince of Damascus had left his family, deserted his troops, and lived as a guest in Hulegu's camp when Ayn Julut erupted.

"Qutuz named joint governors there—Amirs Alam al-Din and Mujir al-Din," Baybars said.

"So the sultan has given Aleppo to a weaker prince with no Kipchak or royal blood and Damascus to loyal amirs?" She closed her eyes in frustration.

"I doubt Qutuz ever had any intention to place me or any other rival in one of the empire's most important principalities."

She nodded. Aleppo and Damascus were jewels beneath only Cairo herself in worth. It was from the riches and influence of these two power centers that past Ayyubid princes had assembled factions to oppose the sultanate in Cairo.

"The sultan did not even offer you control of one of the smaller principalities?" she asked.

"No. He granted most of the Ayyubid princes their former governorships, regardless of whether they had submitted to the Mongols or not—even al-Ashraf of Homs, who rode with the Mongols at Ayn Julut."

"So al-Mansur kept Hama, al-Mughith still has Karak?" she asked.

"Yes."

She sat in silence, taking in what was said. "The Ayyubids will be of no threat to Qutuz in these smaller princedoms. What will you do?"

"I do not know. But Qutuz has made it clear—all of Syria now answers to him. Everyone," he said, frowning.

After that meeting with the sultan, Baybars joined the rest of the army for the trip back to Egypt. The first piece of gossip to fall upon the Bahriyya's ears was that the sultan felt the Bahri had fled from Ayn Julut. Qutuz apparently suggested that Baybars' regiment skirting east at Gilboa to attack the fleeing Mongols in the Jordan Valley illuminated the commander's faintheartedness. Esel heard that Baybars received this word stone-faced, giving no reply.

During the journey west through the Sinai, the Bahri held their heads low. They were wearied from the weeks of fighting, but Esel knew Baybars' Mamluks quietly fumed at Qutuz's insult, plus the loss of the anticipated fiefdoms and prestige that would have been theirs if the sultan had made good on his pledge of Aleppo. What would be the Bahriyya's future in Cairo under Qutuz, now that the shared Mongol enemy had been halted for the time being?

Esel walks to the edge of the encampment, where she is to meet the others for today's hunt. Hundreds of staked and hobbled Arabians feed on the short grass. She is heartened by the sound of ripping grass that fills the valley. While she is early this morning to the gathering place, two mounted men have arrived first. Even from a distance, she identifies the Bahri's Amir Zeki by the bulk in his shoulders. As directed by the sultan, both men are without bow and quiver.

She wishes Zeki and Amir Anis a pleasant morning. She takes the reins of her bay from the ghulam, who stands obediently with one hand behind his back.

"Thank you," she says. She runs her hand beneath the girth strap to check its tightness and double-checks the other fastenings.

He offers a cupped hand to assist her into the saddle. She denies his aid and springs atop the animal with a vigor that belies the gray in her hair. She offers the slave boy a smile and farewell and turns her horse toward the men, who back their mounts to make room for her in their conversation.

"Nice morning for a hunt, eh Esel?" Zeki asks.

"Perfect," she says. "Although I'm not quite sure why Baybars would invite an old lady along, amid such important men."

The Bahri chuckle.

"We might have been important last moon," Anis says, "but no longer."

The dejection from the sultan's insults seems to have moved down the ranks, she thinks.

Zeki changes the topic. "Anis said you were the one who introduced Baybars to most hunts, when he was just a lad. Is that so?" Zeki asks.

"Well, me and plenty others. But if nostalgia is Baybars' reason for inviting me, for breaking custom, then I suppose I am grateful."

She looks about the quiet bivouac. Men begin to stir about their tents. Baybars must have detected her melancholy since her ordeal with the Mongol capturers and Jacinta's death. Perhaps he brings her along to cheer her up. Or maybe Qutuz suggested her presence for some odd reason, although she cannot think of one.

Two wrinkle-faced Bedouin clomp toward them on camels. Nestled in leather pouches on either flank of their animals sit a pair of Qutuz's hunting dogs, his Salukis. She beams, having come across Bedu over the years who worked similar dogs to hunt birds, gazelle, fox, and even wild ass. Accustomed to riding in such perches, the Arab hounds sit facing outboard, their eyes alert to all around them.

She understands these Bedouin, the sultan's hound keepers, arrived in camp from Cairo yesterday, traveling the Via Maris, "The Way of the Sea." Once nearing the al-Salihiyya encampment from the west, the Bedu scouted the thick brush and side trails for hares, figuring Qutuz would be itching for a hunt.

Esel nods upon seeing the hounds' green paws hanging over the thickened leather edge of their enclosures, a sign of these Bedu's love for their animals. The compassionate among the Bedouin hunters mix the olive-colored henna powder with their strong tea and a touch of molasses, which acts like glue. They apply the concoction to their dogs' paws just before a hunt, or "coursing," as they call it, to further protect the hounds' thick pads from sharp rocks and thorns.

These men bow their respects to the amirs and then Esel. Knowing their place among this company and speaking little Turkish, the Bedu stay a respectable distance away. They chat quietly among themselves, their eyes glancing back and forth between the glowing eastern horizon and the sultan's royal pavilion. The elder pets the smooth heads of his prized canines.

The Arab peoples have made companions with these desert hounds for thousands of years, the breed sharing the greyhound as an ancestor. She heard that the Hadith, Islamic law, mentions the Saluki as the only clean dog, the sole canine a devout Muslim may use on a hunt. The Quran even forbids men of faith from eating game killed by common hounds, the only exception being that dispatched by Salukis.

In fact, the Bedu whom Esel has met do not consider their Salukis to be dogs at all. The Bedouin so admire the physical qualities and speed of these hounds that Salukis are the only dogs allowed inside Bedu tents and upon their camels. A litter of these pups ranks in significance just behind the birth of a son or a purebred Arabian—all three being precious gifts from Allah to His people. The best hunting hounds receive burial rituals as sacred as those provided for family members.

Amir Anis turns his horse, his face gone stern.

Baybars and Qutuz approach, with two of the sultan's guards between the commanders. While the sultan and Baybars carry only swords, the pair of Mamluks also wear strung bows across their shoulders, as would boys.

Even given the extra weapons that the sultan's men carry, Esel is astounded that Qutuz would risk venturing into the scrub away from the army's protection, much less accompanied by Bahri amirs, leaders from a regiment whom he openly fought against only two years past. But what does she know? She is merely a bow maker and former kitchen slave. Qutuz is Egypt's ruler.

The sultan raises his hand in greeting to the Bedu.

Being the senior in their group, Anis moves forward. "Good morning, Sultan," he says. He then nods to the other amirs.

Qutuz half-grins. "Good morning, indeed." He glances to the sun-hardened Mamluk beside him, the old *Furusiyya* instructor, Cenk. "Better chasing hares than those damn Mongols," the sultan says.

"Yes, my Sultan," Cenk says, rubbing the bags under his reddened eyes.

"You have met Cenk." The sultan looks to the younger guard beside him. "This is *Boynuz*."

Boynuz means "Horn" in Turkish. Esel picks out the Kipchak features in the young man's dark face. A half-breed. She wonders if his nickname was coined in the old country, his family being carvers who made thumb rings for archers, or perhaps musical instruments. Maybe the man's father was a horn-blower, a signal man for his fellow Kipchaks in battle.

The Bahri amirs acknowledge the trooper with slight nods.

Qutuz eyes Esel and then addresses Baybars. "I see you have summoned your bowyer. Since when do women accompany amirs on a hunt?"

"Bowyer, but also my aunt, Sultan, the woman who raised me. I hoped you would allow her presence, as she did much to assist in equipping our force before Ayn Julut and is very fond of watching the dogs work."

Cenk scowls. Qutuz tries to disguise his upper lip raised in mild disgust. "I suppose that is fine."

Esel wishes she could leave. She knew it was inappropriate for her to be here. This hunt feels unnatural to her, void of blissful anticipation and full of tension. She glares at Baybars, not only for putting her in this position, but also for neglecting to mention her as a legitimate rider and hunter.

Baybars avoids her stare.

"Shall we?" the sultan asks, pulling around the head of his horse, clearly with no intention of waiting for a response.

CHAPTER 54

Eşel

East of al-Salihiyya

October 24, 1260

The nine hunters head north along the Via Maris, falling in line behind Qutuz, Baybars, and the Bedouin hound keepers. Esel brings up the rear, the morning chill pleasant across her cheeks. She savors the lemony fragrance of *homath*, the scent from its green leaves and dried spring flowers roused by the hoof stomps.

The elder Bedu turns in his saddle toward Qutuz. "We picked up some sign ahead, a game trail at the next western offshoot," he says, referring to one of the lateral trunks that intersect the main road. "With your blessing, we could try that one first, my Sultan?"

"Of course," Qutuz says.

They clomp along the path, widening their offset column to better flush game. The amirs appear content to take in the morning quietly, away from the probing eyes of soldiers and the onus of endless worries which have plagued each man for moons. Their experienced eyes comb the nearby ground and hills, places where a spooked hare might expose itself.

One hound on the old Bedu's side pouch whines in anticipation. The man snatches her by the scruff of the neck and turns her head toward his. "Patience, my love." The dog's eyes never leave the scrub.

Esel stares at the hound's cropped ears and lean body, recalling years ago the words from another Bedu "slipper," as the hound keepers are called for the slip collars they use on their dogs. "What makes a good Saluki is the length of the dog and the flexibility in its spine." He put his hand across his hound's rear end. "And hips. When four fingers fit here, that is perfect. But in the end, it is about a dog's balance and stamina and stride length."

She is excited to watch these dogs run. Salukis are sighthounds, beasts adept at using their keen eyesight, more so than their nose or ears, to track game. Blessed with exceptional speed, they are born to run down quarry.

They reach a stretch of undulant hills just as the sun cracks the horizon. The old Bedu opens his left palm respectfully to the sultan, who guides the party to the side trail. Fresh hoof prints pock the trail from where the two Bedu scouted the path yesterday.

Only a few hundred paces westward, the track becomes speckled with dark, round dung and blotches of urine-soaked sand. Fresh sign of the hare. Farther along, runways crisscross the lowlands with soft-footed depressions in the sand, disclosing the offset bound of the creature.

A hare feels their hoof clops. It flushes. A streak of white flashes across a wide knoll nearby. The varmint charges uphill, bounding seven, nine feet per leap.

The Saluki on the right side of the old man sits up higher in his bag, quivering. A broad smile forms on the younger Bedu's face. Another hound attunes to his litter mate's response and whimpers in anticipation. This becomes contagious. All four hounds softly whine.

The old Bedu waits for the hare to separate about three hundred paces from the riders. He releases the slip collar from the hound on his left. He lifts the animal from its bag by the scruff of its neck, exposing a red-painted handprint upon the dog's thigh. This pressed right hand is the *hamsa*, symbolic of the Hand of Fatimah, after the daughter of the Prophet Mohammad. For centuries, Muslims across the realm have rendered this ancient symbol for good luck and protection against evil.

The hound quakes in his hands. The Bedu leans over and gently tosses the dog toward the hare from atop his camel.

Like a shot arrow, the dog bounds northward across the sand, a curved blur of black and tan. The hound holds his narrow head low, his large eyes focused upon the exact point where the hare breached the foothill.

The sultan nods to Zeki and then cocks his head toward Cenk, wordlessly inviting the two to join in chase after this first hare.

Cenk appears confused. He eyes the Bahri and then glares a short, subtle warning of vigilance to Boynuz, the sole bodyguard at Qutuz's side. Reluctantly, Cenk pulls his horse's head toward Zeki. Both men are quick to the gallop, attempting to catch the sand-churning Saluki. The dog and trailing riders drop over a rise, out of sight.

The sultan apparently intends to pair a Bahri with a Muizziyya on each chase. Esel wonders if Qutuz envisions this hunt as a means to help soften the opposing Mamluks' differences over the years. But surely a man in his position could not be so naïve.

The sultan's betrayals against the Bahri started six years past with the murder of the Bahriyya's leader, Aqtay, when Qutuz was but a counselor to the Sultan Aybeg. Qutuz had not relented in his disloyalties to the Bahri since, the reneging on his pledge of Aleppo to Baybars being just the latest.

Yet all journeys begin with a first step. Perhaps today is the sultan's initial action toward some type of reconciliation between the regiments. Such is needed. Maybe once in Cairo, Qutuz will exert more effort to reward and reunite this old family of Mamluks.

The remaining hunters continue west, the ground gradually flattening to their south and rising slightly to their north. Amid the scrub, narrow game lanes become more concentrated with the powdery tracks of their quarry.

A hare bolts near Esel's horse on the north side of the trail. She circles her stomping mount to the south, where yet another hare scampers from the oak scrub. This flushed game tears southward across the flat ground.

For the first time this morning, the old Bedu is excited. He points to his junior while pulling a "feathered" white hound from his right-side bag. "Hip, hip, hip, hip." He incites the slender bitch, while gently guiding her thin snout in his hand to the north, where the hare runs midway uphill, more than a bowshot away.

His dog locks on the prey. A rush of adrenaline sets the canine's legs to trembling. The Bedouin looses her in the direction of the fleeing hare, grinning.

The sultan nods to Anis. This amir needs no further invite. He turns his horse toward a clearing in the scrub. He charges up the first knoll along an angle of pursuit that will assist him in closing on the hound.

Qutuz grins at Boynuz. "Go with him." The obedient Mamluk does not question his sultan. He is off.

Baybars attempts to locate the second hare to the south. The younger Bedu has already released the slip collars on the cream-colored male and longer-haired red. These dogs charge diagonally over a sandy ledge toward the open desert, darting effortlessly across the sand, the quintessence of elegance and symmetry.

"The hounds are tracing, my Amir," the Bedu tells Baybars, his way of urging Baybars to simply follow the dogs, who are already on the hare. Baybars looks to the sultan.

"We go," Qutuz says.

Baybars smiles, giving his horse some heel.

Esel puts her gray to a canter, loping in trace of the Mamluks. She stands in the stirrups to watch the men hurtling southward away from her. She grins, her view evoking Baybars as a lad, racing across the boundless steppe grass.

She stops on a rise. Sayal trees and mounds of shrubbery dapple the valley, the gravelly flat terminating miles away into folds of tan-striped mountains. The eastern fringe thickens into higher bush and dense groves of younger sayal thorn.

The pair of Salukis run nearly side-by-side in the open country, vaulting in short, quick bursts. Covered in short hair, the male's chest ripples with muscle. His strides reach so far that his legs parallel the ground when extended. The hounds seem to fly across the shingle, all outstretched paws off the ground at the same time.

She ponders on the similarities between these Salukis and the Tazy hounds of her native steppe. The Tazy were also slight of build, their light frames keeping them atop the snowy crust, while their prey often sank deep. Wily enough to catch marmots and bearing the ferocity to kill a badger, it was no wonder that more than one Kipchak had given the hand of his daughter in return for a mating pair of Tazies. But surely the desert sighthounds here are faster, the gods somehow choosing to create the most efficient speed machine for these sandy places.

When Esel loses sight of the riders, she eases her horse down the talus and into the wadi. She follows the hoof prints up a broad knoll and again stops to look.

She locates the red hound first, the far off bitch wagging her tail. Baybars walks his horse into a clearing with the mangled hare at the tip of his riding stick. He and Qutuz appear to exchange pleasantries.

The men return the way they came, reaching her on the high ground. The light-colored male passes her, the green stains about his paws and forelegs having gone orange, as the paste does when exposed to the air, after cracking off. The Saluki's feet now appear as if made red hot during his running.

"Good run, gentlemen?" she asks.

"Aye," Baybars says with a smile.

The sultan nods his head for Esel to lead the way back. As they re-enter the wadi, the dogs nose the scrub, occasionally lifting their heads to the wind. She follows their tracks and the natural bend in the drainage.

The hair raises on the back of Esel's neck as she hears the familiar zip of an arrow in flight, then another, seeming to come from a copse of trees to their right.

A grunt behind her. The Sultan has taken an arrow in the side.

She ducks and reaches for her bow that is not there, quickly remembering that she was not allowed to bring it. She looks into the sun and can make out no shooter.

Instinctively, her heels go to her horse's side. She plows through the scrub off the pathway, steering northeast around the bigger trees. She reaches to her boot and feels the bone handle of her dagger.

A safe distance away, she reins in and listens. Nothing. She wipes the sweat from her face, across scars just healed—reminders of her last encounter against armed men.

She keeps her horse at the walk arching southward, looking for tracks. Seeing nothing, she turns west into a break in the vegetation, the direction from where the arrows were shot. She again stops to listen. A sole raven squawks as it flies past.

Esel eases through the brush, her heart drubbing a frantic cadence against her chest, the memories of the Mongol chase still fresh in her mind. Her stomach turns. Her nephew is armed only with a sword. Baybars had survived months of danger in battle. She cannot bear the thought of him now being wounded or killed by bandits while on a leisurely hunt.

Shaking her head, she pulls the dagger from her boot. Underarmed and unfamiliar with the ground is no way to enter a hunt. She wishes she had a bow and knows full well the absurdity of an old woman stalking thieves with just a small blade. She continues, regardless. She will not let some assassin kill her nephew, even if she must fight them with a mere dagger.

Esel comes across a pair of horse tracks, the prints oriented from the northeast. She follows the tracks for a hundred paces west, until the vegetation becomes too dense to ride. She ties her horse under the canopy of a sayal tree.

On foot, she follows the hoofprints. Every six steps she looks behind. She wipes the sweat from her dagger hand. She peers around a tree trunk. The horses of Amir Anis and Boynuz stare back at her.

She rests her forehead against the tree and sighs. At least she will have help from these two warriors. Anis and Boynuz must have seen the brigands approach from the higher ground to the north, or somehow known there was trouble.

The hammering in her chest lightens. Fortunately, Boynuz carries a bow. She follows their boot prints to the thickest edge of the valley, near where the arrow shots originated.

She hears a man scream. Baybars? Her heart sinks. Harsh words, muffled from the scrub—those from her nephew. She runs toward the ambush site. She breaks through the bush line into a small clearing, gasping.

The three men snap a glance to her and then resume their focus upon the downed sultan, their backs kept to her. She drops the dagger to her side and gawks in disbelief.

Baybars, Anis, and Boynuz encircle the sultan with swords bared. Qutuz lies with two arrows sticking from his side and a slash across his neck. The sultan looks up defiantly, blood coursing down his neck.

Baybars leans over Qutuz. "You thought you might use my men for your own purposes and then break your promises to us? Lead the Mongols to you like goats to the butcher, and leave us with nothing?"

The sultan looks up to Boynuz, his bodyguard who now leans his forearm upon the top limb of his bow. "Traitor," Qutuz mutters. Only the young Mamluk could have been the one who shot his master. "You will burn in hell."

Boynuz looks down at the sultan with no expression.

Baybars points the tip of his mottled steel at Qutuz. "You rewarded the Ayyubids with their principalities—some who bent their knees to the Mongols and accommodated the Franj invaders for years, rather than honoring your fellow Mamluks who drove out the infidel horde."

"You expected me to provide for your mob of caravan raiders?" The sultan looks up to Baybars. "Dumb enough to play hare to the Mongol dogs. Dumb enough to be kicked back into the desert to scrounge with the jackals." Qutuz coughs up some blood. He spits it toward Baybars and collapses to his back.

"Of course," Baybars growls. "You, the great victor." He spits upon the sultan's chest. "The savior of Islam," he says cynically. "Your battle lasted a morning, ours lasted three moons."

Baybars places his sword tip high between Qutuz's ribs. "You thought us unaware of your design for the Bahri? Putting us in the worst spots at every turn, trying to kill off as many of us as possible?"

Baybars looks into Qutuz's eyes as he leans into the hilt of his sword, burying it slowly into Qutuz's ribcage. "In the name of my forty-six Mamluks lost—those who fought valiantly and gave themselves for Egypt."

Amid the sound of parting gristle, Qutuz groans his last breath. His eyes go glassy; his mouth hangs open.

Baybars stands. He meets the gaze of the other Mamluks. "He is gone. It is done."

Baybars mounts his horse and turns north for the trail. He looks back to Boynuz. "Unlike Qutuz, I will keep my promise. You will be duly rewarded for your work here." Baybars departs with the bloody sword clenched in his fist.

Esel's head spins. Her nephew has just killed a sultan—all planned without her knowing. Her hands begin to shake.

Anis and Boynuz exchange unenthusiastic looks of relief. They avoid Esel's eyes and recede into the thicket to retrieve their horses.

She gapes at the bloodied Qutuz lying in the sand, his vacant eyes gawping skyward. A fly lands on the dead man's eyeball. Another on his opposite eyebrow. The sultan had expected a glorious reception from the admiring crowds in Cairo in just two days. Instead he is left for the jackals and vultures, unattended in the desert.

She retrieves her horse and finds the path just south of where Baybars slowly rides. He turns to see her and continues northward from where they came. She lingers behind, leaving him alone in his contemplations.

When they reach the trail crossing, they find Anis and Boynuz sitting their horses with swords drawn. The Bedouin stare at the horizon as if they watch a looming storm, ignoring the dogs that sniff the brush and frolic in the sand.

Anis lifts his chin to Baybars. He cups his ear and points to the east.

Hearing the approaching hoof clomps, Baybars nods. Boynuz nocks an arrow. The six wait for the riders to arrive.

Cenk and Zeki make the final turn in the path from the east. They stop ten paces opposite the other hunters. Cenk eyes the group. His jaw drops as he notices Qutuz not among them. He looks down at Baybars' bloody sword and then to Boynuz's bow made ready.

Cenk nods and leans forward on his pommel. He stares at his horse's striated hoofs. Zeki draws his sword and comes alongside Baybars.

Cenk pushes himself up in the saddle. Sad-eyed, he seems to look through them, his posture gone round-shouldered. A gloom sets upon his weathered face. Despite Cenk's likely participation in the schemes against her nephew, Esel feels a strange pity for him.

Cenk begins mumbling to himself. Tears fill his blood-shot eyes. He asks some unheard question, which he quietly answers himself. He looks heavenward, while unbuckling his belt. His scabbard falls to the ground with a clunk. "Yes, Amir Turkmani," he says softly. "I know. Time to do as you said. My duty is done. There is none worthy left to serve."

Anis rides forward, looking to Baybars as he passes. "Allow me to finish this, my Amir."

"Wait," Baybars says.

Cenk ducks from underneath his bow and flings it into the brushwood. He mutters to himself, ostensibly unaware of those around him. He reaches back and unstraps the quiver from his saddle. He drops it atop a purple-flowered sakraan bush. He stares at the poisonous plant, the one the Bedu teach their kids to avoid, its name meaning "drunk" in Arabic.

Anis follows the order and backs his horse. He looks to Zeki. "Who does Cenk address?"

"Turkmani was his first patron, his amirate commander killed in battle, more than twenty years ago," Zeki says.

Cenk uncorks the skin around his neck and takes a few slugs of the spirit. He rubs the back of his hand across his mouth and beard. He looks to the slayers of his ruler. "I am not reckless enough to fight you. Not spineless enough to flee." He shrugs his shoulders. "Kill me now or let me fetch my sultan—I care little which you chose."

Anis looks to Zeki in suspicion of Cenk's words and then to Baybars, who rests his hilt atop his thigh as he watches Cenk.

"Retrieve your sultan, Cenk," Baybars says.

Cenk dismounts and pulls a pair of wide lashings from a saddlebag. He unfastens his "butt bag" from behind the cantle.

He elbows it aside, letting it fall upon the shrubbery. He gently lays the straps across his horse's rump. He leans his turbaned head against one. He stammers to himself, rolling his forehead side to side across the cracked leather.

Baybars runs the stained blade against his trousers and returns it to his saddle scabbard. "He is a short ride south. Our tracks will lead you to him."

Cenk looks up to the sky. He slurs. "I should have done as you advised. I tended to Aybeg's wishes, and Qutuz's, but not to my own family's needs. I will do this now." He takes another draw from his skin and mounts his horse.

He turns to Baybars. "Do not think your sparing of me will gain you my backing."

"I understand. Go," Baybars says.

They watch as Cenk follows the hoof prints southward toward his patron. Slumped in the saddle, Cenk waves his hands, as he explains some unheard point to the ghost with whom he speaks. The straps across his horse's rear drag in the dirt behind him. Puffs of sediment mushroom on each sluggish hoof strike until he is out of sight.

"My Amir, please," Anis says to Baybars. "Cenk is as guilty as Qutuz. His is a coward's ruse. His madness is like that of an actor's, faked to save his own skin. Let me send him to hell."

Zeki looks to Baybars, his face suggesting that he agrees with Anis.

"We came to kill one man. And he is dead. We will gain nothing by killing Cenk here."

"We will gain by snuffing out a vote against you before it is cast," Anis says.

Baybars shakes his head. "Cenk is but a single man, a single raised hand. We kill him now and we will lose backers from some in the Salihi, amirs whose votes could go either for or against me. We do not want amirs in any regiment viewing me as another Qutuz, one willing to slay valuable men for not taking his side."

Zeki nods his head. "Baybars is right. Those teetering between support or resistance may come around wholeheartedly later. We just need a majority of hands today."

Baybars looks to Anis. "Remember, only two years past Qutuz executed twenty-six Salihi not far from here for taking the field with me in opposition to him. I refuse to slay more than one." He shifts his attention to Boynuz of the Muizziyya. "I eliminated Qutuz to reunify our corps, to bond all who wear the scarlet and gold in the defense of Egypt, not to throw Mother Cairo into greater chaos."

Votes. An election. If back on the Kipchak steppe, Esel knows their old law would be clear on the matter before them: he who killed the ruling khan would become khan. Yet she recalls the story of these Mamluk amirs ten years past, after their murder of the sultan Turanshah, son of their adored patron al-Salih. Immediately after killing al-Salih's detestable offspring, the amirs gathered in the sultan's pavilion in Fariskur, determined to not leave the place until Turanshah's succession was settled. Her nephew must expect the same will happen today. But what will happen to Baybars if they do not accept him?

"Quickly, back to camp," Baybars says, turning his horse. "Let us see if this corps will choose a man who will put aside past ills and move the sultanate forward. If I gain the amirs' pledges of allegiance, we will break camp and push the vanguard toward Cairo, keeping them well ahead of the main body. We will secure the citadel in Cairo before the rest of the army comes up, before they know Qutuz is dead."

Zeki nods. "Let the Egyptian army arrive in Cairo in time to join a procession that not only celebrates a victory over a supreme foe, but also hails the rise of a new sultan."

The Bedouin stare at Baybars wide-eyed, perhaps stupefied by the audacity of the man and his design. Anis collects Cenk's weapons.

Baybars looks at the Bedu and chuckles. "Agonize little, my friends. If I win a show of hands today, our army will do nothing but hunt and train for war for as long as you live. Your pack of hounds will only grow in skill and size, just like my single corps of Mamluks."

Esel takes a deep breath. Her nephew will soon become either a king or a corpse. How shortsighted she had been to not have seen this coming. Of course Baybars would act decisively when given the opportunity to rid the ultimate menace from the Mamluk flock. Her mind roves to a springtime celebration on their steppe homeland twenty-two years past—to Baybars as a lad and the lone wolf that he chased into camp that day.

> *"No! Stop!" the saman screamed, running from where the musicians and Kipchak dancers stood aghast.*
>
> *Esel winced. With his left heel hooked on the pony's flank, Baybars yowled in time with the downward stroke of his sword blade to the bitch's neck. The wolf's front legs crumbled, her momentum toppling her rear legs overhead.*
>
> *The animal slid to a rest belly up, her left paw gently clawing at the air.*
>
> *Her nephew jumped from his mount to finish.*
>
> *The saman broke from the group of observers and ran toward Baybars. "No! Do not!"*
>
> *Baybars grabbed the animal by the white neck fur and lifted it with all his might to look into the animal's eyes, as if allowing the beast to recognize her slayer, before the last light of life departed. With his lungs heaving and his fist full of bloody fur, he stared sideways into the creature's face, its curled hindquarters resting on the ground, the canine's head flopped askew.*
>
> *The saman stopped short of Baybars. He circled wide to face him. "You have not been granted the role of 'wolf taker.' The gods—"*
>
> *Their khan pushed aside the holy man. The broad-shouldered chieftain cuffed Baybars across the back of the head, sending the lad tumbling atop the beast.*

Baybars sprang to his feet, still clutching the wolf with one hand. Gaining his bearing, his eyebrows furrowed. The boy just now seemed to fully comprehend that he was in the tower's living area and surrounded by his people. He let loose of the animal and looked up to the soured face of their khan.

The khan's eyes glowered with an angry fire. Their leader picked up the sturdy youth by the tunic, until Baybars' boots no longer touched the grass. "You have shed the wolf's blood on the same grass that our gers occupy. You know the ill fortune this can bring upon us?"

Baybars glanced at the hulking lump of gray and white fur beside them and then back to the khan's face. "For years, this beast has killed many of our sheep," Baybars protested. "And this spring, she would have bred more of the devils. She is now dead at our feet, incapable of producing young. Is this the bad fortune you speak of?"

Holding the youth aloft by a fist of wool, the khan reared back and punched Baybars in the face. The impact threw the boy to his back. "Fool!" the khan roared.

The tower stood in silence.

Baybars crawled to one knee and pressed a sleeve to the cut above his eye. He tottered. Collecting himself, he strode past the wolf and his waiting pony to the sword that lay in the grass, the weapon gifted to him by Gozde, the injured Mamluk who stayed with their tower for moons and bonded with the lad while recovering. He picked it up and ran the flat of the blade against his trousers on each side.

He looked up to meet his tribesmen's faces, their stares shifting between the mangled wolf and the ivory-handled weapon in his grip. He walked to his pony and slipped the blade into the saddle scabbard. He uncoiled his rope, tied a hasty knot, and placed this slip above both of the canine's rear hocks.

Without turning back, he mounted and put his pony to the walk. His rope went taut, cinching the knot. He dragged the creature away from the tower, leaving a path of crimson-matted grass behind him.

CHAPTER 55

Cenk

Cairo

October 29, 1260

Cenk trudges north of the Cairo citadel through *el-Mansuriya*, the blacks' quarter. He takes a swig from his wineskin and shifts a leather kitbag to his other shoulder. The bag is stuffed with quill and pen wells, candles and papyrus sheets—his personal effects from his small workspace in the citadel. He grumbles to himself, oblivious to the approaching locals whom he forces off the edge of the walkway.

For almost a decade, the bag's contents have helped him serve Sultans Aybeg and Qutuz. He pored over scrolls by candlelight in that stone-walled chamber until his blurry eyes would not stay open. Countless mornings he awakened on that lumpy cot, scarcely remembering having laid down. So much planning, too much at stake to leave work. How disgraceful that one of Baybars' trolls will soon occupy his desk.

Five days ago, Cenk had returned alone from the hare coursing with the slain Qutuz draped over the back of his horse. At the vanguard's encampment near Salihiyya, Mamluks from the Muizziyya and Salihi met him solemnly, their eyes moving between the dead sultan and the royal pavilion, where the amirs in support of Baybars were already making their pitch in why the murdering Baybars should become the empire's next ruler.

Cenk entered Qutuz's marquee and was ignored by Baybars and the gathered commanders. All seemed to acknowledge that Cenk was used up goods; he would serve no purpose in whatever regime succeeded. Knowing the majority of the army was still traveling a day's march behind them and that Baybars' chances of winning any election were better with mostly the sympathetic Salihi and his Bahri on hand, Baybars and his cadre pushed for the amirs to cast their votes now in assent to his leadership.

The regiments' leaders argued. Despite the objections made by Cenk and some of the Salihi to voting before the bulk of the amirs arrived, the Mamluks held the poll. Cenk cast his vote against Baybars, but the Bahri's commander won the showing of hands. Cenk and most of the Muizziyya considered the entire procedure a mockery. With only a fraction of the decision-makers' consent, Baybars, the king-slayer, became ruler of an empire. For now.

Baybars ordered the camp broken down and the vanguard to make its way back to Cairo. He forbade this advance guard from exchanging any communications with the main body, a ploy to keep a lion's share of the army ignorant of Qutuz's death. At the time, Cenk thought Baybar's maneuver laughable: the Bahri's commander actually believed he could sneak his way into the sultanate. Still, Baybars spurred ahead of the forward element with a troop of staunch Bahriyya.

They arrived in Cairo in the dark of night. First to meet Baybars was al-Hilli, an amir who Qutuz had appointed as vicegerent before leaving on the Mongol campaign. After learning of the election and receiving promises of gold made by Baybars, al-Hilli quickly recognized Baybars as the new sultan. The vicegerent secured vows of allegiance to Baybars from the garrison at Cairo's fortress. He then handed over the citadel, and hence rule of the Mamluk Sultanate, to Baybars.

Expecting to greet the victorious Sultan Qutuz with vigor, the populace had decorated Cairo and made preparations for a great festival. Wall coverings in arabesque hung from every balcony, the patterns of intertwining plants and curvilinear designs stretching almost continuously for miles along the main roads. Banners glorifying Qutuz also adorned the streets: "Reviver of justice among all; father of the poor and miserable; liberator of Islam."

The people of Cairo awoke the next morning to a summons bidding them to pray for God's mercy in receiving the spirit of the deceased Sultan Qutuz and to beseech the new sultan, al-Malik al-Zahir Rukn al-Din Baybars. The population discreetly rolled up any banner that glorified Qutuz by name.

Some quietly latched their shutters and stayed inside, recalling eight years ago when the Bahriyya pillaged their homes and raped their daughters, the Bahri's reckoning against Sultan Aybeg for slashing the Bahri's pay and perhaps giving Cairo reason to call for another leader who might better keep order. Of course, Aybeg responded to this belligerence by killing Aqtay, the Bahri's leader, and running most of the Bahriyya regiment out of town. The sultan dismantled the Bahri's citadel on Rawda Island.

Cairo delayed her festival. Baybars then announced the abolishment of the emergency tax, which Qutuz had placed on the population to fund the war against the Mongols. When the masses learned this, their reveling kicked off in earnest, some hastily scrawling new banners with Baybars' name, or simply folding over the fabric to cover praises made to Qutuz. Ignorant, short-sighted sheep, Cenk thought.

The Egyptian army arrived through Cairo's gates amid swarms of adoring locals, skins of wine and jugs of beer thrust into their hands. It was only then that they learned who had become their new sultan.

Baybars had secured the sultanate by cold-blooded murder and a dubious election. The remaining amirs of the main body and officers of the state pledged their oaths of fidelity to Baybars; the troopers joined the celebration. Baybars now ruled the land by fait accompli.

Cenk approaches the Zuwayla Gate. Three sun-dried heads remained spiked atop the eastern tower, the only remains of the Mongol envoys executed by Qutuz four moons past. Cenk looks up to their curled patches of leathery skin, dark braids, and bright teeth.

Cenk recalls Qutuz's brazen command. "Take them to the horse market. Have them halved, then beheaded. Hang their gourds at the gate, eyes facing northeast toward where Hulegu and their thousands of brothers departed."

One Mongol head looks as if smiling condescendingly at him. Cenk stops. "Your mates lie dead at Ayn Julut, you have little reason for conceit," he mutters.

A pair of gate guards call down to him from the rampart, troopers who Cenk trained years ago. Cenk's disregards their greeting; his eyes stay to the grinning skull. He feels his blood rise. He drops his bag in the street and takes to the stairs, ignoring the pain in his knees, his fury growing with each upward step.

The guards meet him at the top of the stairs, yet step aside as their old commander goes to the wall. Out of breath, Cenk yanks the smiling gourd from the spike. He holds it in front of his face and looks it squarely in the eye sockets. "Or is your smirk because of the retribution you sowed in death? You laugh having vexed my sultan with the same fate met by your heathen brothers?" He heaves the skull over the wall with a stream of bitter profanities. The brittle cranium shatters on the cobbles below.

He looks to the remaining two skulls, which stare to the northeast. He deems these Tartars show their teeth in fright, not ridicule. The Mongol heads seem to avoid his glare, knowing better than to challenge him. Satisfied, Cenk turns.

The guards eye him warily, one with his long axe across his body at the ready. Below, pedestrians walk around his bag and the braided scalp and the pieces of white pate scattered upon the street. Several look up to the tower.

Cenk lumbers down the stairs. He hefts his sack across his shoulder and continues north through the gate. With eyes to the street, he enters the Amirs' Quarter. He ignores the workers who pull furniture from a Muizziyya amir's house and those who paint over the coats of arms on several fence gates that designated the previous functions of the inhabitants. Baybars, of course, now assigns his own treasurer and armor bearer and master of the robe.

Cenk stops to drain the last of the wine from his skin.

"Thank you for your toil at Ayn Julut, amir," a passing seller says to him. "Blessings for beating back the infidels and saving Cairo."

Cenk looks over to the stranger who stands before him. Chubby cheeks above a thin beard. A bulge of fat rounding the midsection of the merchant's robe. The dealer's smile fades as Cenk's feral eyes look through him. Cenk glowers at the soft-handed money man, swings his bag to the other shoulder, and continues walking.

He looks to the sky. "I know, Amir Turkmani. My first words to them will be an apology for my neglect."

He reaches his house and stands before the stoop. He tries to think of when he was last here. Three, four moons? He pushes open the door and steps inside.

His wine rack stands bare. Two sets of dishes lie tidily arranged upon the cloth-covered table. The floor is swept, the broom and pan leaning in the corner, as if this task was completed just before stepping out the door.

Cenk drops his bag in the entranceway and walks around the corner. His wife Fidan's linen towel hangs folded across her washing basin. The pantry shelves are bare. Her blackened kettles set upside down, tipped against the fireplace brick. The ashes have been scooped out down to the bottom of the heating blocks. A dry purple stain blemishes the stone, his wine she must have dumped on the coals.

He enters their bedchamber. He opens her bureau. Empty. He does not bother going into his daughter Inci's room. He opens his chest and squats to pull a small cask of wine hidden behind his spare boots and gaiters.

He grabs his ceramic mug from its peg and walks back to the table. He taps the keg and pours himself a drink, watching the blood-red liquid gurgle. He takes a long swig. He rolls his head back and sighs.

He looks down at the tableware given to him as a wedding gift from al-Salih, presented at the same time as Fidan herself, a Kipchak slave girl also purchased by the fatherly sultan. She had gone from rags to bridal gown in less than two days; from steppe rat to wife of a Royal Mamluk.

He roars in frustration. Grabbing the cask and mug, he swipes at the teacups and backhands the plates. He snatches the edge of Fidan's tablecloth and flings it to the floor. He stands for a moment, huffing.

He unbuckles his sword belt and lays it on the bare wood. He walks to his small crate near the door, the broken ceramic crunching under his boot steps. He sets the box on the table, as his wife would have forbidden.

He slides his sword from its scabbard and rubs his thumb against the edge to test its sharpness. He eases to a rest on his bench on rickety knees and flops open the crate top. He pulls out the coarse whetstone and adds a few drops of oil to it. He takes another pull from his mug.

From point to chappe, he runs the sword across the stone, back and forth along the weapon's edge, focusing on keeping his blade's angle constant. He flips the weapon and continues. He loses himself in the whisper of steel on stone.

The cracked door eases open. Cenk looks up from his work. Tarkhan steps inside cautiously. His eyes go first to the broom, then the kettles and the broken dishes on the floor. Then to Cenk.

"Come in, it is just me," Cenk says.

"Everything all right?" Tarkhan asks.

"Depends what you think is all right," Cenk says, with one eye closed, the other looking down the blade. He looks up at Tarkhan. "And I will save you from asking—yes, it looks like both Fidan and Inci have left for good this time."

Tarkhan slumps, his eyes fill with sorrow.

Cenk nods to the bench across from him.

Tarkhan sits. "What will you do now?"

"I am doing it. She wanted me to retire. I am there. And now it looks like I can do it without having to hear any whining from them."

Tarkhan shakes his head.

"And what will you do?" Cenk asks.

"My wife and I were thinking of living on the coast. Alexandria. I suppose it depends on what happens to Baybars."

"Baybars is not going anywhere soon. He stole his way into the sultanate and there he will stay," Cenk says, without looking up from his sword.

"Maybe."

"I never should have allowed Qutuz to be so thinly guarded during that hunt," Cenk says. "I will never forgive myself."

"You had no way of knowing that some of our guards had conspired with the Bahri."

Cenk shakes his head. "It was my job to have anticipated such. At the least, I should have stayed at the sultan's side during the entire hunt. He might have stood a chance."

The rasping sound of steel on sharpening stone punctuates their conversation.

"Then you would be dead, too," Tarkhan says. "You did as the sultan asked. You always did as Qutuz asked."

"We should have kept Baybars afar, as we had done for years. Sent him back to Syria straight away. Anywhere. With no governorship and men loyal to Qutuz in every principality, Baybars would have become no more than a thief again. But now the caravan raider is sultan."

"It is done, my friend. No sense beating yourself up now."

"We both know there is little future for the senior Muizziyya here." Cenk stops from his work and looks up to his friend. "Well, for the old rags like me, that is. But your reputation is good. You are younger. Your situation is unique. Baybars will need good emissaries. Level heads. Men who truly understand how the Mongols think. That is you. By Allah, take up work with him. I will not judge. One must adapt."

"We will see. Perhaps down the road." Tarkhan eyes the cask on the table. "You need to quit drinking that poison, or you will not last a year."

"We cannot live forever, my brother," Cenk says.

"As a friend. . ."

"I know. And you are right. But what does it matter? I serve no function now."

"It matters to me. If we move to Alexandria, I think you should come there with us. I could find a property with two houses." Tarkhan raises his eyebrows.

Cenk smiles. "I am sure your wife would like that."

"She has already agreed."

Cenk chuckles. "Poor woman. And what kind of friend would I be to do that to you?"

Tarkhan squints.

"Plus, those of high position who take a fondness to me end up dead."

Tarkhan looks down.

"You know it is true. Every mentor, every senior I served has ended up slain in battle or murdered in intrigue."

"We would be retired. You would not be working for me. Thankfully." He smiles.

Cenk grunts. "I am cursed. I would not want my bad luck anywhere near you and your wife."

"You are not cursed."

Cenk grins, appreciating his friend. He looks down the edge of the blade and then to Tarkhan. "Then my close presence seems to scourge the people I accompany and serve."

"It is the nature of things. Thirty years you have served Egypt. A man so long in the business of war will have people near him die." He eyes Cenk's blade grip sadly, the finger missing on one hand.

Cenk looks up from his sword. "Yes, well." He applies more oil to his whetstone and takes a long swig from his mug. They both become engrossed in the whisping of steel back and forth across the worn stone.

"Let me know on Alexandria, my friend. My offer stands."

Cenk looks up and nods. He goes back to working the blade, reflecting on his patrons. Too many of his friends and mentors killed—Amir Turkmani, the sultans al-Salih, Aybeg, and now Qutuz. The scenes of their deaths mash together in his mind. Blood. Gray skin. Their lifeless faces pass in succession, upon each hiss of his blade on hone. His tears drip upon the grindstone, mixing with the oil.

When he looks up, Tarkhan is gone. The door is cracked open, as the Mongol found it.

Cenk winces to stand. He pushes open the door to take in the street. The sun sets. Merchants walk home. Veiled women pass with their heads down, their shoulder bags filled with fresh goods from the souk to be made into their family's dinner.

Cenk latches the door. He pours another mugful and returns to his task. He eyes the spot on the wall where he will hang the weapon. He envisions it covered in dust and eventually cobwebs. He figures unlike himself, at least the old blade will go to its final resting place with a proper edge.

CHAPTER 56

Esel

Cairo

November 2, 1260

Holding Zane's little hand in hers, Esel walks south along the *el-Khaliq* canal, meandering around the slender-armed peddlers with their pushcarts and men strolling the path both north and south toward the mosques. A crisp breeze off the Nile tosses her curls. She stuffs them back under her head scarf.

She has hardly spoken with Baybars in the week since Qutuz's murder. Concerned for her wellbeing, Baybars persuaded her to stay with the bulk of his Bahriyya in the vanguard while he swiftly covered the final stretch of road to Cairo ahead of them. He promised her a new home in the city, once he secured the citadel and won oaths from the entire army.

She did as he asked and arrived in Cairo during the afternoon, the streets empty and the merchandise stalls picked clean. The locals remained shuttered in their homes, fearful of the Bahri and what their leader-turned-sultan might do. "Stay inside with your door barred," Baybars told her. "If you need anything, or trouble begins, go to the quarters of Zeki or Leander."

Yet, once Baybars declared the end of Qutuz's war tax, the population's anxiety changed to delight. Celebrations filled the streets. Esel watched from her balcony as Cairo indulged in food and drink. Perhaps wary of an assassin's dagger, her nephew made no public appearance.

It made no difference. The festival went on for days.

Now, the city only recently begins to settle down into its more productive bustle.

She skirts the top end of Elephant's Pond, the sun shimmering off the wind-swept water there and farther west on the broad Nile. Between the locals' round-topped huts, she sees a pair of felucca boats clear the northern point of al-Rawda, the prominent island splitting the great river.

She squeezes Zane's hand and points to the angled lateen sails filled with wind. He looks to Esel with gratitude and affection. Esel sees Jacinta in his eyes and the cast of his jaw. A wave of grief moves through her.

Since Jacinta's death two moons past, her nurse friends had initially looked after Zane. After Esel recovered from her injuries, she insisted upon taking over full responsibility of his care. She found the lad's company a godsend, not a burden.

They continue south and east until reaching the east bank of the Nile. A break in the palms on al-Rawda exposes the ruins of the Bahri's River Island Citadel. The tumbled white blocks remain striking among the foliage. She tries to imagine the fortress and al-Salih's old palace still standing, as one local described it to her: "Like white gems atop the islet's crown."

When they reach the first bridge that crosses to the island, she spots a speck of red on a bench in the shaded courtyard. She approaches the seated Bahri from his rear.

"Pleasant evening, amir," she says.

Leander turns, handsome in the red winter uniform of the regiment. Looking at Esel and then to the little hand tucked into hers, a wide smile crosses his face. "Good evening, Esel. Pleasant, indeed."

Zane grins. Leander hoists the six-year-old up by the armpits and stands him upon the bench. "So were you a good boy for your Tita Esel today?" he asks, looking into the lad's face, then over his head at Esel.

She smiles and nods her head, pleased that Leander has begun to refer to her as the child's aunt.

"Yes, Father," Zane says. He points to a family tossing grain to the grebes and plovers that loiter at the river's bank. "May I watch?" he asks.

"Of course," Leander says.

The youth bounds across the grass.

"I heard the troops rounded up the last of the rabble last night," Esel says.

"Those not killed are in irons," Leander says. "Your nephew is not going to let a few stable hands and lowly pages own the night and plunder the shops. He knows the importance of keeping Cairo orderly."

"I hope he is as effective at keeping order to the north."

Leander raises his eyebrows. "If you mean Alam al-Din in Damascus, it is true his allegiance was to Qutuz only. But do not fret. If this prince thinks himself a wiser statesman than Baybars—or one who wishes to win the support of Homs and Hama and then declare his own sovereignty like al-Nasir did upon Aybeg's ascension—he will soon enough find himself outwitted and outmuscled by your nephew."

"Actually, I meant Aleppo. Is it true that the Mongols have crossed the Euphrates?"

"I believe so," he says. "We do not know how many, but surely the Tartars aim to retake Aleppo as a foothold to northern Syria. They are not going away." His eyes turn to the sun setting over the Nile. He shakes his head. "Unfortunately, Prince al-Muzaffar there has gathered about him al-Nasir's Aziziyya and Nasiriyya. These Mamluks still hate Baybars and are prone to stir trouble. They may help fight the Mongols, but they will also try to lead al-Muzaffar away from Cairo's rule."

Esel thinks of the duplicitous al-Nasir from years past. "Is al-Muzaffar so desperate that he would bring these wolves into his ger? Those Mamluks will turn on him in Aleppo, just as they repeatedly betrayed al-Nasir in Damascus."

"I do not know that al-Muzaffar is as desperate, or spineless, as al-Nasir, but a man insufficiently skilled in the martial way—one without the experience to attract warriors to his side—too often feels he must purchase the dependability of his troops."

Esel turns to check where Zane plays and then looks Leander in the eyes. "I worry for Baybars. A disloyal governor in Damascus, an incompetent prince leading Aleppo. The Mongols reorganized and again moving south. And even in Cairo, amirs will want Baybars dead for murdering the sultan who just led the entire Muslim army to victory at Ayn Julut."

Leander nods. "All true. All worrisome. But I lose little sleep."

"You worry little about the man to whom your future is tied?"

"I lose little sleep because of the faith I have in his ability."

She cocks her head inquisitively.

He lightens, lifting his chin to where a small girl shares her crumbs with Zane. The two toss bits to a growing flock of grebes. Esel smiles.

Leander looks beyond his boy to the water, his lips set hard. "Doubtless there are as many amirs in the citadel who would enjoy *taking* Baybars' head from his shoulders as those who would *carry* him upon their shoulders. And methinks this would be true in the fortresses of every Syrian principality. But I do not think it will matter. The disloyal will not succeed."

"No?"

"No. I will not lecture the woman who helped raise him. But I know in my heart that Baybars is the right man to lead the empire."

She looks to the rustling palm fronds at the river's edge to reflect on his words and then back to the Frank as he continues.

"For over six years, since the day we Bahri fled Cairo, your nephew treated us fairly," he says. "Those were difficult times, with plenty of opportunity and reason for his Mamluks to bolt. Few Bahri did."

She nods.

"I wager that Baybars will be as forthright and sensible with Cairo's gold as that which he tapped from the princes in Damascus and Karak years past. Methinks he will use all of Syria's coin, too, for the greater good of the kingdom. He will disperse command, governorships, and iqtas to those worthy amirs, based on merit and performance. Not bloodline or regiment. Such is one of his strengths."

She smiles behind her hijab. She admires Leander's steadfastness, his confidence in her nephew.

Leander's watches the sun kiss the horizon. "In due course, his evenhandedness and know-how will win over Qutuz's Muizziyya and Salihi. And then all of the soldiers in Syria. One unit, one man at a time."

"It seems to me that no man has earned such fidelity from all of Egypt's Mamluks since your old patron, al-Salih. Perhaps my nephew would be wise to emulate this man."

He grins. "I see why Baybars has kept you in such close company for so long. Baybars already displays a charisma similar to that held by al-Salih. But if Baybars is to succeed, he will also need to employ the shrewdness learned from his first patron, Amir al Bunduqdar."

"To survive," she says.

"Aye." He sighs. "I hope Baybars also understands those actions of al-Salih's that he should not repeat."

"Like?"

"I know Baybars would agree that things were best in Cairo when Egypt's Mamluks were one corps—all Salihiyya.

Before al-Salih grew the regiment and formed the Bahri and Jamdariyya."

Esel beckons him to continue.

He looks upward. "Allah bless him, but even if done so unintentionally, I think al-Salih created this bloody legacy of ours. These splinters, these rivalries in the regiments. Our father meant well and was wise to enlarge the best of his force, but al-Salih laid the first course of stones that divided us Mamluks. Each succeeding leader stacked more stones, so that we now face this high wall."

Leander again watches Zane and the girl. His face returns to its former hardness. "Al-Salih's splitting of the regiment was his greatest misstep. When he died, so did Mamluk devotion to one man, one commander. Turmoil and bloodshed were destined to follow. And they did."

He picks up a pebble and rubs its edge. "This rift between brothers has plagued my soul for ten years now. Such infighting was why I left the Crusaders in the first place."

She reaches across and squeezes his arm tenderly. They both watch Zane in silence for a few moments.

"That is the heart of it," she says. "Will Baybars be able to rally *all* of the empire's fighting men when the entire Mongol horde returns again to beat on the gates of Cairo?"

He looks to the water introspectively. "I believe so. But seems to me the greatest hurdles before him are within our own stone walls, not outside them."

She stares at him.

"Deep down, we both know he was fated to rule. But to me it feels the ties of the Khushdash no longer unite us, but rather seem to hold us back."

Baybars had explained the Khushdash to Esel as the code of loyalty between brothers who shared the same initial training at the barracks schools—so necessary in binding the novices at the tibaq and keeping faithfulness among units of Mamluks afield. "How so?" she asks.

He throws the pebble into the water, watching the undulant rings spread. "I have learned to view this seemingly vital part of our system as a cracked foundation—and one supporting too many walls. The Khushdash led to our factionalism. With brothers in training dispersed across every regiment for years, it was acceptable for a man to switch units and loyalties without any loss of honor."

She nods.

"If Cairo, the empire, is to endure," he says, "then Baybars must demolish this maze of walls and rebuild the old foundation." He nods to the toppled remnants of the Bahri's citadel. "Rebuild it, as he intends with our old fortress here."

"Or perhaps replace the compromised foundation and stone walls altogether with a single felt covering," Esel says. "All the Mamluks of Egypt, all of the army, under one felt blanket—thriving in one common ger."

Leander beams. "I think you have it, Tita. Closer to how the Mongols viewed themselves under Genghis Khan—'people of the felt walls.' No more infighting. No more Muizzi, Salihi, or Bahri. Just Mamluk. All of us, just Mamluk."

The muezzin's chant rides the wind from their south, the adhan, the call to prayer, carrying from the high tower at the Mosque of Ibn Tulun. This mournful and penetrating invitation mingles with the voice of another muezzin calling to the faithful from the mosque of ibn Ruzzik, distant to the north.

The little girl's parents wave them a farewell. Zane returns at the run.

"Maybe you will share your vision of this single ger with your nephew soon?" Leander asks.

Esel smiles.

"Well then, until tomorrow morning." He looks down at the lad. "Young warriors must feed to gain strength. Tell Esel good evening."

"Good night, Tita," Zane says.

Leander hugs her with one long arm.

Esel crosses the bridge and walks north to a secluded stretch on the canal, stopping just short of the Greeks' Quarter. The second call to prayer, the Iqamah, sounds louder than the first from ibn Ruzzik's minaret.

She takes a narrow trail off the path that dumps into a patch of low grass, secluded by high reeds on both sides. She waits until the route behind her empties of those making their way to prayer.

She absorbs the beauty of the Nile sunset, the rounded towers and reed-thatched roofs across the canal silhouetted against a wedge of orange-black cloud— a patch of blue prominent in the center.

When the voices from passers-by subside, she removes her veil and head scarf. She kneels, facing north toward her native land near the Black Sea. She puts her nose to Mother Earth. She savors the smell of dark soil and decayed papyrus. A gust whispers through the browning sedge grass that towers above her. She prays to the Respectable Woman:

"Oh Noble One, oh Wise Spirit, please bless the precious boy now in my care and also his mother, who rests peacefully in your felt house in the sky. And favor also my people of the steppe, those scattered in every direction like errant seeds blown far across the plains in violent storm—and those Kipchaks living under the Tartar's fist.

"Please lend wisdom and strength to my nephew as he leads all in this desert land. Help him unite the warriors under his care, as the confederation once bonded your Kipchaks. Pull us together, just as the close of winter drew our people to common pastures before the move to upland grass.

"And please forgive me, Respectable Woman, for falling short of your ideals those two moons past on the Jordan River, when my eyes went temporarily blind, when my mind became clouded with the foolish illusion of an old woman's hunting skills, still thought sharp. Forgive me for thinking myself still the protector, when I had instead become easy prey. Forgive my regretful actions, which sealed the fate of my dear friend, Jacinta. Please pardon this grave sin."

Esel rises from the prostrate position and remains seated upon her calves. The murmuring current of the canal waters settles her. She stares ahead, unblinking, allowing her vision to gloss over in the last of the evening light. The curved rooflines morph into the sprawling foothills of her steppe homeland, the "String of Hills" near her birthplace.

She pictures the Respectable Woman sitting prominently on her knoll, amid the tall spring grass and wildflowers. In her mind, Esel walks toward the stone figure. As she nears the sculpture, a swirling wind picks up, intertwining the waving stalks, heavy with seed heads. She halts. The grass obscures the idol's form. A darkness sets in.

When the squall passes, the feathergrasses part. A soft light gleams upon the smooth rock, revealing lean cheeks and a slight chin, the round-faced features on the statue having melted away. The figure's wide stone hips have shrunk to a more slender form, her large breasts halved in size. The big-boned effigy appears slim, yet strong.

Esel tilts her head in thought. How is it that her vision of The Respectable Woman changes shape? Her eyes flood with tears, trickling down both cheeks. She does not fully understand why. She stays, refusing to wipe or blink the tears away, hoping that if she remains still, the goddess may grant her a clearer view.

Jacinta's face materializes on the carving. The statue's eyes go from stone gray to brown. A soft smile forms on her lips.

Esel extends her hand slowly. A cloud passes between them. When it clears, the face has gone back to rock. Esel places her outstretched hand across her heart.

More tears. She rubs a sleeve across her eyes and looks up to the twilight.

The odd patch of blue in the sky has gone to violet, the color of Hyacinth. Jacinta. Goose bumps rise on her arms. Esel's friend resides in the heavens. In the purpling space between tufts of darkening clouds, the first of the evening stars glitters.

MORE BOOKS FROM BRAD GRAFT

Chains of Nobility:
*Brotherhood of the Mamluks (Book 1)**
by Brad Graft

A Lion's Share:
*Brotherhood of the Mamluks (Book 2)***
by Brad Graft

**A Finalist for the Colby Award, which recognizes "a first work of fiction or non-fiction that has made a major contribution to the understanding of military history, intelligence operations, or international affairs."*
***Awarded a silver medal by the Military Writers Society of America: "The author has created an intriguing and believable world from ancient ideas, settings and characters, a masterful job of both history and fiction."*

MORE BOOKS FROM THE SAGER GROUP

The Swamp: Deceit and Corruption in the CIA
An Elizabeth Petrov Thriller (Book 1)
by Jeff Grant

Meeting Mozart:
A Novel Drawn From the Secret Diaries of Lorenzo Da Ponte
by Howard Jay Smith

Labyrinth of the Wind:
A Novel of Love and Nuclear Secrets in Tehran
by Madhav Misra

Three Days in Gettysburg
by Brian Mockenhaupt

Miss Havilland: A Novel
by Gay Daly

The Orphan's Daughter: A Novel
by Jan Cherubin

Lifeboat No. 8: Surviving the Titanic
by Elizabeth Kaye

Shaman: The Mysterious Life and Impeccable Death of Carlos Castaneda
by Mike Sager

A Boy and His Dog in Hell: And Other True Stories
By Mike Sager

For more please see The Sager Group.net

ABOUT THE AUTHOR

Brad Graft is a businessman who runs a national chain with his partners. A former U.S. Marine officer, he helped develop a military program that assists wounded servicemen and families of the fallen. He continues to steer fundraising for charities serving this cause. An avid fly fisherman and hunter, for decades he has pursued gamefish and predators in remote places around the world. Also a history buff, his research on the Brotherhood of the Mamluks series took him to the Middle and Far East, where he studied Medieval-era routes and fortresses and trekked the Mongolian steppe on horseback, learning the ways of native hunters and nomadic herders.

ABOUT THE PUBLISHER

The Sager Group was founded in 1984. In 2012, it was chartered as a multimedia content brand, with the intention of empowering those who create art—an umbrella beneath which makers can pursue, and profit from, their craft directly, without gatekeepers. TSG publishes books; ministers to artists and provides modest grants; designs logos, products and packaging, and produces documentary, feature, and commercial films. By harnessing the means of production, The Sager Group helps artists help themselves. For more information, visit TheSagerGroup.net

THE SAGER GROUP
Artifex Te Adiuva

Lightning Source UK Ltd.
Milton Keynes UK
UKHW040702241221
396187UK00001B/195